BLUEBELL SEASON AT THE POTTING SHED

BLUEBELL SEASON AT THE POTTING SHED

Jenny Kane

An Aria Book

To all the girls in The Old Well Garden
Centre coffee bar.

A place of smiles.

MARCH

I

Maddie's breath caught in her throat as she saw the glass panel fall towards the gravel path. A vision of half of The Potting Shed's new greenhouse roof being reduced to smithereens flashed through her mind as a workman dived forward and caught it a split second before it hit the ground.

'I can't watch this anymore.' Maddie turned her sister. 'It took us so long to decide whether we should splash out on a greenhouse for my herbs or not, I don't want to look again until it's up. It's too stressful.'

Sabi gave the two men the full force of the haughty glare she reserved especially for tradesmen. 'Let's go inside. We're supposed to be talking battle plans for the nursery's expansion, and I for one could murder for a cup of tea.'

'You know the greenhouse's roof wouldn't have smashed, don't you?'

'Logically, yes.' Maddie placed the biscuit tin in the middle of the kitchen table. 'No point in paying for reinforced glass if it's not going to do its job, but instinct still told me it was going to break.'

'Have you worked out which herbs you're going to grow yet?'

'Almost.' Maddie glanced down as Florrie's wet nose nudged at her hand. 'Yes, I know you want a biscuit, but you've already had one, and they aren't good for you.' She ruffled the puppy's black and white fur, before returning to the point. 'I'll start by increasing production of the herbs I already grow. All the favourites: thyme, mint, chives, parsley, and such. But I also want to produce some less common varieties too. See if I can tempt people to be braver in their tastes. Borage definitely – it's good in a jug of Pimm's; maybe some caraway and chervil.'

'Not coriander and dill? I use all of those – and basil of course.'

Maddie's eyebrows rose. 'You mean *Henry* uses all of those.'

'Yes, well, it's hardly my fault if my husband loves to cook.'

'You're a lucky woman, Sabs.' Patting her sister's arm, Maddie selected another biscuit. 'But I'll leave out those particular herbs for now. They tend to bolt if you don't keep on top of them, and as we can't afford to employ any more staff, I want to keep things low maintenance.'

Sabi delved a hand into her massive handbag, pulled out a state-of-the-art tablet, and opened it at a list of jobs that needed doing. 'Maybe we should have ordered a bigger greenhouse.'

'Anything bigger wouldn't have fitted between the first polytunnel and the path to the car park.'

'I still can't see why it couldn't have been built on the scrap of land at the far side of the nursery.'

'Light.' Maddie bit back the temptation to ask Sabi how many times they needed to have this conversation. 'While the rear of The Potting Shed does enjoy the sunshine, overall, it's lighter at the front of the nursery for longer each day.'

Sabi grunted reluctant acceptance of the situation as she pulled a cookie from the tin, brushing a crumb away as it hit her tablet's screen. 'Notification of the payment of Dad's inheritance tax came through this morning. So, that is something less to worry about.'

Maddie gave a sigh of relief. 'Just a few instalments left for my half of the solicitor's fees, and Dad's death is finally paid for.' She picked up her coffee cup. 'I can't believe how much money we had to find just to sort probate. As if losing him wasn't bad enough.'

'I know.' Sabi fiddled with her tablet. 'I'm sorry we couldn't settle your half too. What with paying two mortgages, Jemima's school fees and...'

Maddie tugged at her chestnut ponytail. 'Really, it's fine. I appreciate it, but I'd never have let you pay my share anyway. At least we have a friendly solicitor who was happy to let me pay bit by bit.'

'Friendly?' Sabi's smile widened. 'Ed's your boyfriend.'

Maddie's eyes strayed to a photograph of her and Ed, stuck to the front of the fridge with a wellington-boot-shaped magnet. 'He wasn't my boyfriend then though, was he. If I'd thought that was why his boss helped us, then...'

'I know, your pride would have stopped you from accepting it.'

Knowing she was capable of being her own worst enemy sometimes, Maddie shrugged. 'It was my decision not to sell

The Potting Shed, so I have to accept the financial hit that goes with it.'

Sabi dunked her biscuit into her tea. 'Dad would be proud of you.'

'Of *us*.' Keen to avoid a rehash of her sister's guilt, after she had initially fought hard for them to sell the nursery to their nearest rival, Big in Gardens, commonly known as BIG, instead of keeping it in the family, Maddie changed the subject. 'Any word on a buyer for your house?'

Raking her hand through her neat bob, Sabi immediately patted her hair back in place before opening a picture of her former home on the edge of Tiverton on her tablet. 'We have a viewing this afternoon. Miriam is hopeful, but then...'

'Miriam could make anything sound rose-tinted.'

'She means well.' Defensive on her best friend's behalf, Sabi exhaled slowly. 'Although I have to admit that I'm less inclined to take what she says at face value when she's in estate agent mode these days.'

'I'm sorry you lost your earlier buyer.'

'Me too. But at least we got to move into our new place. I suppose any house sale that goes at least half right is a miracle.'

Maddie nodded. 'I'm also sorry I haven't been over to see you in Culmstock for a few weeks. How's it shaping up?'

A smile spread over Sabi's lips, lighting up her eyes. 'I love it. I still can't believe I'm living in my dream house. It's frustrating not being able to crack on with doing it up, but...'

'It's hardly falling down around your ears. It's perfect.'

'Not my sort of perfect.'

Laughing, Maddie pointed to her sister's tablet. 'Well,

let's get the work talk sorted, then maybe you can get back to deciding what shade of plum curtains will go best in Henry's study.'

Sticking her tongue out at her sister, Sabi opened a spreadsheet full of figures that Maddie didn't really want to see.

'Since we decided to realise Dad's vision of transforming this place from a nursery into a garden centre, custom has increased, but then so have the costs.' Sabi pulled a face. 'In short, we are closer to breaking even than we were – but there's still a long way to go. Going ahead with converting the downstairs of this place into a shop and the upstairs as a flat for you to live in, means we'll have to watch our budget even more than we are already.'

Maddie surveyed her kitchen, trying to imagine what it would be like to cook and eat upstairs. 'Do you think we should hold back for a while? Leave converting the house until we're on a firmer footing?'

Sabi shrugged. 'I keep changing my mind to be honest. The architect's plans are almost drawn up, so maybe we should just cross our fingers and go for it.'

'Spending money to make money.' Maddie's stomach churned at the thought of the new business loan they'd secured – in theory – with the bank. Paying back the one she'd taken out to get them this far felt like a lifetime's work; the prospect of paying off a second one made her faintly nauseous.

Sabi stared at the figures before her. 'I don't think we can call The Potting Shed a garden centre until we have a larger indoor space to sell from. I know we have more stock for sale, but right now we're just a large nursery. The loan we already have will cover the conversion – but it won't keep it up or fill it for long, nor will it get us the café we badly need to attract more customers.'

Trying not to feel guilty about buying the greenhouse for herbs before they'd started on the conversion, hoping her instinct that the produce raised would ultimately pay for it, Maddie was determined to be positive. 'Weekend trade is much better since Jo's pop-up coffee shop became a feature. He's drawing regulars, especially on a Sunday morning. There is something about seeing a bright orange camper van that warms the heart. Especially when that sight is complemented by the aroma of freshly brewed coffee.'

Sabi agreed. 'Shame Jo can't come on weekdays as well as at weekends.'

'Or even every weekend.'

'What do you mean?' Sabi's head jerked up.

'He can't do the Easter weekend or the first weekend in May. He has a previous commitment. One he can't get out of without letting people down.'

'What about letting us down?' Sabi was horrified.

'Come on, Sabs. Jo has been coming here as a favour to us since Christmas. He said upfront that there were weekends he wouldn't be able to make.'

'Well, yes, but I never dreamt they'd be at such a peak time. *Especially* as we'll need all the help we can get over Easter. We rely on him as a draw to bring people in!' Sabi banged her cup down onto the table with exaggerated force. 'BIG open their new garden centre Easter weekend – only twenty miles' drive away!'

'As if I could forget.' Maddie took a moment to savour her coffee's smooth texture before she went on. 'I'm as fed up as you are about losing out to them over Easter, but I can't see how we can prevent it. It's only been three months since we started to upgrade, and we have nothing like the resources they have. BIG are... well, big. Huge even!'

'But we can't do *nothing*. Even if there was no BIG to compete with, Easter weekend is a popular time for purchasing stuff for the garden.'

'I wasn't suggesting doing nothing, Sabi. That's why we agreed to have this meeting, remember – to discuss Easter.'

'Sorry. Ideas then?'

'A children's club. Gardening for the under tens. Show them how to grow simple things, teach them a bit about nature and the environment. You know the sort of thing.'

'You've never taught in your life.'

'True, but I did help with the school trips to Killerton House's gardens when I worked there. I was thinking, maybe an hour at a time, with a max of five children.'

'Plus parents?'

'Maybe.'

'*Definitely!* They'll stop it becoming a riot.' Sabi opened a new notes page and began to type. 'Where were you thinking?'

'The far polytunnel. There's enough space in there for everyone to sit at the potting desk, plus nothing is growing in there right now.' She paused. 'And before you ask, no, I couldn't have used it for the herbs.'

'I wasn't going to say that.' Sabi shifted in her seat just enough for Maddie to know that had been exactly what she'd been about to say.

'What do you think of the idea?'

Sabi drained her tea as she thought. 'You'd need to have a proper plan of what you'd do in each class. Easter's not far off. Is there time to make it work and attract enough people?'

'That's why I thought five children. Six at a push. A taster session to see if it works.'

'Ummm… It could work. Especially if you got them to plant something they have to come back here to check on every few weeks, to chart its growth.'

'That's an excellent idea.' Maddie grabbed a pen and pulled an unopened bill towards her, writing on the back as she spoke. 'Sunflowers! They could come back once a fortnight to watch them grow and do something else each time too.'

'Brilliant!' Sabi nodded enthusiastically.

'I need to think it through, and I'll see if Ed had any ideas tomorrow.'

'When's he back from his conference?'

'Late tonight. Are you sure you and Jem are okay to watch this place with Jake while we go out tomorrow?'

'How many times?' Sabi rolled her eyes. 'My daughter's name is Jemima! How hard is it to say her whole name?'

'She likes Jem.'

'Well, I don't.' Sabi brushed a hair from her face. 'But yes, of course we'll hold the fort. I think she's finding the school holidays a bit dull. She'd much rather be here fussing over Florrie than at home.'

'I thought I'd take Florrie with me, actually.' Maddie automatically put her hand down to the puppy who, having given up hope of a biscuit, was curled up by her owner's feet.

'Although Florrie adores Jemima – as do the customers – it might be just as well. She does tend to knock stock over when she gets overexcited.' Sabi stared at her spreadsheet as she stroked Florrie's fur. 'While you're catching up with Ed, ask him if he knows anyone else who has a coffee van or some sort of mobile refreshment unit.'

'Hardy likely, is it. The fact he knew Jo through the Dark Skies constellation spotting group was pure luck.'

Sabi drummed a fingernail against the oak table. 'Well, we're going to have to think of something, because having no tea and coffee on offer is a death blow over the Easter weekend.'

Maddie twisted her ponytail around her hand as she stared at the columns of numbers on the accounting spreadsheet. 'We can't afford to hire anyone to come in, not yet anyway. And I can hardly ask Jo to break a longstanding promise to the Northcotts just so he can serve food and drinks here.'

Sabi sat up suddenly. 'The Northcotts? Of Hawthorn Park near Exmouth?'

'Yes. They open the manor's gardens a few weekends a year during Easter and bluebell season. Jo provides the refreshments. Why, do you know them?'

'I've heard of them.' Sabi lowered her gaze to the tablet. *I used to know them... well, one of them. Once...*

2

The kingfisher came and went in a flash of blue. If Ed hadn't seen it too, Maddie would have wondered if she'd imagined the tiny dart of colour that had shot across her vision as they sat, hand in hand, on the bank of the River Barle.

'I always feel so privileged to see nature in action like that. An additional late birthday treat.' As the bird disappeared into the trees, Maddie stroked a finger over the silver brooch of a Border Collie that Ed had given her. 'Thanks again for this. I can't believe how much it looks like Florrie.'

'And I can't believe I had to miss your birthday. Especially as not only was it your thirtieth, but it's also the first one since we've been together.'

'Couldn't be helped.' Maddie picked up a small scone, which had been topped with a generous dollop of cream and jam. 'Plus, it means my birthday celebrations last longer. An Exmoor picnic is always worth waiting for.'

Ed laughed as his girlfriend took a bite from the mini scone. Cream oozed precariously from its top, which Maddie only just caught before it fell down her front. 'I'm glad you're enjoying it.'

'Loving it,' Maddie's brown eyes shone as she licked her sticky fingers.

'So are you, aren't you, girl?' Ed's attention was diverted from wanting to kiss the remaining cream from his partner's lips by Florrie dropping a tennis ball in his lap. 'You want me to throw it again?'

Florrie's paw landed on Ed's thigh.

'I'll take that as a yes.' Swinging his arm right back, he launched the ball into the woods behind them.

'You've got a friend for life there.' Maddie wiped a tissue across her mouth as her puppy bounded into the trees. 'You'll be doing that all day if you're not careful.'

'I like playing with Florrie. I can't believe how much she's grown since Ivan gave her to you.'

'Tell me about it. She's still very much a puppy when it comes to coordination though. Always careering into things and leaping around.'

'That's the springer spaniel in her.'

'Sometimes I wonder if her Border Collie part is tired out trying to keep up.' Maddie opened her arms as Florrie bounded back towards them, the ball in her jaws, before dropping it, and dashing back into the woods to chase it all over again.

Turning back to Ed, Maddie noted the intense way he was staring at her. 'What is it? You've got a funny expression on your face.'

'I was just looking. I've missed you.' Ed leant forward and gave Maddie a gentle kiss. 'And you missed a bit of jam.'

A few seconds later, proudly carrying her ball, Florrie

was unimpressed to find no one showing her any attention. With a polite bark, she nosed herself between the two bodies locked in an embrace between the uneaten scones, a flask of coffee and a bottle of elderflower.

'Oh, Flo!' Maddie sat up with a giggle, her dog clinging to her front as she did so. 'Talk about a passion killer!'

Ed brushed muddy paw prints from his jumper. 'Remind me not to invite you along to all our picnics, hound!'

Maddie wrapped her arms around Florrie's neck. 'Bored with being second best by any chance?'

Giving a short yap by way of response, Florrie wagged her tail so hard, she knocked over the – thankfully stoppered – bottle of elderflower.

Righting the bottle, Ed said, 'I haven't had the chance to ask you how things are going at the nursery since I went away.'

'Not much has changed yet – you've only been gone a month.'

'True, but we tended to stick to non-work chats while I was away. Trade picked up?' Ed helped himself to another scone.

'A bit, but not enough. Opening to the public as well as to traders for six days a week, rather than just part-time a couple of days has helped. We're building up regulars at the weekends, mostly thanks to Jo's coffee van.' Maddie couldn't prevent a sigh. 'To tell you the truth, I'm rather worried about Easter.'

'With BIG opening up the road you mean?'

'I know they'll take the majority of trade that weekend – it's understandable. People will be curious to see what they have to offer – but what if they don't come back to us after that? I don't mean to sound defeatist, and I don't expect to be able to offer as much as BIG do; but with Jo taking his van up towards Exmouth for several weekends until both Easter and bluebell season are over, we can't even guarantee our customers a coffee as they browse around the polytunnels.'

'Hawthorn Park!' Running a hand through his chestnut hair, Ed's easy smile dimmed. 'I'd forgotten about Jo's commitment to Sara.'

'Sara?'

'Sara Northcott. She runs the park.'

'Oh right.' Maddie poured herself a drink. 'It's not somewhere I've ever visited.'

'We should go – it's lovely.' Ed flicked a crumb of scone off his lip. 'I went to see Jo last time he was there. Gets very busy in bluebell season.'

'I'd like that. Although, maybe after Easter.' Maddie grimaced. 'We did ask the Exmoor Drifters farmer's market if they'd like to come for the holiday weekend. They were so popular when they came to us at Christmas; but they're already committed elsewhere.'

'I can imagine. They get bookings years in advance for seasonal occasions.' Ed chewed thoughtfully. 'It might be worth asking the Drifters manager, Ivan, if there are any stragglers? Not every one of the Drifters does every market. Although, none of them could fill Jo's shoes.'

'I know.' Maddie felt the magic of their afternoon begin to fade. 'Sabs and I have worked so hard since we decided to press on with Dad's dream of upgrading The Potting

Shed, but there's a long way to go, and money is tight. I need a draw, something BIG don't have, to attract a few customers our way.'

'Do you have any ideas?'

'I'm going to do some children's classes. Fun stuff about growing plants and nature.'

'That's a great idea. You'll need a DBS check though.'

The colour drained from Maddie's face. 'Oh hell, I forgot about that! How long do they take to clear?'

Ed started to stack their picnic things into a large hessian bag. 'Up to a month.'

'Oh hell! That's that then.'

'*Nil desperandum* – as my Latin teacher used to say. We'll work it out.' Ed checked his watch. 'We ought to go, The Potting Shed will be closing soon.'

'Shame. It's been lovely.'

'And it's not over. I was merely suggesting a change of scene.'

'You mean you intend to eat the rest of the picnic at my place?'

'Sort of.' Ed stretched out his long slim legs as he stacked the remaining food into a waiting tub. 'You'll see. I missed your birthday – that is a crime that needs atoning for properly. A picnic is not enough.'

'Isn't it?'

'No, it isn't.' Ed pulled Maddie to her feet as Florrie helpfully lapped up some scone crumbs from the rug.

The nursery was quiet. Sabi and Jemima had gone home. The Potting Shed's gate was closed and the small shop, which had once been Maddie's father's potting shed – the space that had inspired the naming of the plant-growing nursery when he'd first started out – was padlocked.

'Come on.' Ed held out his hand to her.

'Aren't we going inside?' Maddie watched as Florrie dashed to the front door of her home, expecting to be let inside so she could curl up in her basket in front of the radiator.

'Not yet. I've got something to show you. But first, you'll need these.'

Opening the boot of his car he pulled out the wellington boots they'd taken onto Exmoor, in case of rain.

'But it's not wet.'

'Just put them on.'

Sabi sat in the smallest bedroom of her new home. In time, it would be her office, but for now it bore the usual marks of a guest room.

Ignoring the urge to continue planning its redecoration, she opened the laptop that sat on the table she was using as a temporary desk. Sabi was about to log onto the Internet when she got up and closed the door. Just the act of doing so made her feel guilty. More guilty.

'You're doing nothing wrong. This is pure curiosity. Nothing more.' Talking to herself, Sabi clicked a few buttons on her keyboard and pulled up the website for Hawthorn Park.

Her heart began to beat faster as she searched through the options at the top of the screen. Then a sound from the hallway stilled her hands.

It's only Jemima heading to the kitchen.

Making herself breathe slowly, Sabi gave herself a shake. 'Stop acting like a criminal! You're only looking something up.'

Hitting the *Forthcoming Events* tab, Sabi was immediately confronted with a photograph of Hawthorn Park's formal garden. It was more beautiful than she remembered. A symmetrical patchwork of colour, neat and yet pleasingly eclectic, gave the sense of observing a maze; albeit one in which you wouldn't get lost.

Maddie would love it.

Scrolling down the page, she saw another picture, this time of the park's manor house. A relatively modest building, given the vast acreage of the land, it proudly sported a hotchpotch of architectural styles, where flashes of the original Elizabethan structure were only obvious to those who knew where to look.

Not allowing herself to linger, nor wonder if the interior of the house was as she remembered, Sabi moved further down the page. This time a stunning photograph of the bluebell woods, which ran around three-quarters of the manor house, stole her attention. But not as much as the picture that followed it.

A beaming Jo, stood next to his bright orange VW camper van, was serving coffee to a family sat at a picnic table in the park's grounds. Beneath the photograph the caption, 'Jo Dunn, close family friend to the Northcotts, will be serving delicious, exclusive coffee blends, alongside fresh pastries and cakes, during the Easter weekend and during the weekends while the bluebells bloom their best.'

'Close family friend? Jo?' Sabi's eyes narrowed. She couldn't square the Jo she knew – a quiet, slim, slightly ethereal man, in a grey beanie hat who always wore loose-fitting jumpers and jeans or oversized coats and jackets – with being the sort of person who associated with one of the richest families in Devon.

Knowing Maddie would tell her off for such snobbery, Sabi moved on to search for what she'd been hunting for in the first place.

A minute and a half later she found it. And immediately wished that she hadn't.

3

Maddie hadn't stopped laughing for at least twenty minutes, and her sides ached with the strain.

Puddle water splashed over the top of her wellington boots as Florrie danced between her and Ed, spraying them liberally as she dived from one water-filled pothole to another.

'I can't believe you got Jem to do this!' Maddie steadied herself on Ed's arm as she bent her knees and leapt, landing in a puddle with such gusto that the sandy-coloured water shot off in all directions.

'I couldn't see what else to do. I know how much you love puddle splashing, but as Mother Nature hasn't obliged us with rain, I asked Jem to use the hose to fill in the potholes. Although...' Ed chuckled as he wiped a splash from his face '...I hadn't imagined she'd fill them to the brim. This is puddle bathing, not puddle splashing, especially for someone as short as you!'

'I'm not short, I'm wonderfully average. You're just stupidly tall.'

Sticking his tongue out, Ed jumped into another puddle. 'Fun isn't it.'

'I love it!' Maddie kicked her blue-and-white-striped wellies through a pothole, savouring both the sound the water made and the silky sensation that washed over her boots.

Before she'd met Ed, only Maddie's late father, Tony Willand, had known of her child-like love of splashing in puddles. Whatever problem assailed her, a welly walk, splashing through puddles as she went, always eased any stresses and strains. Now she had someone to share such silliness with, it was even better.

Taking another leap from one puddle to the next, Maddie landed beside Ed, and hugged him. 'This is the best birthday present I've ever had.' She kissed his damp cheek. 'Thank you.'

Holding her tighter, Ed looked at their canine companion. 'Seems Florrie also approves. We'll be ending our day by giving her at least two showers to get the puddle water out of her fur.'

Sweeping her ponytail over her shoulder, Maddie sank down onto an old bench that had been abandoned behind the polytunnel that bordered the back of the nursery and the fields beyond. 'I think I can guarantee, that is not how we'll be ending our day.'

Sitting next to her, Ed winked. 'That sounds promising.'

Maddie rested her head on Ed's shoulder. 'Thanks for taking my mind off work for a while.'

'My pleasure.'

They sat in silence, the only sound coming from Florrie as she arranged herself under the bench, her tail rhythmically thumping against the ground.

'Who owns the land behind the nursery?' Ed broke the peace as he stared across the strip of rough, now rather wet, potholed gravel that divided the nursery from its neighbour.

'Chap called Dennis. I don't know his surname. Nice guy. Farmed the land all his life.'

'Farmed? It's just grass and trees. Hardly farming.'

'You've clearly lost none of your observational skills while being confined in the wicked metropolis. It is indeed grass with a side order of trees.'

'Surely a farmer can't afford to have a field lying idle?'

'It isn't idle. It's a wild area. A field that the relevant government department will pay Dennis to keep uncultivated, providing he mows it once a year. It won't be long before it is a mass of colour. Wildflowers, grasses and so on. When Sabi and I were children, we'd sit on this bench and count the poppies.' Maddie waved an arm to the left, where a roughly circular patch of oak trees spilled shade across the land, leading to some woodland beyond. 'Sometimes we went in there to explore.'

'Sneaked in did you? I can imagine you being a rebel, but Sabi, not so much.'

'Nah. I was too shy to break rules, and Sabi would have been very prim about it if I had. Dennis let us. He and Dad got on quite well; helped at harvest time if the farm was ever up against it.'

'Ummm...' Ed tapped the top of the arm of the bench. 'So, you'd say that you and Dennis were on good terms?'

'We aren't on bad terms. I haven't seen him since Dad died. Why do you ask?'

'Are there bluebells in the wood?'

'Yes.' Maddie waved an arm to their left, where a roughly circular patch of oak trees spilled shade across the land. 'You can just see where the leaves are through already. The flowers are a few weeks away yet, but when they come, they'll be lovely.'

'But who sees them?'

'Me. Jake, if he comes around here for his break – although he isn't here so much now he's started college. This year I guess it'll mostly be me, you and Sabi. And Jem if she plays here with Florrie.'

'Shame.'

Maddie gave her boyfriend a shrewd look. 'What are you building up to?'

'Possibly nothing, but what if... assuming Dennis was willing of course...' Letting go of Maddie, Ed moved to the fence that divided The Potting Shed and the farmland and paced up and down.

'If you're about to suggest building a greenhouse or erecting another polytunnel here, forget it.'

'Nothing like that. I was just wondering about bluebells in general.'

'They're small flowers – mostly wild – my favourites as it happens.' Maddie tilted her head to one side. 'Come in loads of varieties these days due to the number of hybrids, but gardeners have to be very careful. The Spanish hybrid in particular will overrun the British bluebell if...'

Ed interrupted, 'Who owns the wood – is that Dennis too?'

'Yes.'

'I imagine the field is stunning when it's in bloom.'

'A butterfly spotter's haven.'

'I bet it is.' Ed paused. 'I've had a sort of idea.'

'Ed, if you're about to suggest I offer the farmer money

for his field, then I should remind you that I have one or two other expenses to deal with before I start splashing out on more land – even if it was land that was for sale – which I doubt this ever will be. Plus, I am still paying solicitor's fees to your boss.'

'Sorry about that.' Ed looked awkward for a moment.

'Not at all. I'm very grateful to you for finding a way for me to pay in instalments,'

'How grateful?' Ed teased playfully.

'Behave, Mr Solicitor, or I'll have to report you to the Law Society for improper behaviour.'

Ed laughed, before he saw a cloud cross Maddie face. 'What's wrong?'

'Nothing. I'm probably being silly.'

'Tell me anyway.'

'Mentioning the Law Society reminded me.' Fiddling with her fingers, Maddie sighed. 'You know we have some planning permission requests in with the council to convert the ground floor of the house into a shop, and the upstairs into a flat for me.'

'And me, hopefully, when I'm allowed to come and play.'

'Absolutely.' Maddie took Ed's hand as she went on. 'The thing is, I can't help but worry about Leo Creswell.'

'BIG's solicitor?'

'He was so bitter about losing The Potting Shed land, not to mention not being thrilled by you threatening to report him to the Law Society. What if he uses his influence to hold up our planning permission application?'

'I wouldn't have put it past him,' Ed agreed, 'but in this case you can breathe easy. Somehow, Creswell managed to sweet-talk himself out of trouble and he's moved on. Got a job in London.'

'You have *got* to be kidding!'

'Nope. I had the dubious pleasure of his company at the conference. As you can imagine, he gave me a very wide berth.'

'For which, I'm sure, you were very grateful.'

'Too right! The man is a snake, and almost certainly doesn't deserve whatever fortune he's now earning, but at least he isn't here making your life a misery.'

Maddie released a relieved breath. 'I can't pretend I'm not glad he isn't with BIG anymore.'

Ed hooked an arm around her waist. 'You really are worried about losing trade to BIG, aren't you. Don't forget, you're aiming for a different, although slightly crossover, clientele to them.'

'I know, but... Easter weekend is such an important time in the gardener's calendar. What if no one comes here at all?'

'They will.'

'But all I've dreamt up is the kids' club idea, and if I can't get as DBS check in time then...'

'We'll apply for one as soon as we go inside. It might come through quickly. It's not like you've got a criminal record to worry about.'

'True.'

'And...' Ed peered back across the field towards the woods '...all the more reason to think in terms of bluebells.'

'You're suggesting I grow up more bluebells bulbs to sell on?'

'Not exactly. Grow more yes, but how about planting them here?'

'Here?'

'Right here.' Ed pointed to the ground beneath their feet. 'Why not develop this strip of land? Make it a picnic and bluebell area.'

Maddie glanced downwards. A thick layer of gravel, compacted by years of use, gave way here and there to the mud-lined potholes Jem had filled for them. Already, the water was seeping into the soil. 'But it's a mess here. Scrap land.'

'Scrap land with a stunning view.'

'True.'

'Although, it would mean I couldn't set up a fake puddle splash for you again.'

Maddie kissed his cheek. 'I loved it, but I can live without the potholes if it's for the greater good.'

'Spoken like a true businesswoman.' Ed tapped the ground with his welly. 'So, how much would it cost, do you think, to dig this lot up, turf some of it and plant bluebell bulbs across the rest? With Dennis's field behind, it could look incredible. The perfect picnic site.'

'I don't know.' Maddie tried to picture what Ed was suggesting. 'Picnic benches aren't cheap.'

'Could you get some second-hand?'

'Maybe.' Maddie sucked in her bottom lip. 'Having a picnic area would mean people could bring their own drinks in while Jo's not here.' She kicked at the ground. 'It's not a quick fix though, Ed. No chance of it being sorted by this Easter.'

'No, but as a long-term plan?'

'I rather like it.'

4

S ara Northcott had read the text three times. Picking up her mobile to read it again, she got cross with herself and slammed it back against her desk.

Habit sent her hands upwards, as they went to run themselves through her long hair, only to meet the back of her neck, and the short bob that she'd had for less than a week.

'Jo is coming just as he promised he would. That's *all* that is happening. He will serve coffee, tea, hot chocolate, slice cakes and pastries. He will be nice to everyone, and he'll be nice to you – but no nicer than usual. There is nothing more he can offer.'

Her fingers hit her computer's keyboard with a sense of frustration – not at Jo, but at herself. 'You know the situation, woman. Why can't you let it go?'

Sara saw her father's gaze assessing her from a photograph on the desk. Her fingers paused over the keys. It had been just over a year since his death, but the sense of loss hadn't diminished. 'Oh, Dad, how am I supposed to run this place on my own?'

★

Jo unhooked the catch that kept the camper van's awning in place. His Saturday and Sunday visits to The Potting Shed were becoming the highlight of his week. Not only was he building up regular customers, but he fitted in there.

Jo slid the van's side door open and had his hands full of folded chairs when he saw Ed heading his way. 'Have you come to help me set up, or are you making a run for it, back to Exeter, before Maddie ropes you into helping?'

'Both.' Ed grabbed a chair and unfolded it. 'I'll help you, then I must get home, air the flat, and put the washing machine on.'

'Came straight here after the course and conference then?'

'Wouldn't you have?' Ed smiled. 'It was a long month, but at least the two events running back-to-back in the same city meant I got them over with in one go.'

'Worthwhile?'

'The course was – future career wise. The conference, absolutely pointless – but aren't they always?'

Unloading four folding tables from the van, Jo agreed. 'Ticking corporate boxes. I did a lot of that when I worked for the council. I don't miss it.'

'I'm sure.' Ed saw a shadow cloud his friend's expression. 'You okay, Jo?'

'I'm always okay.'

'Yes, you are, but...'

'Thinking back to my time in the business world always casts a gloom. I'm fine.' Jo put a table into position and grabbed two chairs to twin with it.

Not completely convinced that Jo was his usual

unflappable self, Ed said, 'Maddie tells me you're off to Hawthorn Park for Easter.'

Jo paused in the act of unfolding the next table. 'I feel bad about that to be honest.'

'About not being here?'

'Maddie's been so good to me. I'm abandoning her just when she needs all the firepower she can get on BIG's opening weekend.'

'We all understand why you have to go. It's a promise you made ages ago.'

'True.' A crease appeared on Jo's forehead. 'I might make this the last year I go to Hawthorn Park.'

'I got the impression that it was your biggest income of the year bar Christmas?'

'It is. A captive audience if you like. The garden is stunning and there's a huge wood to walk around, and no other refreshment provider. I usually do well.'

'Don't give it up through loyalty to The Potting Shed. You never hid the fact you couldn't always be here. This is your livelihood, Jo. Maddie and Sabi understand that.'

'Thanks.' Jo slid a hand into his jacket pocket, cradling the weight of his mobile in his palm.

If I could talk to anyone about Sara, it would be Ed.

He tried to picture himself asking Ed out for a drink to the pub to talk it over. That's what blokes did, wasn't it? Said: *Do you fancy a drink later? Pub trip maybe?* But the words stayed firmly locked in his throat.

Ed frowned. 'You sure you're okay?'

'Yeah.' Jo switched on his coffee machine. 'Just thinking, that's all.'

'Have you had the chance to talk to Jo today?'

Maddie clutched her phone to her ear as she emptied an extra bag of ten-pence pieces into the shop's till. 'Not beyond a hello and a wave. He's been busy and, mercifully, so have we. I was going to start putting herb plants in the new greenhouse, but I've not had time to do more than give it a sweep-out. This is the first lull for hours.'

Ed smiled down the line. 'Excellent. Bodes well for the future.'

'Why were you asking about Jo?'

'He seemed a bit down this morning, something more than worrying about letting you down over Easter.'

Listening to her boyfriend stuff dirty washing into his washing machine, Maddie lowered her voice, aware that Jo wasn't far away, and that he'd hate people to be talking about him, even if it was because they cared. 'I have told him it's okay. That we understand.'

'I know. Like I said, this is something else – or maybe not. I could be reading things into a situation that doesn't exist.'

'I'll go and see him in a bit. Sabi's due for a shift running the shop soon. And…' Maddie broke off as her sister poked her head around the door. 'Talking of which, she's here.'

Sabi brandished a roll of tracing paper out before her. 'I've got the plans from Henry!'

'I've got to go, Ed. Sab's got the conversion plans. See you later!'

*

Only after two customers had been served with a variety of fledgling vegetable plants and another had discussed the pros and cons of pampas grass as a border plant, did the sisters have the chance to unroll the plans across the till's desk.

'The advantage of you being married to the architect is, not only do we get to watch over Henry, so he plans exactly what we want, but there's no massive bill either.'

Sabi laughed. 'Charging us for his services would be rather counterproductive.'

'I'm so grateful. Henry can't feel as if he's had a day off work since this started.' Maddie smoothed out the sheet of conversion plans her brother-in-law had sketched, showing how her house could be converted from a four-bedroomed home into a two-bedroomed flat above a shop. Each wall had been measured, checked, and remeasured from every conceivable angle.

It had been difficult deciding which rooms to convert, and which to leave as they'd always been, but eventually, after much soul-searching, Maddie had opted to keep her bedroom as her own, make her father's bedroom into the living room and Sabi's childhood room would be a spare bedroom-cum-office. The final bedroom was to become a small kitchen-diner.

Then, ultimately, once they started to make a profit, the current kitchen space would be cleared out, refitted, and converted into the production and serving part of the café – which would then spread out into the old dining area for seating.

'The space downstairs will seem much bigger once they've taken out the front door and some of the surrounding wall to make room for glass sliding doors.' Maddie traced a finger over the paper.

'Henry is convinced that's the best place to have the main entrance. It'll be wide enough for wheelchairs and pushchairs, and it will meet fire regulations.'

Keeping her attention fixed to the plans, Maddie examined how Henry had changed the remainder of the downstairs. The lounge and dining room would be knocked into one large space, from which to sell a selection of tools, seeds, and houseplants. The washroom, which currently served as a place for herself and Jake to scrub the mud off their hands between jobs, was to become a public toilet, with disabled access and a counter that could be used as a baby changing area.

'We will need to expand that in time.' Sabi stared at the plans. 'One toilet for everyone won't be enough.'

Maddie grimaced. 'What if it is enough though? What if no one comes after BIG open on the 9th of April?'

Sabi tilted her head to one side. 'We have to think positive, but...'

'But?'

'Okay, so...' Sabi leant forward, her tone practical as she said, 'Henry and I have been talking about worst-case scenarios.'

'And?' Perspiration suddenly dotted Maddie's back as she waited to hear what her sister was going to say.

'If trading as a garden centre, albeit a small one, doesn't work out, then we'll have to scale back. Stick to being a bigger nursery, selling houseplants and a few tools from the new build, and using Dad's old potting shed as – well – a potting shed rather than a shop.'

Maddie's shoulders sagged with relief. 'I thought you were going to say we'd have to sell up after all.'

'No way, not after all we've been through.' Sabi tucked a strand of hair behind her ear. 'But listen, Mads, we are going to have to be sensible – give ourselves a time limit. Set up financial goals that we have to hit. No wavering – if we say we need to earn a certain amount in such a time, we *have* to stick to it, or we'll be forever chasing our tails and making excuses for not paying loans back.'

'I agree – I hate owing money.'

Sabi nodded. 'So then, shall we say, if we haven't paid back the loan you took out to pay for the conversion, and covered the costs of all we have paid out so far, by the end of May, then we won't take on a new loan – and we'll have a rethink.'

'The end of May?' Maddie paled. 'That's less than two months!'

'I know – I'm not saying we have to be in profit by then. We just need to have paid off the current loan and break even. It's essential to be bringing in enough to cover daily costs and new stock.'

'Make sense.' Maddie felt slightly sick. 'Dare I ask how much money we need to make in that time?'

Sabi showed her sister the tablet.

'Oh God! That's a fortune!'

'It's doable if we work hard.' Sabi gave her sister's hand a squeeze. 'If all else fails, we'll rethink being a garden centre; consider our strengths and capitalise on them. Expand on the sales of vegetables and fruit to the local hotels and greengrocers instead. Be a supersized nursery.'

'I'd like to do that anyway. People like Tim Robertson

at the Blackdown Hotel have been loyal customers for so long, that I don't want to let them down now we're expanding.'

'We'd be fools to do that, but can we sustain the amount of growing we'd need to do, and run this place as a more public concern? There are only so many hours in the day, and I have a lot to get on with at home. You can't do everything.'

'Jake still helps when he is home from college.'

'He does, and I'm not knocking his green fingers, Mads, but his college course is taking up four days of the week, and I can't imagine him wanting to work here every weekend now that his girlfriend is stationed near Plymouth.'

'I haven't asked, but I get the impression that Petra and Jake aren't finding the practicalities of a long-distance relationship easy.'

'Hardly long-distance – they're both in Devon.'

'Sabs, not everyone can afford a car and the petrol to travel from one side of the county to the other every week.'

Flushing slightly, Sabi said, 'Petra could have a car if she wanted one. Her parents would buy her one. Miriam was only saying the other day, how fed up she and Nigel were with Petra's stubborn determination to do everything herself.'

Maddie couldn't help but laugh. 'Only Miriam would see her daughter's desire to stand on her own feet as a character flaw. If Petra was my daughter, I'd be proud of her determination to support herself.'

Not wanting to be drawn into a discussion about her best friend's shortcomings, knowing she occasionally suffered from many of them herself, Sabi said, 'The point I was trying to make was, once Jemima goes back to school, I want to crack on with updating my place. Are you going to be able to handle all the work involved in growing the new crop of plants, advise customers, walk Florrie, and man the till all on your own?'

5

Jake opened the folder containing his course notes. Two seconds later he closed it again.

If Petra had been there, she'd have helped him. Although his literary skills had improved since they'd become a couple, the idea of reading more than a few paragraphs at a time remained a daunting prospect. Thanks to an absent father and a mother who cared about nothing but herself, Jake's school years had been a car crash of non-education full of insecurity, self-hate and loneliness, which had seen his teachers brand him a hopeless case. Although he'd upped his efforts since he'd met Petra, he frequently felt out of his depth.

The report he had to read, to discuss in a tutorial the following Tuesday, seemed to be screaming at him from inside its holder. *You're useless. You'll never amount to anything.*

Squeezing his eyes shut, Jake took a swig of lager and, following his girlfriend's advice, counted to ten in his head.

Since he'd started at Bicton Agricultural and Horticultural College, doing a course that needed no entry qualifications, meaning his lack of GCSEs – for once – made no difference, Jake frequently swung from feeling fulfilled when cracking on with the practical side of the college work, to being filled with fear whenever he had to tackle the few written tasks involved. The inadequacies that had led to him drop out of school with little reading, writing and mathematical ability had started to flare up again, becoming increasingly frequent since Petra had left. Not that she knew he was suffering from mild panic attacks at the idea of tackling written work without her on hand.

Reopening the folder, Jake glared at the report explaining various methods of planting fruit canes. 'I know how to plant fruit already. Can't see why I have to discuss it "with the group".' He mumbled into his pint, staring with a mix of fear and resentment at the green folder.

I'm twenty for God's sake. I should be able to read and write a simple report by now.

His wallowing wasn't helped by the memory of a phone called he'd had with Petra at lunchtime. There was no doubt she was loving every second of the gardening apprenticeship she'd been offered with the Royal Horticultural Society at Rosemoor in North Devon. Jake didn't begrudge her that for a second. True, he'd hoped they'd both be offered gardening apprenticeships together, at the same place – but they'd known from the outset it was unlikely, and had vowed to stay together as a couple, however difficult it might be. They had WhatsApp and Zoom and so could at least see each other every day, even if they weren't physically together.

Jake's hand moved towards the phone sat on the table next to the folder. *I could call her now. We could have a virtual pub trip.*

A smile cut through his gloom as he pictured Petra. She was, as both his mother and hers had wasted no time in telling him, 'out of his league'. Intelligent, beautiful, kind, brave and fun; Jake had no idea what Petra saw in him – a high school failure who hadn't got an exam to his name – whereas she had a first from Cambridge. They'd never have met if her mother, the terrifying Miriam, hadn't asked Sabi to find Petra a job at The Potting Shed. It had been a ploy to teach her daughter a lesson – to show her that she should be grateful for her expensive private education and follow the legal career her parents had decided she should take.

But Petra had had other ideas. She wanted to work outside, preferably with plants. Being sent to work with Maddie, Petra claimed, was the best thing that had ever happened to her; not only had she met Jake, but she was also following her dream – their dream – of developing a career in horticulture.

Sabi wasn't sure why she hadn't told Maddie about her discovery. She should have told Henry – although that would have felt like a confession, and she hadn't done anything wrong.

The excitement of sharing the plans for the conversion of Maddie's home had taken the edge off her initial attack of unexpected grief. But now, alone in her kitchen, stacking the dishwasher while her husband and child watched an old episode of *Doctor Who*, tears pricked at the corners of Sabi's eyes.

She hadn't thought about Simon Northcott in years. Every now and then, while driving around Devon, she'd seen brown tourist road signs for Hawthorn Park, and a few memories had surfaced, but she'd never gone back. Life was for moving forward. But not for him – not now.

They'd met during their first week at university. Simon had been a mature student, returning to studies after a teenage marriage had ended in heartbreak after a fatal car crash, while Sabi had been a fresh-faced eighteen-year-old. They had marvelled that they'd met while studying when they lived so close to each other back home. Sabi had fallen in love with Simon before she'd known he was from a wealthy family; it was some weeks later, when he'd shown her he photographs of his home, that she'd been unable to believe her luck. In the twilight hours of night, Sabi had found herself imagining herself living at Hawthorn Park as Simon's right arm, months before she'd even visited it.

Switching on her dishwasher, Sabi sank into the wingback chair Henry had bought her as a moving-in present. She despaired of her former self. Of course, her plans hadn't worked out. It had been the fact she'd had them in the first place that had proved their undoing. If she'd kept her mouth shut it would have been alright – but she hadn't.

After they'd been a couple for six months, Simon had invited her to visit Hawthorn Park. His parents had been away, and they'd had the whole estate to themselves. He'd told her he had a surprise for her. Sabi cringed now as she remembered imagining him proposing or showing her a garden that he would develop just for her, to watch grow as they grew as a couple.

The day had been blissful at first, the weather warm despite it being early spring. The trees had still been naked as they'd scrunched their way through the woods on endless frosty walks, talking about everything and anything.

He'd given her a tour of the house, during which she'd complimented anything and everything, from the curve of the banister to the tiles on the kitchen floor. Sabi closed her eyes as she recalled how Simon had found her later, on returning from fetching them a takeaway, trailing a hand across the bookshelves in the small library. He'd been surprised and a little put out to find her exploring his family's home more without him.

The following day they'd been sat together at the kitchen table, eating breakfast, when he'd asked if their age difference bothered her. Taken aback by the question, Sabi had said that it didn't – it was only seven years – the same gap had existed between her mother and father.

He'd gone quiet then, saying he had something important to tell her, but first he'd like to know – if she could pick anything – what it was she wanted most of all from life. Caught up in the moment, Sabi had eagerly told Simon how she'd love to live at Hawthorn Park with him and a large family, running the house while he maintained the grounds. He'd said nothing to contradict her – but later, thinking back, she saw there'd been a distance between them she'd not been able to breach for the rest of the visit.

Two days later Simon had ended it. He'd driven them back to university, sat her in her student room, but hadn't sat down with her. Hovering by the door, he'd jangled the keys in his pocket the whole time he'd spoken. Sabi could still remember his opening words as he ended them.

I can't do this, Sab. I can't be with someone who loves my home more than me.

Everything she recalled after that was a blur of disjointed words and phrases. She remembered protesting, saying she loved him not his inheritance – but he'd countered, saying he'd seen how she looked at his home – more lovingly than she looked at him. He'd accused her of being materialistic – a snob in the making. She'd cried then – but her tears had stopped abruptly when he'd told her about his daughter. A child he'd kept secret all that time.

Sabi shivered as she relived the shock that had swept through her. She'd known he was a widower – but not a father.

He thought me a snob who wasn't fit to know about his child. Sabi groaned. *If that had happened now, at my age, I'd have told him where to go – but back then, in the grip of a naïve first love...* Her thoughts morphed into a puffed-out sigh.

It had been six months until her broken heart had healed enough for her to even consider moving on, and then, like a miracle, she'd met Henry and learnt to laugh again. That laughter had brought with it the knowledge that what she'd seen as forever love was nothing of the sort. It had been love with Simon – but not the lasting kind.

'Good old Henry.' Sabi patted the arm of her chair. Her husband hadn't told her he was going to buy it. She hadn't even realised he'd noticed her point it out in an interior design magazine she'd been scouring for ideas for the house. Then, the day after they'd moved into her dream home in the village of Culmstock, she had come home from helping Maddie sort through the nursery's accounts, and it had been sat in the corner of the kitchen waiting for her.

'I do love you, Henry.' Sabi breathed the words into the empty kitchen as she wiped a tear from her eye.

So why am I so sad at the death of a man who dumped me years ago?

Sabi thought back to the picture of the young woman in the photographs on the website. Sara. Simon's daughter. A woman who'd be in her early twenties by now. She'd been stood in a new part of the garden – a memorial garden to her father, grown soon after he'd lost his fight with cancer.

'Ed won't mind, will he?' Jake asked as his boss placed a glass of shandy on the table.

'Don't be daft.' Maddie settled into the wooden chair on the opposite side of the table. 'Better to ask me now than tomorrow when we'll both be busy.' She gestured to the folder on the table. 'What do you need help with?'

'Fruit canes.'

'Go on.' Maddie pulled the folder closer and flicked through the first few pages.

'I have to talk about this paper in a tutorial on Tuesday.' Jake ran a hand over his shaved head. 'And there are some words I can't...' He groaned. 'You must think I'm very stupid.'

Maddie fixed her friend with a hard stare. 'For the last time, Jake, I do not consider you stupid. I never have.'

'I know I could just type each word I don't know into Google, but Petra says that if I work them out for myself, or use a dictionary in book form, then the words have a better chance of staying in my head, so I recognise them again.'

'Another reason why I like Petra so much, although I'm

sure she wouldn't be against you looking things up on the computer while she isn't around to help.' Maddie spoke more gently. 'How about at Bicton? Are you making friends at horticultural college?'

Jake shrugged.

'Have you tried to?' Maddie found herself reminded of the Jake she'd worked alongside before Petra had come into his life. Shy, and self-conscious to the point of morosely cutting himself off from everyone who might have befriended him, so sure was he that he'd be judged as pointless company because his education was somewhat lacking.

'It's not that easy and, well…' Jake unhunched his shoulders '…on the practical side of things, I've left all the others behind. I know what I'm doing, and I just get on with it. The written stuff, however… There isn't too much, and I was honest about my abilities when I signed up, but although I can do it, I'm slow and I hate doing it.'

'Have you spoken to Petra about this?'

'No. She's busy having the time of her life doing her apprenticeship at Rosemoor. I don't want to bring her down.'

'You're a good chap.' Maddie smiled. 'When are you seeing her next?'

'No idea.' Jake ran a hand over his head. 'Now I'm living back at home it's not easy to be together. Petra hates coming to my place. Mum is not exactly welcoming to me, let alone anyone else, and as for her place…'

Maddie swallowed. 'I'm really sorry I can't have you as a lodger anymore Jake – what with the conversion and…'

'I totally understand.' Jake gave his boss a brave smile. 'I was very grateful for staying when I could though.'

Keen to change the subject, Maddie tapped the folder with her fingertip. 'Come on, let's deal with one crisis at a time. Tell me what you've managed to read so far.'

6

'It's arrived!' Maddie announced to the empty room as Monday morning started with the arrival of an email in her inbox. 'Blimey, that was quick.'

Scanning through the attached letter from the Disclosure and Barring Service, she saw she was entitled, for the next twelve months at least, to hold group sessions for children and vulnerable adults.

'Thank goodness Ed was wrong about how long it takes.'

Making her way into the living room, Maddie picked up Henry's plans. 'I just hope the planning application goes through as quickly as the DBS check did.'

Knowing that was probably a hope too far, Maddie had shut down her laptop before it hit her.

'Oh God! I've passed the DBS check. That means I actually have to run a children's club and design the classes.' Her heart hammered in her ribcage as a mild sweat crossed her palms. 'Come on, you helped do school visits when you worked at Killerton, and this will be just the same.'

Apart from the fact you'll be doing it on your own, without Dan to support you.

Thinking back to Dan, her former boss and mentor, when she'd worked as a gardener for the National Trust,

Maddie smiled. She knew what her old friend would say: 'Stop fretting, girl. You'll be great with the kids.'

I bet he'd offer to help, if I asked him; just like he did when we were fighting off BIG.

Blowing out a puff of air, Maddie pulled herself together. 'You're perfectly capable of doing this without dragging Dan out of retirement. It'll add to the "breaking even so we can keep going" fund.' Maddie studied the plans in her hand and had just gone back to visualising how the space would appear once the wall before her was knocked down when her phone rang.

Sabi raced across the kitchen and hugged Henry as if her life depended on it.

'Steady on, love.' Henry took a step backwards. 'A chap needs to breathe.'

'Sorry, but I was beginning to think we'd never sell our old house.'

Henry looked up quickly. 'That was Miriam?'

'Yes! We're officially under offer!'

'Thank goodness!' Henry sank onto the wingback chair and patted his lap, for Sabi to snuggle up next to him. 'When the sale Miriam first lined up fell through, I wasn't sure how we'd manage. Two mortgages would have been doable on their own for six months or so, but well, we are not without expenses.'

'We're alright though, aren't we?' Sabi felt an unfamiliar twinge of financial unease. They'd only moved because she'd fallen in love with their new home, thinking it looked like a doll's house she'd always wanted when she was a child.

She loved it – but if they hadn't moved then they would still be secure.

'We're fine, but all our savings are gone.'

Sabi's heart contracted as she listened to her husband, guilt assailing her as he gave an uncomplaining account of how she'd so causally spent all the money he'd spent his working life saving.

'The move, our half of the solicitors' fees and tax for the nursery, plus the few things we couldn't hang back from getting so we could live here, took everything. The buffer we're used to having is no more.' Henry kissed the top of his wife's head. 'I know you're dying to crack on with changing the interior design of this place, but we're going to have to refill the coffers a little first.'

Hoping the disappointment she felt, despite her guilt, didn't show in her eyes, Sabi said, 'Waiting is fine. I have plenty to help Maddie with right now. It'll give me time to work out exactly how to decorate each room.'

Henry hugged her to his side. 'It won't take long for us to get on an even keel again. The company has lots of work coming in. That's why we took on an assistant at the office. Graham and I can't do everything anymore.'

'How's she getting on? Hazel, isn't it?'

'Early days yet, but she came highly recommended from her previous employers at the county council. I'm planning to bring her over to The Potting Shed later in the week to write up the order of events for the builders, once planning permission is granted, so you'll meet her then.'

'You're sure it *will* be granted?' Sabi bit her lip. 'If it isn't, I'm not quite sure what we'll do.'

'There may have to be tweaks here and there – there

often are – but otherwise I can't see a problem. After all, they were willing to give BIG planning permission to do something far more radical with the site.'

'I hadn't thought of that. Obvious really.' Sabi paused, before voicing the nagging doubt that had begun to circle her head. 'What if our house sale collapses again?'

'Let's work on the theory that it won't.' Henry stroked his wife's hair. 'I think we should go to see Miriam at her office to discover the full situation. Find out how long it is likely to take for everything to be completely sorted.'

'Good idea.' Sabi checked the time on her phone. 'When works for you?'

'Graham's out of the office today. I've got a couple of meetings I can't reschedule this morning, but I could leave Hazel to keep things ticking over this afternoon. How about two o'clock?'

'You're sure she'll be okay?'

'Our PA, Donna, is there too; she'll keep an eye on things.'

'In that case, I'll give Miriam a call to make sure she's going to be there.' Sabi kissed Henry's cheek. 'I'd better call Maddie too. I was going in with Jemima this afternoon to take Florrie for a walk and see if I could think of any more ideas re Easter weekend custom.'

'You could still drop Jemima off there. I doubt she'll think it fun hanging around an estate agent's office.'

'True.' Sabi picked up her phone. 'At least it'll be quiet with no customers.'

'Still don't think it's worth opening to the public on a Monday then?'

'We toyed with the idea of opening seven days a week,

but it isn't practical. It's the only day Maddie can get on with any serious gardening, and as Jake is at college Tuesday to Friday, she is doing most of that these days. They need Mondays to tend the plants properly.' Sabi examined her perfectly manicured fingernails. 'I earn half the profits so… sometimes I think I ought to help with the plants. If I…'

'You do enough.' Henry cut through his wife's latest bout of remorse. 'You do the accounts, the stock ordering, and you liaise with Ivan at the Exmoor Drifters when they run their occasional markets at The Potting Shed. Maddie never expected you to do the actual gardening.'

'Occasional is the word.'

'Sorry?' Henry reluctantly pulled on his suit jacket.

'The Exmoor Drifters' markets. I had hoped after their successful Christmas and New Year visits, they'd come at least once a month, but they are so booked up. Years in advance in some cases.'

'Perhaps you should secure them for next Christmas now, then.'

'Already have. Did it the second the last one was over.' Sabi clambered to her feet. 'Perhaps I'll call Ivan on the off-chance they can do a day in the Easter holiday. Cancellations are not unknown.'

'Unlikely though.'

'Very, but you never know.'

'Florrie, will you get out of there.' Jemima flicked her ponytail over her shoulder, giggling as the puppy disappeared into a large cardboard box, once used for daffodil bulbs, and now destined to be filled with books.

Maddie grinned as she saw the tip of a tail wagging out of the box. 'I've told her she'll end up at the charity shop, but she seems determined to be packaged.'

Hauling Florrie out of the box, Jemima gathered up a pile of old gardening magazines. 'Do you really think the charity shop will want these?'

'No. I want those.' Maddie took the well-thumbed paper pages from her niece and held them protectively to her chest. 'There's a lifetime of wisdom in those. Dad pored over them for hours. Said that, with the exception of *Gardeners' Question Time*, they could answer every query a gardener ever had.'

'What's *Gardeners' Question Time*?'

'Programme on Radio 4. Been running forever. You can phone in your horticultural issues and gardening experts will help you out with advice.'

'Can't gardeners use Google then?'

Maddie couldn't help but laugh at her niece's confusion. 'Not every answer is on the Internet you know.'

Horrified at the notion, Jemima said, 'Are you sure?'

'Well, no, I'm not, but sometimes a few different opinions from experts can be nice. And a human voice is friendlier than a machine, don't you think?'

'I've never thought about it.' The eleven-year-old threw a few more books into the box. 'Aunt Maddie, do we have to do this?'

'Sorry, love, you must be bored stiff. Emptying out my spare room isn't exactly fun Easter holiday stuff, is it.'

'It's just... all I seem to have done since I got home is

pack or unpack suitcases or boxes between the end of the boarding school term and moving house.' Jemima pointed towards the window. 'Isn't there anything I could do outside? Could we plant something?'

'Really?'

'Yeah. I used to love helping Grandad fill pots with stuff.'

'So, you did.' Maddie felt a tug of sadness at the memory of Jem at six or seven years old, sat on her grandfather's knee, soil being liberally pushed – often far too tightly – into rows of flowerpots in the potting shed, now the nursery's shop.

Now the shop is going to be downstairs, perhaps Dad's old space should go back to being the potting-up room again and…

'Aunt Maddie? Are you alright?' Jemima ruffled the fur on Florrie's head as she dived out of another empty box.

'Sorry, yes. Just thinking.' Maddie put down the magazines and headed to the bedroom door. 'I could do with some fresh air too. Let's go and prep some flowerpots for vegetable cuttings to go towards that "Grow a Smoothie" idea you had before Christmas.'

'Do you really think it's a good idea?'

'I think it's brilliant. I'm going to put some kits together when I have time. Recipe cards, seeds, pots and – when relevant – potted starter plants.'

'That sounds fab.' Jemima leapt up with so much enthusiasm that Florrie let out a bark of excitement. 'I can't wait to drink my first plant.'

Maddie opened the bedroom door. 'It really is an excellent idea of yours, to grow plants specifically for juicing.'

'I could do the recipes on my computer!'

Grateful for Jemima's enthusiasm, knowing she could just as easily have been at home, playing computer games, listening to music, and messaging her friends, Maddie smiled. 'If you wouldn't mind, that would be great.'

'No problem. I'll do a spinach and something one first.'

'Spinach and…?'

'Not sure?' Jemima took a step backwards as Florrie bounded past her. 'What grows fast?'

'Nothing grows that fast – unless cress would work?'

'Not much to juice in cress.'

'True. How about blueberries?'

'Oh yes! Spinach and blueberry smoothies are delish! Can I grow some?'

'Sure.' Knowing Jake would have something to say about them encroaching on his fruit-planting territory, Maddie reasoned that he was hardly there, and everything still needed doing. 'We have some young plants started, but it would be good to bring on some more. March is a good time to plant them.'

'When will they have fruit on them?'

'September.'

'That's ages!'

'Not for growing fruit it isn't.' Maddie passed Jemima her coat as they reached the back door. 'Actually, there's something else I wanted to pick your brains about.'

'Do you need more ideas to make money?'

Maddie snorted as she worked her way down the stairs. 'I'm always going to need more ideas for making money, but it's an idea I've already had I need some help with.'

'Like what?'

'Like, what would you want to do if you came to a children's gardening club?'

'Oh, that's easy?'

'It is?'

'Yeah. I'd want to grow blueberries for a smoothie!'

7

Sabi sat in her almost-office and listened to the silence of an empty house. She ought to have gone straight back to The Potting Shed after the trip to see Miriam at the estate agents, but the desire for a few minutes alone had been too strong.

Pushing her feet into the slippers she kept under her make-do desk, Sabi recalled Henry's relief when Miriam had explained how the new prospective buyers had already sold their home and had a pressing employment need to be in Tiverton. 'Perhaps we can all relax a bit now,' Sabi told herself as she opened her laptop.

Resisting taking another look at the Hawthorn Park website, she pulled up the Word document she'd made, containing all the contact details for the Exmoor Drifters. Finding their manager, Ivan Porter, on her list, she fired off an email.

Good afternoon, Ivan,
I hope you are well, and that Sheba is behaving herself. Florrie is proving a total delight at the nursery, although if she doesn't get some puppy training soon, I fear it will be too late!

She is rather good at leaving chaos and broken flowerpots in her wake.

I'm writing on the off-chance that the market is free over any of the Easter weekend – even if for just one day. A long shot I know, but if you do have cancellations, Maddie and I would be delighted to host you.

Warmest wishes,

Sabi

As soon as she'd sent the email, Sabi found her mind reverting to her former boyfriend.

'I should be elated! Celebrating the probable sale of our old home.' Sabi headed to the kitchen to make some tea. 'So, why am I obsessing over the loss of a man who hurt me?'

Addressing her mug as she dropped a teabag into it, a weak smile edged its way across Sabi's face. It hadn't been long ago that she'd never have drunk from a mug, always preferring her tea from a cup and saucer. And she'd certainly never have used a teabag, opting for fresh leaves and a state-of-the-art brewing teapot. No one had ever asked her the reason why she had drunk her tea that way, but she knew why – and the reason embarrassed her.

It wasn't that she didn't like the taste of the tea if quickly made, or the sensation of drinking from a mug, it was simply that making tea the 'proper way' was something she felt she ought to be seen to do in case someone important came round to the house while she had a cuppa on the go.

I hadn't realised quite how much of a snob I could be until Dad died. Cradling the mug, a bone-china one covered in pictures of roses that Jemima had bought for her, Sabi closed her eyes. An image of Simon immediately appeared behind her eyes.

'This is ridiculous. Why am I thinking about Simon so much? Is it because the nursery suddenly has a tenuous connection with Hawthorn Park?'

A new thought entered her head as she fetched some milk from the fridge.

If he was still alive, would I be making excuses to go and check on Jo while he's up there, in the hope I'd catch a glimpse of Simon?

'This *must* stop. I have nothing to prove, and it wasn't as if Simon was honest with me. I had no idea he had a child until the day he split up with me.' Sabi put the milk on the counter with a sigh. 'I'd have liked him to know I'm not the shallow snob he ended up believing me to be... Except, sometimes, I am.'

Taking her tea upstairs to her office room, Sabi pushed her shoulders back, knowing she'd come a long way since her father's death. 'I'm *not* the person Simon took me to be in the end. Not anymore.'

This time she did open the Hawthorn Park website and, once again, found herself face to face with a picture of Simon and his daughter.

'I wonder what you'd think of me, Sara. Did your dad ever warn you to stay away from men or women who would only love you for your heritage?'

Knowing she was being irrational, Sabi blew across the top of her mug to cool the contents. 'There's no reason on earth Simon would have ever mentioned me to you.'

With a sharp shake of her head, Sabi hit the button that closed the website's window, forcing her attention back to her emails.

She was surprised to see that Ivan, not known for his speed in responding to emails, had already replied to her message.

Sorry, Sabi lass, the Drifters are well and truly booked up for the time being. Next free day for the whole market is June 6th!

However, if a one-off stall would help, I'm happy to come along one day over the Easter weekend – providing it isn't raining. Can't manage more I'm afraid, but my cheese stand is your cheese stand if you'd like it.

As to Florrie – I'm imagining a puppy-sized jumping cracker! I'll bring Sheba over and see if she can't calm her down a bit.

Let me know about Easter,

Ivan

'Mum!' Jemima waved as she saw her mother heading across the nursery.

Florrie, not wanting to miss out on a greeting, dashed out of the polytunnel and almost bowled Sabi over in her keenness to be fussed.

'Hello, darling.' Sabi bent down to Florrie. 'You really do need training classes very soon, or you'll be flooring a customer.'

Maddie came to the polytunnel's door and waved a soil-stained hand in her sister's direction. 'I was thinking the same this morning. Goodness knows when we'll find the time.'

'Ivan said he'd bring Sheba to calm her down, although I'm not sure how that would work.'

'Sheba is a very calm Labrador. Maybe she'd be a good influence.'

'While she's around perhaps, but once she's gone again…'

'Back to being a live firework!' Jemima giggled as she wrestled the puppy.

'Ivan called her a jumping cracker.'

Maddie headed back into the polytunnel, calling over her shoulder, 'How come you've been talking to Ivan?'

'I emailed to double-check the Drifters hadn't had any Easter weekend cancellations. Even one day here would have been good.'

'No chance, right?'

'Ish. Ivan said he'll come. Just his cheese stall, if we want him for one day.'

Passing her niece a dustpan and brush, so she could sweep up the soil they'd unintentionally sprinkled on the floor, Maddie was surprised. 'Really? Why isn't he working with the others? It's his market.'

'He didn't say. Just said he could be with us for one day.'

'I hope Ivan's okay.' Maddie started to stack filled flowerpots onto a tray.

'I wondered if he was okay too, so I called him, telling him I wanted to confirm his email. Thinking back, he didn't sound his normal forthright self. Now I'm wondering if he was just trying to sound as if he was okay.'

Maddie smiled. 'That would be just like Ivan.'

'So, if he is serious about giving up a day of his holiday – assuming we're right about that – would you prefer him to come on Saturday or Sunday?'

'Sunday.' Maddie chewed on her bottom lip. 'I'll do the children's club on the Saturday. If Ivan came on Sunday, we'd have a small attraction each day, although nothing for the Bank Holiday Monday.'

'It's not a lot compared to BIG on their opening weekend, I don't suppose, but it's something.'

Jemima tapped the contents of her dustpan into a waiting bucket. 'Are you planning to go up to see what BIG's new place is like?'

The sisters exchanged an uneasy glance, before Maddie said, 'I suppose we ought to suss out the competition. At least no one who works there would recognise us.'

'True,' Sabi agreed. 'Still feels a bit like a betrayal of Dad though. I've almost opened their website several times but couldn't quite face it. It's bound to have lots of photographs of their newest store, as well as a list of opening events.'

'I think I'd rather do that – look at them online rather than visit I mean. Although, at the same time, I'm not sure I want to know.'

Jemima looked at the adults as if despairing of them. 'Grandad would say there is no point burying your head in the sand.'

Maddie smiled. 'He would have, wouldn't he.'

'Maybe we'll log on later and see exactly what we're up against,' Sabi agreed.

Changing the subject, Maddie brushed her hands down her jeans as she asked, 'House move chat go okay?'

Sabi put her arm around her daughter. 'I'm not counting my chickens, but we're hopeful that the sale will work out this time. So, tell me, what have you two been up to while I was away?'

8

Ed waved as his image appeared across Maddie's laptop screen. 'Hi, love, good day?'

Adjusting the volume on the Zoom call, Maddie waved back. 'Not bad, thanks. I managed to get some planting done. Jem is a dab hand at setting blueberry plants.'

'Green fingers must be in the blood.'

'For which I am very grateful.' Maddie sipped her wine as she balanced her laptop on her knees. 'I've decided to use Jem's "Grow a Smoothie" idea as the main draw for the children's classes.'

'Sounds good.' Ed pulled off the tie he wore around his neck and undid the top two buttons of his shirt. 'In the hope that the children book for a series of workshops and come back to see their plants grow?'

'And then, ultimately, drink them.' Maddie waved a notebook in front of the screen. 'I've been sketching out a few workshops and timings. I'd have to go at roughly the pace of the plants we grow, so Sabi's idea of sunflower planting would be good too.'

'If I was a kid, I'd definitely be impatient to see my plants pop up fast.'

'That's why I thought we'd go traditional – if not predictable – as well.'

'Cress?'

'Cress.' Maddie put down her glass. 'In a later class. I know they'll have all grown it before, but if I can find a different angle… maybe grow it with a purpose then…'

Ed suddenly leant forward, so his face was full in the screen. 'A picnic purpose!'

'I'm sorry?'

'Our idea about growing bluebells at the back of the nursery and adding picnic tables.'

'Your idea.'

'It's a good one. You agreed it was.'

'It is. But I can't take a load of kids to have a picnic there at the moment, Ed. It's all potholes and there's nowhere to sit.'

'But by the time their plants have grown it could be ready – and if you leave planting the cress until the summer…'

'Ummm, I see what you mean.' Maddie put her glass back down. 'It isn't a bad idea though – a picnic with cress sandwiches.'

'And, if the smoothies are ready by then, perhaps with orange juice squeezed from real oranges.'

Maddie snorted. 'If you think I can afford to buy in enough orange trees for…'

'No, I mean, the idea is to show children how plants work for us, right? You can't possibly grow them all – so how about a class about how some things are harder to grow than others, because of the weather or the soil conditions or the light or cost or whatever? You could buy in some oranges, let them juice them, and they could drink it.'

Laughing at the note of triumph in Ed's voice, Maddie asked, 'You'll be coming along to this picnic to sample the cress and juice then?'

'If I'm invited, I'd love to.'

'Would you?' Hoping she didn't sound too keen or presumptuous, Maddie added, 'I did wonder if you'd like to help me run the classes, but I know it's a lot to ask on your weekends off so…'

'Actually, I was going to ask if you needed an extra pair of hands, but I didn't want you to feel you had to ask me.' Ed winked. 'I come ready DBS-checked too.'

'Thanks, Ed. I'd love that.' Maddie relaxed back against the sofa, peering around the room as she did so.

'You okay?'

'I was just wondering what it'll be like sitting on this sofa upstairs, rather than in here. This was where Dad and I sat most nights, talking plants and putting the world to rights.'

'You'll get used it.'

'Hope so.' Maddie gestured to her right. 'I've got a copy of the plans laid out over there. If permission goes through, I want to be ready to get the ball rolling and start sourcing builders.'

'What will you do when said builders start pulling walls down?'

'Move around the house, living in different rooms, until they've finished, I suppose.'

'Don't be daft. You'll have to move out. Health and safety and all that.'

'But I can't move out!' Maddie was horrified. 'I need to be here. Onsite. Keeping an eye on things. Anyway, we can't afford to do everything in one lump. If we stick to the idea of earning enough to break even by the end of May – the idea of which seems increasingly unlikely…' She exhaled slowly. 'It's all going to take time and…'

'Don't worry. The money will come in and you'll be on site when it matters.'

'But where will I go if I do have to move out? Hotels are too expensive, although…' Maddie paused. 'I suppose if I asked Tim over at the Blackdown Hotel near Wellington, he might give me a good rate. We've been supplying him with fresh veg for years and—'

'Maddie, honestly! You can stay with me.'

'What did you tell him?'

Sabi unlocked the garden shop and pushed the door hard to open it, wincing at the high-pitched squeak its hinges made. 'This needs a spot of WD-40 or oil or something. I swear it gets harder to open every day.'

'I'll tell Jake.' Maddie pulled out her phone and then stopped. 'No, I won't, he's at college.'

'Not having him or Petra around is getting difficult, isn't it.'

'Just a bit. Jake's worked here so long, I keep forgetting he's studying.' Maddie passed her sister the float money for the till. 'I'll go and fetch the oil can now before I forget.'

'Oh, later will do. So, what did you tell Ed?' Sabi's tone gave away the excitement she felt at the prospect of her sister's relationship moving forward. 'Are you going to stay with him while this place is expanded?'

'No.'

'No?' Confusion creased Sabi's brow.

Maddie pushed a wedge under the shop door with her foot to hold it open. 'You sound surprised.'

'I am.'

'So was he.' Maddie tried to dismiss the memory of the disappointed expression that had crossed Ed's face when she'd rejected his offer. 'It's a nice idea, but it isn't practical.'

'Because?'

'He lives in Exeter.'

'You make that sound like Outer Mongolia! It's only twenty or so miles away.'

'Twenty-five to Ed's place, and anyway, it isn't the mileage. You know as well as I do that, although it's not a bad run up the motorway to Exeter, driving through the city is a nightmare. Residentially, the streets just weren't designed for motor cars. It's slow and it's always impossible to park.'

Sabi opened the till but didn't start filling it. Instead, she looked straight at her sister. 'Methinks, the lady doth protest too much.'

Maddie groaned. 'I think that's the impression Ed got too, although he didn't say so. He was very... stoic.'

'You mean gutted, but he's too nice a man to say so.'

'Maybe... yes, I suppose so.' Maddie stopped what she was doing and faced Sabi. 'It's just, I'm not sure that I'm ready.'

'To move in with him?'

'Or for him to move in with me. It doesn't mean I won't want to in time, but...' she raised her hands and dropped them again in defeat '...so much has happened over the past year. Ed and I haven't been together that long.'

'Three months?'

'Almost four.' Maddie could hear Ed's voice in the back of her head. *I know it's only been four months, but we get on so well, and it seems silly for you to have to pay out to stay somewhere when it's not unknown for us to spend the night together.*

'You stay at his place sometimes though, don't you?'

Wondering if her sister could read her mind, Maddie said, 'No, that's just it. I don't. I've been there, and it's a lovely flat and everything. But when it comes to staying over, Ed always comes here. It's easier, with the nursery being so twenty-four-seven.'

'So, he's always the one who makes the effort. With the travelling I mean.'

Her sister had spoken gently, but Maddie still felt the slight. 'You think Ed is the one putting all the effort into our relationship?'

'I said with the travelling, but, well... he does come here a lot doesn't he.'

'He likes it here.'

'I know but look at it from Ed's point of view. You don't want him to think he's all give and you're all take, do you?' An image of Simon Northcott flashed through Sabi's mind. 'I know you're not, but...'

Maddie picked up an undercurrent in her sister's tone. 'Are you okay?'

'Yes, of course, why wouldn't I be?'

'Now I *know* you're not okay.' Maddie frowned. 'You only say "why wouldn't I be?" when something's wrong. What's up, sis?'

'Don't deflect your guilt onto me by inventing a reason why I might not be alright.'

Maddie gave her sister an examining stare. 'I wasn't. I know I've hurt Ed, even though I didn't mean to – and I know I have to make it up to him. It isn't that I don't love him or don't want to be with him – but I can't be so far from The Potting Shed while it's undergoing surgery. He said he understood.'

'You don't think he does though.'

Maddie sighed. 'Not yet. Not completely.'

'None of this addresses the question of where you'll stay during the renovation.' Sabi ripped open a bag of ten-pence pieces and clattered them into the till's drawer. 'Although, obviously, you can stay at our place. Plenty of room, and not too far to drive in every day.'

'Really?' Maddie, not entirely sure that she wanted to stay with her sister either, but knowing it was the most sensible option, said, 'Are you sure? You've only just moved in. Aren't you decorating?'

'Chance would be a fine thing.'

'Sorry?'

'Oh nothing.'

'Sabi?'

With a puff of regret, Sabi confessed, 'I'm always here, so I've had no time to implement any of my plans. And even if I was, there's no spare money. All my interior designs dreams are on hold. And…'

A second wave of guilt hit Maddie. 'If it wasn't for me… for this place…'

Sabi held up her hand. 'I'm glad we saved The Potting

Shed and I do not mind working on the tills, Mads, or doing the books from home. I was just saying I wish I had a bit more time to do my new place up – but then, so would anyone who's just moved house.'

'True.' Maddie gave Sabi a relieved smile as she went on.

'When Jemima's home it's fine. She loves coming here at the weekends and in the holidays. Plus, she can walk Florrie for us.'

'She's a dab hand at planting too.'

'But we need to face facts, Maddie. We *have* to get new staff. You and I aren't enough. I know you feel loyal to Jake, but we need regular help.'

'But if we have more wages to pay, then it'll be harder to break even before the end of May.'

'We were paying Jake – we'll use that money.'

'Only some of it. He still gets paid for the hours he does.'

Sabi put a reassuring hand on her sister's arm. 'I know you're worried about not making our first financial goal – but Mads, how on earth can we expand this place, if there aren't enough staff to run it when it's this small?'

9

'Here you go, Dad. The first step towards expansion is open for business.'

Placing the final pot of chives next to a row of mint plants, Maddie picked up a handful of price labels and poked one into the soil next to each herb. 'Not quite on the scale that BIG have, but at least I grew everything in here myself.'

Leaving the doors to the greenhouse open, to let both customers and fresh air in, Maddie surveyed the nursery's grounds. The past few days had been relatively quiet customer wise. Although that wasn't great, it had meant she'd managed to get the herb greenhouse just as she wanted it and she had fully planned her children's workshops. Having decided to call the group the Little Acorns Gardening Club, Maddie had sketched out one meeting a fortnight, lasting until early September, when, hopefully, they'd all get to drink the fruits of their labours as one of Jem's smoothies.

Now, as she meandered into the shop area, Maddie picked up one of the posters she'd printed off, advertising the classes, and was suddenly hit by a sense of it all being rather pointless.

'Sabi's right – who *is* going to run this place while I take the workshops?' She swallowed as she remembered what her sister had said about her and Ed. He'd said he'd help her at weekends, but should she let him when he worked such long hours all week? *Am I taking him for granted?*

Hearing her mistress sigh, Florrie peeped out from beneath the desk, her tail wagging.

'You're offering to help, are you?' Crouching down, Maddie gave her dog a cuddle. 'I'm sure you'd be excellent at counting out a customer's change, wouldn't you.'

Florrie agreed with a short yap as the sound of approaching footsteps made Maddie stand up again.

'Ivan!'

'Hello, lass.' The manager of the Exmoor Drifters market peered over the counter. 'Well then, young Florrie, let's be seeing you.'

At the familiar voice, the puppy leapt out from under the counter.

'How's my little jumping cracker?' As Ivan bent to greet Florrie, Sheba, Ivan's black Labrador, sat patiently in the shop doorway.

Coming out from behind the till, Maddie gave Sheba a hug. 'Florrie is just fine, but nothing like as well behaved as this beauty.'

'That's what I've come to talk to you about. That and Easter.'

'Sabi said you could bring your stall over. She did confirm Easter Sunday with you, didn't she?'

'She did. Very efficient, your sister.'

'That she is.' Maddie brushed some dust off her legs as she stood back up. 'How come, if you don't mind me asking, you aren't working with the rest of the Drifters over the Easter break?'

'Ah.'

'Ah?' Maddie's eyes narrowed. 'You're alright, aren't you?'

'My normal response would be, "Right as rain", but I'd be lying, and I've never liked doing that.'

'Ivan?' Maddie went cold. 'What's wrong?'

'Nowt to stress about.' As Ivan stood back up, Sheba came to his side, as if knowing he needed moral support. 'Touch of arthritis, that's all. Doctor has advised me to give up the length of time I spend standing in the open air during the colder seasons.'

'But you run a market and...'

'You've hit the problem right there, lass.' Ivan kept a hand on Sheba, as if drawing strength from her presence. 'But time ticks on, and I'm not getting any younger.'

'You make yourself sound old.'

'Fifty-six.'

'That's nothing! You're not going to give the Exmoor Drifters up, are you?'

'I'm a good few years off retirement yet, but I am having to accept the fact that I will have to be more of a hands-off organiser during the autumn and winter.'

'But what about your stall? Surely you need to sell your cheese to...' Maddie stopped abruptly. 'Sorry, I didn't mean to pry.'

'Not at all.' Ivan gave her a warm smile. 'The nicer weather is already poking its head above the parapet. I have spring and summer ahead of me before autumn strikes, but I ought to get into a sensible routine from the off. The Drifters are good people. They're quite happy for me to organise the gigs and only actually be there when I can.'

'You'll miss it though, the camaraderie of the group, I mean.'

'I will. Which is why I was so grateful when your sister called. I'd be very happy to set up my cheese stall here on Easter Sunday.' Ivan flexed his left leg as if to show Maddie where the root of his problem lay. 'The forecast for Easter weekend is dry, so I won't have to worry about my knee stiffening up in the rain.'

'I'm so glad you can come. Your cheeses and chutneys are fantastic. And don't forget, you'll be doing me a favour by being here.' Maddie tilted her head to one side. 'Would you prefer to be undercover though? On the Saturday I'm using the far polytunnel for a children's class, but it'll be empty on the Sunday. We could put up plenty of "Ivan's cheese this way" signs so no one can miss the fact you're here.'

Ivan shuffled as if embarrassed. 'I don't want to be putting you out, lass.'

'You aren't. You're doing *me* a favour.'

'Talking of favours…' Ivan appeared uncomfortable. 'I was chatting to Elspeth. You remember her?'

'Absolutely. Elspeth sells the best homemade beauty products in Devon, if not the country.'

Ivan chuckled. 'She'd be chuffed to hear that, lass. And you're right of course. Well, she wondered…'

Maddie leapt in, 'Please tell me that she wants to sell here on Easter Sunday too!'

'I take it that's a yes then?'

'She does? Really?'

'I was chatting to her about my stepping back from some of the markets, and she confided she was thinking of giving up the selling side of things, and just making her hand creams and so on. She hopes to find a retail outlet for them instead of being at the helm of the marketing herself. Elspeth's a remarkable woman, but she's long past retirement age, and the constant setting up and taking down of a trader's stall is beginning to take its toll.'

'Well, we'd love it if she was here too over Easter.' Maddie clapped her hands, making both Florrie and Sheba look at her. 'So that's how to get your attention, Flo!'

Ivan rubbed a hand over his beard. 'That was the other reason for popping over. Sabi mentioned that Florrie could do with a bit of sorting out.'

Some of Maddie's jubilation dissolved as she confessed, 'I know I should have taken her to puppy-training classes at least a month back, but there just isn't...'

'The time or money. I know.' Ivan held up a hand. 'And before you apologise or explain, I knew your situation when I gave her to you, so how about I have a go for you. I trained Sheba, and she's not a bad soul.'

'Sheba's the most well-behaved dog on the planet! I can't imagine Florrie ever being that good.'

'Nor can I.' Ivan patted the puppy's head affectionately. 'But we can improve things a bit. Stop her knocking things over with her tail and yapping when yapping is not helpful.'

Maddie felt awkward. 'This is very kind of you, but aren't you supposed to be staying inside more?'

'If I was with the dogs I'd be moving about. That is positively encouraged by the doctor. It's sitting or standing still in the damp and cold that's not so sensible.'

'Well, I—'

'And before you say you ought to pay me for doing this, then save your breath. This is the sort of thing I love to do.

I promise, you'd be doing me a service by letting me help – stopping me getting old before my time and winning me brownie points with my physiotherapist by keeping me on the move.'

'In that case, thank you!' Maddie beamed. 'I'm so glad you came. I was just having a gloomy moment. Then you arrived and solved two problems in one.'

'Two problems?'

'Not having enough of a draw for custom on Easter Sunday and training Florrie!'

'I can't promise Elspeth and I will bring in extra trade, but we'll do our best.' Ivan bent back down to Florrie. 'As to this little dynamo, we'll have a great time, won't we?'

By eleven o'clock, Maddie had sold three herb plants and had managed to talk a customer into bringing her granddaughter along to the first Little Acorns Gardening Club on Easter Saturday. Still buoyed up by Ivan's visit, she was about to call Sabi to let her know that Elspeth was on board, when another familiar face walked through the door.

'Jo!'

'Morning, Maddie. Love the greenhouse.'

'Thanks.'

'It's steady out there, people wise, I mean. Car park has got more cars in it than I expected for a Thursday.'

'Thursdays can be a bit hit and miss, but we're slowly getting more folk through the doors. Mostly pensioners and young mums with toddlers looking for somewhere to go.' Maddie ran a hand through her hair. 'I'm not sure we'll keep them once BIG opens, but for now, I'm grateful for their custom. When they actually buy something, that is.'

Jo shifted awkwardly. 'You'd have more chance of keeping customers if you had a café.'

'Ultimately, we will, but as yet...'

'There's a lot to do first, I know. The thing is, I wondered, over spring and summer – when I'm not booked elsewhere – if you'd like me to bring the van here on Thursdays and Fridays as well as over the weekends?'

'Are you serious?' Maddie's face lit up.

'I am. What do you think?'

'What do I think?' Maddie laughed. 'I think I'd like you to start tomorrow!'

'Ten till four?'

'Deal!'

IO

Maddie was bouncing around the polytunnel with such enthusiasm that it was a miracle the contents of the mug she held weren't spilling everywhere. Her phone was pressed tightly to her ear; she couldn't get the words out fast enough.

'I can't believe it, Ed! I was so worried, and now, miraculously, I have two fabulous extra selling points on Easter Sunday *and* Jo is going to work here two extra days a week during spring and summer.'

'I know! You told me last night.'

'Yeah, I know I did, but now I've had the cherry popped onto my cake. Henry just called. Planning permission for the first stage of redevelopment has been granted. The Potting Shed really is going to grow!'

'That's fantastic! I'm so excited for you.' Ed's voice was full of encouragement. 'I can't wait to come over later to see the plans in person.' He paused. 'They went through fast. How did Henry pull that off?'

'Something to do with his new assistant. Apparently, she used to work in the council planning office and knew how to get things fast-tracked.'

'Handy.'

The cautious tone of Ed's reply made Maddie anxious.

'You don't think she's dishonest like Leo Creswell was, do you? I'd hate to cheat the system. That would make me no better than him.'

'I'm sure it is all above board. Henry wouldn't have any dealings with someone he didn't trust.'

'That's true.' Remembering what Sabi had told her about being all take and no give where Ed was concerned, Maddie said, 'Enough about the nursery though, you must be sick of hearing about it. How's it going your end?'

The note of surprise in Ed's voice was embarrassingly telling as he replied. 'It's good thanks. Are you okay?'

'Yes, why?'

'You don't normally ask about my work.'

Her joy evaporating, Maddie admitted, 'I know. I've been more than a bit self-focused lately. Sorry, Ed.'

'Not at all, and that wasn't what I meant. My work is mostly confidential, so I can't share it with you.'

'I know, but I should ask about it more often. I've been so wrapped up in things and now the building should start soon...'

'Let me guess...'

Maddie found herself holding her breath as she heard Ed rest back against his office chair as she waited to hear what he was going to say.

'...you're feeling bad about saying no to staying with me while you've got the builders in.'

'I am. Dreadfully.' Maddie pulled out a stool from under the potting up bench and sat down with Florrie at her feet. 'It truly *isn't* because I don't want to be with you, it's just—'

Ed interrupted, 'Too much too soon?'

'Partly. I would like to stay at yours sometimes though. I

wasn't casting aspersions on your flat or you. But you're far away when I need to be here all the time, and then parking in Exeter is...'

'Maddie!' Ed spoke firmly but gently down the phone. 'I know you're good at digging, but right now, you're digging yourself into the wrong sort of hole!'

Attempting to pull herself together, Maddie hugged an arm across her chunky jumper. 'What I was clumsily trying to get to, was that I love you and I'm sorry it's been so "all about me and the nursery" ever since we met. If you'd put up with me, I'd love to come over tonight, but I'm not ready to do the total living together bit. Not yet.'

'I would love you to come over tonight, but how about I come to you?'

'But you always come here. I was trying to...'

'I know what you were trying to do, and it's appreciated, but I want to see the plans Henry has put together now that they're official. I want to see how it's all going to work in situ. I'm excited for The Potting Shed.'

Maddie smiled. 'I don't deserve you, Ed Tate.'

'True, I'm not all heart though. Before I come over to yours later, I'm taking Jo out for a pint. We don't get to catch up so much out of Dark Skies season, and I'm sure something's bothering him.'

'He seemed okay when he was here yesterday, but I know he always plays his cards close to his chest. Make sure you buy him a pint from me.' Maddie hurriedly added, 'I'll give you the money back. I just want to thank him for bringing his coffee van here more often.'

'Don't worry, I knew what you meant.' Ed nodded. 'I admit I was disappointed you didn't want to stop here, but

I totally understand why, and I don't think you take me for granted.'

'Did Sabi talk to you?'

'No, why?'

'She accused me of doing just that.'

'Well, just for once, she was wrong.'

'Still want to have your wicked way with me?' Maddie giggled.

'Often and always.'

Maddie was hit with a sense of joyous relief. 'Really?'

'Really.' Ed paused, and Maddie suspected he was gathering himself before he carried on. 'Ultimately, I hope we can live together – but not until you're ready. Is that okay?'

Maddie's pulse zipped up a notch. 'That's very okay.'

The sound of a faint knock told Maddie that Ed had to go. 'First client of the day?'

'Yup. Better go.'

Maddie could hear her boyfriend stand up. She pictured him in his grey suit, morphing from relaxed gardening helper to city solicitor. 'Don't go offering them hot chocolate and biscuits to dunk if it's a gorgeous young woman.'

Ed laughed quietly as he recalled the first time they'd met. 'Fear not, Madeline Willand, that specialist treatment was just for you.'

Buoyed up from the good news that the last twenty-four hours had brought her, and relieved that she had cleared the air with Ed, Maddie headed to the shop.

'Thanks goodness it's Friday!'

'What are you talking about?' Jake peered up from where

he was sweeping out the small area beneath the till. 'You work all weekend, it's hardly the end of the week.'

'But it means you're here!' Maddie smiled. 'Your presence is missed Tuesdays, Wednesdays and Thursdays, believe me.'

'Oh, right.' Jake carried on with his sweeping.

'How did the tutorial about fruit canes go?'

Jake shrugged. 'It was okay. Thanks for helping me.'

'My pleasure. Anytime – really. Never be afraid to ask. You're a great gardener. Once you have this qualification, you'll be able to apply for much better jobs than this one.'

'Actually—' Jake abruptly stopped talking. 'No, it doesn't matter; it's only a small thing anyway.'

'What doesn't?'

'I'm not supposed to say. Not yet. Not 'til it's all official. And I don't want to jinx it. It's probably too good to be true anyway.'

'Or whatever it is, might be amazing.' Maddie smiled. 'Honestly, Jake. A little self-belief wouldn't hurt you know.'

Not bothering to answer, Jake finished clearing the floor. 'Who planted all those extra blueberries in my fruit tunnel?'

'Me and Jem. They're for the children's gardening club. I'm starting it on Easter Saturday.'

'The *what*?' Jake looked up in horror.

'Don't worry, I'm not asking you to run it.' Maddie quickly added, 'Although, if you wouldn't mind running the shop while I'm taking it…'

'Couldn't Petra do that? She is much better with people.'

'Petra?' Maddie's face lit up. 'She's coming to help at Easter?'

'Yeah. She volunteered. Didn't I say?'

'No.'

'Only if you want her to help, but she thought, you know, Easter is a busy time in the garden, and it'll add to her hours of gardening work. It all goes towards points for her studies.'

Maddie gave Jake a massive hug, much to his discomfort. 'That's fantastic. Just when I thought Easter was going to be a disaster, everything is coming together.'

At precisely quarter to ten, Jo pulled his bright orange camper van to a halt on its usual patch of ground near the shop and jumped from the driver's seat, ready to open for business on the hour. Although, beyond popping a quick announcement up on his social media platforms, he hadn't had time to advertise that he was going to be there that day, he experienced a tug of satisfaction as a few of the nursery's early customers enquired how soon it would be before they could have a drink.

Assured of at least a few sales, he set about activating the coffee machine and unstacking the tables and chairs. As he worked, the buzz of the mobile in his pocket sent a shot of adrenalin through his chest. He still hadn't replied to Sara's last text. *Surely that isn't her again?*

Knowing he was mean for not responding to her before, and that the only reason he hadn't was that he didn't want to hurt someone he cared about – again – Jo read the text.

Relieved to see that it was Ed asking if he was up for a drink at the pub after work, Jo tapped in a positive response. His conscience, however, still pricked him.

*

Sabi whispered out of the side of her mouth. 'Henry did *not* tell me his new assistant looked like that!'

'I'm a scarecrow by comparison.' Maddie muttered as she saw her brother-in-law's immaculately turned out employee stride confidently across the car park towards them.

'Since when did you start worrying about things like appearance?' Sabi whispered back.

'Since about thirty seconds ago.' Maddie brushed her palms over her old jumper and mud-stained jeans. 'No idea why! What did you say her name was?'

'Hazel Cooper.' Sabi lowered her voice further as the briefcase-carrying woman in a designer business suit got closer. 'As much as I'd like to hate her on principle for looking that good in those clothes, she has managed to fast-track the planning permission.'

'True,' Maddie admitted, 'I promise not to hold the fact she can walk on stupidly high heels across gravel without falling over against her.'

'Stupid things to wear here. She must have known she was going on site today,' Sabi grumbled, glaring down at her own boots. They may have been several hundred cuts above Maddie's battered walking boots, but the items on Hazel's feet were in another league altogether.

'I think your husband is paying her too much,' Maddie muttered.

Sabi looked at her sister in surprise. 'That's not like you – that's more like – well, me!'

Maddie gave her sister a quick hug. 'Sorry. I'm just nervous – I want this to go smoothly so badly.' Knowing it was time to be a grown-up, she nudged Sab's arm. 'Come on, let's go and greet Henry's new employee.'

After ten minutes Maddie knew three things for certain. The first was that Hazel Cooper was not someone it would be easy to argue with. The second was that they were not destined to be friends. The third was that, according to Hazel, Henry had already secured them some builders, and she had to be out of her home in two days' time.

II

'This will be a no-go area for some time.' Hazel threw open a few cupboard doors as she prowled around Maddie's kitchen. 'I'm surprised you haven't moved the contents out already.'

'But I didn't know the builders were booked until you arrived ten minutes ago.'

'You knew it was going to happen though.'

Feeling as though she was being told off by a disappointed headmistress, Maddie found herself floundering. 'Obviously, I am aware of what needs doing, but...'

Already determined to report his new assistant's high-handed manner to her husband, Sabi cut in with icy calm. 'Miss Cooper, while we appreciate the speed at which you've helped encourage the turnaround of the planning permission, we do *not* appreciate being treated like naughty children. My sister and I have many skills, but clairvoyance is not one of them.' Before Hazel could respond, Sabi continued, taking the cut-glass edge off her voice as she asked, 'Now, these builders, I'm assuming my husband has sourced them from a pool of workers he has employed before, and therefore trusts?'

'Naturally.' Continuing as if the admonishment had

never happened, Hazel extracted some paperwork from her briefcase. 'R. K. Andrews – a family firm from Taunton – will be doing the work for you.'

'Sounds good.' Maddie knew her father would have approved of using local tradesmen. 'And they are beginning by stripping out my kitchen?'

'As I said. Yes.'

'I think,' Sabi screwed her hands into fists as she experienced a totally uncharacteristic urge to give their visitor a slap, 'what my sister is asking is, why is her kitchen going first when we are not planning on upgrading it into part of the café area until next year?'

'I am aware of the order of your upgrade plans. However, with planning permission, the most sensible process in a situation like this, where work is being done on a piecemeal basis, is to get in all the permissions at once. Mr Willand-Harris informed me that you wouldn't be in residence during the renovation, so therefore starting in here will not matter.'

'But I'll still need to be able to use this kitchen until the new one upstairs is sorted.' Maddie felt panicked at the thought of having the facility to make coffee and toast taken away from her. 'I was planning to nip in and out to use it, even once the new sales area was open.'

'There'll be no need for that.' Hazel gave a dismissive shake of her head. 'The conversion of the fourth bedroom into a kitchen-diner will be done as soon as this old kitchen is dealt with. My thinking being that you'd be able to move back in sooner if there was somewhere to eat, and that having drinking water available on the floor in which you are living established from the off might be helpful. And so...' undeniably smug, Hazel took, a patient breath '...the builders will have to dismantle the cooker from here and rerun the water supply from downstairs, so they can establish the new kitchen area.'

'Ah, right. I see.' Maddie blushed. It seemed so obvious when it was put like that.

Ed collected two pints of Stag, his favourite of all the Exmoor ales, and headed to the far corner of the pub, where Jo had grabbed the last free table. 'Busy, isn't it.'

Jo nodded. 'I'd forgotten what Friday night in a pub was like. It's been quite a while.'

'I've not been lately either and I've never been to Maddie's local before.' Ed looked around the stone walls of The Cider Press. 'Not that she goes to the pub much, and if I go out for a drink, it tends to be in Exeter, or somewhere for a meal with Maddie.'

Taking a mouthful of ale, Jo said, 'She could have come too.'

'In normal circumstances she would have, but right now Maddie is running round like a headless chicken with Sabi and Jem, filling cardboard boxes with kitchen utensils and moving them into the spare room.'

Jo went to stand up. 'Shouldn't we be helping?'

Raising a hand to gesture for his friend to stay where he was, Ed said, 'I offered, but Maddie didn't think we'd all fit into the kitchen at once – and to be honest, she has a point. I'll take over once Sabi and Jem have gone home.'

Jo lifted his glass. 'I'm glad that the conversion is starting, but I'm surprised Henry didn't give more warning.'

'Not as surprised as Maddie.' Ed's forehead furrowed

as he recalled how panicked his girlfriend had sounded when she'd phoned him during his lunch hour. 'Apparently Henry's new assistant is a force to be reckoned with. I take it you didn't have the pleasure?'

'I've been full on with the van. Sounds like I missed a treat.' Jo grinned. 'Is Maddie moving in with you while the upgrades are going on?'

'No.'

Hearing Ed's blunt response, Jo lowered his glass back to the table. 'Sorry, I just assumed.'

'I offered, but she wants to be nearby during the upgrade.'

Jo tilted his head to one side. 'I can see her point. The nursery, it's like a person to her. A family member in its own right. She told me it's like waiting for a loved one to go in for surgery.'

'I hadn't thought of it like that.'

'You two are okay though, aren't you? I'm sure you were disappointed that she's not moving in, but her reason is good.'

'I was a bit disappointed, but no, we're fine. Explanations were given and the air is clear.' Ed placed his palms on the table. 'Anyway, I got the impression that it was you who had something on your mind.'

'Did you?' Taking refuge in his drink, Jo pulled his grey beanie further over his ears, trapping his shoulder-length hair against the sides of his face.

Recognising the gesture as Jo feeling insecure, Ed asked, 'Is it just the lack of constellation gazing that's unsettled you, or is there something you want to talk about?'

Shuffling in his seat, Jo stared into his drink. 'Look, Ed, I don't tend to do the sharing thing.'

'I know, and I respect that.' Ed's stomach grumbled, tempting him to go and fetch some chips to nibble alongside their beer. 'If I've got the wrong end of the stick then…'

'You haven't.'

'Right.' Beginning to wish he hadn't changed out of his work suit before leaving Exeter, knowing he always felt more equipped to deal with people's confessions when he was in solicitor mode, Ed waited for Jo to elaborate.

'You know I feel bad for going to Hawthorn Park over Easter and part of May.'

'And you know that Maddie and Sabi accept you have a long-standing arrangement with the Northcott family. They don't hold it against you.'

'It isn't that. Well…' Jo paused to take a drink, wondering how to explain the situation '…not just that.'

'Go on.'

'There's a complication at Hawthorn Park… no, that's not fair. She's a friend, not a complication, but…' Jo put his glass down with a light thump. 'God, I sound awful. Forget it. It's a non-problem.'

Ed realised he was in danger of gawping. Jo was thirty years old, and yet he'd never heard him mention a woman beyond the realm of friendship before. 'Are you sure it's a non-problem?'

Jo kept his gaze fixed firmly downwards. 'I believed it was sorted, that Sara understood that we can't be more than friends, but… I have a feeling she's still hoping. Maybe I'm wrong. I hope I'm wrong.'

Sweat trickled between Maddie's shoulder blades. She had

been running between the nursery and the house ever since Hazel had strolled regally away on her killer heels. The resulting stack of cardboard boxes, packed rather more haphazardly than she would have liked, stood like a mini Leaning Tower of Pisa in the corner of the spare room that was to be the kitchen. It was only now she'd got them upstairs that she realised that they'd all have to be moved again once the builders had finished stripping the old kitchen.

'Why didn't I just put them in Dad's bedroom?'

Wishing that she'd accepted Ed's offer of help before he'd gone to the pub, Maddie pulled off her jumper and ran a hand over her forehead. Sabi had left half an hour ago when Jem's need for her dinner had overruled her desire to be helpful. A yawn escaped Maddie's lips as she considered how much needed to be done before the builders arrived on Monday morning. The kitchen, now devoid of saucepans, plates, cutlery, non-perishable food and the giant pile of papers, post and useful bits and bobs that she kept on the table, felt wrong. Her stomach grumbled.

'I should have made dinner *before* I emptied the kitchen.'

Closing her eyes, trying not to think about the amount of work she had to do over the weekend, while also running the nursery, Maddie ignored her hunger, and dashed into her bedroom to pack a suitcase.

Ed ordered two portions of chips along with two glasses of lemonade and headed back to Jo. He was sure that he wasn't the only one wishing they didn't have to drive, and so could have a second pint.

'Do you mind me asking how long you've known Sara,

or would you rather I changed the subject and we talked about coffee blends or the weather?'

'Almost three years.' A flicker of a smile crossed Jo's face as Ed sat down. 'Although, I hear the weather is going to be kind over the Easter weekend, which will help everyone.'

Opting not to follow the conversational weather option, Ed asked, 'How did you meet?'

'Her father, Simon, came to Dark Skies once. He was a lovely chap, but the lying still and watching the night sky didn't work for him in the way it does for us.'

'Couldn't switch off?'

'Precisely.'

'But you must have become friends anyway?'

'The situation wasn't too dissimilar from the one I have with Maddie. Simon needed a part-time coffee supplier, and I was available.'

'And so, you went to Hawthorn Park and there was Sara.'

'On her summer holidays after her A levels.'

'She was eighteen?'

'Almost nineteen.'

'A susceptible age.'

'Yes.' Jo hid his expression with his lemonade glass for a moment. 'It would be so easy to make it sound romantic, but you know that isn't how things work for me – I'm much older than her and, well, I don't have those feelings. I...'

Ed raised a palm, indicating that he understood, and it was alright. 'I know. Do you want to go on telling me?'

'There isn't much to tell. That's half of the problem.'

'Because Sara would like there to be a lot to tell?'

'Exactly.' Jo sat back as a waiter deposited two plates of

steaming-hot chips onto their table. 'It was fine at first. We really hit it off. I told Sara about… things. She understood.'

'You *told* her.' Ed was surprised. 'You hardly ever tell…'

Jo picked up a chip. 'She guessed before I got as far as stating things.'

'I see.' Chewing his food, Ed found himself thinking, *Jo must really trust this woman to talk about being trans with her. He hardly ever does that.*

'Occasionally people see it. Sometimes they ask, sometimes they don't.' Jo selected another chip. 'Anyway, Sara guessed and asked me about it. And it wasn't an awkward asking. It was as if it was the most normal thing in the world. Like it was okay.'

'It *is* okay.'

'I know.' Jo dropped the chip back to his plate before it got anywhere near his lips. 'But not everyone thinks so. It can be… Sometimes it isn't a very nice world to live in.'

Not sure what to say, Ed took refuge in eating his supper, letting Jo have a minute to decide if he wanted to continue.

'Sara is clever and fun to be with, but she's also shy and lonely.' Jo abruptly added. 'Not that she's ever said she was lonely, but it doesn't take a rocket scientist to work it out.'

'Not many friends?'

'Not that she mentioned, and no siblings. Her mother died when she was a baby. When I met Sara, it was just her and Simon running the whole of Hawthorn Park.'

'With a few staff surely?'

'Two gardeners, and they employ a seasonal tree surgeon. But the house doesn't open to the public, and it isn't that big in stately home terms, so apart from a twice-weekly cleaner it was just them. And now, it's just Sara.'

'Oh.'

'Her father died not long after discovering he had cancer.' Jo took a gulp of lemonade. 'So, when Sara called to check I could still do the pop-up café for Easter and the bluebell season, I could hardly say no. I was booked in anyway, but even if I hadn't been…'

'Of course, you couldn't back out.' Ed swallowed. 'But if Simon hadn't died you might have done?'

'Last Easter Sara asked me out on a date.'

'A nonfriend date?'

'Yep. She hardly paused for breath when she asked me. I could see her physically gearing herself up to do it. It was just after her father had died. It took guts to ask me and… well, it went on and on, in a long stream of words telling me how who I once was didn't matter, and that it was who I am now that's important. About how well we got on and how much her dad had liked me.'

'What did you say?'

Jo pulled off his beanie and scrabbled a hand through his hair, before quickly hiding beneath it again. 'I said, "I've got to go, see you next year," and disappeared like a bat out of hell.'

APRIL

12

The back of Maddie's Jeep resembled that of a parent taking a child to university for the first time. A large blue rucksack and a suitcase were jammed next to her laptop bag, a mountain of coats and two boxes of books, work folders, phone chargers, hairdryer and a hundred other things she wasn't sure she could live without, were piled in a semi-organised heap.

Maddie groaned as she stomped into her eerily empty kitchen. All that remained was a handful of bits and bobs to get her through the weekend, before she vacated the premises first thing on Monday morning. Sabi had tried to persuade her to move out that same night, so she had Saturday and Sunday night to settle into her temporary home with her sister in Culmstock, but Maddie had no intention of leaving until the last minute. Part of her couldn't stop hoping that the builders would be more relaxed about where she lived and would allow her to stay – health and safety or not.

Heavy from lack of sleep, she was staring at the pile of packing up that still awaited her practical attention when Ed, his hair wet from the shower, appeared behind her, folding his arms around her waist.

'Take a breath. If the current kitchen and the room that's

to be the new kitchen are empty, the rest can happen more slowly.'

'There's just so much stuff. Even with Jem and me having already sorted some of Dad's books, there's heaps to sift through.'

Ed surveyed the scene. 'A lot of it can stay where it is for a moment. There's nothing structural happening to your dad's old room. It's more a furniture removal situation.'

'True.'

Florrie chose that moment to help and bounded through the door of the bedroom.

Maddie watched helplessly as her puppy knocked into a pile of – thankfully empty – cardboard containers, sending them scattering to the floor. 'Oh, Flo!'

'Hey, come on.' Seeing she was close to tears, Ed pulled Maddie into a hug. 'This isn't like you. What's wrong?'

'Nothing. I mean, there shouldn't be anything wrong.' Maddie experienced a sense of being rudderless as she watched her puppy gleefully bury herself into a former bulb box. 'It's happening. The upgrade *is* happening. The planning has gone through, and we have builders coming in two days' time. *And* we have a few attractions, so we won't completely lose out to BIG over Easter…'

'But?'

'I just want to run away and hide!' Maddie extracted herself from Ed's arms. 'Why do I feel like that? I should be over the moon. I should be running round all excited and packing as if my life depended on it.'

'Which is exactly what you have been doing.' Ed sat on the edge of the bed and patted the space next to him, encouraging her to sit. 'You were so happy before you heard about the builders. What went wrong?'

'The suddenness of it all I suppose.' Maddie wrinkled her nose. 'I was just about managing everything, but now… And what with Easter around the corner and hardly any staff. I mean, BIG are *twenty* miles away. That's nothing in shopping terms! Who are we kidding here?' A sense of helplessness overtook her. 'And the amount we have to earn to meet our first goal so we have the confidence to keep going keeps growing rather than shrinking.'

'Okay.' Ed looked Maddie in the eye. 'Let's tackle one thing at a time. First, you need breakfast and then you must open The Potting Shed.'

'Right.' Grateful for Ed's practical tone, Maddie nodded.

'While you are doing that, I'll carry all the packed kitchen boxes into your dad's bedroom.'

'Life would be so much easier if I could just stay in there.'

'True, but it wouldn't be much fun with nowhere to cook and no water and electric.'

'Why Hazel couldn't leave the downstairs kitchen operational until the upstairs one is fixed, I don't know! At least she said we can reuse the old units – and not have to buy new ones.' Maddie harrumphed, before apologising. 'Sorry, Ed. *Again*. It's just, Easter is only a week away, I've hardly done a thing to advertise what's happening here and… what if, after all my friends have done so much to help me, that I let everyone down because I haven't even stuck an announcement on Facebook?'

'You won't let anyone down. Put social media on

today's list.' Pulling Maddie to her feet, Ed pointed her in the direction of the door. 'Go and open up. I'll bring some coffee and toast out to you in a minute.'

'Thanks, Ed, coffee would be wonderful. As for toast – good luck finding wherever Jem packed the toaster.'

Sabi looked longingly at the notebook she kept by her bed. It was full of everything she planned to do with her new home. So far, all she'd done, despite having lived in the house for almost three months, was cross out a few of the more expensive ideas as wishful thinking.

She checked the time on her mobile. It was already almost nine o'clock. Maddie was expecting her at the nursery in half an hour.

Sabi muttered as she patted the closed notebook. 'Be fair. Mads had said she'd manage with just Jake today – right up until Hazel arrived like a whirlwind and turned our plans upside down.'

It had taken an immense amount of self-control for Sabi not to make her dislike of Hazel vocal over the family evening meal the night before. Only Jemima's presence had calmed her desire to vent. Henry had briefly asked how Hazel had got on, but he'd been so pleased with himself for being instrumental in getting the reboot of The Potting Shed underway so quickly, that Sabi hadn't liked to be churlish and complain about his assistant's brusque manner.

'Are you two ready?' Calling up the stairs to hurry Henry and Jemima into action, Sabi tugged on her boots. For a moment her eyes lingered on the neat pair of court shoes she wore when she went out shopping on a Saturday. *If you don't go shopping, there'll be more money for upgrading this place when you have time.*

'Ready, Mum.' Jemima skittered in from the lounge. 'Where's Dad?'

'Upstairs. Could you go and hurry him up, love? Auntie Maddie needs all the help she can get today. You two getting Florrie out of the way by taking her for a nice long walk will be a great start.'

As her daughter dashed up the stairs, Sabi picked up her mobile and opened the Hawthorn Park website. She stared at the photograph of Simon's daughter for a second, before sliding her phone away just as her husband jogged down the stairs.

Sara pressed send, holding her breath as the text disappeared into the ether.

'I just want your opinion Jo – that's all. Who else have I got to ask?' Staring at her phone, willing a reply to pop up, Sara muttered at her mobile, before casting it aside and turning to the calendar on her office wall. 'Hope, you're a cruel woman. I'm a fool on April Fool's Day.'

Easter weekend, only a week away, was circled in bold purple pen, as were the first two weekends in May. Opening her computer, Sara started updating the design of the parking tickets, adding fifty pence to the three-pound parking charge they'd asked for last year.

'Or maybe it should be a pound more?' A wave of insecurity washed over here. *Well, Jo isn't answering, so what would you do, Dad? Should I charge more to help with rising heating costs for the house? Or is that greedy?*

Having left a reluctant Jake in charge of the till until Sabi arrived, Maddie decided to tackle the forthcoming holiday weekend old-school-style. Sat on her father's favoured stool in the far polytunnel, she pulled a notebook and pen out of her pocket ready to write a list.

'I think you'd like Ivan and Elspeth, Dad. They are so full of life and great fun. I'm going to set them up in here on Easter Sunday. First though...' Maddie scribbled down a few notes '...I need to clear enough space so that five children – hopefully five anyway – have room to pot some blueberries and plant some sunflower seeds.'

Maddie smiled as she looked around her, remembering how Henry and Sabi had surprised her the previous Christmas, by converting the space into a Santa's grotto. Going back to her pad, she scribbled, down *contact local primary schools*, before underlining it twice.

Wishing Petra was there to do the social media side of things as she used to, Maddie took a broom from the side of the tunnel and swept the floor. 'What do you think, Dad, should I set everyone up on the floor to pot things, or would it be better if we used the potting bench?'

A voice at the back of her head asked, *What would Jem prefer, do you think?*

Maddie abandoned the broom and spun round towards the long thin potting bench that ran the length of the polytunnel to clear it of the various bits and bobs that she'd put on it, often because she didn't know where else to put them. 'Jem would want to be treated like a proper gardener, not like a child who happened to be gardening.'

Adding, *find five tall stools* to the list, Maddie abruptly stopped what she was doing. 'If I don't tell people about next weekend soon, all this will be pointless.' Flicking her phone onto Facebook, Maddie pulled up the nursery's page, before stopping again. 'I need a poster.'

Feeling she was taking more steps backwards than forwards, Maddie sat back down. 'But they take ages.'

You don't need a poster. Just put out the information and add some photographs from the last market, as well as one of the nursery's sign.

Maddie reopened her phone. Mumbling 'thanks, Dad', she had soon selected a few of the pictures she'd taken of Ivan's cheese stall and Elspeth's beautiful creams during the Christmas market, as well as a few of The Potting Shed in general.

Five minutes later, she'd shared the notification across six popular local pages and groups.

Eight minutes later, her mobile rang.

Twenty minutes later she'd taken her second booking for the children's gardening club. 'Maybe I'll make it six children, rather than five.'

Ed unfolded a set of chairs he'd just freed from the camper van. 'Did you call Sara?'

Jo tugged at the van's awning, yanking it into position. 'Almost. I was about to, but she beat me to it. Sent another text about half an hour ago.'

'Can I ask what it said?'

Concentrating on what he was doing, Jo mumbled, 'She asked if I'd like to go for a drink at the house before opening so we can talk over the Easter weekend set-up.'

'And is that something you'd normally do or...'

'Or is it Sara making up an excuse to chat to me alone?' Jo's shoulders slumped as he collected another two tables from his stack. 'It's not unheard of, but I suspect the latter is carrying the weight of motivation here.'

'Right.' Seeing the closed expression that had formed on his friend's face, Ed changed the subject. 'If you're okay setting up, then I'll go and see if Maddie's alright. The builders coming so soon has thrown her rather.'

'I'm good here.' Jo slid open the side of the van. 'I'll do it now. Text Sara, I mean.'

'It's for the best, mate.'

'I know. I just wish I knew what to say.'

13

Sara was halfway through refilling the handwash bottles in the visitor's washrooms when, from the depths of her coat, her mobile announced the arrival of a text. Since she'd sent the extra message to Jo, she'd been cursing herself. She might be missing her father, but the last thing she wanted to do was come across as needy.

Bit late for that!

Telling herself that such behaviour had to stop while she had some pride left, Sara resisted the urge to stop what she was doing and grab her phone. Only when she'd finished squeezing the clear, gloopy liquid into the push bottles and washed her hands did she retrieve her phone.

'Jo.'

Her pulse cranked up a beat as she read.

Sorry for delay in reply. I would be OK to meet before opening. I am working on Thursday until 4pm. I could pop over at 6pm for a work chat. Jo.

Gripping her mobile, Sara replied.

Why not stay over Thurs night, as you'll be working here
from ten on Friday morning anyway? Plenty of rooms
free.

Sara hadn't known she was going to ask him to stay
until she'd done it. Now, as she put the mobile on her desk,
convinced it would be hours before he replied – a reply
which she would include an excuse as to why he couldn't
stay – she was about to berate herself for coming across as
more rather than less needy, when a message flashed across
her phone's screen.

Thank you. Be good to save petrol.

'Save petrol.' Sara felt flat. Not 'be good to see you', just
'be good to save petrol'.

Pulling her jacket over her shoulders, Sara marched out
onto the estate, muttering angrily to herself, 'You only have
yourself to blame. What did you expect? Hearts and roses?'

'I'm beginning to think you are bluebell-obsessed.' Maddie
grinned as Ed came into the shop, pushing a wheelbarrow
of potted bluebells.

'I intercepted Jake bringing these over. He's gone back to
checking his veg. Should I stack them along the windowsill?'

'Thanks Ed.' Maddie came out from behind the till to
help arrange the display. 'I've been thinking about what you
said about having a bluebell garden.'

'Bluebell garden?' Sabi, with Jemima hot on her heels,
stepped into the shop, Florrie at their side.

'Just an idea, possibly impractical.' Maddie wrinkled her nose. 'It's not like we don't have anything else going on.'

'I love bluebells.' After fussing Florrie until she could be persuaded to sit down, Jemima picked a pot out of the wheelbarrow. 'Can we plant them in the children's club?'

'Well, I...'

'That's a brilliant idea!' Ed paused in the act of distributing some price tickets. 'That would speed things up no end. The children could plant the bluebells around the back.'

Maddie was horrified. 'Ed! I can't use the Little Acorns for that! It would be tantamount to child labour!'

'Course it wouldn't. They'd be playing a vital role in designing a new garden. I'd have thought that was exciting when I was a kid.'

Jemima looked up at her aunt. 'Could we really design a garden? That would be epic!'

'Would it?' Maddie was surprised by her niece's enthusiasm. 'It would be all digging and shovelling gravel and, in short, bloody hard work.'

'Maddie!' Sabi snapped, making her daughter raise her eyes to the ceiling.

'Honestly, Mum, I hear worse in the playground every day!'

Sabi was horrified. 'Then I need to have a word with the staff. Your dad doesn't pay all that money for—'

Seeing that they were in danger of going off at a tangent, Maddie reeled her sister in. 'Come on, Sabs, think it through.'

'I suppose so... It's just...'

'I know, but it's the world we live in.' Maddie switched her attention back to Jemima. 'Would you honestly have enjoyed that when you were younger?'

'Digging and seeing a garden form. Sure. I still would!'

Maddie remained unconvinced, but Ed had seized on Jemima's enthusiasm. 'It would mean some heavy work, which obviously the adults would have to do – and eventually some paving stones would have to be laid – perhaps some turf – but in the short term, it would work with just some clearing and planting.'

Sabi pushed a rogue strand of her brown hair behind her ear. 'What made you think we needed a new garden in the first place?'

Maddie explained Ed's idea for having a picnic space and bluebell garden behind the back polytunnel, as a temporary solution to having nowhere for refreshments.

Sabi nodded slowly. 'It's a good idea. Not something we could get done fast – and it would cost – plus, it's next weekend we really need such an area for.'

Ed nodded. 'That's true, but if we made a start, and the children helped, then by May, when the bluebells are at their height, there'd be an area to sit outside.'

'Only if we started right now. And even then…' Maddie's chest tightened at the prospect of the additional work being proposed '…when would I fit it in? I have lots of bluebells, but I hoped to sell them, not plant them. I'm already freaking out about money – I know nothing awful would instantly happen if we didn't hit our earning goal for the end of May, but if we can't break even over a busy gardening time of year, then…'

As her sister's concern faded into a thoughtful silence, Sabi's mused, 'Would they ultimately pay for themselves though – if we have an area of bluebells that people want to come and see? Maybe pay to see?'

'But, Sabs, it wouldn't be an area big enough to walk through. Is just having a patch of bluebells as your view while having a picnic enough to charge for? And I should add that we don't have any picnic benches.'

'Perhaps we could get some.'

'Sabs, have you gone mad? We are expecting the builders any minute and a big bill will come with them. I still have some inheritance tax to pay off. I can't just go and buy picnic benches, even second-hand ones.'

From her position kneeling with Florrie to keep the puppy sat still, Jemima peered up at the adults. 'You're so defeatist! If it'll help The Potting Shed, shouldn't we find a way?'

Sabi agreed. 'Jemima's right. I tell you what, why don't I do some research? I could go up to Hawthorn Park and see how it's set up there. After all, it must work for them, otherwise Jo wouldn't go there to sell his coffee.'

'But that's a *whole park*!' Maddie pictured the collection of potholes that made up the strip of land that divided them and the neighbouring farm.

'Even so...'

'I think you three are forgetting who'll have to do the work connected with this idea.'

A second's silence hung in the air before Ed conceded the point. 'Sorry, Maddie. I was getting carried away. I am happy to help when I can though.'

'I know.' Putting an arm around his waist, Maddie gave Ed a squeeze. 'I'm just a bit overwhelmed.' She turned to her niece. 'Are you honestly sure that helping with some landscaping would be something the children's group would want to do?'

'Yeah.' Jemima grinned. 'As long as it doesn't interrupt the smoothie making.'

It was almost the end of the working day before Maddie had time to leave her customers and go off in search of Ed. Eventually, she found him stacking bags of compost along the sides of the first polytunnel.

'Thanks for helping Jake today. I'm sorry I've hardly seen you.'

'Don't worry.' Ed brushed his hands down his jeans. 'I'm having a lovely time.'

Maddie gave him a gentle kiss on the cheek. 'It takes a special type of man to happily lug compost on his day off.'

'You might not think me so special when I tell you I've had a few more ideas about the bluebell garden. Less special, more pain in the arse.'

Despite herself, Maddie laughed. 'Dare I ask?'

'Go one – dare!'

Maddie tilted her head to one side. 'Ed?'

'No need to sound so suspicious. Don't forget, I'd help with any schemes I concoct. Let's go and see the site.'

As they wove their way through the remaining shoppers, Ed suggested, 'What if, in the first instance, you didn't go the whole hog... what if you made the potholes work for you?'

'What do you mean?'

'You know that you...' Ed stopped talking as Maddie came to an abrupt halt. 'Are you okay?'

'Hazel.'

'What?'

'Over there.' Maddie let go of Ed's hand and pointed as she saw her brother-in-law's assistant heading towards her home. 'That's the woman who works for Henry. Why is she here on a Saturday?'

Changing direction, they made their way towards the house. They were almost there when Maddie drew in a sharp breath. Hazel Cooper wasn't stopping to knock on the door. She was letting herself in with a key.

'What the...' Maddie broke into a run.

Ed jogged at her side. 'Did you give her a key?'

'No. I can't imagine Sabi letting her borrow hers either. Not without telling me anyway.'

'Henry?' Ed frowned.

'Doubt it.'

Their unexpected guest was already in the kitchen, her briefcase open on the table, when Maddie and Ed came in.

'Miss Cooper?' Maddie struggled not to sound angry at the intrusion of her personal space. 'Can I ask what you are doing here?'

'And how you acquired a key?' Ed asked bluntly.

Hazel calmly brushed a stray hair from her jacket's collar. 'I didn't expect this place to be so full of people.'

Not caring for the element of disbelief in Hazel's tone, Maddie ignored the slight. 'That doesn't answer our questions. Why are you here?'

'The builders are due. I'm to show them round.'

'*You* are to show them round?' Ed put a hand on Maddie's arm. 'Today?'

'Yes. Mr Willand-Harris has entrusted the working of this project to me.'

'I was told the builders would arrive on Monday.' Piqued at her precious expansion project being relegated to an assistant's starter project, Maddie repeated Ed's earlier question. 'Did Henry give you that key?'

Hazel's gaze switched to her briefcase. 'I couldn't find you, so I asked the person tending the vegetables. I borrowed his key.'

Maddie shook her head. 'Jake would never give you a key just like that.'

Ed gestured a hand towards the window. 'And you didn't think to ask in the shop? Mrs Willand-Harris would have been happy to help you.'

Hazel knocked a set of papers against the table. 'I put my head around the door, but she was surprisingly busy, so I left her in peace.'

Offended that Hazel found it surprising they were busy, Maddie said, 'I'd like you to leave please.'

'I can't do that. As I said, the builders will be here to assess the working space soon.'

Maddie opened her mouth to respond, but their visitor's certainty, not to mention her cheek, had left her speechless, so Ed took over.

'Miss Willand is perfectly capable of showing them around, thank you. And in the future, if an appointment is made, be it for the builders or yourself to be here, it would be appreciated – not to mention professional – if you informed Maddie first, so that arrangements can be made to suit all parties.'

'I assure you I am *always* professional!'

Ed turned to Maddie. 'Were you expecting the builders today?'

'No.'

'I see.' Ed fixed Miss Cooper with a stare. 'A professional would not have borrowed a key from a junior member of staff and let themselves into someone's home without their knowledge to prepare for a meeting that their client did not know was going to take place.' Ed's tone dripped disapproval. 'Your employer is not going to be impressed.'

For the first time since her arrival, Hazel wavered. 'I assure you I was trying to help. Henry said you wanted minimum disruption, so...'

'That does not give you the right to ask builders over without my knowledge or walk into my house uninvited. What did you say to Jake to make him give you the key?'

'Umm...'

'Umm?' Maddie crossed her arms as she regarded the suited woman.

'That you'd said it was alright to give it to me.'

'I beg your pardon!' Maddie bit her lips together, not trusting herself to say anything else.

'Miss Cooper.' Ed walked to the kitchen door and held it open. 'I suggest you leave. Now.'

Jo closed the side of his coffee van with a satisfying click. His busiest Saturday of the year so far; he'd run out of pastries by half past one, and his supply of fruit teabags was getting low.

Resting against the van's orange bonnet, he began to make a list of the supplies he'd need to restock before the following day, when he froze mid-thought.

'No. No way... it can't be.'

Jo closed his eyes and immediately opened them again, hoping his senses were making fun of him – punishing him for being mean to Sara, however unintentionally.

But he wasn't imagining the woman marching across the nursery in an expensive business suit.

Diving around to the other side of the van, he jumped into the driver's seat. He'd fired the engine into life and steered his way to the exit with far more speed than he'd normally risk in a populated area.

By the time Jo had joined the main road his hands were sweating.

14

'Jake, really, I'm not angry with you. I am angry with Hazel.'

'Petra was livid when I told her last night.'

Maddie smiled as she wedged the greenhouse door open. 'Is Petra still coming to help at the weekend?'

'She's looking forward to it. Be here from lunchtime on Good Friday, but she'll have to leave halfway through Easter Monday to get back to Plymouth for Tuesday.'

'I'm ever so grateful. Have you warned her that we have a kids' club happening?'

'Yeah.' Jake grimaced.

Maddie chuckled. 'Don't worry, I know it's your idea of hell. As Petra will be here, and Ed's going to help me with the Little Acorns, you're safe from any teaching or parental entertainment duties. I'd be grateful if you'd take care of the tunnels and listen out for anyone who needs help carrying anything heavy to their car.'

'Petra assumed she'll be doing the till, but she is happy to do the club with you if you want her to. I wasn't sure if your sister would be here or not.'

'Sabi's coming on Sunday, but if we get busy, she'll drive over to help on Saturday as well. Henry and Jem are going to take Florrie for the day. Love her as I do, I don't think an overexcited puppy would be a good idea while I have six children to entertain.'

'You got all six places filled?'

'Yep. There was a flurry of booking via Facebook last night. There's even two extras on the waiting list.'

'Oh. Good.'

Maddie smiled. 'Ten out of ten for trying to sound sincere, Jake!'

Jake laughed as he waved a hand towards the newly arrived orange camper van. 'Why isn't Jo getting out? He normally leaps into action the second he's parked.'

'Probably taking a call.'

'I'll miss his coffee next weekend.'

'We all will.' Maddie forced her mind away from the lack of refreshments over Easter and towards the imminent upgrade. 'I had the builders here after closing on Saturday. They confirmed they'll be starting tomorrow. At eight in the morning apparently – although I'll believe that when I see it.'

'I bet if that Hazel woman has told them eight o'clock, they'll be here on the dot. She's scary.'

Jo remained in his camper van as he looked across the nursery. Sundays were usually hectic for him here these days. Many of his regulars arrived just after opening, ready to enjoy a warming beverage and some cake.

He knew all he had to do was to ask Maddie if she'd had a meeting with Hazel, or if her being at The Potting Shed yesterday was pure coincidence, and he'd be out of his misery. He had told himself again and again that she was probably just a customer and that the chances of her coming back were remote. But the fact she been wearing her business suit and carrying a briefcase nagged at the back of his head. Hazel had always been ambitious, but he couldn't imagine her wearing work clothes on a Saturday unless her job dictated it.

'It has to have been about the planning permission.' Jo stifled a yawn. His sleep had been plagued by images of Hazel, which had merged into visions of Sara. But while Sara had been quietly sad, Hazel had been vitriolic with anger – and both had told him precisely what they thought of him.

Ed stacked three trestle tables at the back of the far polytunnel, ready for Ivan and Elspeth to use a week from now. The six stools for the children due next Saturday were already in place by the potting bench and a pile of flowerpots sat, waiting to be filled.

Checking the list that Maddie had given him, Ed gathered a handful of trowels and placed one on the bench in front of each stool. Then he opened a sack of compost and started to fill three buckets.

Ed hummed to himself. A sense of contentment consumed him as he carried out the simple tasks Maddie had assigned him. Lifting the buckets of soil up onto the bench, ready for the children to use when filling their pots, he brushed loose mud from his palms as a growl from his stomach reminded him that breakfast had been hours ago. As Maddie's kitchen was currently devoid of equipment, he'd need to rely on Jo for food to keep him going.

Fishing out his mobile to ask if Maddie would like anything, he was saved the trouble as his girlfriend arrived, complete with two of Jo's coffees and a paper bag, which he hoped contained food. 'You must be a mind reader.'

'I was starving, so I guessed you would be too.'

Ed took his proffered drink. 'I've had a ball setting this up. But it is definitely coffee time.'

'It sure is.' Maddie opened the bag. 'I got us blueberry muffins.'

'Perfect.' Ed pulled out two of the stools he'd positioned. 'Shall we picnic?'

'Actually, I wondered if you'd like to come around the back?'

'Oh?' Ed wiggled his eyebrows. 'And what physical excesses will I have to indulge in once I get there?'

'Well, if you're very lucky, I might let you move the old bench into the sunshine before we sit on it, rather than us have to lurk in the shade.'

Sara opened the sash window to the guest room that neighboured her bedroom and inhaled a lungful of fresh air. The driveway to the house, with the woodland veering off to each side, looked as majestic as ever. Almost all the trees were sporting the fresh leaves of spring. Buds were forming on the occasional rhododendron bushes that bordered the drive, while others were already heavy with full bright pink blooms.

As she listened, Sara could hear birds exchanging songs, but nothing else. By the end of the week the scene would be very different. The drive would play host to a long stream of cars parked along its right side. People, often in twos or fours, sometimes alone, sometimes in large family groups, would be trailing up the drive, before peeling off along one of the many paths set out through the bluebell woods. There would be pushchairs and walking boots, walking sticks and Zimmer frames, as well as Nordic poles for the more serious ramblers, and a host of backpacks, binoculars and cameras.

Tears formed at the corners of Sara's eyes. She let them fall, but no sound left her lips. The routine was the same every year, and while it was time-consuming organising everything, it wasn't difficult. But this was the first time she'd done it alone.

'That's why Jo's still coming, even though he clearly doesn't want to. Because Dad isn't here.' Taking a tissue from her sleeve, she dabbed her eyes as she turned towards the double bed she'd made up for him to use on Thursday night. 'He's coming because he's a nice person.'

Leaving the room, she shut the door behind her. 'Sometimes I wish he wasn't.'

'Before Hazel interrupted us yesterday, you said something about making the potholes work for us.'

Ed sat on the bench they'd repositioned, so that they were in full spring sunshine as they watched the field and the woods beyond. 'It's a bit of a mad idea.'

'Another one?'

'Cheeky.' Ed flipped the top off his coffee cup to let his

drink cool to below scalding. 'I was thinking how much fun it was on your birthday when we puddle-splashed here.'

'I loved it.'

'How about doing that with the kids? A reward for their hard work after helping plant some bluebells.'

Maddie took a bite of her muffin, as she pictured what Ed was suggesting. 'I bet they'd like that. I've already told the parents to put them in wellies and old clothing. But the thing is, Ed, good idea though it is – the area isn't ready to be planted. So, they can't plant bluebells into the ground. Into pots yes, but the ground – no way.'

Ed stared at the broken-up land that ran between the fence and where they sat. 'What would we have to do to make it plantable?'

'The gravel would need scraping off, then the earth beneath must be broken up with a fork before topsoil and compost are dug in. Ideally, it would need time to settle, then it would have to be dug back over and...'

'Okay. I get it. You weren't kidding about it not being a quick thing.'

'And it's April. The bluebells should be in the ground already.'

'It's only the second day of April, and surely if they're making progress in a pot, they have a head start.' Ed paused before adding, 'And couldn't some bluebells be planted as bulbs as well? That way the kids might come back next year to see them bloom for the first time.'

'I suppose so.' Maddie chewed her muffin. 'But that doesn't make the land magically ready.'

'But if it was... just a small section perhaps, nearest the

fence... Like we said the other day, it would be a great lesson for the children in how a garden is developed from scratch.'

A frisson of excitement tripped through Maddie as she allowed herself to picture the scene. It was exactly the sort of project she'd have loved when she was young.

Jemima held Florrie on a short lead as she made her way towards Jo's van. Her dad had given her three pounds to treat herself to a smoothie, and this was the first time all day that there'd been no queue.

'Hey, Jo.' Keeping a hand on Florrie's head to prevent her from bounding forward and greeting Jo with more enthusiasm than was safe so close to a coffee machine, Jemima took one glimpse of her friend and asked, 'What's wrong?'

'Nothing at all. Smoothie?'

'Please. Do you have a spinach one?'

'Spinach and kiwi. And a bowl of water for Florrie?'

'Yes please, to both.'

'Sit over there then. I'll bring them over.'

Observing Jo as he moved around the van, Jemima remained convinced something was bothering him.

'Here you go.' Placing a glass full of green liquid on the table, Jo bent down to Florrie, who'd settled herself at her young keeper's feet. He snuck her a biscuit alongside the freshly filled water bowl.

'Thanks.' Jemima took a satisfying suck through her straw.

'Good?'

'Perfect.' Making sure no one needed Jo for a moment, she patted the seat next to her. 'Unlike you clearly.'

'Pardon?'

'You're not yourself. Something's wrong.'

'Really, I'm fine.'

'I go to boarding school with hundreds of teenage girls. Believe me, Jo, I know a fake smile when I see one.'

15

Maddie reluctantly climbed out from beneath her duvet. Although the builders shouldn't have to go into her bedroom at any point, she wanted to have the bed made just in case they should pop a curious head around the door. 'And,' she told her pillow as she plumped it into shape, 'if there does turn out to be a way I can stay, then my bed will be ready for me.'

She had just finished dressing and thrown her toiletries into an overnight bag, the last of her things to take to her sister's home after work, when a hearty knock on the front door, sent her heart thudding.

'This is it, Dad. The builders are here.' She checked her watch. It was exactly eight o'clock.

Not for the first time, Jake regarded his boss as if she was mad.

'Say something.' Maddie had just finished explaining Ed's idea for making the area behind the polytunnel into a bluebell garden.

'Totally converted by May. Seriously?'

'Not totally – just mostly. In time for people to sit and enjoy a few of the bluebells this year.'

'But, even with the kids' help – which will only work if you can get the land to the planting stage in time – it's a big job.'

Knowing he was right, Maddie tried to dismiss the list of other tasks that needed doing and said, 'How about if we started now. You and me.'

'You want us to clear the gravel now? Today?'

'Yes, Jake.'

'But the plants need tending and I have some potatoes to get in if you want late-season crops to sell to the hotels and greengrocers come October. I've left it late already. They *have* to go in today.'

'You're right.' Maddie pulled her gardening gloves over her hands. 'You go and do that, then if there's time, you can join me later.'

'You're insane.'

'Thanks Jake!'

'Sorry, Maddie, I just meant, why do this now? If you want to compete with BIG, clearing a bit of scrubland isn't going to do it. You can't even see this area from the main nursery.'

'I know.' The determination Maddie had woken up with wavered. 'But if it works…'

Holding his hands up in defeat, Jake said, 'Fair enough. I'll help. Spuds first though.'

'Always!'

Her wheelbarrow was half filled with gravel before ten o'clock.

'Jake's right, this is insane.' Pulling off her gloves, Maddie wiped the back of her hand across her forehead.

She hadn't realised she was going to follow Ed's advice until the builders had arrived. R. K. Andrews, who'd turned out to be Robert and Kevin, two well set up men in their late forties who oozed confidence in their abilities, and their teenage apprentice, Ahmed, who had the shyest smile Maddie had ever seen. They had told her that they'd be dismantling her kitchen today, so if she wanted to grab a last cuppa, now was the time.

As she'd walked away from her home, Maddie knew she needed something to do that was so all-encompassing she wouldn't have time to think about the desecration of her home. The bluebell garden was that something.

She pulled her gloves back on and shovelled up another pile of gravel. 'At least it's soil underneath here, Dad, and not concrete.'

Telling herself it was worth it, and that it would be a nice surprise for Ed, not just that she'd made a start, but that she valued his ideas and suggestions, Maddie moved the barrow forward. Now the surface gravel was largely cleared, she could concentrate on an area, about four metres by four, nearest the fence.

'Well, if a child falls over while they are helping, at least they won't get loose stones embedded in their knees, like we used to in the school playground when we were kids.' Memories of TCP and wincing as the teaching assistants dabbed at her legs, pulling out grit, set Maddie's teeth on edge. 'Not that health and safety rules allow me to put so much as a plaster on a child if they hurt themselves these days, so best to have as few hazards as possible.'

Taking a broom from where she'd propped it against the fence, she swept the area she'd chosen as an initial planting ground. 'What do you think, Dad? Can you picture this full of bluebells?'

She'd only made one sweep across the compacted earth when a loud crash made her drop the brush and sprint towards the house.

Jake zipped out of the veg tunnel and was on her heels in seconds. 'What the hell was that?'

The kitchen sink was sitting forlornly in a broken heap, next to a pile of cupboard doors.

'Oh my God.' Maddie stared at the mess. 'I assumed they'd reuse everything.'

'Move the sink and cupboards upstairs you mean?' Jake was flushed from the unexpected sprint.

'Hazel said that was the plan.'

'Looks like the builders didn't get that plan.'

Maddie kicked at a convenient stone. 'Where's Sabi when I need her?'

'Getting ready for you to stay at her place probably.'

Maddie's sighed. 'I was being rhetorical, Jake.'

'Being what?'

'It doesn't matter.' Maddie regarded the pile of discarded furniture. 'I'd better go and see what's going on in there.'

'Shall I nip into the shop and boil the kettle, boss?'

'That is the best idea I've heard all day.'

★

'Hello? Robert?' Although it was her own front door, Maddie felt self-conscious as she poked her head around her it. 'Kevin? Ahmed?'

'Miss Willand?' Kevin's round face appeared around the kitchen door, a reassuring expression already in place. 'Are you alright?'

'Um, well... not totally. Why is my kitchen in pieces outside?'

'Because it was unsavable, lass.' Stepping into full view, Kevin beamed wider as he shoved his checked shirtsleeves up past his elbows. 'The units were barely hanging together. They must have been there since the seventies.'

'Yes, but...'

Clearly used to their customers having a wobble, Kevin's tone was placating. 'We explained to Miss Cooper that this would happen. The space for your kitchen upstairs is wrong for the units you had anyway. They couldn't be transplanted.'

'Oh.' Wondering why neither Henry nor the uber-efficient Miss Cooper had mentioned this to her – Maddie asked, 'But, umm... I was told one of the advantages of you doing this room first, was that some things *could* be transplanted – could save us money.'

'We would have transplanted if we could, but as I said to Miss Cooper, it's a question of doing it well or doing a rush job. If you want a kitchen that's going to last, then...'

'Of course.' Maddie hunched her shoulders. 'And has my new kitchen been picked out by someone else, or do I get a say in what it looks like?'

Kevin's face lost some of its assurance. 'You *really* didn't know the direct transfer of your kitchen wasn't a certainty?'

'No.'

'I see.' Running a hand through the token gesture of hair that clung to his head, Kevin beckoned for Maddie to step inside. 'I think you'd better come up.'

Two minutes later, Maddie found herself sat on an upturned bucket, holding a brochure displaying a series of small fitted-kitchen units.

'And Henry picked one of these cupboard door designs for me?'

'That one.' Robert stabbed a stubby finger at the page. 'Although, we'd rather assumed you'd picked them.'

Maddie studied a photograph of plain cream cupboard doors, with silver plastic handles. 'The cheapest option?'

'And the quickest to put up from our point of view.'

'Have you fitted them before?'

'Once.'

'And you hoped not to ever again?' Maddie hadn't missed the significant glance Robert had exchanged with Kevin.

'Let's just say they aren't the most hardwearing option.' Kevin turned to his apprentice. 'Fetch a sample door and handle from the van Ahmed, there's a good chap.'

As soon as Ahmed had disappeared, Robert asked, 'You are aware of where the cupboards will be placed within your new kitchen?'

'Oh yes.' It was Maddie's turn to be reassuring. 'I approved all the plans, but clearly, I made a few assumptions.'

Robert chuckled as he changed the subject. 'This must be a lovely place to work.'

'It is. Although, there's always something that needs my full attention, and if we don't want to lose all our customers to BIG, then...' Maddie stopped talking. 'Sorry, you don't need my troubles, especially when I'm holding you up.'

'Not at all.' Kevin's smile was now firmly back in place. 'You must have what you want. You're the customer.'

The sound of Ahmed's trainers rushing back through the front door was soon followed by his arrival. The door he carried was as Maddie suspected. Basic, functional, and designed not to last forever. The handles were the type of plastic that would come off in her hand after a few months.

'And how much to swap to the next design up?'

'Twenty quid per door, and another fiver per handle.'

'Ouch!' Maddie winced.

'You happy for us to use the dearer ones instead?' Robert tilted his head. 'It would mean money well spent in the long run.'

'To be honest, the appearance of the doors doesn't bother me much, but I can't afford to have to do all this again in a year's time. Plus, I can just imagine what my sister will say when she sees these. I'll have the upgrade.' Maddie put down the plastic handle, trying not to think of the extra money she was committing herself to spending. 'Thank goodness I only have a small kitchen.'

'I'm sorry about all this.'

'It's okay. It was just a shock seeing everything in a heap. I've lived here so long, and my dad, he...' Maddie stopped talking and swallowed hard. 'I guess the original kitchen space will need more hardwearing cupboard doors and a better sink when it's a café. Upstairs it's just me, so no one will care.'

'When we get to the café design stage, Miss Willand, I promise we will check with you before we start, so that you know exactly what we've been asked to do.'

'I'd appreciate that. I'll let you get on.' She paused as she reached the doorway. 'Oh, and please, call me Maddie.'

Jake passed Maddie a flask before producing a packet of biscuits from their hiding place on a shelf beside the till. 'You okay?'

'Just weird seeing the kitchen all bashed up. The builders are on it though. Nothing to worry about.' Maddie hoped her concern didn't show as she poured some tea. 'Thanks for this, Jake. How's the planting going?'

'Getting there.' He wiggled his mobile. 'I've been checking out the competition.'

A swarm of nerves somersaulted in Maddie's stomach. 'You've visited BIG's website?'

'Yeah.' Jake was suddenly uncertain. 'You must have had a look to see what they're doing.'

Taking a cookie from the packet, Maddie admitted, 'I haven't dared.'

'Why not?'

'Because I know we can't match whatever they do.' Maddie sighed. 'We haven't their budget. Knowing what they are doing isn't going to make it any easier.'

'Sorry.' Jake stared at his feet.

Immediately regretting her tone, Maddie apologised. 'I didn't mean to snipe at you. I'm a bit tired. You're right – we should know what they're up to. Jem was trying to get me to look the other day. I've been a bit of an ostrich over the whole thing if I'm honest.'

'Head-in-the-sand syndrome?'

'That's the one. You might as well tell me then. What are BIG planning for their opening weekend?'

16

'I hope you can explain yourself.'

Henry regarded Hazel as she sat on the other side of his desk. His head was still ringing with his wife's indignation after she'd spoken to her sister the night before. An indignation she had repeated over breakfast that morning in vivid detail.

'With hindsight, I can see I was wrong to ask the assistant for a key, but I couldn't locate Miss Willand and your wife was busy.'

'The problem is *not* that you asked Jake for a key, but your implication that you had permission to take his key, when that was not the case.'

'He must have misunderstood me.'

Picking up a pen, Henry fiddled it between his fingers as he sat back in his seat. 'Despite appearances, Jake is a sensible young man. He also has exceptional hearing. If he heard you say you were expected, then that is what you said.'

Sitting a little straighter, Hazel held up her palms. 'Then I can only apologise for a poor choice of words. My intention was to cause as little disruption as possible.'

Holding eye contact with his employee, Henry said,

'Never again will you let yourself into someone's home without their knowledge. Before you visit anywhere, you will call ahead first. You have Miss Willand's mobile number; why you didn't use it on Saturday?'

'As I said...'

'You didn't want to disrupt anything.' Henry checked the time. 'I have another meeting in five minutes. Were you planning a trip to The Potting Shed to check on the builders today, Miss Cooper?'

'No, I'll go on Thursday. Give them the chance to make some progress. They are builders you told me you trusted, so I see no need to check up on them so soon.'

'Very well. I don't have to spell out why it is important to this company that this project goes well.'

'I can assure—'

'I'm sure you can.' Putting the pen back down, Henry leant forward. 'Just remember, whatever we do in this job, whoever we are working with, respect for the fact we are on other people's private property must never be forgotten. Consider this a warning. Everyone is allowed to make mistakes, but you have to admit, you haven't made the best impression since your arrival here, and it's our company reputation you are playing with. If Miss Willand wasn't family, I doubt she would have been so forgiving. Such a professional lapse will not be tolerated a second time.'

'Understood.' Standing abruptly, Hazel brushed her hands down her pencil skirt. 'Talking of professional reputations, I was *very* surprised to see Jo Dunn working for your wife and sister-in-law.'

'Jo?' Henry's eyebrows rose. 'Why?'

'He used to work at the council too. Left under a cloud.'

'A cloud?' Henry regarded his assistant; her expression was unsettlingly passive.

'I don't suppose it matters now.' Picking her briefcase up off the floor, Hazel headed to the office door, calling over her shoulder, 'After all, despite evidence to the contrary, it was *decided* that nothing could be proved.'

'Decided?' Henry frowned.

'Apparently my word that Jo was untrustworthy wasn't proof of fact.' Hazel put her hand on the office door. 'If you'll excuse me, I'll get on with my work.'

Ed was surprised to have a call from Maddie as he was walking around Exeter's cathedral square during his lunch hour. She quite often sent a text to see how he was around midday, but as she rarely took a break herself, they generally didn't speak until the evening.

'You alright?'

'Jake showed me the BIG website this morning.'

'Ah.' Ed made his way to the nearest bench and sat down. 'Now you know what they're offering, how do you feel?'

Maddie was about to reply when it dawned on her that Ed hadn't asked what they were offering. 'You've already looked, haven't you.'

'I have.' Ed hurriedly added, 'And I would have said, but you made it clear you didn't want to know.'

'They have celebrities coming! How can we even begin to compete?'

'That was the other reason I didn't say anything. I knew

you'd freak out about that.' He tried to sound soothing. 'They don't have celebrities coming until May. All BIG are doing for the Easter weekend is relying on being new and having an opening offers sale.'

'So, we have that to compete with too.'

Maddie sounded so defeated that Ed had to fight the temptation to get into his car and go and give her a hug. 'You don't need to compete, love. Come on, we've been through this. You just need to keep doing what you do. The Potting Shed has a good reputation. Remember, you are providing things BIG don't provide, personal service, a kids' club, and a family atmosphere. So, why not worry about what you're doing, not what BIG, or any other garden centre, are doing?'

As Ed's words soothed some of her anxiety away, Maddie said, 'I'm sounding like a stuck record, aren't I?'

'Just a bit.'

Twisting the end of her ponytail through her fingers, Maddie said, 'I'm sorry, Ed. In fact, I'm sorry for being sorry all the time.'

Ed gave a rueful smile. 'The apologising does get a bit wearing.'

'Sorry – it's just I've wanted this for so long, but so much could go wrong.'

'Even more could go right.'

'I prefer that way of thinking.' Maddie pulled herself together. 'Enough of my whinging. How's your day going?'

'Slowly. I'd much rather be helping you. Are the spuds in?'

'Jake's almost there. I'm working on the bluebell garden.'

Ed sat up. 'Really? But I thought—'

Maddie rushed on, 'And I thought too – and what I

thought was that you were right, and if we want to have this garden up and running, then I have to get on with it so the children can pop the first bulbs in the ground on Saturday.'

Jemima threw the door to her home open as her aunt's Jeep parked on the drive. 'I'm so glad you're here.'

'Thanks, Jem.' Maddie climbed out of the driver's seat and hooked her overnight bag onto her shoulder. 'Has Florrie behaved herself today?'

'Ish.' Her niece's voice became conspiratorial. 'It's been fun watching Mum trying not to mind the dog hairs on the furniture. I suspect it's driving her mad.'

Maddie groaned. 'Oh hell. I didn't think Sabi would want Florrie here. It was kind of her to ask us to stay but…'

Seeing her aunt's concern, Jem jumped in, 'No really, it's all fine. Mum's even bought Florrie her own basket. Let me show you your room.' Slipping her arm through Maddie's, she pulled her forward. 'All your stuff's in place. I was supposed to be doing my homework, but I escaped for a bit so I could make it cosy for you. I hope you like it.'

The coyness in her niece's voice reminded Maddie how young she was. 'Of course I will. I already love that you spent time on it for me. Thank you.'

Having been greeted by an ecstatic Florrie, Maddie followed Jemima upstairs, with the puppy bouncing around them in excited circles. 'The sooner Ivan takes you in hand the better!'

Once they were in the main guest room, Maddie shut the door so that Florrie couldn't continue to gallop up and down the pale cream stair carpet. *Just the thought of muddy paw prints on it must be giving Sabi hives!*

'It's beautiful.' Maddie took in the perfectly made, queen-sized double bed, covered in a dark burgundy quilt. The curtains matched, as did the lightshade. 'I didn't think your mum had had time to accessorise the rooms or anything yet.'

'She hasn't, but she was getting stressed about you sleeping in a "sub-standard" room, so she hit the shops this morning.'

'Sub-standard? Seriously? This place is ten times more well-kept than mine.'

'You know Mum.'

'True.' Maddie slid open a well-waxed drawer and prepared to fill it with her clothing. 'It's probably just as well she wasn't at The Potting Shed today. The mess in what was once my kitchen would make her want to cry.'

As Maddie opened her rucksack, Florrie gave a flying leap and landed in the middle of the duvet, circling round and round, chasing her own tail, until Jem was in hysterics and the bed was a mess. It was only a call from downstairs, telling them that dinner was ready, that brought them down to earth.

'That's Dad – we'd better go. Mum has got him to cook your favourite meal.'

Shame at the dishevelled state of the room – after her sister had gone to so much trouble – hit Maddie as she looked at Florrie. 'You're going to get me into a lot of trouble while we're here, aren't you?'

Wagging her tail, as if to wholeheartedly agree with the

assumption, Florrie slumped into her basket by the bed and curled into a ball.

'Worn yourself out, have you?' Jemima stroked the puppy's fur. 'Come on, Aunt Maddie, let's leave Florrie here so we can eat dinner without her offering to help lick our plates clean.'

The homely aroma of beef casserole assailed Maddie's nostrils as she took a seat at the dining room table. Having been instructed by Henry that he didn't need any help, she found herself experiencing hotel-style service as her sister poured her a glass of red wine.

'Dinner smells incredible. I can't remember the last time I had a proper home-cooked meal.'

Sabi chuckled. 'I almost did you a side order of toast, in case you got withdrawal symptoms.'

Laughing, Maddie raised her wine to her lips. 'Just because I'm a beans-on-toast-level cook, does not mean I can't survive a meal without bread. But I have to say, Sabs, I'm ever so grateful for this. I won't be expecting silver service treatment the whole time I'm here though. You guys should just get on with your lives. I can sort myself out.'

Sabi stood firm. 'I can't see Henry wanting you invading his kitchen. He's hardly let me cook since we moved! And I'm not that keen on finding your toast crumbs everywhere if I'm honest.'

'So sure I'd make a mess?'

'Yes.'

Unable to deny it, Maddie raised her wine glass towards her sister. 'Well, as I said, I'm very grateful, not just for the food, but for the lovely room. You shouldn't have gone so much trouble.'

'Of course I should – you're my sister.'

Any reply she might have given was stopped short by Jemima opening the door, a plate of steaming hot dumplings in her hands, followed by Henry carrying the largest casserole bowl Maddie had ever seen.

'I hope you're hungry.' Henry picked up a ladle ready to portion some food onto his sister-in-law's plate.

'Famished. I've been clearing and digging all day.'

'Really?' Sabi spooned up a dumpling and placed it on her casserole. 'Weren't you and Jake planting potatoes today?'

'Jake did that; I decided to listen to Ed. I've made a start on a new garden, so we can plant bluebells with the children on Saturday.'

'Not sunflowers and blueberries?'

'Those too.' Maddie turned to Jemima. 'By the way, Jake has found us a type of blueberry that will give us plenty of fruit in September.'

Jemima clapped her hands. 'Yeah. Bring on the smoothies!'

'You've smoothie-obsessed.' Henry grinned at his daughter. 'Is the land ready for the kids then, Maddie?'

'Nowhere near. I'm hoping to get a bit of time on it tomorrow. It'll depend on how busy we are, and if anything else goes wrong with the builders.'

The second the words were out of her mouth, Maddie regretted them. She was about to qualify her statement, when Sabi pounced.

'Wrong? What's gone wrong?' She immediately swung round to Henry. 'You said these men were reliable.'

'Whoa.' Maddie raised her hand. 'It wasn't that

something went wrong. Just something happened that I hadn't expected.'

'But we went through all the plans. There shouldn't be anything unexpected.' Sabi laid her cutlery down as she waited for an explanation.

Wishing she'd kept her mouth shut, Maddie picked up her wine glass. 'Hazel told me the kitchen units would be transferred from downstairs to upstairs. I was quite pleased as it would save money. But the cupboard doors weren't transferable and fell to bits as they were moved, as did the sink when they threw it outside.'

'They literally threw it out?'

'Because it wasn't needed.' Maddie stirred her fork through her dinner. 'It was a bit of a shock seeing it in pieces by my front door.'

Henry looked from his wife to Maddie and back again. 'You did say you wanted a new kitchen.'

'A new kitchen, as in a room being a kitchen rather than a bedroom, not a new kitchen as in new units et cetera.' Maddie bit her lip. 'It's okay, I must have misunderstood early on or not made myself clear.'

'I don't remember you choosing new doors, Mads?' Sabi's eyes narrowed.

'I didn't. Henry picked them. They we're okay, but I did ask Robert for an upgrade today – no offence, Henry, but the ones you chose were so flimsy they wouldn't last two minutes.'

'Actually…' Henry spooned a second dumpling onto his dinner '…I asked Hazel to deal with everything. Are you telling me that she didn't ask you which cupboards you'd like, but selected them on your behalf?'

'I'm afraid so.' Maddie dropped her gaze to her plate. The last thing she wanted was to start a row. 'But it's okay, I've sorted it with the builders.'

'That's as may be, but she shouldn't make those sorts of decisions. It's your home she's playing with.' Seeing his wife's dissatisfied expression, Henry added, 'I'll have another word with her tomorrow.'

'You spoke to her about the key incident then?' Sabi asked.

'I did. I'm rather disappointed in her to be honest. She was so good in the interview, but both Graham and I are beginning to question our decision to employ her.'

'She's probably just trying to impress you and went a bit too far.' Maddie plunged her fork into a cube of beef.

'Or she's a high-handed madam.' Sabi was less inclined to give her husband's assistant the benefit of the doubt.

'She did say something a bit odd.' Henry hesitated, unsure if he should continue in front of Jemima, but it was too late to backtrack. 'That she was surprised to see Jo working for you. Apparently, he left his council job under a cloud. She claimed he was untrustworthy.'

'What sort of cloud?' Sabi was becoming more suspicious by the moment.

'She didn't say, but it made me wonder. What do we know about Jo?'

'You don't think there's anything dodgy about Jo, do you?' Jem whispered to Maddie as they headed upstairs after dinner.

'Not for a moment. Sounds to me like Hazel was trying

to deflect attention from herself. She knew she'd messed up and couldn't handle it. Wanted your dad to worry about other things to take the heat off her.'

Jemima was unusually quiet for a moment, before saying, 'I'm afraid I might have upset Jo.'

Seeing the concern on her niece's face, Maddie gave her a hug as they got to the top of the stairs. 'I'm sure you've done no such thing.'

'I hope you're right.' Jemima shrugged. 'I knew something was bothering him, so I asked what was up. His smile wasn't real, if you see what I mean.'

'The lips were turned upwards but the eyes weren't shining.' Remembering what Ed had said about Jo not being himself, Maddie added, 'I think he's feeling bad about not being able to work with us over Easter, that's all.'

'Really?'

'Really. Now…' Maddie put her hand on her bedroom door '…let's see what horrors Florrie has unleashed on this room while we've been downstairs.'

17

'Why are you whispering?' Ed moved closer to the phone screen as Maddie glanced apprehensively over her shoulder.

'I don't want anyone to hear me.'

'Why not?'

Maddie was about to reply when Florrie bounced across the bed. 'Oh, Flo! Come on, settle down.'

'She's enjoying luxury life in Culmstock then.' Ed's chuckle was cut short by the pained expression on his girlfriend's face. 'Or not?'

'This is only the third night, but I know Sabi's already struggling not to throw us out.'

'As bad as that?'

'Every time Florrie so much as brushes the furniture, she winces.'

'Ah.' Ed gave a sympathetic nod. 'And I take it Jem can't amuse her all the time.'

'Jem's been brilliant, but even she needs some puppy-free time occasionally. She goes back to school straight after Easter and has homework to do.' Maddie lowered her voice even further. 'It isn't just Flo. Sabi's routine is so set.

Mealtimes and stuff. Everything is so rigid. Like a really posh hotel. And... well, then there's the lovely furnishings. I know Sabi wants to replace lots of them, but I'm still scared of getting things dirty or spilling my food. Florrie almost sent a vase of flowers flying this evening. Luckily, I was on my own with her at the time, but...'

'You can't relax.'

'Not for a second. What with that and wondering how the builders are doing all the time and being nervous about the weekend, I'm getting jittery, and that's making me snappy – which isn't helping.'

Ed gestured around his flat. 'You could still come here. Florrie and all.'

'To tell you the truth, I'd love to. I regretted saying no as soon as you asked me – and I only said no in the first place for practical reasons... but I can't. Sabi would be so offended if I left. She's gone out of her way to get in food I like. She's even bought a bedspread and stuff for me and a basket for Florrie to sleep in.' Maddie ruffled her dog's head. 'Not that you stay in it for more than a few minutes at a time, do you, you annoying hound.'

'What progress on the build today?'

'Slow. They are working though. I have no lazy builder complaints, but they have another job on elsewhere, so it's me in the mornings, and they head off elsewhere in the afternoons.'

'Did you know that was going to happen?'

'Not until today, no. Robert was very embarrassed. He assumed I knew.'

Ed rolled his eyes. 'Any sign of the notorious Miss Cooper today?'

'Not a peep thankfully.' Maddie paused. 'Did you think of anything that might have made her be mean about Jo?'

'Not really. Perhaps Jo beat her to a promotion or something when they were both at the council.'

'Jem's genuinely worried she's upset him.'

'I'm sure she's imagined it. Jo isn't like that. He'd never make anyone uncomfortable on purpose, especially not Jem.'

'That's what I keep telling her.' Maddie reached out to hug Florrie as she climbed out of her basket and popped up to see Ed's face on the screen.

'That reminds me, I spoke to Ivan today. He's looking forward to Sunday.'

'That's good. I'm hoping he'll be able to take Florrie in hand soon.'

'He hasn't forgotten, just been busy arranging the Exmoor Drifters for the next few weeks. He might not be going out with them, but he still does all their management stuff.'

Maddie rested back against the bedhead. 'I hope Ivan gets a few customers on Sunday.'

'You aren't going to start flapping about the weekend again, are you?'

'No, I've come to see you're right. I can't compete with BIG, and we're so different to them. It'll be okay.'

Ed peered closer to the screen. 'Who are you and what have you done with my girlfriend?'

Maddie stuck her tongue out. 'Yeah, I know I've been a nightmare, but I'll make it up to you.'

'I'll look forward to that.' Ed winked. 'Shall we talk about something else for a while before we go to bed?'

'What a good idea.'

Jemima made a beeline for Jo's camper van as soon as she and Florrie jumped out of her aunt's Suzuki Jeep.

Nerves swam in her stomach. Jo had always been so friendly towards her, but despite her aunt's reassurances, his blunt dismissal to her enquiry as to his wellbeing had left an unpleasant taste in her mouth. Determined not to leave things uncomfortable between them, she approached with an apology forming on her lips.

Florrie leapt ahead of Jem, nudging Jo's leg.

'Sorry, Jo. She got away from me.'

Fussing the collie's head, Jo gave an apologetic smile. 'It's alright. I'm glad you're here. I wanted to say sorry for being so grumpy last week.'

'It's okay. That's why I'm here. I wanted to apologise for being nosy. I was worried about you.'

'You have nothing to apologise for.' Jo hooked a smoothie off the shelf. 'Here. A thank you for caring gift.'

'Really?'

'Sure. You were right. I wasn't myself, but I'm fine now. I'm just not used to sharing. It's always been me looking after myself – well and my mum.'

'You haven't mentioned your mum before.'

'She's in a care home. Dementia.'

'Oh, I'm sorry, Jo. Was it her you were worried about?'

'No more than normal, and to be honest, she's happy and cared for, even if she doesn't remember who I am – or who she is – half the time.'

Biting back the urge to ask more questions, Jemima took a sip of drink. 'Thanks for this, Jo.'

'Fancy helping me set up this morning, or has your aunt got jobs lined up for you?'

'I'd love to help, as long as you don't mind Florrie being here.'

Reaching down to stroke the pup's head, Jo smiled. 'I'm sure if we bribe her with a biscuit, we'll be okay.'

'I'll miss you when you're not here over Easter,' Jem whispered as she helped Jo open the side of the van.

'I'll miss you too. It's been nice having a helper.' Jo's tone became serious. 'Do you like boarding school?'

'Yeah. I do. I'm only a weekly boarder, so I get home at the weekends. I have nice friends and I love learning.' Jemima paused before adding, 'I could do without some of the girls though. But that would be the same at any school.'

'True.' Jo pulled a face. 'I assume you mean the popular ones who can do no wrong in the teachers' eyes, but are actually total horrors?'

'That's them. Did you have some like that at your school?'

'Everyone does.' Jo flicked a switch to start the coffee machine. 'And sadly, such people don't always confine themselves to school life. They can loom large at work too.'

Seeing Jemima and Jo happily chatting as she crossed from the shop to the nursery, Maddie felt a sense of relief. Whatever had been eating Jo had obviously passed.

Having promised Sabi that she could leave at eleven so

she could have some time in her new home, Maddie dashed around to the back of the nursery to examine her progress with the new garden.

'The children will be here the day after tomorrow, Dad.' Maddie examined the area of recently forked soil. 'I'm rather nervous, to tell you the truth.'

Wishing that Jake was there to help, she grabbed a fork from the polytunnel. 'This will be my last chance to work the soil over before the first Little Acorns session. Tomorrow I'll be too busy – I hope. Good Friday usually brings people in, and there's no doubt we have more customers now, even though we are still only small. We'll be okay – won't we, Dad?'

Of course you will, lass.

Pushing the fork into the mix of topsoil and compost she'd worked into the ground, a twinge of sadness hit Maddie as she considered how much her father would have enjoyed what she and Sabi were creating. 'I'm going to start with a talk about gardens and how important they are. Then we'll transplant some of the blueberries Jake has already started into bigger pots. I was going to do sunflowers, but I think I'll leave that until next time now, so we have time to plant some bluebells out here.'

The sound of running footsteps behind Maddie made her spin round. 'Jem? You okay?'

'Not really. Well, I am... it's Jo. He's packing up.'

'But it's only half ten?'

Jemima looked worried. 'He said he's had an emergency call and has to go.' She sucked in her bottom lip, as if uncertain to go on.

'What is it?'

'I was with him, and I'd swear his phone hasn't rung all morning.'

Sinking the fork into the earth, Maddie gestured to her dog. 'Why don't you take Florrie for a walk; I'll go and see what's happened.'

'Thanks, Aunt Maddie.'

Maddie hadn't made it all the way to Jo's van, when she saw Hazel Cooper striding towards her. Her heart sank.

'Miss Cooper. How can I help you?'

'I'm here to see how the builders are getting on. I trust you have no objection?'

'I have no objection. I appreciate you asking first this time.'

'As I explained to Mr Willand-Harris, I was simply trying to cause you as little disruption as possible. The sooner we get this upgrade done, the sooner you can open as a proper garden centre. Honestly, I am trying to help here.'

'Well, that's kind of you. But if you could keep me in the loop with your plans then I'd appreciate it.' Maddie could see Jo in the background, he was folding his chairs up with a speed that bordered on panic. 'If you'll excuse me, Miss Cooper, I have to get on.'

Hazel stared at where Jo was closing up. 'I *had* hoped for a coffee before I went in, but clearly Mr Dunn is as unreliable as ever.'

'Why do you say that?'

'He should be here all day, shouldn't he?'

'Yes, but...'

'He's clearly preparing to leave. He'll have an excuse

ready – it'll be believable too. Make sure you get him to pay today's rent anyway.'

Maddie's head suddenly began to ache. 'He doesn't pay rent. He brings us customers by just being here. He…'

'He's not lost his touch then.' Hazel shook her head. 'If you'll excuse me, I'd best get on.'

Running to the camper van, throwing an apologetic glance at a couple who'd obviously been heading towards it with the intention of buying a cup of something, Maddie gasped out, 'Jo? What's happening?'

'Emergency. I'm so sorry, Maddie. I wouldn't shoot off like this if it wasn't important.'

'I know you wouldn't, but—'

'It's… Sara, you know. The one at Hawthorn Park. It's her first Easter opening without her father and she's having a wobble.'

Maddie held up a hand. 'Then you must go. We'll see you after Easter.'

'You will.' Jo's eyes flicked to the house and back again. 'Of course you will.'

18

Easing past the closed sign, Ed pulled into the car park of The Potting Shed just as Maddie was heading towards her Jeep.

'I'm glad I caught you.'

'Umm, me too.' Maddie gave Ed a long kiss, before asking, 'What are you doing here? You said you weren't coming until tomorrow.'

'I wasn't, but Henry called. Emergency summit.'

'Really?' Maddie checked her phone. 'I haven't had any messages and Sabi didn't say before she left.'

'That's because Sabi doesn't know his news. It's a surprise. Come on, I'll follow you in the Jeep.'

'What news?'

'You'll see.' Ed opened his car door. 'Apparently, there's a nice pub near Culmstock. We're all going there for dinner.'

Two bottles of champagne waited in an ice bucket in the middle of a large oak table. Henry, Sabi and Jemima were already sat along one side as Ed and Maddie went in.

'Wow. What a gorgeous place.' Maddie took in the clever interior design that gave the pub a sense that, at any minute, it could transform into a five-star restaurant. 'I can see why my sister would like it here.'

Hooking her arm into Ed's, waving towards her family as they passed a blazing open fire, Maddie suddenly realised there was no sign of her dog.

'What a lovely surprise – but umm – where's Florrie?'

'At home.' Jemima gave her mother a sideways glance. 'Mum says she'll be okay for a while.'

Maddie's insides did a backflip. 'She's never been left on her own before. Sabi, if she damages your home, I'll never forgive myself.'

Henry answered before his wife had the chance. 'Florrie was sound asleep in her basket when we left. She's had a long walk, some dinner, and she relieved herself before we came out. There's no reason to think she won't be okay.'

And if she does cause chaos, it'll just be in my room, damaging only my stuff.

Guessing his girlfriend was wondering what she'd find left of her bedroom on her return, Ed changed the subject. 'So, what's the occasion?'

Picking up a bottle, Henry started to fill the glasses as a waitress arrived with a pile of menus. 'I'll tell you in a second. Dinner is on me tonight.'

'There's no need, Henry.' Maddie pushed her glass towards her brother-in-law. 'Just a drop – I'm driving.'

As he poured a half-glass of champagne into her flute, Henry said, 'There's every need. I owe you an apology for a start.'

'An apology?'

'Miss Cooper. Her manner has not been what either Graham or I had hoped for.'

'Heavy-handed.' Maddie lifted her glass. 'But well-meaning, I'm sure.'

'High-handed and self-serving if you ask me.' Sabi picked up a menu. 'Let's not ruin the evening before it's started by thinking about her. How is the building work going anyway? I didn't have the chance to look today.'

'Fine, I think. The builders are just quietly getting on with it – well, mostly quietly. Some of the bangs and crashes from the house are a little disconcerting, but the few times I've popped in, it seems to be in hand. "Carefully controlled chaos", that's what Robert called it.'

'Sounds like him.' Henry poured some fizz into his wife's glass. 'He's a good bloke. Robert and Kevin have built up a reputation for being calm, methodical and professional. They'll do what needs doing, and although it'll be messy for a while, it will soon start to take shape.

'Actually...' Henry sat back down and raised his glass '... apologising for Hazel wasn't why I asked you all to come along tonight.'

'A planning meeting for the weekend?' Sabi laid her menu back down. 'That's a sensible idea. I know that Petra and Jake will be with us from Friday, and you're helping aren't you, Ed...'

'Sabi.' Henry gently cut across his wife before she got into full organisational mode. 'While there is loads to discuss, I have other news. We have something to celebrate.'

'We do?'

Laying a hand across his wife's palm, Henry said, 'I would like to raise a toast to our new home in Culmstock. My beautiful wife's dream home – and – as of today, our *only* home.'

Sabi had thrown her arms around her husband before he'd had the chance to take a drink from his champagne glass. 'Our house in Tiverton is sold? *Properly* sold, not just under offer?'

'One hundred per cent sold.' Henry beamed. 'Miriam called this afternoon. It's signed and sealed and sorted.'

Maddie laid her knife and fork on her plate and sat back in her seat with an air of contentment. There was barely a trace of her pan-fried steak, cauliflower cheese and parsnip mash left on her plate, and the glass of lemonade she'd ordered had gone. Her sister's joy at the sale of their old home was as palpable as Henry's relief that he'd no longer be paying two mortgages.

While eating her food, Maddie had been happy to let the conversations around the table wash over her. She was vaguely aware that Sabi and Henry had been chatting over décor options for their home now finances were less pressured, and that Ed and Jem were talking about the various constellations you could see from her back garden. Every now and then Maddie's mind drifted to Florrie, and the high chance that, later, she'd find her bedroom in disarray, with a duvet covered in dog hair – or even in pieces. Mostly, however, she found her mind had switched off. For now at least, it was refusing to deal with problems she could do nothing about.

Her pleasant state of numbness was abruptly taken away by Sabi, who had overheard something her daughter had said to Ed.

'What do you mean, Jo left early today? How early?'

'Umm...'

Feeling sorry for Jemima, Maddie interceded. 'About half-ten. There was an emergency. He had to go.'

'A real emergency, or...'

'Or what?' A light sweat broke out on the back of Maddie's neck.

'Well, you know what Hazel said – that he couldn't be relied upon. What if...'

'No, Mum.' Pink-faced, Jemima placed her cola onto the table with a light thud. 'He had to go because a friend needed him.'

'Very gallant I'm sure, but what about his business? What about ours? How can he just—'

'Sabs!' Maddie broke through her sister's fast-building tirade. 'Come on, we're having a lovely evening. A celebration for you selling your old place. Don't ruin it by getting stressed about something that's already happened.'

'But what *did* happen? We can't afford for Jo not to be there when he said he would be. It's bad enough he can't be here this weekend. You know as well as I do that if we don't reach our agreed budget by the end of May, we'll have to scale down – backtrack even!'

'He doesn't know that though, does he.' Tension seeped back into Maddie's shoulders and her head spun with visions of explaining to the bank manager why the original loan wouldn't ever be paid back, while he told her to wave goodbye to the new one. 'His friend Sara, the girl at Hawthorn Park… she lost her dad just over a year ago. She's facing her first open garden event alone and needed help. I'm sure he wouldn't have gone unless it was vital.'

'Well, yes… I suppose…' A bright flush hit Sabi's cheeks that she hoped she could attribute to the warmth of the pub if anyone commented.

'We know what it's like to lose a father, and I get the impression this Sara is much younger than us.'

'She's twenty-one,' Ed interrupted, 'but, more to the point, she's entirely on her own. No relatives to help her out.'

'Oh, right. Fair enough.' Sabi gulped down the remainder of her drink before mumbling, 'It can't be easy for her. Do you know Sara, then, Ed?'

'Only that she is a friend of Jo's and runs Hawthorn Park on her own. That's where Jo is selling coffee over Easter.'

Jemima looked at the adults surrounding her as if they were dim. 'If he hadn't gone, he'd have still felt guilty, but for a different reason. I'm sure he's not untrustworthy.'

'I have to agree with Jemima. Jo was put in a no-win situation.' Ed nodded. 'I hardly like to ask, but have you let your customers know that there won't be a café over Easter?'

'No.' Maddie sighed. 'I didn't want to put people off coming. Nor did I have time to find any picnic tables, so I haven't advertised that people can bring their own food either.'

'Probably just as well if the children will be planting in that space on Saturday.' Ed rolled the stem of his empty wine glass between his fingers. 'How about Sunday, while Ivan and Elspeth are there?'

'How am I going to magic picnic tables before then?'

'No, I mean, why not have a few ordinary tables and chairs set up in the polytunnel with tea and coffee facilities. I'm sure we could rustle some furniture up between us. Put out some squash and biscuits. You know the sort of thing.'

'We aren't cleared to sell refreshments that way. No certificate from the relevant body.'

'You don't need one if you ask people to serve themselves. Just have a donations tin, for anyone who wants to help themselves.'

Henry nodded. 'That's a great idea, Ed. And Ivan could keep an eye on things. Although... would it be safe? I mean, what if someone burnt themselves on the kettle or spilt boiling water or...'

Maddie held up her hands in defeat. 'You know, it's a lovely idea, guys, but I think it's best we leave the refreshments to Jo when he gets back. The last thing we need is to be sued because someone has choked on a crumb from a biscuit we gave them for free.'

Sabi reluctantly agreed. 'No refreshments over Easter then.'

Maddie checked the time. 'It's been lovely, Henry, thank you, but I should go and make sure Florrie doesn't need to go outside once more before bed.'

'And I should head home.' Ed stood up to leave. 'I'll be with you by eight tomorrow, unless you want me earlier?'

'Don't be silly.' Sabi smiled. 'You can stay with us tonight.'

'Are you sure?' Maddie took Ed's hand, delighted at the prospect of having him with her.

'Of course. That's okay, isn't it, Henry?'
'No problem at all.'

Jo couldn't sleep. But then, he hadn't expected to.

Staring at the crack of moonlight that snuck through the tiny gap at the top of the curtains, he let out a muted moan.

He'd dared, just for a few months, to think that life was finally on his side. That all he'd done, all he'd risked, had finally started to pay off, and – more importantly – he was being accepted for who he was. Then Simon had died, and his resolve not to go back to Hawthorn Park again had gone up in a puff of smoke. His kind nature, and the fact that he was very fond of Sara despite himself, had seen him agreeing to return. After all, they'd been good friends before. *She's still a good friend... except...*

The previous evening had been awkward at first. But eventually, small talk about coffee and tree growth had relaxed into animated chatter about Sara's plans for the park.

They'd talked about where he should position his van to sell from over Easter– Sara's suggested plot being different from the one her father preferred – and discussed Jo's range of drinks and foods, and whether he wanted to borrow extra tables and chairs. Sara had told him about a small marquee she'd bought, just in case the weather soured and he wanted to work undercover. This gesture had touched him, making Jo regret hardly communicating with her since that awkward moment, a year ago on Sunday, when she'd tried to kiss him, and he'd backed away with so much speed that any chance of covering it up as an innocent mistake or misunderstanding had been lost before it started.

Afraid that their calm reunion would falter if they stayed up talking too late, Jo hadn't lingered after he'd helped Sara stack the dishwasher with their dirty plates. Pleading tiredness and a long weekend ahead, he had found himself shown into his current environ. Only now did he realise that Sara hadn't spoken a word from the moment he'd announced he was ready for bed.

An image of Hazel Cooper eclipsed one of Sara as Jo tugged the duvet around him even more firmly. Hazel had never been a friend in the way Sara had. She had been something else – something he hadn't understood then and didn't understand now. *Yet, you did what you did – Hazel has every right to hate you.*

He'd promised Maddie he'd go back to The Potting Shed after Easter, but with Hazel prowling around, he wasn't sure he could. Shame washed over him as he recalled his speedy exit that morning. 'Perhaps I should have spoken to Hazel. Perhaps she's forgiven me – moved on.' Jo pulled his duvet up, allowing the bedding to smother his face. 'Who am I kidding? By the time Hazel's finished lacing her poison around the nursery, Maddie and Sabi won't want me back anyway.'

19

Petra bounced into the shop with Florrie-like energy. Jake was close behind her, a contented expression on his face.

'Maddie! It's so good to see you. I've missed this place.' Petra swept her long blonde hair up into a lopsided bun. 'Almost as much as I've missed this one here. I hope he hasn't been too mopey.'

Maddie bit back the urge to laugh as Jake's eyebrows shot up. 'I do *not* mope.'

'Yeah, right.' Poking him in the ribs, Petra said, 'Have you told Maddie your news yet?'

'No. I wanted to tell you first.'

'News?' Maddie looked from one of her assistants to the other. 'Is this the thing you didn't want to tell me about in case you jinxed it?'

'Yes. But, as of yesterday afternoon, it's official.' Jake's cheeks flushed self-consciously. 'And, as I said, I wanted to tell Petra first.'

'Of course you did – but I'm dying to know. Tell me!'

Petra slipped her hands into his. 'I'm bursting with pride! I can't wait to tell my friends at Rosemoor. They'll be so chuffed.'

'Will they?' Jake sounded surprised. 'But they're all clever and—'

'Stop that right there.' Petra placed a finger on his lips. 'How many times do I have to tell you? They're differently clever, that's all. You're a *true* gardener. None of us will ever be a natural at the art like you are.'

'Oh.'

Seeing the wind had been blown from Jake's sails by Petra's heartfelt compliment, Maddie prompted, 'And the good news is…?'

'Oh, um, yes… you know I'm doing the horticulture qualification at Bicton that needs no academic qualifications to take it.'

'Yes.'

'Apparently, I'm okay with the plants, even if I'm not too hot on the writing stuff. My tutor thinks I'm good enough to maybe try for a better course.'

Petra, who'd been hopping from one foot to the other as he'd spoken, could stand it no longer. 'Jake! They did not think you were *maybe* good enough! I've seen the email, remember! It said that the teaching staff had recognised how gifted you are and have invited you to do a level three apprenticeship via the college instead.'

'Oh my God!' Maddie threw her arms around Jake, only to remove them when she remembered how much he hated shows of affection by anyone beyond Petra. 'That's awesome. Congratulations!'

'There's a snag.' Jake looked awkward. 'I need to find somewhere to work from. Somewhere that is accredited to take apprenticeships; otherwise, obviously, I'd have asked if I could work from here.'

'Won't the college find a placement for you?'

'Yeah, but they could send me anywhere. I'd rather find my own so I can stay local-ish.'

Maddie was sympathetic. 'As much as I don't want to lose you completely, Jake, I totally understand. Will you be trying to get a place somewhere near Petra?'

'I'll try, but there isn't much going.'

'I wondered about us asking Dan. Do you think he'd mind if we contacted him?' Petra unzipped her coat and folded it up under the till desk. 'Your old boss was so kind when I was hunting for my apprenticeship.'

'Of course, he won't mind. It's a great idea.' Maddie turned to Jake. 'Why don't you ask him on Sunday?'

'He's coming this weekend?' Petra asked.

'I sent him an email explaining what we were up to and that we'd love to see him.' Maddie turned back to Jake. 'Dan might know someone who can help you, even if he can't help you himself.'

'I'll ask him, thanks.' Jake scuffed a trainer over the floor as he mumbled, 'And for your help. Without you and your dad...'

A lump developed in Maddie's throat. 'Dad would be every bit as proud as we are, Jake. But right now, we need to work on his dream. Today is, hopefully, going to be very busy.'

'Sabi?' Jo was surprised, and a little disconcerted, to see one of his employers at Hawthorn Park. 'No Jemima or Henry?'

'They've taken Florrie for a long walk along the beach at Exmouth. She needs wearing out before I let her back in the house.'

Something about Sabi's clipped voice made Jo wonder what the dog had done. 'She disgraced herself?'

'We left her home alone for a couple of hours last night. It was a mistake.'

'Ah.'

'She tore Maddie's new duvet cover to shreds. The duvet didn't survive intact either.'

'Oh.' Jo didn't know what else to say about the inevitability of the result if Florrie was left alone for too long. 'It's lovely to see you, Sabi, but how come you're at Hawthorn?' A nagging sense of doom nudged at Jo. 'If you're here to tell me that you and Maddie don't want me back after I let you down yesterday, I'll quite understand. I love working at The Potting Shed, but...'

'No, Jo... that isn't why I'm here.' Sabi glanced over her shoulder. 'I umm... I wondered how the set-up here worked. You know, with a mind to expanding at The Potting Shed.'

'Oh, right. Okay. Well, I'm not the person to speak to. You need Sara.'

Hoping Jo didn't notice her face flush at the mention of Simon's daughter, Sabi looked around her. The space Jo had allotted to him was perfect. On the edge of the wood, his usual number of tables and chairs had been increased by a third with a set of wooden picnic tables.

'Where will I find her?'

'Probably in the office. It's at the back of the house.'

'Right.' Sabi's stomach churned as she walked in the direction Jo had pointed. She still had no idea what she was really doing there, nor what she'd say to Simon's daughter when she found her.

'That's the third one.' Maddie stared across the car park to see a disgruntled couple get back into their vehicle only a few minutes after they'd parked. 'We're never going to make enough money to keep going at this rate.'

Ed slipped an arm around Maddie's waist. 'They'll come back once Jo's here.'

'Or they'll drive on to BIG, use their café, and never return.'

Unable to deny the possibility, Ed waved a hand around them. 'You have a steady flow of folk here, and tomorrow you'll have the children, plus parents – so that's a captive audience.'

'I suppose so.' Maddie stuck a large poster onto the fence behind her. 'Hopefully the people who do stay for a wander today will be tempted to come back on Sunday when they see that Ivan and Elspeth will be here with their cheese and beauty products.'

'Does Petra have one of those posters?' A call came from behind Maddie.

'Hi, Jake.' Ed smiled. 'I hear congratulations are in order.'

'Thanks. Yeah.'

'What were you saying about Petra?' Maddie asked.

'Has she got a computerised copy of the poster? She could do the social media thing while she's in the shop, you know, like she used to.'

'I'll send it to her now.' Maddie unlocked her mobile. 'I don't know why I didn't think of that.'

'Too much else on your mind.' Ed spotted some activity by the stacks of soil lined up along the outside edge of the shop. 'I think we might have a compost sale. I'll go and help.'

As Ed went off to help an elderly couple to carry their chosen bags of soil, Jake watched him go. 'I think he likes working here more than he likes being a solicitor.'

'Do you think so?'

Jake plunged his hands in to his pockets. 'Wake up, Maddie!'

Sabi's heart hammered in her chest. *What am I doing here?*

She could see the house ahead of her but wasn't sure if she was going to go and talk to Sara or not. 'What would I say? At best she'd think I was rude for asking her how profitable a bluebell wood is, at worst she'd think I am here to poach her custom.'

You want to help her.

The voice at the back of her head took her by surprise. 'Why do I want to help her?'

Because you don't want her to think of you in the same way Simon did.

'But she has no idea who I am, so it makes no difference. And Simon's gone, so...'

So, she needs help. Anyone who loses a parent young feels lost – but she has no one. She could have had you if Simon hadn't labelled you a snob and—

Sabi cut her thoughts short. 'No! I have Henry and Jemima and I wouldn't change that for the world.'

Hurrying down a path to her left, which swung away from the house and into the thick of the woods, Sabi crossed her arms across her gilet. Her boots moved faster and faster, until sweat clung to her neck and her palms were clammy.

Head down, as she passed through a corridor of trees, Sabi looked up as she became aware of light flooding around her. An opening that led to an unexpectedly formal area of garden stretched out before her. Sabi's hands went cold as she stopped. She'd seen a picture of this on the website.

'Simon's memorial garden.' The words were whispered under her breath as she forced her feet to move forward.

'I wanted to clear the air.' Sara rubbed the toe of one boot against the heel of the other as she stood with Jo. 'Before it gets too busy.'

'So do I,' Jo mumbled. 'I'm sorry I went to bed so early last night. It was a lovely evening, I was just...'

'Running away to avoid things going wrong?'

'Guilty as charged.' He pointed to his van. 'Coffee is ready if you want one.'

'Please.'

'Latte with one sugar?'

'As ever.' Sara smiled.

'Did Sabi find you?'

'Sabi?'

'One of the women who owns The Potting Shed. I think she wanted to talk to you about this place. How you run the bluebell walk side of things and stuff.'

'Really? Whatever for?'

'There's a bit of land at the back of the nursery. They're thinking of having a small bluebell area.'

'How can I help with that?'

'I've no idea.' Jo's forehead creased. 'It is a bit odd, but Sabi never does anything without a reason.'

After pouring the latte concoction into a long slim glass, Jo passed it into Sara's hands. 'You and I talked about all sorts of things last night, but I didn't ask how you were – I mean, how *you* are, not how this place is?'

Sara sank onto the nearest rickety seat. 'Coping.'

'Just coping?'

'If I'm honest, yes.'

'I'm so sorry. Simon was a good man. It's so unfair.'

Staring into her glass, Sara took a second to gather herself. 'Dad liked you. He hoped you and I...'

'I know.' Jo suppressed a sigh. 'If I could, I would... but I can't. If there was ever going to be anyone...' He lowered his voice, unsure if he should have said anything, but knew he'd said too much to backtrack now. 'You do know it would have been you, don't you?'

Lifting her gaze to meet his, Sara's eyes shone with a dozen emotions. 'No, I didn't know. I hoped. But I didn't know.'

Pausing their conversation to serve a family of five with three hot chocolates and two cappuccinos, Jo considered all Sara had said. Now he was here, in her company, surrounded by the beauty of nature, he realised just how much of a fool he'd been. He'd believed keeping his distance had been a kindness to Sara – to them both – but he'd been wrong.

Glad that his customers had chosen to sit on the far side of the seating area, and therefore were out of earshot, Jo rejoined Sara. He peered through his fringe at her elfin face. 'This is the bit where I say sorry for hurting you.'

'Thank you.' Sara clutched her drink in both hands. 'Not that you meant to hurt me. I always knew that.'

'Doesn't help though, does it.'

'Not really.'

A peaceful hush settled between them as they watched a steadily increasing stream of walkers in the distance, amble up the driveway towards the gardens and wood. Knowing it wouldn't be long before Jo was too busy to chat, Sara broke the silence.

'You know why Dad liked you, don't you?'

'We had similar interests.'

'True, but that wasn't it. He liked you because you saw beyond the material. Dad was constantly advising me to avoid people who can't see me aside from what I'd inherit.'

'Sounds sensible.'

'It was. Although it got a bit annoying sometimes.' She gave a sad smile. 'It came from a good place though. Not long after he'd started uni, he fell for a fellow student – it was love at first sight for him. But her love was for Hawthorn Park.'

'I can see how it could bewitch a hopeful girlfriend.'

'Apparently, she had decided on the size of family they'd have together, and how she'd run the house while he did all the maintenance and the "being the face of Hawthorn Park" within a few hours of being here. Frightened Dad to death!' The colour ran from her face, as she mumbled. 'Well, not to death, obviously…'

Getting off his chair, Jo put his arm around her shoulders.

'Sounds like Simon was wise to step aside from this girl, however he felt about her.'

'He thought so. Even though he loved her, he didn't want to live a life where he was second best to his home.'

Sabi froze. A sense of horror tripped down her spine as she stepped behind a set of thickly trunked oak trees, distancing herself from Jo's café van. *So, Simon did warn her about me.*

Sara found herself snuggling closer into Jo's side. 'The woman who was after this place, she didn't know about me, not until they split. That's why she was here... the reason Dad brought her for a visit. He wanted to tell her about me, and hopefully, to have her meet me. I was having a holiday at the seaside with my grandparents while she visited. The idea was that he'd tell her about me just before we were due to come home, and then we'd join them later for tea. He'd told her he had a surprise for her.'

'She'd assumed Hawthorn Park was the surprise, when in fact it was that he had a daughter?'

'You've got it.'

'Ah.'

'Dad returned her to uni before we got back. He was dismissive of anyone who came near him after that. And wary of any blokes who liked me.'

'But I was okay because, well, I'm not a "normal bloke" – and I liked you, not the park.' Jo pulled his hat further over his ears. 'Not that I don't like it here.'

'I know what you mean.' Sara swallowed. 'But drop the "not a normal bloke" stuff, okay?'

'Okay.' Jo wondered if she'd ever understand how important her firmness on that point was to him.

A child of about five, belting along on a scooter, suddenly shot into view. A harassed-looking woman on his heels was approaching them fast. Sara got to her feet. 'I should let you get on.'

Jo squeezed her hand. 'I meant what I said. If I was a relationship-type person, I'd be making a nuisance of myself every five minutes.'

'But you're not.'

Jo exhaled slowly. 'You have always deserved more than I can give you.'

Sabi leant back against the tree trunk and closed her tear-filled eyes. She wanted to go home. She wanted Henry.

20

Having checked Jemima was getting on with her homework, and that Florrie was sleeping after their long walk in the sea air, Henry joined his wife on the sofa.

'What's wrong, love? You've hardly said a word since we picked you up.'

Leaning forward, Sabi placed her china mug on the coffee table and took a deep breath. 'Henry, you know we had a bit of an uncomfortable time before Christmas, when I put in an offer on this house without telling you?'

'Yes?' Henry pulled his arm from around his wife, but placed a palm on her leg, so as not to withdraw himself completely.

'It was the fact I didn't talk to you about it – about my dreams for this place – that was the problem, wasn't it?'

Henry was wary. 'Where are you going with this?'

'I only partly wanted to go to Hawthorn Park to see how it operates.'

Henry swivelled around so that he was looking directly at his wife. 'Go on.'

'Do you remember when we first met?'

The recollection knocked some of Henry's disquiet to one

side. 'I couldn't believe my luck. The most beautiful woman I'd ever seen was talking to me.'

'Oh, Henry.' Sabi brushed her hand over his cheek; the skin was rough compared to when they'd first met.

'Come on, what is it?'

'Okay,' She took a steading breath, before explaining, 'I had been single for six months.'

'And I'd been single for eight. We'd both had our hearts broken, a fact that united us from the start. Why bring this up now?'

'Hawthorn Park.'

Henry was confused for a split second, then realisation dawned. 'Your ex works there? You ran into them today and didn't know how to tell me?'

'Not quite...'

Maddie passed Ed her empty fish and chip box. 'That was perfect. Thank you so much.'

'My pleasure.' Ed scrunched up the paper that had wrapped their takeaway. 'Very little in life is better than fish and chips from the chippy eaten outside.'

Getting up from where she'd been sat, at the potting bench in the far polytunnel, Maddie examined the space. 'Is there anything else we can do to prepare for tomorrow?'

'Short of dragging the kids out of bed to start the workshop early, no.'

Sweeping a hand over the bench, Maddie said, 'At least if we did that, then it would be over.'

'Aren't you excited about your first Little Acorns gathering?'

'I am, but I'm also terrified. What if they're bored? What if I can't engage with them?'

'How about, what if they love it and you end up wishing you'd arranged a longer session? What if they can't wait to come back?'

'I'm so glad you're here.' Maddie crossed the tunnel and gave Ed a lingering kiss. 'You sure you want to help tomorrow? You haven't had a day off work in ages, what with lawyering all week and then helping me.'

'I can't wait. I love kids.'

Maddie's insides melted as she saw how Ed was looking at her. 'You do?'

'Sure. I'd love a family one day. Wouldn't you?'

'Yes.' Maddie held his gaze for a moment, before looking across to the bench set up before them. 'But not of six!'

Ed laughed. 'I was thinking maybe two... but if more came along...'

Maddie's heart gave a leap as he took her hand. 'I love you, Ed.'

'Love you too.' Manoeuvring her gently back so she was facing him, Ed murmured, 'And I hope that when the time for children comes, they'll be ours.'

'Me too.' Maddie whispered the words, realising she meant them. For the first time since they'd been a couple a real sense of security sweep over her. 'Shall we go back to Sabi's?'

Ed trailed a hand through her hair, unhooking her ponytail, sending her chestnut hair cascading around her shoulders. 'Umm, we could do.'

'But?'

'Florrie does tend to get a bit jealous.'

'That's true,' Maddie murmured as Ed's hand continued its journey south, his fingertips dancing slowly down her arm before resting against her hip.

'How about we go and see what state the house is in?'

'Now?' Maddie drew back in surprise.

Ed kissed her nose. 'I was thinking more of checking your bedroom has been left undisturbed by the builders.'

Maddie had her door key in her hand before Ed had even finished his sentence.

'You think you owe this Sara, somehow?'

Sabi kept her eyes fixed on her untouched peppermint tea. 'If I hadn't acted like I did, then perhaps Simon wouldn't have felt the need to warn his daughter about future relationships, and she wouldn't be coping with his bereavement alone.'

'You were young. And a little overenthusiastic perhaps, that's all.'

'I was a snob.' Sabi gulped against her dry throat. 'I'm still a snob, but...'

'You have good taste and high standards. That's not snobbish.' Henry kissed her nose.

'Thank you, but I know my faults, and so do you.' Sabi took a sip of cold tea. 'After Dad died, I saw things a little differently. It took a while to wake up to how much I was trying to be someone I wasn't – trying to keep up with other people like Miriam. But the scales fell from my eyes – better late than never I suppose.' She paused, before adding, 'I can't stop thinking about that girl over there, all on her own.'

'Can I ask you a question?' Henry leant back against the sofa.

A flutter of nerves stirred in Sabi's stomach as she inclined her head.

'You thought being taken to see Simon's home back then was his surprise, but now you know that *Sara* was. How would you have reacted do you think if, back then, Simon still wanted you to be together and he'd told you, out of the blue, even though you'd been dating for a while, that he had a daughter he hadn't previously mentioned?'

'I... I don't know.'

'You were eighteen, love. Wouldn't you have been hurt that he hadn't told you about her up front? Suspicious that he'd kept her quiet? And, more importantly, would you have wanted to take on a child?'

Sabi stared at her hands. 'I honestly don't know.'

Seeing his wife's discomfort, he gently asked, 'How old is Sara?'

'Ed said she was twenty-one the other night.'

'Still young then.' Henry reassured Sabi, 'She has plenty of time to meet someone. Her lack of partner is hardly your fault.'

Sabi thought about Jo but said nothing about that side of the overheard conversation. 'Maybe not, but she's wary and sad. There must be something we can do – I can do – to help her.'

'You think she's lonely?'

'Yes.' Picking up the cold tea, Sabi put the cup down again before it reached her lips. 'I can't help thinking that's my fault.'

'You know it isn't.'

'But it *might* be! If I hadn't made Simon so unwilling to trust, she might have had a stepmum.'

'No, love. Simon lived his own life and made his own choices. If he'd met someone who he was meant to have been with, he'd have gone for it no matter what.' Henry held her hand a little tighter. 'What happened to Simon was horrendous – the loss of his wife and then terminal illness – but you don't owe him or his daughter anything.'

'I'm sorry I didn't tell you about why I wanted to go to Hawthorn Park.'

'You've told me now. I'm glad you did.' Henry slipped an arm back around his wife and kissed the top of her head. 'Secrets are never a good idea.'

'You're an amazing man, Henry Harris.'

'True.' Henry pull himself off the sofa. 'How about I make us fresh drinks and then you can tell me about Hawthorn Park itself. You never know, an idea of how to help Sara may come to us as we chat. If you still want to help her – and if she wants our help. Remember, we're strangers to her.'

Gathering up her cup, Sabi followed Henry into the kitchen. 'We might be strangers to Simon's daughter, but Jo isn't.'

21

The final child allowed his fingers to be prised from his mother's hand before being gently ushered into place by Jemima, who was clearly enjoying her position of authority.

'If she doesn't end up running this place, she'll make an excellent teacher.' Ed gave Maddie a hug for luck. 'You ready?'

'As I'll ever be. You?'

'Yep.' Ed smiled. 'Relax, you'll be great.'

Ten minutes later Maddie's nerves faded away as, proudly wearing the new gardening gloves she had presented them all with, six under-tens started scooping soil into their flowerpots with an enthusiasm that bordered on gusto. Her talk on why gardening was so important had been listened to with wide-eyed politeness and minimal fidgeting, but now, as she and Jem wandered along the short row of happy faces, suggesting more soil – or in one case less soil – in the pots – she wondered why she'd ever been worried. When she'd told the Little Acorns that they were going to be potting on blueberries – and then explained what potting on meant – they'd swooped into action, each one declaring they couldn't wait to taste their smoothie in the summer.

As she made her way along the line of children, Maddie could hear Ed in the background talking to the parents. He was explaining how the workshops would work over the future weeks, and was reassuring them that, if their child was happy, they could leave them while they had a wander around The Potting Shed, or they were welcome to sit in the polytunnel, or even join in. 'Shovels,' he was telling them, 'are always on hand for anyone who wants to help out.'

'Now then...' Maddie signalled to her niece, who immediately picked up two blueberry plants '...when Jem gives you a plant, be careful. Even with your gloves on, it would be easy to be scratched by the mini fruit canes. As you can see, they are little more than a bunch of leafy sticks at the moment.'

'Where's the fruit?'

Maddie mentally thanked her niece for her last-minute suggestion of writing the children's names on sticky labels and popping them on their coats. 'Good question, Noel. The fruit will start to appear in late spring, and then, by early September, we should have enough to eat or add to a smoothie.'

'Are we going to grow the spinach for smoothies too?'

'Yes, Kayleigh, we are.' Maddie smiled at the little girl as she waved to the other side of the tunnel. 'If you look over there, you'll see some sacks. Next time you come, we'll be using that soil to make a growing area for your spinach.'

'Cool!' Noel grinned at his neighbour, Mark, who shyly smiled back.

Engrossed in helping Josie, the youngest member of the group, at just six years old, Maddie didn't notice the parents slip out for a stroll around the nursery. She was therefore surprised when Ed appeared at her side, helping Noel ease his blueberry plant out of its current pot and into the new one he'd prepared.

'Thanks, Ed.' Maddie mouthed as Noel sat back, his first horticultural task successfully complete.

Passing his young charge a sticky label and a pen, Ed said, 'If you write your name on here, Noel, we can stick it to the pot. That way we won't forget it's yours.'

By the time everyone had labelled their pots, Jemima was showing them all where the dust pans and brushes were kept. Seconds later, six happy helpers were sweeping up the soil around their feet and along the benches.

'I think I spy your answer to needing more help around here.' Ed chuckled as the soil was smeared across the floor, before being – mostly – gathered up and poured into the waste sack at the back of the tunnel.

'I wish I could give them orange juice or something.'

'Don't worry, all the parents came prepared. I have a host of squash bottles, water bottles, and cartons of various liquid concoctions waiting over there.'

'Fabulous.' Maddie stepped forwards. 'Right, folks. Excellent work all round. I think you've all earned a break. If you go over to Jem, she'll give you all a squirt of hand sanitiser, before you fetch your drinks from Ed. Then, I'll tell you what we are going to do next.'

★

Petra left the till and stood in the shop doorway. While trade hadn't been non-existent, it was nowhere near as busy as Maddie had hoped.

Catching Jake's eye as he returned from helping a customer place an olive tree in the back of their car, a plant Petra recognised as being left over from the Christmas stock, she beckoned him to her side.

'Where are all the people?'

Jake grimaced. 'At BIG I suspect.'

'Jo not being here isn't helping. I've had two complaints about his absence.'

'Maddie had some yesterday too. Have you sold much?' Jake watched as a couple with a small child in their arms stepped inside the herb greenhouse.

'On and off.' Petra pulled a face. 'I'm glad Maddie is too busy to see how quiet it is.'

'Just as well Sabi isn't working today, or we'd have her stressing.'

Petra retrieved her phone from the till's desk. 'Well, at least tomorrow is something I might be able to help with.'

'Another social media hit?'

'Better than that. I'll call Mum. If she knows that Elspeth is going to be here with her posh unguents, she'll be happy to alert the county set.'

Jake wrinkled his nose. 'As long as you warn me if your mum plans to come.'

'So you can hide in the greenhouse?'

'Nah, in the house. You can see through the sides of the greenhouse!'

★

'Now then...' Maddie stood over the children as they knelt on the edge of the plot of ground she'd prepared behind the polytunnel. 'You all have trowels or forks. These are dangerous tools if you aren't careful. You want to dig the soil. You do not want to chop each other's fingers off!'

As the children squealed, half in horror, half in glee at the prospect, Maddie knelt with them, a hand fork at the ready. 'You all have your own little patch of ground. First, we are going to make sure that it is nicely broken up, so the mud is in little pieces. Then, when it's all crumbly, we'll plant some bluebells.'

'All blue things today!' Kayleigh commented as she plunged her trowel into the earth.

'That's right.' Having not considered this, Maddie added. 'And green and yellow next time.'

'Ohh... what are we doing next time?' Noel asked as he pushed his fork into the ground, his bespectacled eyes fixed on what he was doing.

'Spinach and sunflowers,' Maddie said as she placed a gentle palm over Josie's hand, helping her with her trowel. 'And then, some more green, the time after that. When we plant some cress.'

'We've done cress at school,' Noel piped up, looking less impressed than he had been before.

'I'm sure you have. But have you made cress to grow for sandwiches and eaten them in your own garden?'

'No! Wow, can we?'

'You can.' Maddie found herself echoing words she'd

once heard her father say: 'Everything we are going to grow here will have a purpose.'

'Henry!' Jo hadn't noticed the familiar face at the back of the queue. He'd been working nonstop since Hawthorn Park had opened at eleven o'clock.

'Hey, Jo, how's it going?'

'Can't grumble. Tea?'

'Please, and one for Sabi.'

'And a smoothie for Jemima?'

'Not this time. She's helping her aunt with the Little Acorns today.'

Jo's cheeks flushed. 'I hope Maddie's getting on okay.'

'I'm sure she's fine.'

Passing over the teas, Jo mumbled, 'On me.'

'Really?'

'Definitely. Where is Sabi anyway?'

'Visiting Simon Northcott's memorial garden.' Henry paused before adding, 'She knew him once.'

Jo's hand froze in the act of topping up a caddy with mint teabags. 'She did?'

'They were at uni together. She hadn't realised he'd passed away until recently.'

'It was quite a shock.' Jo didn't know what else to say.

'I'm sure it was. He had a daughter I believe.'

'Sara.' Jo wished someone else would join the queue, so he had an excuse to cut their conversation short.

'Sabi wondered if she'd like to come over to The Potting Shed some time, you know, just for a mooch and a cuppa when you're back. It must be a bit isolated here on her own sometimes.'

'Well, I umm... I could ask if you like.'

'Good idea.'

Jo busied himself with polishing up the coffee machine with a cloth. 'Does Sabi know Sara then?'

'No, but she knows what it's like to lose a father at a fairly young age. She feels for her.'

'Of course.'

An elderly couple came into view. 'I'll have to go, Henry. Customers.'

'Of course. Nice to see you, Jo. Thanks for the tea.'

'Why are we planting some bulbs and some plants?' Kayleigh's confidence was gathering at a rate that made Maddie suspect she was quite a handful at school.

Gesturing for all the children to stop what they were doing for a moment, Maddie explained. 'Do you see that wood on the other side of this fence?'

A chorus of 'Yes, Maddie' filled the air.

'The green leaves you can see around the base of the trees, the long ones, they are bluebells.' She picked up a pot yet to be planted. 'Just like this one. But those plants came from a bulb that was planted into the ground.' Holding up a bulb, Maddie felt a buzz of excitement at the children's rapt expressions. 'We are planting a brand-new bluebell garden here, so we need to have some bulbs in the ground that will come through next year, as well as some established plants with leaves, so that we can enjoy some bluebell flowers this year too.'

'While we wait for the new ones to pop up?' Mark whispered.

'Exactly. Well done, Mark.' Maddie waved to Jemima. 'Could you get the wheelbarrow, so we can bring out another twelve bluebell plants?'

'Sure.'

'Can I help?' Noel waved a hand in the air. 'I'd be a good wheelbarrow steerer.'

Maddie had a sudden panic that every child would want a go at pushing the wheelbarrow, and the control she'd won would be lost, but her niece was ahead of her.

'Come on then, Noel, you can help this time. Next time someone else can have a go.'

As Noel took Jemima's hand, the other children went back to digging holes to put the bulbs in.

Ed came up to Maddie's side. 'Yup, that girl is a born primary school teacher.'

With the children stood either side of her, Maddie admired their work. She had donated far more bluebell plants from her sales stock than was cost-effective, but there was no denying that the result was worthwhile. In the next three to four weeks there would be a small carpet of bluebells reaching from the fence to a third of the way into the area Ed had suggested should be a picnic space.

Turning around, Maddie regarded the space behind her. It was ugly by comparison. Full of potholes, it was far too rutted to put up picnic tables, even if they had any. For now, however, it was perfect. Beckoning for the parents, who'd come to see what their offspring had been up to, to step closer, Maddie saw Ed appear from the other side of the polytunnel, a bright yellow hose in his hand.

'What's Ed doing with that?' Kayleigh piped up. 'Is he going to water in the plants?'

'He is. But first he is going to do something else.' Maddie grinned. 'Why don't you go and tell the adults what you've been up to, and very soon you'll find out what.'

As the children ran to their various parents and grandparents, Jemima picked up a pile of towels they'd secretly stowed in the polytunnel and came to her aunt's side.

'Everyone agreed to photos.' She pointed towards the tunnel. 'There's a pile of signed consent forms inside.'

'Brilliant. Thanks, Jem.' Maddie could hear the children jumping with excitement as they saw Ed start to fill the potholes with water. 'Can I ask you to take some pictures of them puddle splashing on my mobile?'

'No problem.' Jem took the phone. 'On one condition.'

'Which is?'

'When they've finished, I can have a splash too.'

22

Maddie handed her sister the day's float. 'After paying Petra, taking out money for the gardening gloves I gave the children, and costing in the bluebells I planted rather than sold, we took no more money yesterday than on a normal Saturday. The only plus I can think of is that we didn't make a loss.'

Sabi sighed. 'The children will come back though. And next time Jo will be here. I bet they'll all hang around for a café stop after the class.'

'Maybe, but that'll be his profit, not ours.'

'I hate to say it, but we ought to be charging Jo rent, or at the very least, asking for ten per cent of his daily profits, as we would if he was here as part of the Exmoor Drifters.'

Maddie shuffled in her seat as she remembered what Hazel had implied – that Jo would not like the idea of paying rent. 'But he brings in trade for us, just by being here.'

'True, but what about when Jo *isn't* here? And what about those customers who only come for a cuppa and then leave again, without even walking around the place? This is our business, not a hobby. And if we want any chance of meeting our financial target and carrying on with—'

Maddie interrupted, her tone resigned. 'I know you're right. Time seems to be slipping away.'

Sabi nodded. 'It's so tempting to say we'll move the goalposts – give ourselves longer to pay back the first loan. But if we do that...'

'I know, we could be tempted to move it again and again, sending us into a debt we'd never repay. It's just...' Maddie paused. 'I wasn't going to say, but Hazel mentioned something about Jo – about not being surprised that he doesn't pay rent here. Said he hadn't lost his touch – whatever that meant.'

A crease puckered Sabi's perfectly made-up face. 'What touch?'

'No idea. She didn't hang around for me to ask questions, and as Jo was packing up early and I needed to find out why...'

Sabi sighed. 'He isn't coming across as Mr Reliable at the moment, is he?'

'But he's such a nice guy. I'm sure Hazel has an axe to grind.'

'Well, until we know what that axe is, I suggest we keep an open mind – while keeping a close eye on things.'

'Suppose so.'

'So, we'll ask Jo about paying rent then?'

'I think we'll have to. Sometimes I hate the lack of humanity that goes with being a business owner.'

'You're hardly asking him to breach the Geneva Convention, Mads.' Sabi twisted the key that launched the till into life. 'You should have seen how many customers he had at Hawthorn Park yesterday. He must have made an absolute mint.'

'Maybe.' Feeling uncomfortable about the sense of suspicion that now hung in the air whenever they mentioned Jo, Maddie changed the subject by pulling out her phone and scrolling through the photographs Jemima had taken for her. 'Do you think Petra would put some of these on our Facebook page between customers today?'

'I'm sure she would.' Sabi picked up a bag of two-pence pieces. 'If it's as quiet as yesterday, then she'll have heaps of time to do all sorts of marketing.'

Maddie, trying hard not imagine all the hundreds of people that had already passed through BIG's front doors, spoke with determination. 'Today will be better.'

Florrie suddenly sat up, telling Maddie that Ivan had arrived a full five seconds before he appeared around the door of the polytunnel, Sheba at his heel.

'Ivan, we're all ready for you.' Maddie gestured to the double trestle table and chair Ed had put together for him. 'Is this side of the tunnel okay, or would you like the tables moved?'

'Here is great, thanks. I've parked the van by the shop for the minute. Are you alright if I bring it a bit nearer?'

'Of course. Get it as close as you can. Any sign of Elspeth yet?'

'She's with me. I picked her up on the way.'

'Fabulous.' Maddie, who had already promised herself a small treat from the old lady's unguent collection, whether she could afford it or not, was looking forward to helping her set up her stall.

Ivan bent to fuss Florrie, who was nudging his knee for attention. 'And how's my impatient firework then?'

'Still nuts.' Maddie stroked her dog affectionately. 'She isn't enjoying being cooped up in the bedroom with me at Sabi's.'

'I bet she isn't.' Ivan held his hand out and Florrie, who'd been circling his legs like a spinning top, immediately sat down.

'How the hell did you do that?'

'No idea. I've always had the knack.' Ivan patted Florrie's side. 'Good girl.'

Maddie tutted as Florrie stared adoringly at Ivan. 'A bit of that sort of adoration for me wouldn't go amiss, young lady!'

Ivan laughed. 'Do you have her lead handy?'

'Sure.' Maddie uncoiled it from her coat pocket.

Hooking the lead on to Florrie's collar, Ivan adjusted his position so that he was stood next to Florrie's head. Sheba, without being asked, stood and moved to his other side. 'Come on then, let's see how well she walks on the lead.'

By the time they'd reached the van, Maddie was pink with embarrassment. Florrie had tugged at the lead or dragged her heels, slowing to investigate every interesting smell, even though they were only travelling a short distance. 'I'm so sorry. I've been a terrible owner. She gets plenty of walks but...'

'But you let her explore at her own pace.' Ivan's tone was reassuring rather than admonishing, which somehow made Maddie feel worse.

'I suppose so.'

'That's no bad thing. She's loved, well fed, and exercised.

It's just the discipline that needs work. You need to show Florrie that you are in charge. Right now, she is under the impression that she is.'

Maddie put her hands on hips as she looked down at her dog. 'Can't deny that.'

'How about I take her for a bit?'

'Well, I…' Maddie felt a tug of loss as she considered not seeing Florrie every day.

'I'm not saying I won't bring her back. Just for a bit, while you're at your sister's. I'll see if I can't install a few manners to temper her go get 'em attitude.'

Kneeling to fuss Florrie, Maddie couldn't deny that it would be a lot easier at Sabi's place without her puppy. 'Are you sure, Ivan?'

'Completely. Although…' he paused, regarding Maddie more seriously '…I'll need to train you a bit too. Show you how to act like you mean it when you tell Florrie not to do something.'

'Sounds terrifying.'

The purple satin that Elspeth used to adorn her market stall was in place, covered by the striking glass and pewter pots containing her *Bee Lucky* handmade beauty products.

Customers had been coming into the polytunnel in a steady stream since the doors to The Potting Shed had opened at ten o'clock. Ivan had sold over half his cheeses, and he was glad of the lull that half past one brought with it.

Maddie's head popped around the door, two mugs of coffee in the hand. 'Only instant I'm afraid.'

'Anything is welcome.' Elspeth pushed her long grey plait over her shoulder. 'My flask emptied long since.'

'I can fill that up for you if you like.'

'Don't you worry. You'll be too busy for that sort of thing.'

Maddie hoped the sinking sensation she'd been experiencing over the past hour, as she'd watched customers arrive, walk around the nursery, and then leave empty-handed, or carrying one of Elspeth's tissue-wrapped parcels or one of Ivan's brown paper bags, but nothing from her, didn't show. 'Oh, it's fine, I've got time.'

Elspeth set her sharp grey eyes on her friend. 'What's wrong?'

'Nothing. It's good. You're selling well, aren't you?'

'We are, but something tells me you're not.'

Maddie shrugged. 'We knew it would be a difficult weekend.'

Ivan and Elspeth exchanged a glance, before Ivan said, 'The novelty will wear off, you know – with BIG I mean. You offer different things here.'

'That's what Ed keeps saying.'

'And he's right.'

'Maybe.' Maddie crossed her arms protectively over her chest. 'I've had some lovely emails from the parents of some of the children who came yesterday.'

'There you go then. Future customers in the making.' Ivan gestured to his stall. 'This is a new beginning, lass. Things like this take time.'

'I know.' Maddie waved as she headed to the polytunnels opening. 'I'll leave you to it.'

Less than a minute later she wished she'd stayed to talk to her friends. If she had, she wouldn't have heard the middle-aged couple coming out of the vegetable polytunnel saying, 'This place has nothing. Come on, let's go and check out Big in Gardens.'

A wave of hopelessness washed over Maddie. *What am I doing? Am I allowing my house to be destroyed from the inside out, just so I have more space to disappoint people in?*

Her mood wasn't improved by the unexpected sight of Hazel Cooper strolling across the car park. Maddie wasn't sure it was her at first, as she was dressed in jeans and a peacock blue jumper – cashmere on closer examination. Her pursed, slightly disapproving expression, however, made her unmistakable.

Not in the mood for Hazel, Maddie hooked her house keys from her pocket and dashed towards her home. Suddenly she wanted to hide.

Picking up a jar of chutney, Hazel gave it a sniff.

'You'll not smell anything through the glass.' Ivan regarded his latest visitor steadily. 'Would you like to try a sample?'

'Thank you, but no.'

'Fair enough.'

'I should introduce myself.' She thrust a hand towards Ivan, who, after a moment's hesitation took it in his. 'I'm Hazel Cooper. I'm overseeing the conversion of the house for Mr Willand-Harris.'

'Are you now.' Ivan sensed Elspeth watching the exchange as she served a teenager with a cream that she promised would clear acne in days. 'How's that going?'

'Client information is confidential. I'm sure Miss Willand will tell you if you ask her.'

'Right.' Ivan exchanged a sideways glance with Elspeth, who, transaction complete, was staring at their latest browser with open suspicion.

'I *had* hoped to get a coffee today, but I see Mr Dunn hasn't bothered to come to work again. I wonder why.'

'Ah, well, you see, lass – that's confidential information. I'm sure if you asked Miss Willand, she'd tell you.'

'That's if he bothered to give her an explanation.' Hazel screwed up her nose as if she'd smelt something unpleasant. 'It wouldn't be out of character for him to let her down.'

Glad there were no customers in the tunnel, Ivan bit back the reply he'd like to give, saying instead, 'I've known Jo for some time, and I can tell you that such behaviour would be very much *out* of character. Now then...' Ivan drew himself up to his full height, causing Sheba to stand with him '...was there anything we could help you with sales wise?'

Waiting until the sound of Hazel's heeled shoes leaving at speed had faded way, Elspeth muttered, 'What on earth was Henry thinking employing her?'

'I imagine she had excellent references.'

'I bet she did.' Elspeth pursed her lips as tightly as Hazel had. 'Probably because her former employers wanted shot of her quickly.'

'Elspeth!' Ivan was surprised. 'I've never heard you be negative about someone like that before.'

'Well! *Mr* Dunn! Why use Jo's name like that? That young lady is trouble. And what's more, she is up to something.'

'You think so?'

'She wasn't here shopping; she was on a fishing expedition.'

23

'Here you are.'
Ed found Maddie sat on the only chair in the room that had once been a bedroom, but was now an empty space, but for a pile of unpacked kitchen units and a heap of tools. 'I've been searching all over the place. Why aren't you answering your phone?'

'Oh, sorry.' Maddie glance at her mobile and saw three missed calls and several texts. 'I had the sound off.'

'It's almost four o'clock. Ivan and Elspeth have started to pack up and Sabi has sent Petra and Jake home.'

'Sensible.' Maddie stared into space. 'No need for them to waste any more of their weekend when there's hardly anything for them to do.'

Hunkering down next to her, Ed took her palm, noting how cool it was to the touch. 'How long have you been sat here like this?'

'I'm not sure.' Maddie hadn't noticed how cold she was until Ed's body heat began to seep through her system. 'I was thinking.'

'Productive thinking?'

'Honestly, no.'

Making himself more comfortable, Ed sat on the floor next to her. 'Sabi reckons, from a brief till tot up, that today was an okay Sunday. Not spectacular sales wise, but The Potting Shed had a lot of people through the doors, even though not everyone bought something. Means you're getting on the map some more.'

'Because Ivan and Elspeth were here.'

'They helped, certainly.' Hearing the closed-off tone to his girlfriend's voice, Ed wasn't sure what else to say on the subject, so he asked, 'Is your sister alright? She's been very quiet.'

'Probably thinking she should have stuck to her guns and made me sell this place when we had the chance.' Maddie got off the chair and sat on the floor next to Ed. 'I'm glad Jem and Henry didn't come in. They'd have been bored stiff.'

'Look, Maddie…'

'No. I know what you're going to say, Ed, and I appreciate it, but I feared this weekend would be a washout, sales wise, and it has been. I hoped the few things we could offer would make a difference, but they didn't.'

'But Ivan and—'

'Yes, and I'm genuinely pleased for them, but as those customers rightly said, there's nothing here.'

'What do you mean? What customers?' Ed swivelled around so he could see her properly.

'I heard some customers complaining how there was *nothing* here and that they were off to BIG.'

'Ah. I see.' Ed opened his arms. 'You need a hug.'

Maddie stayed where she was. 'How's that going to help?'

'They always help.' Ed slipped his arms around his girlfriend; her breath tickled his neck.

Maddie mumbled through an unexpected rush of silent tears, 'You're right – hugs do help. I'm tired, that's all.'

'It's okay. It's hard to sleep when Florrie is prowling the room at all hours. I'm a bit bushed myself for the same reason.' Squeezing her tight, Ed let Maddie sob quietly into his shoulder, before easing her away so he could see her face. 'So, let's get positive, the Little Acorns group was a success, the bringing in of Ivan and Elspeth worked in that they brought their own regular customers into the nursery. Okay, they may not have spent much money, but they came.'

'But will they come back?' Maddie waved an arm around the empty room. 'It's going to be *ages* before this place is fully functioning as a shop downstairs.'

'Not that long surely? Henry said a month for that side of things.'

'I know, but Hazel has got them starting upstairs and not down, so...'

'What is it with that woman?' Ed scowled. 'Ivan was saying she introduced herself to him and Elspeth. Had a dig at Jo.'

'I saw her arrive, that's why I came in here.' Maddie wiped the back of her hand over her eyes. 'I decided to hide until she was gone. I must have lost track of time. Why is she so down on Jo? She had me wondering if we could trust him again the other day.'

'I honestly have no idea. He's such a placid chap, I can't imagine him upsetting anyone.'

'Nor me.' Maddie frowned. 'To the best of my knowledge he hasn't encountered Hazel while he's been here, so he can't have upset her. She arrived just as he was leaving for his emergency dash to Hawthorn Park.'

'When she arrived – or just *after* she arrived?' Ed raked a hand through his hair.

'You don't think he saw her and scarpered, do you?' Maddie sat up a little straighter.

'Well… Nah.' Ed dismissed the idea. 'Jo'd face out any trouble.'

Maddie shook her head. 'We're imagining things. It was a coincidence when he left. He wouldn't lie about an emergency.'

'You're right, he wouldn't,' Ed agreed, but despite himself, there was a level of uncertainty in his voice. 'Hazel must have an issue with him, but goodness knows what. All I can think is that it stems from their council days.'

Maddie fiddled with the end of her ponytail. 'I don't like how Hazel talks about him, as if he were dodgy in some way. The last thing we need is for her to claim he's untrustworthy in front of customers.'

'Perhaps I should ask him, although he hates talking about his past.'

A frisson of unease that Maddie didn't like crept over her. 'Maybe that's because…'

As his girlfriend's sentence petered out, Ed asked, 'Because what?'

'Because there *is* something he doesn't want us to know. Something that, if we knew, would mean we wouldn't let him work here?'

Ed paused before giving a sharp shake of his head. 'No. I can't believe that.'

Pushing her doubts away, Maddie said, 'I take it Hazel has gone?'

'Must have. I've not seen her.' Ed's forehead creased in concern. 'Why would she visit if she didn't come in here to check on the builders' progress? She did not strike me as a garden centre sort of person.'

'Nor me.'

Ed stared around the empty room. 'I was sure, when we originally went through the plans, that Henry said they'd start downstairs, so we – you – could open sooner rather than later.'

'He did, but Hazel said we needed to have a useable kitchen and bathroom upstairs first.'

'I suppose that's true, but you could have used the downstairs ones for a while at least. You wouldn't have minded going up and down to the kitchen and washroom, would you? It's not like the old kitchen is being converted to a café yet. How long is it supposed to be before Robert, Kevin and Ahmed are sorted upstairs?'

'A couple more weeks.'

'Would you mind if I checked that with Henry? I know it's your home not mine, but that seems a long time. Unless you're expecting perfection before you ship back in?'

'Hell no. I just want my bed, a kettle and toaster.'

'Then, I'll see if things can't be hurried along a bit.'

'Thanks, Ed, and don't think that this is just my home. It's yours too – at least I hope it might be one day.'

'You mean it?'

A hopeful smile crossed Maddie's previously sad face. 'I really mean it.'

Cupping her head in his hands, Ed pulled Maddie in for a long kiss. 'One day can't come soon enough.'

Maddie rested her head on Ed's shoulder. 'I'm sorry I abandoned you. Have you been okay today?'

'Very much so. Jake's been talking me through the veg, showing me what needs doing to them next and when.'

'Really?'

'As he's going away soon, he said you'd need someone else to know what's what, so it wasn't all on you.'

'Oh God.' Maddie ran her hand over her face. 'Jake's going away.'

'You knew he wouldn't stay forever.'

'Yes, but...' Maddie broke off mid-sentence and jumped to her feet. 'This is no good at all, is it. I'm moping around in here, full of self-pity, when there's heaps to do whether we have customers or not! Especially as it's a Bank Holiday Monday tomorrow, so we're open rather than closed.'

'That's the spirit!' Ed kissed her cheek. 'Forward, it's the only direction ever worth going in.'

Maddie laughed. 'You sounded just like Ivan then.'

'Exactly like Ivan actually. I just quoted him. He's in the polytunnel with Elspeth. They'd like to see you.'

24

Sabi was busy helping Elspeth put her few unsold jars into sturdy plastic boxes when Maddie and Ed arrived. 'Mads, where've you been?'

'In the house. Ed and I were wondering about asking Henry if we could change the build schedule a little, you know, get the essentials only sorted upstairs and then crack on with downstairs?'

Realising that she could have her home back if the flat was simply made habitable rather than fully finished before her sister moved back in, Sabi picked up her phone. 'You want me to call Henry, now?'

'It's okay, I'll talk to him at your place later. Apparently, Ivan wants to talk to us.'

'No need to sound so suspicious.' Appearing through the polytunnel door, Ivan put an empty cardboard box, ready to be filled with unsold chutney, onto the table. 'We've been having a ponder about your business and how to help it, that's all.'

Glancing at Sabi's puzzled face, Maddie took hold of Ed's hand, unsure whether to be pleased, wary or offended that her friends had been planning things for her business without her.

Ivan sat back at his now empty table. 'Stop looking so worried, you three. Sit with us a minute.'

As they got settled, Florrie rested her head on Maddie's lap, her big brown eyes boring into her, as if apologising for being away.

'I've missed you too. I hope you have been behaving for Ivan.'

Florrie cocked her head to one side, sending her velvety soft ear flopping over Maddie's hand.

'I'll take that as a yes, shall I?'

'She's been as good as gold.' Ivan patted Sheba's head. 'This one's been keeping a beady eye on her.'

Keen to get home, Sabi said, 'I'm sorry to seem impatient, but you said something about an idea.'

'Yes, we...' Ivan stopped talking as Dan arrived in the tunnel.

Tugging off his cloth cap, Dan brushed a hand through his thinning grey hair. 'Hi all, just popping by to see how it's gone.'

Maddie got up as her former boss made a beeline for an empty chair next to Elspeth. 'Great timing, Dan – I wondered if you had time to talk to Jake and Petra?'

Sabi sighed. 'We weren't busy enough for them to stay. I sent them home early. I hadn't realised you were coming or that you wanted to see them, Dan.'

'Don't worry, they can reach me on my phone. Just drop them my number, Maddie.'

Thinking that Jake was unlikely to be brave enough to call, as he hated calling anyone he didn't know well, Maddie said, 'Thanks, Dan, I'll do that.'

'So?' Sabi zipped her jacket up to her chin as the sun slipped into shadow behind the polytunnel, dipping the temperature considerably. 'You've had an idea, Ivan?'

'First things first.' Ivan picked up a large white envelope and passed it to Maddie.

'Here's mine.' Elspeth followed suit. 'We did well today. Not as good as if we'd been with the other Drifters, I grant you, but not far off.'

Maddie gasped as she opened the envelopes. 'You can't give me this. You earnt it.'

Sabi's eyebrows rose as she saw the bundle of ten-pound notes in her sister's hands.

'We did earn it, but only because you allowed us to sell here today. This is your ten per cent.'

Maddie slid the money back into the envelope. 'Thank you both. I can't say I like taking your money, but I won't pretend it won't come in useful.'

'Does it help, I mean, with the fact you didn't have as many sales as you hoped today?' Elspeth, paused before phrasing her next sentence. 'What I am trying to delicately ask is, would you say we helped sales overall today? Were there many people who came to see us but bought from you too?'

Inclining her head, Sabi placed her notebook on the table before them. 'Some. Not as many as I'd hoped, but some certainly did.'

'And some came simply because you were here,' Ed added. 'I recognised faces from when you were here with the market at Christmas.'

'Right. Good.' Ivan glanced at Elspeth, who gave him a reassuring smile. 'Would we also be right in thinking that, just now, things here are a bit stretched? The conversion is happening, but manpower is low, and you're in that tricky period between expanding and not having quite enough space or staff to do so properly?'

The sisters nodded in unison, neither sure where this conversation was going.

'In that case we have a proposition for you.'

'One we want you to think about properly.' Elspeth reached her hands across the trestle table and gripped both Maddie and Sabi's wrists with a strength that belied her age. 'We mean it. No acting on impulse. No saying yes because you're nice people. Go away tonight and discuss things.'

'Saying yes to what? Discuss what?' Sabi's patience was ebbing away as her need for a bath and a hot meal increased.

Ivan rested his palms flat on the table before him. 'How would you like to rent out part of your space to us? On a permanent basis. A small area from which I could sell my cheese and Elspeth her products, although, in practice, I'd do most of the selling for her. You'd be an offsite trader, wouldn't you, lass?'

'I would.' Elspeth kept up her eye contact with the girls. 'But *only* if you agreed and *only* if you think it's a good idea to have some non-gardening products available here on a daily basis.'

'Well, I certainly like the idea.' Maddie said. 'But the question of where…'

'We wondered about the current shop – once the new one opens. What's going to go in there?'

*

The aroma of beef stew from the slow cooker was incredible. Jo's stomach growled in appreciative anticipation.

'Could you grab some plates?' Sara waved a ladle in his direction. 'They're in the larder.'

'Sure.' After hunting down the plates, Jo collected some cutlery and laid the kitchen table for two for the third night running. 'Dinner smells incredible. I hadn't realised that you were such an amazing cook.'

'It's just one-pot stuff.' She spooned some stew onto the plates. 'After I lost Dad, I taught myself several recipes. Kept my brain occupied.'

'Good idea.' Picking up the bottle of red wine Sara had placed on the table, Jo poured them each a glass.

'It's rather nice to have someone to cook for.' The moment the words had come from Sara's lips she regretted them. 'I didn't mean that. Well, I did mean that… I didn't mean…'

Seeing the blush growing across her face, Jo put her out of her misery. 'It's okay, I knew what you meant. No need to watch your words – I didn't think you were trying to trap me with food.'

'Of course. I'm being silly… I…'

'No, Sara. You're not silly. I've enjoyed eating with you this weekend.' Jo laid down the fork he'd just picked up. 'We need to get past this. Didn't we agree the other night that we were okay as friends?'

'We did.'

The heat of Jo's meal wafted against his face as he gently asked, 'And are we? Okay as we are – just friends. Close friends.'

Stirring her fork through her meal, Sara muttered, 'We are. I just... it isn't always easy. It's not your fault, Jo, but I lost so much and, well, it all happened at once.'

Jo laid down his cutlery and gave her a hug. 'It was a bad time – neither of us was thinking straight.'

'And now?' Sara eased herself away from Jo's embrace and grabbed a tissue from her pocket.

'Now, we give ourselves a stern talking-to and decide never to hurt each other ever again. We eat this delicious dinner and brace ourselves for the final day of the Easter weekend.'

'What do you think, Sabi?'

'I think we should bite their hands off.'

'Me too,' Maddie agreed, 'and if we're going to charge Ivan and Elspeth rent, it'll be much easier for us to ask Jo to do the same.'

'And we could have other products in time.' Sabi picked up her tea mug as they sat at her kitchen table. 'A few good quality artisan products from local crafts folk.'

'Good idea. In the old shop, or in the new build?' Maddie blew across the top of her coffee cup. 'It feels strange thinking of Dad's old potting shed being used to sell non-gardening stuff.'

'I know what you mean, but it would be a good temporary space, until we know exactly what the flat conversion will be like in practice.' Sabi scribbled a few notes on her pad. 'Ivan would need a fridge.'

'He should be near the new kitchen instead then.'

'I agree. The small cold storage unit he uses for the

market would work in the current shop on a temporary basis though. He'd need to be near a few power sockets, so we didn't have cables running everywhere and causing safety issues. And even if they were in there, we could still use the till for everything and...'

Maddie's eyes widened in surprise. 'Move them in straight away you mean? Now, before the build is complete?'

'Yes.' Sabi tapped a pen against her notepad. 'Their rent will help us pay wages for a new assistant. And, well... we agreed to give this our best shot, didn't we?'

'We did. And if Jake gets his apprenticeship far away, I'll be lost with no one horticultural on side.'

Sabi smiled. 'I was feeling quite down about everything earlier, but now we have a way forward, even if it means we'll have to talk to Henry about adjusting the plans – which means a run-in with Miss Ice Cube.'

'Miss Ice Cube?'

Sabi looked sheepish. 'I heard Jemima call Hazel that when she was chatting to Florrie.'

'Good name for her. Perfect even.'

25

Sara blinked in the morning light. 'Did you just ask me if I'd like to come and meet your friends at The Potting Shed?'

'I did.' Not sure if he was doing the right thing, Jo heard the echo of Henry's voice telling him that Sabi had known Simon. 'Although, you don't have to.'

'I think I'd like to.' Sara picked up a handful of sugar sachets and distributed them between the flowerpots Jo used as napkin and sugar holders. 'But I'm a bit out of practice with people. They might hate me.'

'You were fabulous with everyone here yesterday.'

'That's strangers. Potential friend people – I don't know, I get a bit tongue-tied and awkward.'

'You and me both!' Jo's grin became a massive yawn. 'As much as I'm glad we talked properly last night, I'm shattered!'

'Me too.' Sara sucked in her bottom lip. 'Such a relief to know you have forgiven me for...'

Jo put a finger over her lips. 'I was never cross in the first place.' He almost didn't ask his next question, but knew it needed to be said. One last reassurance for them both before they could truly move on. 'And you're one hundred per cent sure you're okay with how things are? If I thought for one second you couldn't move on with your life because of me…'

'Jo.' Sara laid a hand on his arm. 'I promise everything I said last night was true. I need a friend. I do not need anything more. Relationship complications are very much *not* on my agenda. In fact, the more I think about it the more a life with the love of friends appeals far more than one with a partner.'

'And if you meet someone who changed your mind about that and swept you off your feet, you promise to tell me if I'm in the way?'

'I've done a lot of thinking of the past year, and, as I said, I'm honestly not sure I'm a girlfriend-type person, but if that unlikely event happens, I promise I will tell you.'

Jo gave her a quick hug. 'Thank you.'

'What for?'

'For not abandoning me.'

'As if I would! Now then…' Sara brushed some tree leaves off the nearest table '…let's make this the best Bank Holiday Monday ever.'

'Morning, Maddie. I'm here to speak to Jake,' Dan announced as he strode into the shop. 'Is he about yet?'

'Over by the veg tunnel. Petra's there too.'

'As I was saying to Elspeth yesterday, it's time that boy considered his future. He has a woman now and they'll be wanting to support each other and that means proper wages, so if I can help, I will.'

Maddie's eyes widened. 'You think Jake and Petra are at that stage already? They're so young.'

'They aren't. They're two young people in their twenties, starting life's biggest adventure.'

Maddie bit her bottom lip as she remembered the living-together conversation she'd had with Ed. Now she thought back, she realised they'd left things a bit wishy-washy. *I will ask him properly later.*

'Are you with me, Maddie?'

'Sorry, Dan.' Pulling herself back to the moment, Maddie said, 'Feel free to head over to the tunnel.'

'I'll find them in a minute.' The old man flexed his legs and pulled out a stool from beneath the till's desk. 'So, my girl, Ivan and Elspeth were considering selling their products here. Is that going to happen?'

'Absolutely.'

'Excellent.' Dan rubbed his hands. 'That means I can tell you about plan B.'

'Plan B?'

'I went to see Dennis after I left here.'

Maddie was stunned. 'The farmer who owns the field behind us?'

'The very same.'

'But… why? I mean, how did you know I was thinking about talking to him?'

'Ed mentioned it to Ivan, Ivan mentioned it to Elspeth…'

Maddie couldn't help but laugh. 'And Elspeth told you?'

'You got it.'

Wondering where their conversation was going, Maddie tilted her head to one side. 'Do you know Dennis then?'

'We go way back.' Dan smiled. 'One of the advantages of old age is that you have lots of people to draw from in your past.'

'I suppose so.' A cold shiver crept over Maddie as she looked at Dan. It was easy to forget he was well into his seventies. He was the sort of person you couldn't imagine not being there.

Maddie's eyes flicked to the doorway as the sound of approaching feet alerted her to a potential customer.

As an elderly lady came in carrying a pot of chives, Dan made his leave. 'I'll hunt down the young 'uns and come back to talk about plan B later.'

Henry called through to the lounge from where he was pulling his shoes on in the hall. 'Sabi love, are you ready?'

'Coming.' Slamming the photo album back where she'd found it, nestled in a box not yet unpacked from their house move, Sabi's pulse raced. There hadn't been many photos from the time she had dated Simon. Mobiles were just for making phone calls back then, so cameras had to be remembered every time you went out. She wasn't sure what had made her remember the few shots they'd taken of each other, but as soon as she'd woken, she'd been determined to hunt down the evidence of her past.

'What are you doing? Jemima's in the car already. Maddie's expecting us.'

'No rush is there? I can't imagine it'll be busy.' Sabi slammed the cupboard door shut and straightened her back.

'Ed wants to double-check the build plans with me. And I want to see how the conversion is going without Hazel there.'

'I'm coming.' Sabi dashed along the hall and tugged on her walking boots.

'Will Florrie be at The Potting Shed, Mum?'

'I've no idea.' Sabi stared out of the window ahead.

Wishing his wife would snap out of her dismal mood, Henry glimpsed his daughter in the rear-view mirror as he drove into the nursery's car park. 'I doubt it, love.'

'I miss her. I know she was too much in our house, but I sort of got used to having her to cuddle. Do you think she misses me too?'

'For goodness' sake, she's just a dog.'

'Sabi!' Henry glared at his wife as the car came to a halt. 'I'm sure Florrie misses you, Jemima.'

'Thanks, Dad,' Jemima mumbled as she got out of the car and pulled on her wellington boots. 'I'll go and find Aunt Maddie.'

Watching their child shoot off towards the handful of customers wandering from tunnel to tunnel, Henry rounded on his wife. 'What is wrong with you this morning? You and Maddie were happy last night, anticipating talking things through with Ivan and Elspeth before opening.'

'It's nothing.'

'Clearly that isn't true.'

'Okay, it is something,' Sabi admitted, 'but can we talk about it later? As you said, we're late.'

*

Having made sure that Ivan was happy for Jemima to tag along as he took Sheba and Florrie for a walk before the impromptu staff meeting, Henry followed Ed into the house. To all external appearances it was as if nothing had been done, until they opened the old kitchen door.

'O… kay.' Henry nodded. 'So they've gutted the place. Not what I imagined they'd do first.'

'You assumed they'd set the new kitchen up before destroying the old one?'

'Yes, so Maddie could move back sooner.' Henry turned towards the door. 'Let's go and see what the new one is like.'

Ed headed up the stairs behind Henry. 'I was in there yesterday. It's a pile of boxes waiting to happen.'

Pushing the door open, Henry sucked a breath through his teeth as he tapped his phone. 'Leave this to me…'

Maddie pulled out a seat between Ed and Sabi, as Dan, accompanied by his collie, Midge, tottered into the far polytunnel. 'Well, we have an hour – I hope – before it gets too busy to leave Petra and Jake in charge of everything, so can we get to the bottom of this plan B, please?'

'My pleasure.' Dan tucked Midge under his seat and addressed his friends. 'In short, a couple of weeks ago Elspeth approached me about keeping bees for her at Killerton. We used to have a hive or two that we shared years back. Anyway, she needs the wax, and I can benefit from having extra bees around for pollination and so on.

Thing is though, the National Trust now has its own hives and sells its wax on. They aren't keen on me setting up additional private hives. So, I wondered about having some here.'

'You want us to have hives at The Potting Shed?' Maddie's instant excitement at the idea was instantly suppressed by visions of health and safety forms.

'That was my first thought, but then Elspeth and I had a brainstorm. As I said, last night I dropped in on old Dennis. The short version is, that he is willing give me unofficial use of the field that backs onto your land in exchange for a tithe of honey and help mowing the field once a year.'

'What do you mean?' Sabi, who'd been stood to one side of the group, her mind miles away for the most part, stepped forward. '*Unofficial* use?'

'The government pays him *not* to use the land for crops or livestock, so we couldn't breach that.'

'Bees don't count as livestock?'

'There's a loophole.'

'Handy.' Ed laughed. 'That's great, Dan, but I can't see how this affects The Potting Shed, beyond the fact we can watch the beehives from here.'

'I told Dennis about the new garden here, and the possibility of picnic tables and so on. He loved the idea. For all his gruff ways, the idea of children planting a garden really caught his imagination.' Seeing Sabi's impatient expression, Dan cut back to the point. 'Basically, if you want to split the fence at the back of the field, so the path into the small wood on his land is accessible, then you can. All you have to do is let him know when you've done it, make sure it's kept litter-free, and padlock a gate across the opening out of hours. Oh, and pay for the gate to be put up of course – that's the downside of it.'

'Wow!' Maddie gave her old boss a hug. 'Seriously? A bluebell wood walk?'

'Yep.'

'But,' Sabi glanced at her sister, 'why would he? I mean, why would Dennis agree to us having access just like that? He must want something in return.'

Dan shook his head, 'He had a lot of time for your father. Dennis is happy to help. Not everyone wants something in return for kindness.'

'Well, no.' Sabi's cheeks went pink as she mumbled, 'I don't suppose they do.'

Resting a hand on her sister's palm, ashamed that she'd hadn't dropped in on her neighbour over the past couple of years, Maddie said, 'We must go and thank him.'

Dan smiled. 'He'd like that – but I'd leave it for a month. He's off into hospital for a hip op tomorrow, followed by a spell in a convalescence home. Agency workers will be seeing to the farm for a while.'

'Poor Dennis.' Maddie turned to Ed. 'We must remember to visit him once's he's home.'

'Definitely.'

'I can't thank you enough for this, Dan.' The fear of failing The Potting Shed that had been circling Maddie's head, vulture-like, all weekend, lifted a little as Sabi opened her tablet to search the Internet for gate suppliers and fitters.

Only seconds later the women's relief dissolved as two customers' voices floated through from outside the tunnel.

'I've got tickets for Davina!'

BLUEBELL SEASON AT THE POTTING SHED

'Davina Ditz? Really?'

'Yeah. She's at BIG in May. She's my absolute favourite gardening celeb.'

'Me too, she's…'

As the customers words were whipped away by the wind, Maddie groaned. 'Every time I think we might be clawing back some ground, BIG do something to trump us.'

'You knew they had celebs coming.' Ed spoke softly.

'I know, but Davina Ditz – she was Dad's favourite.'

'Never mind.' Dan patted her shoulder. 'The bluebell wood will last forever; Davina is only for a day.'

'I know. I didn't mean to sound ungrateful. Thanks, Dan.'

'No problem. Now then, I want another talk with Jake.'

Maddie, Sabi and Ed had only just started discussing gate prices, when Dan appeared back through the door, his walking stick tapping against the floor. 'So then, you like a spot of hard work don't you, Maddie?'

'I'm not sure I like it; I'm not afraid of it though. None of us are.'

'That's good, because Ditzy will be here on the 1st of May.'

'What?!' Sabi and Maddie spoke as one.

'Yup. She's going to come here before she does BIG. Doesn't like them apparently. Too corporate for her, but her agent did a deal there's no backing out of.'

'Coming *here*?' Maddie stared at her sister in confusion. 'Just like that?'

Echoing her sister's disbelief, Sabi frowned, 'Dan, I don't mean to sound ungrateful – especially after you've already sorted access to Dennis's woods for us – but how can you have arranged for Davina to come here, and so fast?'

'If I thought you were ungrateful, even for a minute, Sabi, then I wouldn't have bothered.' Dan winked.

Maddie regarded her former boss as if he where some kind of magician. 'But how did you...?'

'Don't you worry about that now.' He rubbed his hands together. 'So, you've got a month to get this place ready to roll. Plenty of time to think of a name for the event and get some tickets sold. I'll tell Davina to come, then, shall I?'

26

It was so rare for her husband to lose his temper that Sabi was instantly concerned when she heard him shouting at someone down the telephone. Climbing the stairs of Maddie's home, she found Henry pacing around the living room.

'I know it is a bank holiday, Miss Cooper, but if you don't get yourself to The Potting Shed this morning, you can kiss goodbye to your new job.'

Sabi held her breath as she listened from the doorway.

'You may well protest, Miss Cooper, but I would like to remind you that you are still within your six-month probationary period, and when it comes to The Potting Shed you have been falling somewhat short of expectation.'

Hanging up with a grunt, Henry sat heavy onto the sofa. Only then did he register that his wife was there. 'Why is that woman so touchy about this place?'

'I have no idea.' Sabi joined her husband on the sofa and took his hand in hers.

'She's gone out of her way to be obstructive, and yet, at the same time, she's never here. I thought she'd come by every day to check on progress.'

'She told me she trusted my choice of builders and was giving them time to get on, but you make a good point.'

'This has to be all about Jo, or her distrust of him.'

'I can't think of another reason. Although I dread asking him about her, it's got to be done.'

Sabi pulled a face. 'I think Ed should do it; after all they are good friends. You should ask Hazel about Jo though – in a direct, we-need-answers way. After all, she brought the subject up first, so it's less like intruding. And whatever it is that's rattling her is affecting her work, so you'd be within your rights.'

'I'll see how it goes when she arrives. If she is in a contrite and helpful mood, I might leave that side of things until we are back in the office. Not for her sake, but because I hate to talk about Jo behind his back. For now, I want Hazel to talk me through her proposed order of events here.' He shook his head. 'Perhaps I shouldn't have trusted her with such a big job so soon?'

'She has experience at this though.'

'She does.' Henry tutted. 'And there I was hoping for a nice bank holiday pottering around with my family at the nursery. I'd planned to nip out and get everyone fish and chips for lunch.'

'Ohh... now you're talking.'

'I even snuck a plate for you into the car, as I know you aren't keen on eating out of paper.'

A flush of shame hit Sabi's cheeks. 'I make life so hard for you, don't I?'

'It's just a plate, love. It's more that you make life hard for yourself.' Henry smiled. 'Now, before Hazel Cooper arrives, tell me what you were up to this morning, and why it made you feel guilty.'

'How did you know it made me feel guilty?'

'Because you snapped at Jemima. You always get snappy when you feel guilty.'

'I do, don't I.' Sabi massaged her forehead. 'Something else to add to my huge list of character flaws.'

'Okay, that's enough.' Henry stood back up. 'Ever since you found out that your ex has passed away, you've been down on yourself. Stop already! It is not your fault that his daughter is on her own.'

Beckoning for her husband to sit down, Sabi whispered, 'I found some photographs of Simon. I don't know what to do with them.'

As Maddie headed back into the shop, she could hear Petra in full conversational flow.

'Here we are then, Mrs Johnson.'

'Thanks, Petra. I'm so glad you're back. I've missed your smile.'

'We all have.' Maddie chipped in as Petra boxed up the begonia plugs their customer had purchased.

The old lady's good humour was contagious. 'Not that you don't have a nice smile on you, Maddie love – so did your dad for that matter, God rest his soul. But this lass has radiance.'

'She does at that.'

Petra chuckled. 'Daft pair.'

'Will you be okay carrying this?' Maddie gestured to the box.

'Still muscles in these old arms. Best use them before I lose them.'

'They'll be a stunning deep pink when the flowers come.' Maddie gestured to the plants. 'Lovely to see you, Mrs Johnson. I hope all five of your grandchildren are thriving.'

'Growing faster than I can blink.' Beaming with pride, the old lady added, 'That cress seed I got from you at Christmas went down a treat with them. They had a competition to see whose grew first. Total chaos. Loved it!'

Jake stared at his hands. He knew he should be jumping around with excitement – inside he was – but... *Maddie's been so good to me.*

'Thought I'd find you in here.' Petra stuck her head in the polytunnel devoted to root vegetables. 'Break time.' She waved three tea flasks in front of her. 'Has Dan gone? I've made a drink up for him too.'

'Just missed him, but I could drink two lots of tea if pushed.' Jake blew her a kiss as he unscrewed the lid of his flask.

'Oh, the sacrifices you make for me!' Petra pulled a bag of loose biscuits from her pocket. 'Maddie's just told me that Davina Ditz is coming here during the first May bank holiday.'

'You're kidding!' Jake took a chocolate digestive and snapped it in half so he could dunk it in his tea.

'Nope. Dan has been waving his magic wand. He's also sorted out a deal with a local farmer about the wood behind the nursery, but I'm not quite sure what. Maddie was in

too-much-to-do-to-chat mode, so I didn't like to press her.'
Checking that no customers were about to come into the
tunnel, Petra pulled two stools from beneath Jake's potting
bench and beckoned for him to sit with her. 'How did it go
with Dan?'

'He has spoken to a few of his colleagues on my behalf
about an apprenticeship.' Unease made Jake shudder. 'Do
you think I can do what you do, Petra? I mean – is there a
lot of extra written work?'

'You *can* do it. No question. And yes, there is more
writing, but you are improving all the time, and I'll help.
This is so exciting.' She paused, 'When do you start at
Killerton?'

'I'm not. I said Dan had spoken to his colleagues.'

'So, you're not getting an apprenticeship with him?'

'No. Shame really, as he's always been so kind to me, but
he's mostly retired anyway.' Jake draped an arm around his
girlfriend's shoulders. 'Do you know Arlington Court?'

'Oh my God! That's only twenty-five miles or so from
me at Rosemoor. You'd be so close! Seriously?'

Jake tilted his head to one side. 'You'd be okay with me
being nearby?'

Throwing her arms around her boyfriend, slopping tea
from the flask she was holding in the process, Petra kissed
him hard on the lips. 'You bet I'm okay with it. And wow, a
National Trust apprenticeship – that's so cool!'

'I hope Maddie's okay with it too.' Some of Jake's
excitement dipped as he sat back down.

'Are you kidding? She'll be over the moon for you.'

'I know she will, but what about this place? Dan said,

if I took the apprenticeship, they'd want me straight away. On Monday. That's a week today! It's so quick because I'm converting to the course, rather than starting again. How can I desert Maddie now, after all she's done for me?'

Maddie passed three petunia sets to her latest customer. 'These are the Grand Rapid variety – they'll be purple and white once they flower. They'll look fantastic in your hanging baskets with some trailing lobelia – which we'll have in by next week – if you decide you'd like some. And don't forget, any problems with them, let me know and I'll do my best to advise.'

Hanging baskets. We need some premade ones to sell – and some to decorate the place for when Davina is here.

'Can I help you with that, sir?' Coming out from behind the till, Maddie took the small sack of Jake's home-grown potatoes from her next customer.

Would it be better to pave or turf the rest of the new garden to hide the potholes?

'Pumpkin seeds? Yes of course,' Maddie responded to a customer's question by gesturing to a rack at the far side of the small shop. 'If you get them in by the end of the week, you should be just in time for a Halloween lantern if you wanted one.'

If Ivan sets up in here temporarily, where will I put the seed rack?

Maddie's mind buzzed with endless questions and ideas as she served a burst of bank holiday shoppers. Just as the final customer for the moment left, Sabi arrived.

'I've found a gate. Ed's at the back of the nursery measuring the fence to see what sort of size we'll need.'

'Thank you!' Glad to be able to cross a job off her list, Maddie added, 'I've had customers. Not hundreds, but a nice steady flow for the past hour.'

'Despite no coffee van.' Sabi shared her sister's relief.

'And the fact we have limited stock as yet, compared to a fully functioning garden centre, that is. Although I am ordering in anything people ask for.' Maddie gestured to an open order book, with hastily written requests and phone numbers jotted across its pages. Suddenly uncertain she asked, 'Do you think that's okay – I mean, every order costs us money – and although most customers will collect what they've ordered – some might not and…'

Sabi waved a reassuring hand. 'It's good. Catering for what people ask for is hardly being reckless with our money, is it. Anyway, if we are known to be able to provide a specific customer's needs, they'll tell others and come back themselves.'

Maddie gave herself a shake. 'Sorry – I think this money deadline thing is making me paranoid. Of course you're right. I've had four requests for lobelia, so I think we might as well get in a decent stock. I used to grow it direct, but this year a few things have had to go by the wayside.'

'Let's get it on the home-grown list for next year though.' Sabi consulted her wristwatch. 'It's gone quiet out there, but then it's coming up to lunchtime. Talking of which, Henry has offered to nip out for chips. You in?'

'Hell yes!' Maddie smiled. 'He's a good man.'

'Henry likes being here, just like Ed does. A nice change from being stuck in an office all week.'

Maddie paused in the act of picking up an ordering catalogue. 'Jake thinks Ed would rather be here than at work.'

'I wouldn't be at all surprised. You know he loves being outside.'

'True.'

'On the other hand, he won't want to give up having a solicitor's salary coming in, so I wouldn't have any romantic ideas about asking Ed to give up his career to haul compost around on a permanent basis.'

'As if.' A little of Maddie's elation died as the thought her sister had planted in her head was snuffed out before she'd had the chance to contemplate it.

'What time is Ed off anyway?'

'Off?'

'Won't he need to go home tonight, ready for work in the morning?' Sabi saw a cloud pass over her sister's face as she hurriedly added, 'Not that I mind him staying at ours. He's no trouble and very helpful around the house.'

Maddie grimaced. 'I'd forgotten he had to go tonight. Time seems to be passing so fast.'

'Always does when you're busy – and we are about to get much, *much* busier.' Sabi rubbed her hands together. 'I can't believe Dan has got Davina Ditz to come here!'

'I've had a few ideas about what we should get done before she arrives – assuming she really does come. I'd feel better if we had set times in writing.'

'Me too, actually.' Sabi made a note on her tablet. 'I'll get onto Dan about contact details. But actually, I meant right now – extra busy today.'

'In what way?'

'As of now, until the 1st of May, The Potting Shed is against the clock! We need the cheese and beauty product spaces to be operational ASAP, which means changing everything around in here. We'll need a temporary shop set up in a tunnel if the work in your house isn't done in time, and the bluebell garden has to be perfected. Not to mention the everyday jobs.'

Maddie gulped. 'You keep saying *we*. Does this mean you are off part-time duty for now then?'

'Oh, um...' Sabi coloured slightly. 'Well, I have a few things I *have* to do this week – and I am out all day tomorrow – but after that I'll do my best to be here more often.'

'Or what you're really saying, is that I'll be doing that lot all on my own.' Maddie blew out a sigh. 'Thank goodness I'll have Jake here on Monday then!'

27

Henry glanced at his watch as he saw Hazel's car pull into the nursery's car park. 'One minute to twelve.'

Sabi pursued her lips. 'Technically still this morning I suppose.'

'Technically.'

'Do you want me to come with you, or would this be better off remaining a work thing from your side, rather than my side?'

Appreciating his wife's offer of assistance, Henry spoke quietly so a passing customer couldn't hear. 'I'd better keep this within my company right now. Switch the ringer of your phone on though, and stick with Maddie, so I can consult you both if I need to.'

Seeing Hazel approaching, Sabi muttered out of the corner of her mouth, 'She wears that business suit like armour. I wonder...'

'What?' Henry flashed his wife an urgent enquiry.

'I wonder if Miss Cooper is anything like as tough on the inside as she appears on the outside.'

The air in the dismantled kitchen felt oppressive. Henry

could see particles of dust dancing in the sunlight that streamed through the window.

'Miss Willand tells me that your reasoning for insisting the builders start in here was so that the overall completion of the project would be faster. Something you told her was common with jobs where planning permission was granted, but work was carried out in small doses. Piecemeal, if you like.'

'I did, yes.'

'Do you recall, when I gave you this project to oversee, that I stressed the need for Miss Willand to be out of her home for the minimum amount of time possible?'

'Of course, and this will be sorted soon. Miss Willand will be able to move back in and...'

'After I phoned you, I called Robert Andrews. He told me he didn't like fitting a kitchen that his client hadn't personally approved.' Henry headed to the door. 'Come with me please.'

Clamping her lips together, Hazel followed Henry up the stairs to the room destined to be Maddie's new kitchen.

'I wonder what it was that made you decide that Miss Willand would not want to be consulted about the units she was going to have to live with and use for years?' Henry gestured to the packs of cupboards ready to be set up.

'I was simply trying...'

'To cause as little disruption as possible?' Henry crossed his arms. 'You keep saying that, and yet everything you have done on this particular project has had the opposite effect. I'd like an explanation. A proper one. Because it occurs to me that you hoped Maddie would hate the units you'd picked for her and cause further delays while she chose new ones.'

'No, it isn't that – really, it's…'

'It's what, Miss Cooper?'

'The sooner the work is done the sooner Miss Willand can reopen – I was trying to speed things up.'

'By picking an order of build work that is illogical and slows progress down – the opposite of what you've just claimed?'

Hazel let out a sigh. 'I just thought that, overall, it would work out quicker that way. Slower at first perhaps, but swifter in the end, and… and I'd have to spend less time on site.'

'Because?'

'Because I don't want to be anywhere near Jo Dunn.'

'And can I ask why?'

'It's personal.'

'Nevertheless, it is impacting on your work, so I need to know.'

Hazel's voice trembled for a split second, before she pushed her shoulders back, visibly reining in her emotions. 'Okay, but you won't like it.'

Leaving Petra to take care of the till, Maddie and Sabi stood at the back of the little shop. In their father's time it had held nothing but a potting bench and piles of flowerpots, a small selection of tools and, tucked beneath the bench, sacks of compost and topsoil. Now, it contained a seed packet rack, wicker baskets full of Jake's home-grown veg, bags of bulbs left over from winter, a variety of houseplants, and three trugs laden with trowels, handheld forks and gardening gloves.

'If we move the till's bench to the right of the shop, rather than just inside the door, we'll have more room.' Sabi sketched a rough plan of the space that surrounded them. 'Then Ivan could have his table next to it, in the middle of the right wall. Elspeth's stuff could go on a dresser or bookshelf on the back wall.'

'Acting as an attractive display to entice people walk to the back of the shop, rather than just poking their heads in, or going as far as the till and no further?'

'Precisely.' Sabi drew in the theoretical table and shelving onto her plan.

'I don't suppose you happen to have a nice dresser or shelving unit you don't need, Sabs?' Maddie did a mental inventory of the furniture in her flat. 'I don't have anything I can spare that would work, and it would be nice not to have to buy anything.'

'Mum's stuff!' Sabi's concentrated expression broke into a wide smile. 'Why didn't I think of it before? The oak dresser. It'll be perfect.'

'But it goes so well in your home. And it was part of your inheritance.'

Sabi flushed, as if embarrassed. 'Umm, actually I had considered selling it.'

'What? But you always loved it.'

'I know, and it looked great in the old kitchen, but...'

'It's too pale a wood for your new place?'

'Yes.' Sabi's face coloured. 'You must think me a terrible

snob. It's just I want the house to be perfect. I dreamt of owning it for so long and now I do… I was going to sell the dresser and put the money into this place.'

Watching her sister as she spoke faster and faster, sounding unusually defensive, Maddie reached out a comforting hand. 'It's okay, I get it. And that's really kind of you to think of selling it for the sake of The Potting Shed, but you don't have to, and you certainly don't need to justify to me what you do with your own possessions.'

Sabi stared at her plan. 'You don't think I'm selfish for not wanting it?'

'No, although we could use it in here.' Maddie glanced at her sister. 'Are you okay, Sabs?'

'Absolutely. Bit distracted. Sorry.' Drawing a row of three circles next to the door, she wrote *veg baskets* across them, before adding another three circles for the tools and gloves on the floor, next to the wall, filling the gap between where Ivan and Elspeth's wares could be displayed.

Maddie patted the seed rack. 'What about this?'

'Ah.' Sabi stared at the plan. 'It'll have to go against the left wall at the back.'

'I'm not sure.' Maddie guided her sister back to the door and pointed to the left corner. 'Even with the light that comes through the glass walls, from here the rack would be almost invisible until a customer was right in front of it.'

'I see what you mean.' Sabi paced the edge of the shop. 'Perhaps we should put the bench with houseplants at the very back, and then the seed rack in front of that?'

'Better idea.' Maddie paused. 'Do you think it'll be a bit cramped in here though? We'll need room for customers.'

Sabi tapped her pencil against her pad. 'We could take out the veg.'

'I'd rather not. You'd be surprised how many people pick up a bag of spuds or carrots when they go up to pay for whatever else they're buying.'

'In that case…' Sabi put a line through the labels on her plan, swapping the position of the tools for the veg, moving it back nearer the till.

Maddie moved, so she was facing the open doorway, looking out towards the new greenhouse. 'I could put the houseplants in with the herbs for a while.'

'Would they stay warm enough overnight?'

'Should do. Most houseplants thrive in a conservatory so, if I'm careful with the temperature, it should be okay for the short term. Again, it'll be a little cramped, but at least it'll look better with loads of plants pushed together in the greenhouse than being overcrowded in here.'

Sabi strode into the middle of the shop and slowly circled, taking in every angle. 'I know I mentioned having to use a tunnel as a temporary shop, but would we have to? Couldn't we move Ivan and Elspeth in here overnight, and adjust things around them?'

'It'd be a long night, but yes, I suppose we could. Or, if you think we can hold off until next Monday, we could do it in the day. Jake'll be with me then, so I'd have him to help with lifting things. That would also give Ivan and Elspeth a week's notice. I doubt they expected to be roped into service so fast.'

'That's probably sensible,' Sabi conceded. 'I was getting carried away with wanting to get everything perfect before Ditzy came.'

'I'll not argue with that, Sabi.' Maddie brushed her hands together. 'Which reminds me, how about hanging baskets?'

'To sell or decorate the place?'

'Both.'

'Do it.' Sabi stood aside to let a customer reach the seed rack. 'But keep some back for the 1st of May and let me help with the ones you intend to use for decoration – I've had a colour scheme idea.'

Unable to suppress a chuckle at her sister's earnestness, Maddie agreed. 'No problem. All the colour schemes within The Potting Shed are all yours.'

'Really?' Sabi blushed for the second time. 'I wasn't meaning to be bossy or anything, I...'

'Sabi, are you sure you're okay? It's not like you to come across as insecure. I've noticed you question yourself a few times lately.'

'I'm fine. Honestly.' Sabi glanced up at the ceiling. 'At least this place being largely glass, means it won't take much time when we paint it.'

'Paint it?! We don't need to do that, do we?'

'We do.' Sabi was firm. 'I can't remember the last time the walls were given a fresh coat. If Davina Ditz really is coming, then let's make sure we give BIG a run for their money. You know how much Dad liked her. He'd probably have rolled out a red carpet.'

'Gardening royalty.'

'Exactly.'

★

Henry tapped his mobile phone. 'You know I can check what you're just told me, don't you?'

Hazel dabbed a tissue to her eyes as she sat on a dusty chair in the corner of the soon-to-be kitchen. 'You can ask at the council offices, but all they'll say is that the information is confidential.'

Knowing she was right, Henry held his assistant's gaze. Not entirely sure if her tears were genuine or not, he softened his tone nonetheless as he asked, 'I'd like you tell me why, the moment you saw there was a clash between your private and professional life here, you didn't speak to me straight away?'

'Because Jo is your friend.' Hazel stared at her long thin fingers, rubbing a non-existent blemish off her pink polished nails.

'Even so, his presence has disturbed you.' Henry leant forward. 'You could have simply spoken to Jo. Asked him to keep his distance from you.'

'I do not wish to speak to him.' Hazel shook her head. 'I *did* tell you he wasn't to be trusted.'

'You considered that claim enough?'

'I assumed you'd question him at the very least.' Hazel sat up straighter as she held her boss's gaze with tear-blotched eyes.

Henry paused before speaking again. 'First thing tomorrow morning you will call Robert Andrews and get an estimated date on the completion of this kitchen. They have come too far to backtrack. After the kitchen is done, they will proceed with the knocking through of downstairs into a sales space. Your actions have delayed this project by at least a week. As such, you will no longer be connected with it. I have no right to ban you from coming to The Potting Shed as this is not my business, but I would strongly advise you to keep your distance. As this arrangement will keep Jo away from you as well, I can't imagine you'll have any objections.'

Standing, Hazel brushed down her skirt. 'And my job?'

'I will talk to Graham.'

'And Mr Dunn, will you talk to him?'

28

Jo couldn't remember having laughed so much for so long. Midnight had come and gone, and yet he was still sat on the sofa next to Sara, half-watching old episodes of *Friends*, and half-chatting about anything and everything. Her latest throwaway comment, that he was the perfect cross between Monica and Chandler should not have been funny, but a combination of fatigue, contentment and relief at their renewed friendship had made everything amusing. Now, with his arm draped around her shoulders, warm from the effects of good food and a glass of whisky, Jo had a desperate urge to watch the skies.

'Come on, let's go and see if we can see any stars.'

'But, Jo, it's one o'clock in the morning.'

'No better time.'

'Won't it be cloudy?' Sara jumped to her feet.

'Possibly.' Buoyed up by their alcohol-fuelled relaxed state, Jo headed towards the back door anyway. 'You never came to Dark Skies with your father.'

'I was too lazy to miss out on my sleep.'

'You have no idea what you've been missing. It is the ultimate peace and quiet, although I admit, your father never managed to settle to it.'

'That's probably because Dad was the most restless person I ever knew. Always overthinking, always planning the next thing rather than enjoying the here and now.'

Seeing the happy expression disappear from Sara's face, Jo cursed himself for mentioning her father, and held out his hand. 'Come on, little friend. I'll show you how to relax in the great outdoors.'

'Less of the little!' Sara poked his ribs.

'Woman, you're tiny.'

'Five foot is not tiny; it is perfectly formed. You know what they say about small packages.'

'Well, small package, put your coat and hat on. It may be spring, but it'll be parky out there.'

The biggest clearing between the trees was in Simon's memorial garden. Sara had claimed she was alright with that, and she had been – until, after half an hour of lying on an old travel rug she kept in the boot cupboard, the slightly cloudy sky had suddenly cleared and Jo had taken her hand, guiding it upwards, using it to point out what they could see. That was when she'd burst into tears. That was when she confessed to Jo that it was the first time she'd cried in a year.

'I loved him so much. He was always there. Never let me down. And now...' she sniffed hard into a hanky Jo had passed her '...everything is just so... so... quiet.'

Letting Sara bury her head in his shoulder as they lay on the hard ground, Jo clasped her shaking frame. Staring up at the gliding clouds, which allowed occasional glimpses of the stars in the night sky, Jo knew he should say something, but every word that came to mind felt like a pointless platitude. Only when Sara stopped shaking did he feel able to speak.

'Can I ask an impertinent question?'

'Uh-huh.' Sara sniffed hard as she buried herself closer to his side.

'Why don't you employ a cook or a housekeeper?'

Surprised by the query, Sara pushed herself up onto one elbow. 'I don't need one.'

'You're a great cook, and I was not knocking your housework, but if you had someone else in the house...'

'A paid companion?' Sara's expression echoed her tone of disapproval.

'More, a person moving around the house – doing something useful – so that the sheerness of the silence is taken away.'

'Oh, I see.'

'My home is a fraction of the size of yours.' Jo paused. 'Actually, it's a fraction of the size of your living room, but even so, sometimes the silence when I get home after work is almost deafening.'

'Maybe *you* should get a housekeeper, then.'

Jo's laugh came out as a half-hearted grunt. 'They'd run out of house to keep in twenty seconds, and besides, my budget and yours are rather different.'

'Fair enough.'

'Or you could have lodgers or open as an Airbnb.'

Sara sat up abruptly. 'Airbnb?'

'Sure. Why not? You're only open to the public for

a few weekends a year. Aren't you bored the rest of the time? I know you had plans to go to university, which you abandoned when your father became ill, but what do you want to do now – for *you* I mean?'

'I don't know.' Sara drew her knees up to her chest and stared out across her domain. 'This land takes work all year round, and lots of it.'

'It does, but is that what you want to do yourself, or do you want to employ someone to do it for you?'

Sara hugged her knees. 'In all honesty I have absolutely no idea what I want.'

Not having Florrie spinning around in her basket or flopping her weight across the end of the bed on and off all night was proving as distracting as having her there.

Maddie threw back the duvet. It was only four o'clock in the morning, but she knew sleep wasn't going to happen. When she hadn't been missing her dog, she'd been wondering how on earth she'd get everything at The Potting Shed done on her own. Jake's announcement that he was leaving, just after closing yesterday, had meant she'd be without him after the following Sunday, and although she was delighted for him, she wasn't so thrilled for herself.

Pulling on her dressing gown, Maddie wandered towards the bathroom Sabi had declared was all hers while she was in residence.

There was no denying that life was easier in Culmstock without Florrie. The atmosphere was less tense and Sabi's tongue-biting was notably absent. Nonetheless, Maddie wasn't sure she could live with her sister for much longer.

'I should never have turned down Ed's offer to move in with him.' As she stepped into the state-of-the-art power shower she wondered if Ed's absence was another reason she hadn't slept. The idea made her stand still beneath the stream of water, an unlathered squeeze of shower gel in her palms. 'I more or less asked him to live with me last Sunday.'

The four nights he'd stayed with her in Sabi's home had been the longest stretch of consecutive nights they'd spent together since they'd got together the previous December. And although they'd be relatively chaste, thanks to Florrie's presence and the knowledge that Jemima slept in the adjoining bedroom, Maddie realised she'd quickly got used to waking up with him. Liked him being there. *Loved* him being there. And now it was Tuesday morning, and Ed was in his own bed in his own home, so he could go back to work. She'd be without him again until the weekend.

'I'm a fool.' Maddie clicked off the shower. 'I should have gone to live with him in the first place, and now, even if I asked him if I could change my mind and come and stay, I'm so busy that I can't spare even ten minutes' driving time every day, let alone half an hour.'

Resolving to talk to Ed about moving in with him on a temporary basis after the 1st of May, if her flat wasn't ready by then, Maddie pulled on her clothes and rushed downstairs as quietly as she could. Then, leaving a note for Sabi, telling her she wanted to get an early start at work, Maddie grabbed a couple of slices of bread and butter, filled her water bottle, and stepped into the dawn light.

*

The pleasantly cool soil coated her hands as Maddie lifted it by the palmful and dropped it into the first of three hanging baskets set out on the potting bench.

'I know I could use a scoop or a trowel, Dad, but I needed to run the earth between my fingers this morning.'

Arriving at the nursery in the early hours, Maddie had felt as if she was intruding. A blanket of quiet hung over The Potting Shed alongside the early morning mist. Avoiding looking at her home, Maddie pulled on an old coat of her father's, which she kept in the middle polytunnel, before examining a variety of bedding plants.

'Sabi wants to do a set colour scheme for some of the baskets, Dad, but I'm going to start with some multicoloured ones. They always sold well when you used to make them to order.'

Scooping some earth from the centre of the first basket, Maddie tipped up a fuchsia, taped the base of its pot to loosen the soil, and gently placed it in the centre of the basket.

'What do you think, Dad? The trailing lobelia arrived late yesterday, so how about adding that and some impatiens?'

Humming to herself, Maddie let the magic of her work soothe away the voices at the back of her head, all of which were shouting out the jobs she needed to do.

Finish the bluebell garden.
Put up a gate to the woods.
Tend the plants.
Look after the customers.
Watch the builders.

Replace Jake.
Advertise…

The only voice she allowed herself to listen to was her father's.

Make sure you confirm Davina's visit, lass. I'd love her to come here.

'You okay?'

'Nervous.' Sabi glanced up at her husband. 'It is the right thing to do, isn't it?'

'You have pictures of her father she'll never have seen. If the situation was the other way around, you'd want them, wouldn't you?'

'I would,' Sabi admitted, but she still couldn't stop wondering if she was about to interfere where she wasn't wanted. 'But you ought to be going to work, and Jemima needs to finish her homework before going back to school tomorrow.'

'I'm not abandoning you to do this alone. Anyway, Jemima is looking forward to a long walk with Florrie before term starts. I've called Ivan; he is expecting us to pick her up on the way.'

'But what about Hazel Cooper? If you're not at work this morning, she might use it as an excuse not to call the builders.'

'Then she will be sacked.' Henry held up a hand. 'And before you say you ought to be helping Maddie, if you don't get this sorted, then you'll be too distracted to be much use anyway.'

Knowing she'd run out of excuses to back out of going to Hawthorn Park, Sabi grabbed her handbag. 'Sara might not be there. The house isn't open to the public again until next month. If the gates are closed, then it could be a wasted trip.'

'Let's try anyway.'

29

Waving to Robert, Kevin and Ahmed as their van pulled into the drive, Maddie carried the third and final hanging basket towards the shop. Unwieldy, its heavy weight pulled at her fingers as she sat it outside the shop alongside those she'd already hauled into place.

'Okay, so it took almost four hours to do fifteen baskets, but they are beautiful. And you've swept all the paths, cleaned the washroom and opened the greenhouse. Today, *anything* you do beyond manning the till is a bonus, so don't even think about giving yourself a hard time, Madeline Willand!'

Unlocking the shop, Maddie continued her pep talk. 'Yes, there is a lot to do, but it can be done. And if you can run the place alone today, then you can do anything.'

Checking the time, seeing there was still an hour before opening at ten, Maddie clicked on the kettle they'd hidden under the till and made up all three flasks. 'Sabi and Jake won't be needing theirs, so I might as well get myself prepared for the long haul.'

Having made two flasks of coffee and one of tea, Maddie then addressed the seed rack. 'Let's see if you need topping up, shall we?'

*

Ten minutes later, having added in a handful of random seed packet types to the display, she stood back to examine the eclectic collection of houseplants, and tried to picture the shop without them. 'Dad always had a few houseplants in here. Not many, but some.' Maddie picked up an azalea that was just showing glimpses of a pastel pink bloom and included it in her conversation. 'Do you remember the row of cacti that sat in the window for years before Petra came along and sold them within minutes of her arrival?'

Wondering if she was going slightly mad by asking a plant about events it wasn't there to see, Maddie focused on picturing Ivan's cheese stall in situ. 'I have no trouble imagining Ivan selling well within The Potting Shed, but in here... I can't see it somehow, not long term.'

'I agree.'

Maddie spun round, her heart beating fast as the unexpected voice broke through the hush, only to breathe out in a tremor of relief when she saw her old boss stood in the doorway.

'Dan! You scared me to death.'

'Sorry, lass.' Dan leant in the shop's doorway, Midge at his feet. 'I knew you'd be up and doing.'

'Lots to do.' Maddie smiled. 'Actually, I was going to call you later. Davina Ditz. Is she *really* going to come? I mean, if she has a gig up the road, will she want to come here too?'

'I told you, she is going to BIG out of duty; she *wants* to come here.'

'But why? You didn't say before.' Maddie peered around her, suddenly seeing the place as it must look to a stranger: clean and tidy, but in need of a lick of paint and a good dose of TLC.

'She's a friend.'

'She is?'

'Yup.'

Maddie fixed Dan with an enquiring stare. 'Okay, but she's your friend, not mine, so why help me out like this?'

'Okay.' Dan held up his hands in defeat. 'I never could fob you off with a half-truth. Ditzy owes me a favour. I knew she was coming this way, so I called it in.'

'Dan!' Maddie was already shaking her head. 'No way. I don't want her here because she feels duty-bound.'

'Hang on, Maddie. That is not the case at all. She's been on at me for years to let her pay me back.'

'For what?'

Resting a hand on top of Midge's head, Dan said, 'I trained her. I always knew she was special – she had an instinctive touch for horticulture, not unlike your Jake. Unlike Jake however, Ditzy has confidence and a bubbliness about her that breeds enthusiasm.'

'That's true.' Maddie remembered her dad saying something similar about the celebrity gardener. 'She won a competition that ended up wither being employed by the BBC, didn't she?'

'She did, and I was the one who spotted the ad for the competition and got her to apply. It was to design, and then grow, a small garden plot without spending more than £20. A tough assignment even back then.'

Maddie thought of the Little Acorns garden. It had cost

double that in bluebell plants alone. 'How did that lead to her becoming a presenter?'

'There was an advert for a new presenter a short while later. A minor role on the BBC, mostly for the radio. Anyway, after seeing her interact with the judges during the competition – many of whom were famous at the time – and seeing how relaxed and unfazed she was around them, I press-ganged her into applying.'

'Press-ganged?'

'I took her to the studio where they were holding the auditions. Told her we were going to visit the *Gardeners' World* garden on a work outing. I didn't let on why we were really there until it was too late to back out.'

'You never did!'

'I did. Applied in her name and everything.'

'Oh my God, Dan! How did you manage that?'

'No idea. I'd never get away with such messing now the world is all technological, but forty years ago things were different.'

'Percy Thrower's time?'

'The god of gardening himself. Indeed.' Dan inclined his head. 'He was an old man by then of course. I only had the pleasure once, but what a gentleman.'

Maddie sank herself onto the nearest stool. 'Not for the first time, Dan, you have left me speechless.'

Passing her a slip of paper with a phone number on it, Dan chuckled. 'Well, I'd get your voice back quickly. Ditzy is expecting you to call her to discuss what you'd like her to do.'

'Do?'

'Her standing by the seeds and saying "buy these" isn't going to be a crowd puller – well, not a big one.'

Maddie sucked on her bottom lip. 'You sure she's okay with me having her number?'

'Promise.'

Suddenly remembering her conversation with Jemima over her father's gardening magazines, Maddie said, 'How about we do a question time?'

'Sounds perfect. Ask her.'

'Right, I will.' Maddie stared at the piece of paper. 'I'll do it now, before I bottle out.'

'Good girl. And then call the papers.'

A cold sweat formed on Maddie's forehead. 'Whatever for?'

'Ditzy is news. No point in her coming to bring in people if no one knows about her visit.'

'I haven't even asked her yet.' Maddie gave her former boss a shrewd look. 'You haven't arranged anything yet… have you?'

Dan grinned. 'As if I would?'

'*Dan?*' Maddie's eyes narrowed. 'If any papers are to be called, it ought to be me or Sabi who calls them.' Speaking more softly, she quickly added, 'Please don't think I'm ungrateful. You've done so much for us, especially lately, but I'd hate you to think we couldn't run our own business or…'

Dan shook his head, 'I would never think that. If I gave that impression…'

'You didn't. Not really.' Maddie sighed, 'I'm sorry. This is all a bit overwhelming. One minute we have no bluebell wood or draw to compete with BIG. Now we have wood access and the queen of gardening coming! I don't think I'll ever be able to repay your kindness, Dan.'

'I don't want anything other than to enjoy coming along to see Ditzy.'

'Thanks Dan.'

'I do think you should call the papers though. Think how proud your dad would be to see an article about The Potting Shed in the paper.'

'But it wouldn't be about The Potting Shed. We aren't newsworthy. It would just be an ad for Davina coming here and...'

'Not newsworthy?' Dan slipped a lead onto Midge's collar, so he could walk her into the shop to be nearer his friend. 'Look around you. Your father died, you kept going, you battled through the pandemic, you stopped a major competitor from taking over your business, and now you have the most popular female gardener in the UK coming to visit. That is *news*.'

The moment Dan had gone, Maddie punched Ditzy's number into her phone. Her heart thudded in her chest as she heard the line ring.

Dad, I'm calling Davina Ditz! This is madness. Why would she want to...

'Hello. Davina here.'

'Oh hi, I'm sorry to bother you. My friend Dan said...'

'Dan!' Davina laughed down the line. 'Then you must be Maddie.'

'Yes.' Gathering herself, Maddie tried not to think about the fact she was talking to her dad's heroine. 'He mentioned you might like to do an event at my garden centre.'

'The Potting Shed, yes?

'Yes.'

'I'd love to – what did you have in mind?'

'Well, ummm… How about a gardeners' question thing – ask an expert evening?' Maddie hurriedly added, 'Assuming evenings are okay for you?' We can easily do…'

'Evenings are fine. Relax, Maddie.'

'Sorry, I'm not used to calling famous people.'

'I'm not sure I count.' Davina's familiar laugh echoed in Maddie's ear. 'By the way, there'll be no fee.'

Maddie couldn't believe it. 'But surely…'

'*No* fee. This is something I want to do. Dan has told me how hard you've been working, and I'd love to help. The likes of BIG can pay me – but you're a real garden centre.'

'I don't know what to say.'

'How about giving me your home address, email address and talking dates?'

Now the early morning mists had burnt away, a blanket of baby blue sky warmed Hawthorn Park. Stood by the back door, pleasantly full of porridge and strong coffee, Jo's gaze fell upon his bright orange camper van.

I ought to go home. I ought to have gone yesterday. So why didn't I?

As if in answer to his thoughts, Sara appeared, locking the door behind her.

Because I've been happy here. With her. Last night was fun. But as soon as I've helped Sara prune the flowers in her father's memorial garden, I'm leaving. I must go home today.

The sound of a car engine in the distance drew Jo from his musings.

'There's always someone who thinks we're open all the time after they've been once.' Sara sighed. 'I should have gone and locked the main gate last night, but I was knackered.'

Jo raised an arm towards his van. 'I could have nipped down to close it.'

'Don't worry.' Sara strode towards the sound, which was growing louder all the time. 'I hate sending people away, but I've done it for Dad before. Everyone is usually okay about it.'

Not so confident that everyone was always nice, Jo fell into step with Sara. 'I'll come with you anyway.'

'If we're quick enough, we should reach them just as they get to the bit of the drive that's wide enough for a three-point turn.'

'Sensible.' Jo found himself walking a little faster as they headed towards the approaching vehicle. Two strides later he stopped dead. 'That's not visitors – that's Henry.'

30

The car pulled over to the side of the driveway. As Jo saw Jemima waving to him from the back, Florrie at her side, he muttered, 'I can send them away.'

Sara, feeling invaded and robbed of her private time with Jo, directed a polite smile at their unexpected visitors, while mumbling, 'Why are they here? To see you?'

'They didn't know I was still here.'

'Oh.'

Jo laid a hand on Sara's arm. 'I mean it, I can send them away.'

'You said I should meet your Potting Shed friends.'

'I did, but I imagined you'd go to see them, not the other way around.' Letting go of Sara, Jo tried to ignore the sense of foreboding that hit him when he saw the sombre expression on Henry's face and the anxiety in Sabi's eyes.

'This is a surprise.' Jo bent down as Sabi's electric window smoothly wound open. 'Is everything okay at the nursery?'

'The Potting Shed is fine.' Sabi's eyes flicked nervously towards Sara. 'We were on the way to Exmouth to walk Florrie, when we saw the gates were open.'

Henry opened his door and stood up. 'Don't worry, we know you're closed. Sara, isn't it?'

'Yes.' Sara took a step closer to Jo. 'You must be Henry and Sabi. Jo has told me all about The Potting Shed.'

'Have you?' Henry sounded surprised. 'I must say, Jo, I didn't expect to find you here.'

Sara suddenly felt defensive on Jo's behalf as she said, 'Jo stayed over. He's a friend.'

'Sorry.' Henry nodded. 'I didn't mean to sound intrusive. It's good to see you, Jo. Perhaps it's as well you are here. I was going to call you later. Do have time for a chat?'

'Sure.' Jo's throat went dry. 'About the coffee van?'

'It's connected.'

Hooking her arm through Jo's, glad of his presence, and increasingly confused, Sara switched her gaze from Henry to Sabi. 'Jo said you were looking for me the other day, but you didn't find me. Can I ask why?'

Sabi climbed out of the car and took her husband's hand. 'It's about your father. I used to know him.'

Florrie bolted ahead of Jemima, stopping every so often to sniff out a particularly enticing aroma between the trees, before haring off again through the woods. Several paces behind them, Henry and Jo strolled. An awkward silence hung between them.

After a few more minutes of an uncommunicative Henry's company, Jo forced himself to ask, 'Did you really want to talk to me, or did you want to make sure that Sara and Sabi were able to speak alone?'

'Both.' Henry kept his eyes on the figure of his daughter in the near distance. 'I'm sorry it seems so cloak-and-dagger. Not our intention. I told you that Sabi knew Simon.'

'You did. Sara is still in a tough place bereavement wise. I didn't tell her about the connection – I wasn't sure it was my place.'

'That was very considerate.'

'Why are you here, Henry? You I mean, not just Sabi?'

'Supporting my wife.'

'And?' Jo stopped moving, his booted feet planted firmly against the well-trodden path.

'Okay.' Henry pulled his gaze from where Jemima was throwing a ball for the puppy. 'The girls need to ask you to pay rent for your pitch when you come back. They feel rather awkward about it, seeing as your being there is so essential to bring trade in, in the first place, but money is tight.'

'No problem. It's a great spot for me. Just get Maddie or Sabi to drop me an email about the rate they want.' Jo frowned as he saw the brief, but undeniable flash of surprise that had crossed his friend's face. 'Maddie didn't think I'd refuse to pay, did she?'

'Of course not!'

'You said that rather fast.' Jo felt his shoulder muscles tighten. 'Is there something I should know?'

Henry took a deep breath. 'Hazel Cooper.'

An unwanted image of his former work colleague came into his head. It was edged in red. Whenever he pictured Hazel, she was angry. And that anger was focused on him.

Eyeing Jo carefully, Henry coaxed, 'She made it quite clear that she finds you untrustworthy. I don't want to believe that.'

'I don't want you to believe it either.' Jo wasn't sure if he felt relieved or afraid. 'And she indicated that if I was asked to pay my way, I'd make excuses not to?'

'Not in so many words, but...'

'And you believed her?'

Henry shook his head hard. 'Of course not.'

'I've been expecting this. From the moment I saw her march regally across the car park at The Potting Shed... I had hoped she hadn't seen me. I hoped she was there for any other reason than to plant seeds of poison...'

As Jo's words faded into silence, aware of how sound could carry in the open air, and wanting to keep their conversation from Jemima, Henry spoke softly, 'A bright orange camper van selling coffee... it's going to give you away.'

'She has made her distrust of me crystal clear, then?'

'In glorious technicolour.'

'But not the rainbow strips of Pride.' Jo muttered.

'Pardon?'

'It doesn't matter.' Jo watched Florrie dive into the trees and emerge with a tennis ball between her jaws. 'I shall miss The Potting Shed.'

The finality in Jo's voice took Henry by surprise. 'Why? Where are you going?'

'You're here to ask me not to come back – aren't you? The rent – is it really needed? If it is, of course I'll pay. But... was asking me to pay it just a test? A way to see if Hazel was right about me?'

'What? No.' Wrong-footed, Henry found himself floundering. 'The Potting Shed needs all the income it can get right now. And more to the point, I need to know why my employee would bad-mouth my wife's colleague. Was I wrong to assume that Hazel is running a personal vendetta?'

Jo rested his back against the nearest tree. 'You weren't wrong. She does have a problem with me, and yes, it is personal. But mud sticks – I've been here before.'

The hush of the still air closed in on Henry as he stood with his friend. Jo's expression had become introverted, his body language tight. Unsure what to say, wanting to ask a whole host of questions, but already knowing answers would not be forthcoming, Henry was glad of his daughter's antics ahead of them. For now, it was balm to see her running around as if she was six again, rather than on the verge of her teenage years.

Jo's whisper was barely audible. Henry wished he hadn't heard.

'Please thank Maddie for me. And Sabi of course. Despite what you all may think of me, I truly loved working with them. I hope Jem will understand. I'm very fond of her.'

Henry was speechless as he watched Jo disappear between the trees.

'Dad loved grasses of all colours, but mostly the dark reds and almost black shades.' Sara trailed a hand through a tightly planted section of grass leaves.

'The colours complement each other perfectly.' Sabi nodded approvingly, glad that the focus of the memorial garden gave them a talking point. 'My sister would be able to tell you their names, but all I can say is that whoever designed this garden has an excellent eye for style, for what goes with what.'

'Really?'

'Absolutely.' Sabi pointed to a collection of wildflowers at the foot of a willow tree. 'Even the wild growth has been tailored. You must have an excellent team of gardeners.'

'Actually, it was me. I did this.'

'You did?' Sabi was aware of her mouth dropping open. She closed it quickly. 'All on your own?'

'I have gardeners who help in the woods and with the formal garden, but this one is mine. I umm...' She faltered for a moment. Now she'd allowed her grief to show with Jo, it was harder to keep it contained. 'I wanted to do this alone.'

A lump formed in Sabi's throat. 'That, I totally understand.'

'Jo said...' Sara paused, unsure if she should go on, but then carried on anyway. 'He said you'd lost your father too.'

'And Mum, although that was much longer ago.'

'Me too.'

Sabi's heart rate accelerated. *This is the moment. She has given you an opening. Take it.* 'I know. That's sort of why I'm here. I knew your father – after your mum passed. I have some photographs of him. I wondered if you'd like them?'

Sara lit the fire. She wasn't cold, but the act of laying the papers and twigs, adding logs, and coaxing some flames into life, gave her an excuse to be quiet and think while her unexpected house guest sat on the sofa. The moment Sabi had explained she was interested in interior design, and was currently working on her own home, Sara had known bringing her into the house would provide a temporary distraction. Time to digest what she'd heard so far.

Once the fire was flaming safely, Sara sat back on her haunches. Staring into the flames she asked, 'When did you know Dad?'

Sabi swallowed. 'At university... he, umm... I think he may have mentioned you to me.'

'At uni? He's only talked about one person from uni, and she was...' Sara's words trailed off as she saw the embarrassed shame on her companion's face.

'A snob? Someone who wanted this place more than your father?' Sabi stared at her hands as they held each other tight. 'Guilty as charged for the first, but not of the second. I was in love with you father... but when I came here I...' Sabi stood up abruptly and came to stand next to a crouched Sara, joining her as she gazed into the dancing flames. 'I was so amazed by this place. So overwhelmed... I loved it instantly. Who wouldn't...? I wanted Simon to love me more because I loved Hawthorn Park too. But I gauged it wrong... said the wrong things... I'm sorry.'

'You *did* love him?' Sara clambered to her feet. Light-headed, her mind swam with the implications of what she was hearing. 'For himself, not for this place?'

'He was my first love. Head over heels and all that.'

'But...'

'I know. I'm sorry. It was only when I heard you talking to Jo over Easter that I realised the consequences of my clumsiness.'

Sara's expression darkened. 'You were listening in on me and Jo talking?'

'What? No, I...' Sabi quelled her tone. 'I was coming up for a coffee, walking through the trees on Easter Saturday. Sound travels and I heard... I swear I did not mean to listen, but once I'd heard you mention a woman who'd hurt your father and how... I knew it was me.' She paused before whispering, 'He was the one who dumped me. I assumed he didn't love me.'

Sara clamped her lips together as her eyes bored into the stranger stood before her. *Jo says she's a good person.* She pointed to the sofa. 'I think I need to hear your version of events – from the beginning.'

Sabi wiped a single tear from her eye as she perched on the edge of the sofa. 'The first thing I should tell you was that I didn't know about you until *after* I'd visited here when I was eighteen years old...'

Sara's hands trembled as she stared into the face of her father. She only vaguely remembered him looking like he did in the photo she held, but then, she'd only been four years old at the time.

'It was so long ago,' Sabi said as Sara fixed her attention on a shot of Sabi and Simon stood in front of a fountain in the university's grounds. They were waving into the camera. 'I can't even remember who took the picture.'

Sara touched the picture with the tip of her finger, touching her father's face. 'You both seem happy.'

'We were happy. That photo was taken before I visited Hawthorn with him and messed it up. I didn't realise quite how much, until recently.'

'What do you mean?'

'I mean I'm truly, truly sorry.' Sabi reached out and tapped the photo gently with her fingertip. 'If I hadn't made Simon think I wanted this place more than I wanted him, then maybe he wouldn't have been so wary of other relationships, and you wouldn't be alone and so…'

Sara glanced up in surprise. 'You blame yourself for the fact my father didn't remarry?'

'Well… yes.'

'No, Sabi. I can't deny that you hurt him – however unintentionally – but Dad already had cause to be wary about starting a new life. He'd lost his wife to a car accident when they were very young. I was the reason for a shotgun wedding leading to a marriage that lasted only a year.

'My grandparents, Dad's mum and dad, they didn't approve of the marriage, but once I came along, they loved me anyway. They became my parents in a way, especially when Dad went to uni. They encouraged his degree – thought he should have a chance to restart his life after Mum died before they'd had time to get used to being man and wife. My mum had no living parents, so it was just me and Dad and my grandparents. Then just me and Dad. A lot happened to Dad, Sabi – very little of it was your fault.'

Jemima slipped Florrie's lead onto her collar as they reached the front of Hawthorn House.

'Wow! Jo's friend lives here. Nice!'

'Very.' Henry tried to smile, but he wasn't sure he'd pulled it off. His head swam with thoughts of his wife here as a teenager with another man – a man she'd loved before him. Then images of Jo and Hazel merged into one of him explaining to Maddie why The Potting Shed could no longer expect the return of the coffee van.

'You okay, Dad?'

'Bit tired.' Henry gave Florrie a gentle pat on the head. 'Now then, are you going to behave, or are we going to have to tether you outside?'

Jemima's eyes lit up. 'I love poking around old houses.'

Henry's smile became genuine. 'You are so like your mum sometimes.'

'Really?' Jemima's nose wrinkled.

'In a good way!' Henry laughed. 'Come on, your mum texted twenty minutes ago, saying we should come inside. She'll be wondering where we are.'

Relief swamped Henry as he entered the living room. He'd dreaded finding the women in tears or mid row, but instead, they were sat together on a sofa before the fire, chatting over the photographs that Sabi had taken with her.

'You two getting on alright then?'

Sabi leapt to her feet. 'Henry, Jemima, this is Sara.'

'We know, Mum, we met before our walk.' Jemima's eyes narrowed. 'Are you okay?'

'I'm fine.' A subdued Sabi asked Sara: 'Is it okay for Florrie to be in here?'

'No problem.' Clutching the photographs of her father, Sara took refuge in hostess mode. 'I was about to make us a hot drink; would you like one, and perhaps a bowl of water for Florrie?'

'That would be lovely, thank you.' Getting to her feet, slipping a hand into her husband's, Sabi said, 'Let's all go to the kitchen, Florrie is bound to slop her water. I seem to remember the floor is tiled.'

Sara's eyes rose. 'You remember the kitchen floor?'

Sabi blushed. 'It's more that I remember gushing about the antique nature of those tiles rather too enthusiastically.'

'Ah. I see.' Sara laid the pictures of her father carefully on the table, before leading the way to the kitchen. 'Let's get that kettle on. Tea, coffee, or hot chocolate? I can't promise a Jo level of beverage of course but... Hang on, where's Jo?'

31

'G one?'

Henry nodded. 'I assumed he'd be with you two, but his van's gone.'

Sara's face fell. 'He didn't say he was going. What happened when you were walking?'

'Well, I...' Henry paused, not wanting to repeat his conversation with Jo in front of Jemima.

The relief she'd felt when Sara had neither shouted at her, nor declared her the source of her loneliness, dipped as Sabi took in the expression. 'He didn't take it well?'

'Take what well?' Sara clicked off the kettle before it had boiled. 'What's going on?'

Jemima turned to her dad. 'Jo's okay, isn't he?'

'I don't honestly know.' Henry turned to their host. 'Sara, I'm sorry. I didn't want to burden you with this. I hadn't expected Jo to be here. This was supposed to be about Sabi apologising and giving you the photos.'

'Burden me with what?' Increasingly defensive, Sara took a step away from the family and tapped a quick text out to Jo as she looked expectantly at Henry.

'Jo worked at The Potting Shed and—'

'Works,' Jemima interrupted. 'He still works there... doesn't he, Dad?'

'Henry?' Sabi stood back up in alarm. 'We need him! What did you do?'

'I didn't *do* anything?' Henry bit back his annoyance at the accusation, 'I asked him about paying rent and about the situation with... well, you know.' He flicked his gaze to his daughter and back, hoping Sabi would get the message and shut up.

'Oh... of course.' Sabi groaned. 'And he walked away?'

'He did.'

'I didn't want it to be true,' Sabi mumbled.

Sara's head shot up. 'Didn't want *what* to be true? What situation?'

Henry frowned. 'I don't think Jo would like us talking about him behind his back.'

'He's my best friend!' The emotion of the last twenty-four hours threatened to catch up with Sara as she stared at her phone, mentally pleading with it to flash up a reply. 'If he's in trouble...'

'Jo is a good person.' Jemima crossed her arms tightly over her chest. 'I want to know what's going on. Jo's not been himself for days. If you two know why, then tell us!'

'Jemima! Don't talk to us like that!' Sabi snapped.

'Sorry, Mum, but I'm worried.'

'It's okay.' Henry rested a hand on his daughter's shoulder, as he spoke to Sara. 'I'll explain, but I'm asking for your trust on this. Jo is so private and... well, even though he just walked away without denying anything or defending himself, I still don't want to believe it.'

'Believe what?' Sara and Jemima spoke together.

'Jo said he'd be happy to pay rent – although I think I accidentally gave him the impression that I was asking him to pay it simply to see if he would refuse. As if I was testing Hazel's claims about him.'

'Oh hell.' Sabi rubbed her forehead.

'I didn't have the chance to ask him about what else Hazel said.'

Sara stared at her guests. 'Are you telling me Hazel Cooper has run into Jo?'

'Yes.' Henry frowned. 'Didn't he tell you when he got here? I'm glad you're okay though. The emergency sorted?'

'What emergency?' Sara sat down slowly as Sabi's mouth dropped open.

'He left The Potting Shed at high speed one morning – just after he'd set up. Said you needed his help urgently.'

Sara swallowed. 'And... and was Hazel there at the time?'

'She'd just arrived.'

'Oh.' Sara closed her eyes for a second before opening them again. 'There was no emergency. Looks like Jo didn't come here to help me out, or because he wanted us to be friends again. He only came to me because he wanted to avoid *her*.'

Sabi looked at Henry. She didn't know what to say.

Jemima shook her head. 'No. This is all wrong. Jo would never...'

'And yet he has.' Sara crossed her arms protectively over her chest. 'So, tell me, Henry, what else did that woman say?'

'You've heard of her then?' Sabi glanced at Henry.

'She's a former colleague. He doesn't talk about her. So, what *did* she say?'

'That Jo has a dark secret.'

The laptop was sat on the kitchen table before her, Sabi, Henry and Jemima. Maddie wished Ed was in the room with them, rather than on the other end of a Zoom link.

'Look, guys, I've known Jo for a few years, and I can confirm that he did work for the council. I know that he was unhappy there, but he would never say why. Only that the corporate world wasn't for him. He didn't like the sort of people it produced.'

'People like Hazel Cooper.' Maddie grimaced.

'Presumably. Hence preferring to work alone.' Ed sighed. 'Can I suggest we listen to common sense here?'

Sabi's head jerked. 'Common sense isn't going to change what Hazel told Henry, or the fact he misled his best friend into thinking he'd visited to help her – when in fact he was just avoiding Hazel.'

'We don't know any of that for a fact. He could have intended to go, just later in the day.' Maddie gave her sister a stern glare, before turning back to the laptop. 'Go on, Ed.'

'If you'll forgive me for going all "solicitor" on you, let's examine the situation properly. Firstly, we have all met Hazel Cooper, and I am sure we can agree that she hasn't made a good impression at The Potting Shed.'

'And then some.' Maggie sighed.

Ed looked grave. 'So, I think we can assume that her very presence, because of what she says she knows about Jo, is what's frightened him away.'

Close to tears, Jemima wrapped her arms around Florrie's neck. 'It's bad enough that we have to take Florrie back to Ivan in a bit, I don't want to go to school missing her *and* worrying about Jo as well.'

'I know, love.' Sabi put an arm around her daughter's shoulders. 'Go on, Ed, you were saying?'

'Secondly, Jo has been good for The Potting Shed.'

'More than good,' Maddie chipped in. 'I don't know what we'll do without him. He's got regular customers, who then spend money with us too – and with Davina Ditz coming—'

'Exactly,' Ed interrupted. 'Thirdly, I know that Jo's comfortable at the nursery. He told me he'd not felt so at home in years – around work colleagues, I mean.'

Jemima leapt to her feet. 'We have to find him! Let's go there now. Where does he live, Ed?'

'I don't know. Maddie?'

'I don't know either… Sabi, did you get his address when he first started working with us?'

'No, I thought you did.'

The adults all looked at each other as Jemima stood up, aghast. 'Are you saying that not one of you knows where our friend lives?'

Ed shrugged. 'It's never come up. If we meet outside of the Dark Skies group, it's always at the pub, and – to be honest – that doesn't happen that often. Jo travels around the county a fair bit with his van.'

'What are we going to do?' Maddie wasn't sure if she was asking about Jo, or The Potting Shed's refreshment situation, or both.

'I'll try calling him again.' Ed wiggled his mobile at the laptop screen. 'If you all send messages as well, then at least Jo will know we are worried about him. That we care, rather than suspect him of anything underhand.'

Sabi took a deep breath. 'That's true. We *are* worried about him. But the fact remains…' she paused, not enjoying being the one to voice the unspoken suspicion '…how well do any of us know Jo?'

'Where are you?'

'Home.'

'Where is that these days? You never said while you were here.' Sara could hear the sharp edge to her tone. She'd told herself she needn't be hurt, that her imagination had run away with her, and that Jo had come to her when he'd fled from Hazel because he felt safe with her. Yet the little voice at the back of her head that said he'd only come to Hawthorn Park because it was convenient wouldn't be silenced.

'Doesn't matter.'

'Jo!' Sara pushed her mobile closer to her ear as she threw an extra log on the fire. 'You walked out on me in the middle of a visit from your friends! Friends who are worried about you. Especially Jem!'

'Jem.' Jo groaned. 'She's such a good kid, but she's better off without me. You all are.'

All of a sudden, something inside Sara snapped. 'That's it! You stop with the self-pity right now!'

'You don't understand.'

'No, I don't, because once again, rather than talk to me, you've grabbed your van keys and run away. Because that's what you do, isn't it. You run away.' Sara could hear the words spilling from her mouth. Words she knew she didn't mean but didn't seem able to stop saying. 'That's the only reason you turned up at my place this time, isn't it? Oh, you dressed it up like answering my summons to talk about the Easter weekend – but that wasn't it at all – you just needed a bolthole to avoid a woman you didn't get on with at the council. And good old Sara was there, delighted you'd come over earlier than duty forced you too. How foolish I am! Well...' she paused, before lowering her voice '...if I can face the fact that I'm nothing but a convenient friend to you when it suits you, then you can face up to the fact that someone from your past is stirring trouble – trouble you need to sort out before it ruins your life a second time!'

Jo was speechless as he heard Sara gathering her breath down the end of the line. The idea of her simply being convenient had never crossed his mind. 'Sara, I never meant to...'

'Well, whatever you meant or didn't mean, the fact remains that a horrid human has spread rumours about you, and that you've run away when you should have faced up to her. Talked to her. Been an adult.' Sara's eyes flicked to the three photographs Sabi had left on the coffee table to the right of the room, her anger subsiding into grief. 'And what's more, right now, I need my best friend as much as he needs me.'

Picking up on the sob building in Sara's voice, Jo asked, 'Why? What's happened?'

Sara felt a quiver of hope as she heard the urgency in Jo's voice. 'Sabi brought me some photographs of my father. She was the one – the one who stopped Dad ever dating again. The one who caused him to lecture me about being careful who I fell for.'

'Oh God.'

'Quite.'

'I'm so sorry, Sara.'

'Will you come over? There's no one here; no one would know you've come back.'

'But... but why would you want me there? I honestly didn't come to you as a place or person of convenience – but I can't deny the bolthole thing.'

Sara puffed out a long breath. 'Why didn't you tell me about Hazel?'

'I didn't want you to think less of me. I know I should have spoken to her – but I can't honestly think she'd want to talk to me, and if she'd made a scene in front of The Potting Shed customers... There's stuff you don't know. Things I'm not proud of.'

'Then come here. Tell me about it. I promise I won't shout at you for taking me for granted if you don't do it again.'

Jo paused. He knew he'd like nothing better than to go back. 'I can't.'

'Why not?'

'Because I have a bright orange camper van. It's easy to spot.'

Sara's hackles shot back up. 'Jo, will you stop being so stupid! I live in a big house in the middle of a huge garden and wood, there are a million places to hide a van, whether it is bright orange or painted in neon rainbow stripes! It has been an emotional roller coaster of a day, and right now we both need a hug. Yes?'

'Yes.'

'Then either tell me where you are, so I can come and see you, or get your butt out of wherever you're hiding, into that van, and drive here. Now!'

32

'Sorry, Maddie, I can't. Don't get me wrong, I'd love to spend the night with you tonight, but I have a hellish early start tomorrow. New client, and it's a big one. Ronald would normally take them on, but he wants me to do it.'

Disappointment gripped Maddie as she sat in the driver's seat of her Jeep, facing the empty nursery. 'But I was offering to come to you in Exeter; I wasn't expecting you to come to Culmstock.'

'I realise that, and I really appreciate it, but I have to drive to Bristol. I'll be leaving about six in the morning, and – well, I'm going to need a full night's sleep. We never sleep all night when we're together.'

A light flush came to Maddie's cheeks. 'We do at Sabi's.'

'When we had a furry chaperone and Jem in the next room – but Jem's at school and Florrie is with Ivan, so there would be no reason for me to keep my hands off you.'

'True.' Maddie giggled despite her disappointment.

'I wondered if you'd like to go for a meal with me on Friday night?'

'That would be lovely.' Maddie quickly added, 'I could come to you after that – if you like?'

Ed chuckled down the line. 'That would be fabulous; then we can drive to The Potting Shed together on Saturday morning. I'm sorry I can't see you before then – really, I am.'

Maddie climbed out of her Jeep and locked its door. 'It's okay. Work first and all that. I assume you haven't heard from Jo?'

'Nothing.' Ed blew out a frustrated puff of air. 'The number of times I've checked my phone since yesterday afternoon is bordering on paranoia.'

'I don't think he's coming back.' Maddie stared at the place where Jo parked when he was selling his coffee.

'He isn't due to be with you today though, anyway.'

'True, but it's Thursday tomorrow, and customers have been asking if he'll be here. What do I say?'

'I think you'll have to say he's unwell, and you hope he'll be back soon.'

Maddie had to concede that was better than saying he wasn't coming back, risking losing customers in the process. 'Sabi is taking Jem to school this morning. The poor kid is cut up about Jo.'

'I can imagine. Hopefully she'll be so busy and happy to see her friends that she'll be okay. Maybe he'll be back by the time she's with you at the weekend.'

'Hope so.' Maddie unlocked the door to the shop. 'I'm going to have to go. I've got a delivery of compost coming before opening and no one here to help me move it.'

'You'll have to sweet-talk the delivery driver.'

'This is when I miss Petra the most! One flash of her smile and the couriers are putty in her hands.'

'I'm sure you could do the same.'

'Spoken like a loyal boyfriend.'

'A loyal boyfriend who has to get dressed, or he'll be late for work.'

'Go on with you then.' Maddie pushed the shop door open. 'You will tell me if you hear from Jo, won't you?'

'Promise.'

Sabi was glad to be busy. She always hated the moment when she took Jemima back to school. Even though she knew her daughter loved her life at school and that, as a weekly boarder, she'd be back again on Saturday, the house always felt empty without her.

Flicking through the third out-of-date phone book in Taunton's library, her finger running through every Dunn, Sabi realised her promise to Jemima was going to be almost impossible to keep.

You will find Jo, won't you, Mum?

Knowing there was a high chance he could be ex-directory, Sabi had opted to search through historical copies of the phone book, as well as the more recent versions.

Once that avenue of research was exhausted without success, Sabi closed her eyes to think. She'd already put Jo's name into Facebook, but with no positive results, and she'd tried Google, but, apart from a connection with the Exmoor Drifters, there was nothing.

'The Drifters! Of course, obvious!' Grabbing her handbag, Sabi dashed outside and pressed Ivan's name into her phone.

Two minutes later her hopes were dashed. 'If you're after

asking me for Jo's home information, Sabi lass, I'm afraid Ed has beaten you to it. I don't have an address for him. I'm only required to ask for an emergency contact, and that was his mobile number.'

'And he isn't answering that.'

'Precisely.'

'Thanks anyway, Ivan.' Sabi stifled a sigh. 'Are you alright for moving into The Potting Shed on Monday still?'

'One hundred per cent. Can't wait!'

'At least we'll have you and Elspeth's wares to bring people in.'

'Not the same as a good cuppa and cake though'

'True.'

'He'll turn up; he's a good bloke.'

'So, everyone keeps telling us, and I want to believe that...' Sabi strolled towards her car '...but the fact is, he upped and left without a word of explanation. Why would he do that if he was such a good bloke?'

Ivan sighed. 'Elspeth was right about that girl – she is trouble.'

'Sorry?'

'Hazel Cooper came to look at our wares on Sunday. She couldn't wait to dish the dirt on Jo. Soon gave up when she realised we weren't biting.'

'I hate to ask, but for the sake of the business I have to – Ivan, do you think there is anything we should know about Jo that could damage The Potting Shed?'

'Sabi lass, I've worked with Jo for several years. Money has never gone missing, and no one has whispered in my ear about bad language or poor customer service. He is always on time and always helps close the market after a long day when we're all tired and want to go home. I promise, with Sheba as my witness, there is nothing that would lead me to think that Jo Dunn is anything other than a good bloke.'

'Thank you. I wish I hadn't had to ask.'

'Me too, lass. Me too.'

Maddie hadn't needed to attempt to charm the compost delivery driver. *Not that I would have*, she'd told her herself, *I'm perfectly capable of moving forty bags of soil.*

Just as the lorry had pulled into the car park, the R. K. Andrews van had arrived. Within minutes a jovial Robert and Kevin had made short work of placing the compost against the car park fence, while Ahmed had headed into her home to start laying dust sheets.

'There you go, Maddie.' Robert brushed his hands together as he exchanged the nod of a job well done with his brother. 'The least we can do after you've been so messed around by Little Miss Perfect.'

Maddie couldn't help but smile. 'Miss Cooper hasn't endeared herself to you two either then.'

'I don't have a lot of time for people who bugger others around.' Robert pushed up his jumper sleeves.

'Nor me.' Kevin rolled his eyes. 'Still, now Henry has got the situation in hand, by the end of the day we should be back on schedule.'

'Really?' Maddie was delighted. 'Does that mean you are now working to Henry's schedule of works, not Hazel's?'

Robert tucked his hands into the bib of his overalls. 'We are. As I told her, you can have the work done quickly, or you can have it done well – things take a certain amount of time; they can't be rushed.'

'She was hardly rushing – the other way around if anything.'

'Ummm... you know what, Maddie, Kevin and I have been thinking about that, and we reckon she was neither rushing nor dilly-dallying as such. Looking at it with hindsight, the schedule of work she gave us was designed to ensure she spent as little time here as possible.'

'Meaning she wouldn't have to come in often?' Maddie frowned as she thought about this. 'But she turned up unexpectedly every now and then – even on her days off.'

Kevin and Robert exchanged knowing glances before Robert said, 'Henry told us a little of what's been going on. If we're right, your friend Jo is an itch Miss Cooper has to scratch with those horrid red claws of hers. Kev and I are just bumbling builders, but it occurs to us that she was trying to avoid him – and yet she couldn't keep away either.'

Maddie looked from one brother to the other. 'You two are far from just bumbling builders. And what's more, I think you might be right.'

'We'll tell our wives.' Kevin chuckled. 'They'll say there's a first time for everything. Anyway, assuming we have no more disruptions, you should have a shop and flat, in three weeks.'

'That's fantastic.' Three weeks was still a lifetime away, but it was better than the six that she'd been previously quoted. 'I wonder, is there any chance of me living in the flat at least for the last day of this month?'

Kevin pursed his lips as Robert scratched his head. 'That's just under the three isn't it… I don't know.'

'I have an important event here on the 1st of May, and it would be much easier to be on site twenty-four-seven.'

Robert inclined his head. 'I can appreciate that. Tell you what, we'll do our best. We have structural work to do, what with knocking out walls and stuff, so I can't promise more than that. I'd hate you to be living somewhere unsafe.'

'Thank you.' Maddie glanced at her watch; it was almost half past eight. 'I'll pop in later. I'm sorry I haven't had the chance to see how you're getting on lately.'

'No problem. Proves you trust us.' Kevin opened the back of the van and pulled out two huge pots of paint. 'We prefer that to customers who fuss and flap every five minutes.'

'Painting the new kitchen?'

'Yup. The units are in, and the sink is plumbed.' Robert paled as he gestured to the butter yellow paint in Kevin's hands. 'You did know it was going to be this colour, didn't you?'

'Absolutely.' Maddie chuckled. 'My sister would have had something to say if she hadn't personally checked the suitability of the colour scheme at least three times.'

Sara sat in her old Nissan Micra in the nursery car park and watched as customers came and went. Trade wasn't busy, but nor was it dead. She wasn't entirely sure why she was there.

Despite her pleas, Jo hadn't returned to Hawthorn Park, nor had he told her where he was.

'I shouldn't have got angry with him.' *You had every right to.* 'I know, but it didn't help anything, did it?'

Realising she was having a one-sided conversation with her steering wheel, Sara was about to get out of the car to have a look around The Potting Shed, the place Jo had claimed to be happy until Hazel Cooper had come along, when she spotted Sabi walking out of a part-glass, part-brick building and heading towards a polytunnel.

A shot of nervous tension shot through her. She had no idea what to think about Sabi Willand-Harris. Unintentional or not, she had been the woman who'd broken her father's heart; a fact that, due to being overtaken by current events, she hadn't had time to process.

A few minutes later, still sat in her car, Sara saw another woman leave the glass and brick building. She looked a bit like Sabi, but her hair was much longer, swept back into a ponytail, and her grubby combat trousers and old jumper made her appear far more at home in her surroundings.

'That must be Maddie.'

Maddie headed to the young woman hovering on the other side of the till desk. 'Can I help?'

'Um, are you Maddie?'

Unsure if she should be wary, or if this was someone about to enquire about the Little Acorns group, Maddie nodded.

'My name is Sara Northcott, and I—'

'Jo's friend!' Maddie interrupted. 'Have you heard from him? I've been so worried!'

Sara's shaky smile faded. 'You haven't heard from him

either? I had hoped he'd have been in touch about coming back to work – or not.'

'Not a word. I'm embarrassed to say I don't even know where he lives.'

'Nor me.' Sara's cheeks blushed at the admission.

'But you're his best friend – aren't you?'

'It isn't that straightforward. With Jo it's always...' Sara broke off as Maddie's mobile burst back into life.

'I'm so sorry. I really must take this call...' Maddie answered her phone. 'Hi there.' She only just stopped herself saying, "Davina" as the gardener began to tell her about the long-range forecast she'd got from the Met Office. 'And they're sure about that...? Well, a picnic sounds rather good... Thank you for thinking ahead for me. I'm really grateful. I'll see if I can borrow some money to buy some picnic benches. Thanks again. Must go. I'll call later.'

Seeing that Maddie was about to apologise again for the phone interruption, Sara put her hands up. 'You need picnic benches?'

'Yes, we have an event soon and without Jo...'

Sara plunged her hands into her pockets. 'I have loads of them. You can borrow some if you like.'

'Really?'

'Sure.'

'But, as much as I appreciate the offer, Sara, I'll need them for May 1st – May Day. Aren't you open to the public that day, needing every bench you have?'

33

Sabi stopped dead on the threshold of the shop when she saw Sara leaning against the till, chatting to Maddie.

She had been about to sneak out again when Maddie spotted her. 'Sabs, come and see Sara. She's going to lend us some picnic tables.'

'Oh, really?'

'Sure. I've got far more than I need, even during an open weekend.'

'Well, thank you, Sara.' Feeling awkward, Sabi turned to her sister. 'I was just coming to see if you wanted a break from the till.'

'I would. Thanks.' Maddie passed the till's keys to her sister.

'Any news of Jo?' Sabi turned to Sara. 'Jemima's beside herself.'

'Nothing. I hoped you might have heard something. Seems he's gone to ground.'

A sense of foreboding trickled through Maddie as she asked, 'Has he done this before?'

Sara nodded.

'How long was he gone?' Sabi stood closer to her

sister; the unspoken issue of whether to start looking for a replacement coffee provider hung in the air.

'About a year.'

'A year!'

Seeing the sisters' horrified faces made Sara feel defensive on Jo's behalf. 'He hadn't done anything wrong; he was just protecting himself.'

'From what?' Sabi lowered her voice as a customer came in.

Sara lowered her voice. 'He was bullied at work. A few years back now. It got too much, and he left. While he was gone... things changed.'

'Bullied.' Maddie felt sick. 'Even the word makes me angry. Was the bully Hazel Cooper, by any chance?'

'I assumed so.' Sara closed her eyes. 'I don't know the full story – I could have things wrong. Jo's always been tight-lipped and well, we had a row – I'm not sure how we left things.'

'Oh hell. I'm sorry.'

'I accused him of using me as a convenient bolthole, taking me for granted – you know the sort of thing.'

Sabi sighed. 'We didn't exactly help by turning up at your place uninvited, did we.'

Sara mustered a smile. 'You came with good intentions.'

Not sure what to say, Sabi merely nodded, before scooting off as a customer chose that moment to need serving.

'Do you have any idea what's behind all this?' Maddie whispered as Sabi left them. 'With Jo, I mean?'

Uncomfortable sharing Jo's secrets, but knowing it was for the best, Sara inclined her head. 'I don't know for sure, but I got the impression that he went out with Hazel for a while. But it could never work.'

'They were a couple?!' Maddie was stunned. 'But Jo is so down to earth and Hazel... isn't.'

'I don't think she was always so devious.'

'I'd better call Henry. It sounds as if Hazel's claims were driven by a broken heart.'

'What exactly *did* she claim, Maddie?'

'Bullying in the workplace.'

'Jo!' Sara's face went puce. 'Jo bullying *her* – not the other way around? Are you insane?'

Taking Sara's arm, Maddie gently guided her outside, as a few browsing customers glanced their way in alarm. 'Let me show you the new garden.'

Sat on the bench overlooking the field of wild grasses and flowers, Maddie and Sara took a collective breath of fresh air.

'It's beautiful here.' Sara examined the scene. 'You're going to have a nice spread of bluebells when the time comes.'

Sensing that Sara would welcome a change of subject, Maddie took refuge in sharing her plans for the space. She explained how the potholes were to be filled and that their neighbour had given permission for their visitors to walk in the woods on the other side of the fence.

'That's wonderful.' Sara watched a pair of butterflies weave through the air as she asked, 'Is this where you need the picnic benches?'

'Yes. We have an event soon. I have a guest coming, and she's suggested we have a picnic while she's speaking.'

'Hence needing the picnic tables. That's a great idea.' Sara's palms prickled. 'Because Jo won't be here to provide coffee?'

'He wouldn't have been anyway. He had an arrangement with you for May Day.'

Sara stared at the bluebell leaves. 'Sorry.'

'Not at all. I never minded that Jo had a previous booking. He was honest about it from the start. I didn't know we'd have an event at the same time back then. I'd rearrange it, but it's the 1st of May or not at all, and with BIG just opened up, we need all the help we can get.'

'Jo told me.' Sara hardly liked to ask. 'Is his absence having an impact?'

'Afraid so.' Maddie waved a hand towards the main body of the nursery. 'We're doing okay, but the weekends are feeble compared to what we need them to be long term. Ed, that's my boyfriend, thinks the novelty of BIG will wear off, and people who like a more personal service will drift back here.'

'I suspect he's right. At worst, they'll use both facilities. BIG for a general wander round and a cuppa, but here for plants and advice.'

Maddie regarded her guest with renewed interest. 'I could live with that. In the meantime, we're trying to bring in people in different ways. A children's club – the Little Acorns – they made this garden; and then a guest – although that might cause issues, as she's going to BIG too. I dread to think how they'll react when they discover we have poached their star attraction.'

'Poached?'

'Well, more arranged to have her here first, so anyone desperate to see her will come to us before BIG – or maybe attend both gigs.' Maddie tugged at the ponytail that hung over her shoulder. 'The person I was on the phone to when you arrived, that was Davina Ditz.'

'No way! She's amazing.'

'And miraculously, she's coming here for a Q&A event, but there is so much to do before she gets here.' Maddie climbed to her feet. 'Would you be awfully offended if I worked while we chatted?'

'Of course not.' Getting up, Sara smiled. 'Perhaps I can help. I'm quite green-fingered in my own way.'

'You like gardening?'

'Love it. Although, I'm more into designing gardens than growing them.'

'Like my sister. Well, she's more into design and the appearance of things generally, not just gardens.' Maddie led the way into the nearest polytunnel. 'That's why I'm in here, to put together colour-coordinated hanging baskets, as per Sabi's instructions, to decorate the place and to sell.'

'Sounds good.' Sara inhaled the aroma of soil and plants waiting to be potted on.

'You really want to help?'

'If you want me to. I don't want to interfere.' Sara suddenly felt self-conscious. 'Helping would help keep my mind from worrying about Jo, though. I can't stop thinking about him. I wish I hadn't lost my temper, but I felt so – so...'

'Used?'

'Yes.' Sara paused. 'That bullying allegation – it isn't true.'

'I'm inclined to believe you.' Maddie headed to

her workbench. 'One of the good things about being understaffed is that I'm too busy to think much. On top of everything else, my house is being converted into a flat and shop at the moment, but I haven't so much as peeped at what the builders are up to for days.'

'You're brave. I'd need to check every five minutes in case they weren't doing what I wanted.'

Maddie grinned. 'You really are like my sister!'

Unable to stop herself from wondering how her dad would have reacted to the comparison, Sara focused on the row of fuchsias on the potting bench. 'Nice plants. Beautiful purple and cream petals.'

'Thanks. Their variety name is Deep Purple. These ones are particularly good as, once the rest of the hanging basket's occupants have died away, they can be transplanted into the garden. They'll create a beautiful display for years if cared for.' Maddie abruptly stopped talking. 'Sorry, I forget people don't always want the Law and the Prophets, plant wise.'

'Not at all. It's fascinating.' Sara lifted a pot of lobelia. 'A matching purple flower?'

'As near as I could get.' Maddie picked two more pots up and placed them on the side next to the fuchsia. 'These will go around the outside of the main plant. I also have...' she picked up two smaller flowerpots '...some cream violas to complement the paler part of the fuchsia.'

'They are going to look wonderful.' Sara picked up a trowel. 'Shall I scoop some soil into the basket, while you deal with the planting?'

'Sounds great. Thanks.' Maddie showed Sara where her

father's special mix of soil and compost sat and arranged three sets of flowers for three hanging baskets, while her helper worked. 'This is really kind of you.'

'Happy to help.' Sara was amazed to find how relaxed she was in Maddie's company. 'Jo said you were lovely.'

'He said the same about you.'

'Did he?' Sara paused mid scoop. 'Really?'

'Yes.' Maddie felt a rush of sadness for the girl next to her. 'You like him don't you, I mean, really like him.'

'More fool me.' Sara shrugged. 'But it's okay, Jo and I have discussed it and him being a close friend is enough.'

'Is it?' Maddie immediately regretted asking the question. 'Sorry. That was rather personal. We've only just met!'

'It's okay.' Sara funnelled a trowel's worth of soil into the closest basket. 'Actually, it's rather nice to have someone to talk to. It's usually just me. Since Dad died, I've not really done people. I know the public come in on occasion, but that's not the same as people to chat with. I have been toying with going back to my degree or finding work beyond the house, but what with sorting out the estate on my own and... Let's just say, me helping you now is a major step after a year of solitude – more or less.'

'Well, if you'd like a part-time job, then just say the word!' Maddie took the first soil-filled hanging basket from Sara's hands. 'I'm about to lose my regular helper to a gardening apprenticeship and Sabi only wants to be here part-time, so I'll be advertising soon anyway.'

Taken aback, Sara brushed a hand across her face, leaving a smudge of soil on her cheek. 'But you've only just met me.'

'I like you. Jo likes you. I'm not saying I'd be making any

assumptions about how long you'd want to stay; I'm just offering a few hours a week – minimum wage I'm afraid. No pressure. Have a think. It might help you get used to being around people again.'

'I'd like to.' Sara gulped. 'I'd really like to, but what about the May weekend when Hawthorn Park is open? You'll need me here, but I'll have to be there.'

'It's okay, I was having to manage anyway. Ed helps out over weekends, as do Sabi and Henry. My niece, Jem, she'll be here for the bank holiday too. She's dying to ask our guest what she thinks about her "Grow a Smoothie" idea.'

'That sounds great!' Sara remembered how Jemima had defended Jo against the uncertainty of her parents. 'I love the smoothie idea, and I'm sure Davina will too. I can't believe she is coming here! My dad loved her.'

'So did mine.'

'Not hard to see why. A stunning woman. Excellent gardener too.'

Maddie smiled. 'True on both counts. Bit old for your dad though.'

Sara muttered, 'She was safe though. Women who you can't have can't hurt you.'

Catching the undertone to her visitor's voice, Maddie asked, 'Your father must have missed your mother very much.'

'I'm sure he did, but she didn't break his heart – well, her death did, but no. That was your sister.'

'My sister? Sabi?'

'You didn't know?'

'I didn't even know they'd met!'

34

Having explained the connection between Sabi and her father, Sara had taken her leave. Promising to let Maddie know soon if she wanted to work at The Potting Shed on a regular basis, she had disappeared with all the speed of a frightened rabbit after her revelation.

'What's the betting I never hear from her again, Dad?' Maddie sat on her bed and took a bite from a cheese sandwich. She could hear the builders in the next room. One of them was issuing forth a tuneless whistle as they painted the kitchen walls.

Maddie had already poked her head around the door, experiencing a stab of relief that everything was in order. The kitchen units – including the doors she had chosen, rather than the ones Hazel had picked – and the sink were in place just as they had told her they would be, and the shade of yellow they were applying to the walls was as welcoming as Sabi had promised.

'Did you know about Sabi and Simon Northcott, Dad?'

She had been surprised by Sara's news and hurt that her sister hadn't told her about the connection she had with Hawthorn Park. 'I bet guilt at her behaviour back then stopped her telling me.'

The whistling stopped, only to be replaced by a low humming of a tune that was possibly 'Waltzing Matilda', but possibly not.

Resisting the urge to climb under her duvet and go to sleep so she could forget all her troubles for a while, Maddie stifled a yawn. She knew there was only so long she could keep working from five in the morning until seven at night.

'It's the only way to get everything done, Dad. Sabi has her eyes on the accounts, and she is great with the customers and the till, but gardening wise...' Maddie's mutterings to the memory of her father faded as she thought about Sabi. Their weekly finance chat was due today, but she wasn't sure she could face it. Suspecting they weren't taking enough money across the till to justify going ahead with the expansion was one thing. Knowing it for sure was another.

Maddie closed her eyes and lay back on the bed, her head sinking gratefully into a familiar pillow, which was squashed and old, unlike the brick-firm new pillow her sister had given her.

'It's not that I don't approve of Sabi having had a relationship with Simon, Dad. She was single back then, but why didn't she tell me? And now, I've offered Sara a job! If I'd known about Simon, I'd never have done that without talking to Sabi first.'

Groaning into the dark behind her eyelids, Maddie mumbled, 'But we need help, and I like Sara. Jo is supposed to work here tomorrow. If he doesn't appear, I'll have no choice but to hunt for someone to replace him.'

Forcing her eyes back open, she lifted her phone, holding it in front of her face. 'It's already the 12th of April. That's only nineteen days until our version of *Gardeners' Question Time*. I haven't got a name for the event, or even advertised it, so no one is coming yet. I have no back-up questions planned in case hardly anyone comes once I have advertised, the garden I'm holding the event in isn't completed, and I know Sara offered to lend us picnic tables, but we might not see her again now I know about her father and Sabi…' Maddie dragged her hands through her hair, pulling out her ponytail in the process. 'I told her it didn't matter, Dad, but she was obviously feeling awkward, and what with Jo and everything… that poor kid.'

She's twenty-one, hardly a kid.

'She feels like a kid right now though. She's lost.'

She has friends.

'She only has Jo.'

She has you and Sabi.

Having decided that it was more sensible to leave Sabi in the shop and get on with creating more hanging baskets while she could, Maddie had fled to the safety of her polytunnel, trying not to mind that she didn't pass a single customer on her way.

'I'm not avoiding talking to Sabi, I'm just working on the practical stuff while I can.' Maddie tried not to think about all the weekly jobs Jake normally did. They'd soon be hers to do on top of everything else.

'I should write a list. A list to go with the list I need to write specifically for the 1st of May.' Suddenly seized with the need to talk to Ed, Maddie checked the time. It was just gone one o'clock.

Seconds later, her phone's video screen burst into life as Ed answered her call.

'Hello, love. You okay?' Ed smiled at her from his office chair, his hands continuing to tap at his laptop.

'Ish. Better for seeing you. Busy?'

'Insane. Not even going to get my lunchtime stroll.' He paused in his typing to wave a shop-bought sandwich in front of the phone. 'No rest for the wicked.'

'In which case, I must have done something really evil.'

'Lucky for me.' Ed winked suggestively, before asking, 'Feeling the pressure?'

'A bit. And I discovered that Sabi used to go out with Sara's dad.'

'Simon? You're kidding!' Ed lowered his sandwich in surprise.

'Nope. It seems that Sara's father mistrusted all women after Sabi. Never dated again, and now…'

Ed's desk phone burst into life. 'Sorry, Maddie, I have to answer this. I'll call later.'

As her phone screen dimmed with the abrupt ending of the call, Maddie picked up a pot of pansies, knowing she couldn't put off talking to her sister about Simon for much longer. Aside from asking her why she'd been withholding information from her, there were hundreds of other things to discuss – not to mention asking if she'd told Henry that Hazel once had a relationship with Jo yet.

★

Henry's meeting with his business partner, Graham, had been long and uncomfortable. In all the years they had worked together, building up their design and architect consultancy business, they'd never had to discuss an issue like this one.

On receiving his wife's call, telling him that Hazel's connection with Jo had been potentially romantic as well as work-based, Henry had spoken to Graham. Several off-the-record phone calls to associates in the local council offices later – including the manager who had written Hazel Cooper's reference – and Henry felt they'd done remarkably well to only have drunk a pot of tea while they talked. A bottle of whisky would have been more welcome.

What they had discovered had left Henry saddened, but not surprised. He dreaded to think what his daughter would have to say about it all.

He could see Hazel through the window of his office. Sat at a large desk, on the opposite side of a well-lit room from Donna – their ever-patient receptionist and PA – Hazel was tapping away at her PC as if her job depended on it. Which, right now, it did.

Graham had agreed that they couldn't just sack her. Neither wanted to contemplate the fuss she'd create. But as she was still within her probationary period, they could decide not to extend her contract once that period was at an end. Something both men were ready to do. Unless she changed – unless she was prepared to be honest.

Heaving himself off his chair, Henry opened the office door. 'Miss Cooper, could I have a word, please.'

Seeing her hands freeze over the keyboard for a split second, Henry noted the fleeting look of apprehension that crossed her eyes before Hazel pressed save on whatever she was working on and stood up.

'Mr Willand-Harris?' Hazel spoke his name as a question as she was signalled towards an upright armchair in the corner of her employer's office.

'Miss Cooper.' Henry sat on the other armchair, wishing he was a million miles away. 'This conversation is not official, but it might become so, depending on what you tell me, and what happens once I have relayed that information, where relevant, to Mr Davies, Miss Willand and my wife.'

Hazel sat a little straighter in her chair. 'Your tone suggests I might need a lawyer.'

'And yours suggests a lack of cooperation.' Henry lifted the plans for The Potting Shed off the table next to him and rested them on his lap. 'I am not about to rake over old ground concerning your unorthodox ordering of the work at The Potting Shed. I am, however, interested in a matter that affects the nursery.'

'Then why aren't your wife and her sister here?'

'Because I wanted to give you the opportunity to talk off the record. I was giving you the benefit of the doubt.'

Hesitant, Hazel said, 'Benefit of what doubt?'

'Jo Dunn. You accused him of being untrustworthy. You have spoken to various people connected to the nursery, making implications – without saying anything specific – about Jo's lack of character. You clearly wanted to plant the seeds of doubt in all of us about him. Then, when I pushed you for a motive to this behaviour, you accused him of having a dark side – and when pushed further, told me this pertained to bullying in the workplace. You also said I could check because there was proof.'

Seeing the pinch of pink in Hazel's cheeks fade, Henry leant back in his chair. 'Ah, I see. You didn't expect me to make enquires. You assumed I'd take your word for it.'

'My word should have been good enough.'

'It might have been if you'd proved yourself a trustworthy employee, or if so many people hadn't got so many good things to say about Jo Dunn.'

'I told you. *They* are not the kind person they appear to be!'

'But you *are* bitter, Miss Cooper.'

Hazel stood up sharply, her palms curling into fists, before she gathered herself and unclasped them. 'I was a victim of...'

'Rejection. Heartbreak maybe?' Henry patted the arm of her armchair. 'Sit down please, Hazel.'

After three long seconds, Hazel retook her seat, the wind blown from her sails.

'Now then.' Henry straightened his tie. 'I have spoken to some contacts at the council. You worked with Jo when you first arrived at the planning department. I'm told you had trouble settling in, but Jo took you under his wing. Showed you the ropes.'

Hazel said nothing, but Henry could tell from the expression in her eyes that what he'd learnt was right.

'You got on. Jo was good at his job, but he'd never really fitted in, and you were new and young and friendless in a strange place. Goodness knows it's always hard joining an office where everyone else already knows the rules of how to get along. It's harder still when, like you, a new employee is not from the local area.

'I believe, and this was conjecture on my contact's behalf, that you and Jo went out a few times. He showed you the area.'

'Yes.' The admission was barely above a whisper.

'You had things in common perhaps?'

'We grew up in the same part of the world.'

'I see.' Henry stretched out his legs. 'I'm not asking you for details, but, for whatever reason, one day Jo asked to be moved to a different office so that he didn't have to work with you anymore. After that you never missed a chance to criticise him. Nothing major, just – and I'm quoting your former manager now – "a slow drip of snipes".'

'I—'

Henry held up his hand. 'Then, Jo took a sabbatical for six months. On his return he found that you had been promoted to a different part of the office block – you didn't even see him – but you knew he was back. Two months later, he wrote a note stating he couldn't work in the same building as you and left. At no point did you make a bullying complaint against him, official or otherwise.'

Hazel's gaze shot up, and she stared straight at Henry. 'He fled when he saw me at The Potting Shed because he knew what he'd done. He knew he was guilty.'

'Of what, exactly?'

'Of pretending. Of leading me on… of making me think that…' She stood up again, swaying slightly on her heels. 'Not once did he call me over the six months he was away. Not once! We had history – he owed me an explanation! I deserved to know why he did what he did!'

'It is my understanding, Miss Cooper, that he called no one at all in that time. Not even his best friend.'

'What?' The little colour that had been left in her face drained away.

'Jo cut himself off from everyone and everything. I'm sure he had his reasons, but they are his alone.' Henry pushed himself up off the chair. 'I am sorry he hurt you; I suspect he is too. But I need you to be honest with me now, did he bully you at work, or did he just mislead you into thinking you had a future as a couple, humiliating you in the process?'

'It's the same thing!'

'With respect, Miss Cooper, it is not. Not by a long shot.'

35

'How was Bristol?' Maddie embraced Ed as he got out of his car.

'Interesting.' Ed ran a hand through Maddie's hair. 'How about I tell you all about it over dinner?'

'That would be lovely.' Maddie glanced at her mud-spattered clothes. 'I'd better get cleaned up. Won't take long, I brought a bag of overnight things from Sabi's, seeing as we're off to your place.'

Locking his car door behind them, Ed smiled. 'Fab. Do you need anything doing before we go?'

'Well, if you're offering…'

Ed laughed. 'I take it that's a yes then?'

'Maybe.' Maddie grinned. 'Just one job, I promise. Would you mind helping me carry the seed rack out of the shop?'

'Come on then. Best do that before you change.'

Grabbing his hand in hers Maddie walked towards the shop. 'I wasn't going to ask for help with this until tomorrow, but if we do it now, it'll be something I can cross off my list.'

'A list which, I imagine, is incredibly long.'

'Of epic proportions. Every time I cross something off, I add two more things onto it.'

'So, where are we moving the rack to?'

'First polytunnel.' Maddie led the way into the shop, clicking on the light switch as she went. 'I've already emptied the seed packets off, so it won't take long.'

Picking up one side of the rack, Ed was surprised by how light it was. 'I was expecting to have to put my back into this.'

'It isn't heavy, just unwieldy. I could have dragged it I suppose, but I didn't fancy it toppling over and crashing into anything else.'

'Fair enough.' Ed peered around the rack as they backed it towards the doorway. 'It's going to be very different in here once Ivan and Elspeth's goods are installed.'

'It'll only be temporary. In here I mean. It doesn't seem fair to ask Ivan to use his small generator full-time, so I've asked the builders to add that to the list when it comes to doing the refit.'

'What did Hazel Cooper have to say about that?'

'No idea. She is officially off the case when it comes to The Potting Shed.'

'Is she now?'

'Yup. Henry called earlier. The bullying at work charge was fabricated. It was all down to unrequited love. They haven't told her yet, but Henry and Graham won't be keeping her on after her probation period.'

'Serves her right.' Ed mused as they manoeuvred the rack gently through the doorway and out into the fresh air: 'I wonder why Jo didn't defend himself when

Henry challenged him with Hazel's bullying accusation, though?'

'Perhaps he felt bad for not loving her back.' Maddie rested the end of the rack down a moment while she unlocked the polytunnel's entrance. 'I got the impression from Sara that Jo would like someone in his life, but something in him is afraid to let that happen.'

'She likes him too. Sara, that is.'

Maddie was surprised. 'You knew?'

'Jo told me. He didn't know what to do about it. They are good friends; he didn't want to hurt her.'

'And then hurt her in the process of not wanting to hurt her?'

'Got it in one.' Ed waited for the signal from Maddie, and then picked his side of the rack back up. 'I haven't heard from Jo since he did his disappearing act. I'm not sure if he's getting my messages, although I can see he hasn't blocked my number.'

'If he's switched his phone off and isn't checking his computer, it'll make no difference how often we try to contact him, though, will it.'

'It's so frustrating!' Ed shuffled forwards as Maddie edged the rack through the polytunnel's doors and along its right-hand side.

'It's very weird that no one knows where he lives.'

'When he does surface, I'm going to make sure I find out.'

Maddie paused. 'You don't think he lives in the coffee van, do you?'

Ed shook his head. 'No room. Every space is taken with up stock and folding tables and chairs.'

'Good point.' As they lowered the rack to the ground, Maddie asked, 'You still think he'll reappear?'

'He was happy here. He could be again. He'll realise that when he stops to think.' Ed checked the rack was balanced, so it wouldn't topple over in the night, and then took hold of Maddie's hand. 'How about we leave talking about Jo for now? Let's have one evening when you forget all about The Potting Shed.'

Maddie grimaced. 'I promised myself I wouldn't go on about work with you all the time, and I've been doing it again, haven't I.'

Ed silenced her with a kiss. 'I was not criticising or complaining. I love The Potting Shed, you know that. I'd just like your opinion on something else.'

'About?'

'I'll tell you over dinner.'

Maddie hadn't been concerned when Ed had turned right instead of left, out of the nursery's car park; assuming he was going to drive home via the country lanes rather than taking the motorway. Now, however, as he went straight on at the roundabout, rather than going right, she started to pay more attention to her surroundings.

'We're going the wrong way?'

'Depends on where we're going, doesn't it?'

'Where *are* we going?'

'The Blackdown Hotel.'

'But…'

'You need a proper night off.' Ed slid the car up a gear. 'And, if we are a little closer to The Potting Shed than you would be if you stayed at my place, then you might relax more.'

'Have I ever told you that you're wonderful?'

'Nope.'

'Well, you are.' Maddie rested her head back against the seat. Cuddling her overnight bag, she let out a puff of air she hadn't realised she'd been holding in. 'It'll be lovely to see the inside of the Blackdown. I've been providing vegetables to its owner, Tim, for years, but I've never seen beyond the back door, despite his offers to show me round.'

'Too busy to take the tour?'

'Yep. Even before Dad died, work was always full on. I used to do the veg deliveries back then, and the hotel was my first stop. If I'd hung around for a tour, then all the other customers would have been kept waiting.'

Ed looked at her in admiration. 'I'm not sure other people would have been so conscientious in the face of curiosity.'

'I'm not other people.'

'For which I am incredibly grateful.'

The dining room was full. Every table, tastefully covered with a white linen cloth, had at least two people seated at it. Positioned next to a large picture window that displayed the hotel's lawned garden, Maddie's eyes moved from Ed to the outside world; immediately meeting a complex bird-feeding station.

'That's fabulous. I don't think I've ever seen so many different types of feeders in one place.'

'I bet we'll see a few birds when we come down in the morning.' Ed surveyed the array of fat-ball holders, coconut halves, seed trays, and some mealworm and peanut dispensers.

'I hope we get this table for breakfast.' Maddie peered harder at the array. 'What's in that feeder do you think? The one nearest the tree?'

'Grasshoppers.' A shadow cast over the table, making Maddie and Ed turn as one. 'It's great to see you, Maddie, and you must be Ed?'

'Tim!' Maddie beamed as she saw one of her oldest clients stood next to their table, menus to hand. 'I didn't expect you to be on waiter duty?'

'Only for special customers. I'm so glad you are finally getting the chance to sample your own goods.'

'That's one of the reasons I chose this place.' Ed got to his feet and shook Tim's hand. 'It's high time Maddie saw the positive effect that her hard work at The Potting Shed has beyond its walls – well, tunnels.'

Maddie opened her mouth to respond, but Tim got in first. 'Good for you, young man. Maddie here, and her father before her, bless him, have been a solid and reliable source of good veg – and summer fruits in season – for years.'

A light blush came to Maddie's face as a couple of the other diners glanced in their direction. 'That's very nice of you, Tim, but don't underestimate how important it is for us to have clients as reliable as yourself.'

The hotelier passed over the menus. 'You are kind to say so. Now then, I can recommend everything, but if you want to enjoy your own produce, then the lamb shank and roast vegetables, the beef wellington and ragu mix, or the spinach quiche with Hasselback potatoes and Mediterranean salad, would be the best bets.'

'Got to be the lamb shank for me.' Ed passed his menu back to Tim.

'I'll give the beef a whirl.' Maddie lifted her wine glass in a silent toast to her client. 'But only if you tell me which birds you attract by having grasshoppers in your garden?'

'Treecreepers and woodpeckers.'

'Wow. I tend to get robins and blackbirds, and not much else, although I can't say I feed them as such. They just grab the toast crumbs when I'm passing.'

Ed watched as the feeders outside swayed in the breeze. 'You could have a set-up like that in the new garden.'

'I bet the kids would love it.'

'*I'd* love it!' Ed grinned.

'Me too, actually.' Maddie looked up at Tim's puzzled face. 'We're building a new garden at the back of the nursery – all part of our plan to become more of a garden centre than a nursery over time.'

'What a fabulous idea.' Tim gestured to the window. 'I'll make sure you have this table at breakfast. The feeders will be alive with birds from six in the morning.'

'Thank you.' Maddie smiled.

As Tim headed into the kitchen, Ed reached a hand across the table, cupping Maddie's palm in his. 'I can just imagine some bird feeders set up at your place. What do you think, set a little back from the fence, maybe near the wood?'

'Wasn't it you who said we weren't going to talk shop tonight?'

'So, it was. I rather love the nursey though.'

Maddie found herself remembering what Jake had said about Ed preferring being at the nursery to the office. 'I'm very glad you do. It's part of the package when you date me.'

'A gorgeous package all round.'

Although he sounded sincere, a tremor of unease hit Maddie as her boyfriend dropped his gaze as he was talking.

'Are you alright, Ed? You said you wanted my opinion about something.'

Keeping hold of her hand, Ed said, 'We both love The Potting Shed, that's clear...' His words trailed off as he tried to work out how to phrase what he was about to say.

'Why do I suspect the next word in your sentence would have been a "but" if you hadn't stopped talking?'

'I'm not sure how to say it – and in truth, I don't know what to do. The only thing I do know is that I don't want to lose you, but...'

Maddie's stomach clenched. 'Another but?'

Ed sat up straighter. 'Perhaps I'll just say it.'

'Please, Ed, you're freaking me out.'

Placing his other hand on top of the one he was already cupping, as if he was making sure he could keep hold of Maddie, should she have an urge to flee when he'd spoken, Ed blurted out, 'I've been offered a senior partnership post at another solicitors – in Bristol.'

36

'Bristol!'

'You made that sound like Australia.'

'But…'

'It's a good promotion, Maddie.'

Knowing she was being selfish but was only reacting in that way as she didn't like the idea of him living so far away, Maddie leant across the table and gave him a kiss. 'It is. Well done, Ed. You deserve it; you work so hard.'

'Thanks. I wasn't expecting the offer.'

'That wasn't why you went to Bristol, then? It wasn't an arranged interview?' A sense of wariness swept over Maddie as let-downs from former boyfriends assailed her.

'Not at all. The company I went to see, they are dealing with a complex conveyance, which I'm helping with this end – I can't say much obviously, and it's all rather dull anyway – but the owners of the property being sold live in Exeter and the buyers, and the property, are in Bristol.'

'And you hit it off with the boss of this firm at a time when they happen to have a vacancy?'

'That about sums it up.' Ed freed one hand and took a drink from his glass of Merlot. 'Obviously, proper interviews have to be held.'

'So, you don't have the job yet, then?'

'No.' He placed his wine glass back on the table. 'I'm not going to take it if you don't want me to.'

'Oh, Ed!' Maddie cried. 'You can't put that on me! You are so good at what you do. I'm not going to stop you following your career path. Especially not after you've helped so much with mine. If it wasn't for you then I'd have lost The Potting Shed.'

'But I don't want to stop seeing you.' Ed lowered his voice, his tone earnest as he held her gaze. 'It would mean no more nipping over on the occasional evening or helping out with the nursery early in the morning before heading to work on the nights I stay over. In fact, there'd be far less staying over altogether.'

A sinking feeling rushed over Maddie. 'No more weekday cuddles.'

'Not many, no.' Ed lowered his gaze. 'I'm not sure I can do this… It's just, if I *do* take the job then—'

Suddenly afraid of what he might say, Maddie interrupted. 'How about Ronald? Wouldn't you take over from him in time – if you stay. Become senior partner when he retires?'

'There are no guarantees, but that is the usual way.'

'Isn't there someone in Bristol who is expecting to step into the senior partner shoes ahead of you?'

'The junior partner, a nice woman called Fran, who I met yesterday, has decided to give up the law. Going to retrain as a teacher.'

'I see.'

'Maddie. The thing is, if I take—' Ed found his sentence cut short as Tim reappeared, two plates of piping-hot food held out before him.

Glad of the interruption, Maddie inhaled the combination of delicious odours. 'This looks incredible.'

'Thank you, I'll tell the chef.' Tim placed their meals carefully onto the table. 'Enjoy the fruits of your labours, Maddie!'

I would like to know that you are okay, even if you don't say anything else, let me know you are alive. I'm not texting ever again if I don't hear back from you.

Sara sent the message, placed her phone on the table, pushed her shoulders back, flicked on her laptop and picked a mug of tea.

'That's the last text you are sending Jo. Employ some pride, woman. If he wants to talk, he'll be in touch. Time to stop being the one who does all the running. It's up to him now.'

Despite her determination, Sara found herself thinking of Jo as she read through the Airbnb website, to see what would be involved if she decided to add her property to their lists.

'I'm just investigating the possibility,' she told herself as she took a sip of her drink. 'I might not do it.'

It would be nice to have people around though. Sara could hear, running through her head, Jo's list of suggestions of how to stop the house feeling so empty. 'Or I could go to university.'

But who would care for this place?

'I could do a part-time degree from here and run an Airbnb.'

Could you manage this place at the same time?

'I could hire a manager.' The words that came out of her mouth took Sara by surprise. While money wasn't a problem thanks to the legacy left to her by her grandparents, she had never taken it for granted. Her father had always worked on the principle that anything could go wrong at any moment, and if the roof blew off, having the savings to replace it would be essential. *How would Dad feel about me employing someone to make the decisions about Hawthorn Park? Or maybe I should make the park work harder for its keep? I could open it all year round, rather than only for a few weekends.*

Or I could sell up.

'NO.' Sara shouted the thought away. 'No, I belong here. This is my family's home.'

But you have no family.

Reminding herself that she wasn't yet twenty-two, and there was plenty of time to have a family of her own, Sara took another swig of hot chocolate. 'I could take Maddie up on her offer. Work for her part-time while I'm sorting myself out.'

Wondering what Jo would say if he did appear at work again and found her pottering around the polytunnels, Sara returned to the Airbnb information. She had only read three sentences, when her phone buzzed.

Telling herself it wouldn't be Jo, but a circular from her phone provider or an advert from Amazon, Sara waited a full five minutes before she picked it up.

I'm sorry. Tomorrow, Wellington Monument, 10am. I'll
understand if you don't come. Goodnight, Sara. Jo

Ed laid down his knife and fork. While the food had been
excellent, the easy atmosphere that had existed across
the dinner table prior to the mention of Bristol had not
reasserted itself. 'That was truly delicious.'

'It was.' Maddie swallowed her last mouthful of beef.
'I must remember to tell Jake tomorrow how good his
potatoes taste in a restaurant situation.'

'It's his last day on Sunday. What will you do once he's
gone?'

'Miss him.' She gave a rueful smile. 'I'm so proud of him,
though. Dad would be too. The Jake who first came to us
was so lost. A lifetime of belittlement... This will be the
making of him.'

'I agree.' Ed poured some more wine into their glasses.
'But what about you? What will you do with no staff?'

'I'll have to advertise, although I did offer a part-time job
to Sara, if she wanted it.'

'To Sara?' Ed sat up straight. 'When was this?'

'Sorry, I totally forget to tell you. She came to the nursery.
We got on well and she has green fingers, so I offered her
a job, just while she was working out what to do with
her life.'

'That's an excellent idea. Did she come looking for Jo?'

'More hoping we'd heard from him.

'Well, if she hasn't had word from him, I can't see why we

would have.' Ed paused. 'I won't go to Bristol if you don't want me to.'

Maddie sighed. 'I don't want to be responsible for you not doing what you love, so you have to do the interview at the very least.'

'Well, I—'

'How about we don't talk about your work either?' Pushing her chair back, Maddie abruptly stood up and held out her hand. 'Let's go and forget about everything for a while.'

'Good morning.' Tim held a jug of coffee in one hand and a teapot in the other. 'I trust you slept well.'

'Best night for ages.' Maddie gestured to the silver pot. 'Coffee, please. And thanks, Tim.'

'Thanks?'

'For reserving this table for us. I can see what you mean about the birds.'

Tim followed his guests' gaze out of the window in time to see a robin join some coal tits and a blackbird jostling around a mealworm container. 'I never get tired of seeing them.'

Maddie agreed, 'It is rather wonderful.'

'Talking of wonderful.' Tim put down the pots and pulled a rolled-up newspaper from his back pocket. 'Seems like you have a hell of a scoop at the nursery.'

Ed and Maddie exchanged glances as a picture of Davina Ditz beamed up at them from page two of the *Western Morning News*.

'But I haven't had the chance to talk to the press yet.'

'Perhaps the paper called Ditzy's agent after hearing she was going to BIG. It's a great piece. Everyone loves Ditzy!' Tim smiled. 'Full English each?'

Agreeing to the assumed breakfast order, Maddie said, 'I guess a random journalist could have arranged the interview with Ditzy – or even BIG?'

'Maybe.' Ed picked up the paper. 'Shall I read it out?'

'Go on then – although I'm not sure I want to hear.'

'It'll be fine.' Ed folded back the page. '"Renowned celebrity gardener, Davina Ditz, known as Ditzy, is coming to Devon this May. She will be visiting the locally popular family-run nursery, The Potting Shed, on the 1st of May. While there she will be presiding over a *Gardeners' Question Time*-style panel with a difference, when..."'

'With a difference?' Alarm stirred in Maddie's chest.

'Hang on.' Ed pushed her coffee mug closer to her. 'Have a caffeine shot while you listen.'

Doing what she was told, Maddie kept her eyes on the photograph of her father's favourite gardener.

'So, "*Gardeners' Question Time*-style panel with a difference, when she will partake of a picnic in her honour in the nursery's new bluebell garden".' Ed took Maddie's hand. '"Ditzy is thrilled at the prospect of meeting the nursery's Little Acorns Gardening Club – a new generation of future gardeners. She commented that, 'The Potting Shed's attitude to the art of horticulture and family-centred gardening is one that larger concerns would do well to adopt'."'

'She said that?' Maddie's mouth dropped open. 'Who told her about the Little Acorns?'

'Must have been Dan.'

'I haven't told him about them yet.'

'Doesn't mean that Ivan or Elspeth haven't. They're all old friends.' Ed lifted the paper a little higher. 'It goes on to say, "Talking of larger concerns, Davina will also be appearing at the newly opened BIG garden centre across the Somerset border on the 2nd of May, where she will be signing copies of her autobiography, *Being Ditzy*."'

As Ed lowered the paper, Maddie saw Tim approach with two plates of breakfast. Tempting scents of bacon, sausage and fried egg assailed her nostrils, but she wasn't sure she'd be able to eat a single bite.

Only when Tim had gone again did she dare ask, 'Was that really all she said about her gig at BIG?'

'Yep.'

'And that dig about larger garden centres learning from us – what are BIG are going to make of that?!'

37

'I swear, if you apologise to me one more time, I'm going to pull this car over, drop you in the nearest lay-by, and go back to Exeter.'

Maddie looked at Ed's annoyed expression in alarm. 'It's only... I feel awful that, after all your efforts, you didn't even get to eat your breakfast.'

'I know, but I am not cross – well, I am now – but only because you keep going on about it. One apology is plenty, not that there was any need to apologise. It was my idea to cut and run.'

'But only because you are so kind. I...'

Ed gripped the steering wheel harder. 'Why can't you accept I'm okay with us not getting a proper breakfast, or that I don't mind talking about The Potting Shed whenever you need to? Look, I've noticed this happen before and not said anything – but if we're going to be together you've got to stop turning these situations into some sort of martyr-like guilt trip whenever work interrupts our time together...' Ed's words trailed off as he slowed to overtake a tractor.

Almost saying sorry again, Maddie gripped the newspaper in her hands. She couldn't deny that she'd probably been testing Ed's patience for the last hour, as a renewed sense that she was taking him for granted had overtaken her. 'If you want to go home, I'll totally understand, but if you could face it, I'd really, really appreciate you being with me today.'

'That's better.' Ed patience sounded less strained. 'As long as you promise not to apologise. If you hadn't noticed, you haven't done anything wrong.'

'Suppose not.' She waved the paper. 'First thing is to call Ivan, see if he is up for a bit of till training. I'm going to need all hands on deck.'

'I can do that if you like.'

'That would be great, thanks.' Maddie threw the newspaper onto the back seat.

They lapsed into silence for a while before Maddie placed her hand on Ed's leg. 'Thank you for taking me to the Blackdown. I loved it.'

'Me too.' Ed threw her a smile. 'I'm sorry I threw Bristol at you.'

'Hey, I thought we weren't allowed to apologise.'

'We are – but not incessantly!' Ed crunched the gearstick as he changed from fourth to third. 'I'm sorry I got cross. I'm feeling a bit guilty myself. We never did have a proper talk about me maybe taking the job.'

'I think you should do the interview.'

'And make a decision after that?'

'Exactly.' Maddie ignored the clenching in her stomach at the prospect of Ed living further away. 'When is the interview anyway?'

'May sometime.'

'That's good. Gives you time to research the company.'

'And it means I can help you prep for the visit from

Davina.' Ed paused. 'So, what will you call the event? You can't use *Gardeners' Question Time* as that title belongs to the BBC – wouldn't surprise me if they'd trademarked the name, in fact.'

'Good point.' Maddie sucked in her bottom lip as she thought. 'Q&A with Davina Ditz?'

'Bit dull. How about Ditzy's Garden Clinic at The Potting Shed?'

'Better.' Maddie conceded. 'A bit medical-sounding though. What about Ditzy's Garden Answers?'

'Oh, I like that.' Ed slowed the car to let a motorbike whizz past. 'Or Ditzy's Garden Answers at The Potting Shed.'

'Better still.' Maddie grinned.

'Or a combination of all of those ideas. Ditzy's Way: Answers to your garden queries at The Potting Shed.'

'Nice, but too long. We should include the nursery's name, so people don't confuse it with her gig at BIG.' Maddie stared through the passenger window across the Devon countryside. 'I know! Ask Ditzy at The Potting Shed?'

'Perfect! Simple and to the point.'

'Thanks.' Maddie glanced back at the newspaper. 'I hadn't planned on the children from the Little Acorns being at the event.'

'Looks like they'll have to be there though – or be invited at least.'

'Won't they be bored stiff?' Maddie tried to visualise Noel staying still for more than ten minutes and completely failed. 'I've no idea what they could do when Davina is with us.'

'Couldn't they help?' Ed pulled up at a crossroads that

led to the A38. 'You know, do little jobs around the place? Sweeping up, helping people find their seats, making sure everyone was okay.'

'They're all under ten!'

'And friendly and keen, and we'd be there too. And Jem – I'm assuming Jem.'

'Absolutely. She'll be home for the May Bank Holiday.' Maddie lifted her phone, ready to text her sister. 'Jem's emailed me a few times, asking if we've heard from Jo.'

'She's a good kid.'

'The best.' Maddie waved her phone in front of her. 'She sent the recipes for her "Grow a Smoothie" idea too. I just need to get some designs sorted for recipe cards and find a good printer.'

'Would Petra do it? The designing at least.'

'I doubt she has time, but I could ask.' Maddie sighed. 'She was only with us a while, but I miss her being around.'

'Perhaps Sara will join the team. When did you tell her to let you know by?'

'I didn't. I just said she should think about it. That the offer was there if she wanted a job. Not that she'd join us on May Day – Hawthorn Park is open then.'

Indicating left, Ed eased into the opening to The Potting Shed's car park. 'Can you do the gate?'

Hopping out of the car, Maddie unlocked the padlock on the gate, pushing it open so Ed could drive in.

I wonder if Jo will turn up at Hawthorn Park on the 1st.

Sara could see the orange camper van nestled under a group of trees as she drew into the National Trust car park. The

Wellington Monument, hidden from the car park by an avenue of trees, stood proudly in the distance, its 175-foot structure towering across the Blackdown Hills, doffing its cap to the duke whose name it bore.

Parking a little way from where Jo had pulled up, Sara stayed in her seat. Unhooking her phone from the cradle in which it sat when she used it as a satnav, Sara muttered, 'At least he's turned up.'

Jo's stomach had clenched into anxious knots as he'd watched Sara's car pull up. He wasn't sure what he was going to say, but her message last night had frightened him into action. The idea that she had got to the point of giving him an ultimatum had brought him up short.

'I can't lose her too.' A sense of his own selfishness swept over Jo as he watched Sara's car.

Perhaps she isn't getting out? Perhaps she only came to see if I'd be here, but has no intention of talking to me? Perhaps... Jo stopped and gave himself a shake. 'Get a grip! This is Sara – she's probably just programming her phone for the directions home again.'

It hadn't been that long since she'd seen him, yet Sara was sure Jo looked older than he had – and anxious. *You're being fanciful, stop it.*

Sara climbed out of her car as he got closer.

★

She looks good. That's a forced smile though. Jo blew out a long-held breath. *Just relax. You are going for a walk with your friend, that's it. Say whatever you'd normally say.*

'Satnav got you here then?'

'Clearly.'

Stupid opening line. Jo cursed himself as he waved a hand towards the car park ticket machine. 'You need to pay if you aren't a member.'

'I've been in the National Trust all my life.' Sara waved her membership card at him. 'I'll just go and scan this for my free ticket. You done yours?'

'Yep.' Jo rubbed clammy palms down his faded jeans. 'I got here early.'

Waiting for her to fetch her ticket, Jo flexed his fingers into fists, before breathing out as he unclenched them. *This is already getting ridiculous. Do something about it.*

'Got it.' Sara waved the small square piece of white paper ahead of her.

'Good.' Jo tugged his grey beanie lower over his ears. 'How about we stop being all awkward with each other, remember we're good friends and just enjoy a walk?'

'Did you know this is the tallest three-sided obelisk in the world?'

'I can't say I did.' Sara stared up at the towering structure as they reached the foot of the monument. 'I wonder what made them build that rather than just a statue of the duke.'

'It almost was a statute.' Jo followed Sara's gaze to the top of the pinnacle, making himself a little dizzy in the process. 'The idea of having something commemorating the victory at Waterloo was first mooted in 1815. Then, in 1817 they held a competition to design a monument. Chap called Thomas Lee Junior won and designed a pillar with a cast-iron statute of the Duke of Wellington on the top. It would have been massive – the final project was supposed to be 140 feet high.'

Sara tried to imagine the imposing sight. 'Why it is a giant obelisk instead then?'

'Ran out of money. You can just imagine how much such an undertaking would have cost. Work ceased when it was only forty-five feet tall. In fact, the statute itself was never commissioned in the end.'

'So, they just made the column higher?'

'Eventually. It stayed as it was until 1850 when, after two lightning strikes it was declared dangerous and a repair plan was put into operation. It wasn't until 1892 that repairs were finally sorted, and it was changed into what we see today.'

Sara fell into step next to Jo as they circumnavigated the path around the base of the column. 'How come you knew all that?'

'Tempted as I am to appear as an all-knowing oracle, I read it off a sign by the entrance.'

Sara gave his arm a friendly punch. 'And there I was being impressed by your local knowledge.'

'I was getting nervous waiting for you, so I had a wander. Read the information boards a few times to keep my mind from driving itself mad.'

'Idiot.'

Jo shrugged. 'I wasn't sure you'd come.'

Sara took a deep breath. 'I know I've asked before, but before we do this, I need to ask again. An honest answer, please. Did you run to Hawthorn Park after seeing Hazel because you wanted to see me, or because you knew she'd never find you there?'

Jo was surprised to find the truth tripped easily from his lips. 'I wanted to feel safe. To be safe. You're my safety. Not Hawthorn Park – you.'

Sara's mouth opened and closed for a few minutes, before – resisting the temptation to hug him, she said, 'How about we skip the bit where I tell you off for worrying me stupid, and I share my news? After that you can tell me where you've been and why you went quiet.'

'O... kay...'

'Jo, I'm serious. I have information you need to know, but I'm not sharing it if you don't come clean about where you've been hiding and what exactly happened between you and Hazel Cooper.'

Jo's heart gave a lurch as he saw the determined expression on Sara's face. 'Tell me. Then I'll tell you where I went and why I disappeared.'

'Promise me you'll be honest about everything.'

'Promise.'

'So, my news first.' Starting to walk again, Sara headed into the woods that flanked the right side of the monument. 'The short version is that Hazel has admitted she lied, and that you did not bully her at work. Henry has decided not to keep her on after her probation period. He has also banned her from working at The Potting Shed.'

Jo stopped dead. His voice was hushed, as if fearing that, should he speak too loudly, what he'd just heard would not be true. 'She admitted lying?'

'She did. But I need to know, Jo, why, when she accused you of being a bully, didn't you deny it or defend yourself?'

'Because – because she was telling the truth.'

38

'Can I buy some tickets please?'

'Tickets?' Sabi glanced from the eager customer, across the shop at Maddie, who was busy tending the houseplants, and back again.

'For your *Gardeners' Question Time* with Ditzy of course.'

'We're calling it Ask Ditzy at The Potting Shed.' Sabi gave the gentleman her best smile. 'You saw the article in the paper?'

'And very good it was too.' He stood up straighter, his chest puffed out as he spoke with almost paternal pride. 'We can rely on Ditzy to support local businesses over the corporate machine.'

'Indeed, we can.' Sabi pulled the notepad they kept by the till closer. 'For environmental reasons, we are keeping a list of bookings rather than issuing paper tickets. If you give me your name, phone number, the number of seats you'd like, and an email address, then we'll send you the details once we have finalised timings with Ditzy.'

'Perfect.' He clapped his hands with delight. 'Can't wait. It's Marcus Talbot and I'd like two tickets please. Do we need to bring anything?'

Maddie crossed the room, in time to say. 'A picnic, if you want one – and a gardening question if you have one, please.'

'Fabulous! Will do. One question per guest?'

'That's right.'

'So, how much do I owe you?'

Sabi, already impressed by how much they had winged it, having not had a chance to talk about the newspaper article yet, was about to pluck a figure out of the air, when Maddie took a deep breath and, hoping she wasn't about to make the man run away, said, 'Twenty-five pounds per person.'

'Done.'

As Marcus Talbot presented his bank card to Sabi without batting an eyelid, Maddie saw Dan come through the door.

'Dan! You said you were going to phone.'

'Always easier to talk in person.'

Gesturing to the door, Maddie led the way towards the new greenhouse.

'How much are you charging for tickets?'

'Twenty-five pounds each.'

'Good girl. I was afraid you'd undercharge and ask a tenner or something. I suspect if you'd said forty pounds a ticket people would still have come.' Habit made Dan pick off a withered head from the nearest herb as he said, 'People won't blink at handing over twenty-five quid to see Ditzy.'

'For which I'm very grateful.' Maddie paused. 'But, Dan, that article in the paper. What were you thinking?'

'Nothing to do with me, that was all Ditzy.'

'But that stuff about Little Acorns…'

'I told her you had a Facebook page. Ditzy always does her homework. I bet she looked you up. That's how I found about the kids' group – brilliant idea that.'

Maddie stared at her old boss for a moment, before

leaping forward and hugging him. 'I'm so grateful to you for sending her our way.'

'My pleasure.'

A new idea came to Maddie. 'Do you think that, if we asked her, Ditzy would agree to saying that she took part in our inaugural event as a garden centre, or is it too soon to say that when the conversion of the house is not quite finished?'

'I think that's a great idea, especially if you make something of the conversion. You know, tell people about it. Shout loud and proud that you are developing here – that you are following through your father's dream. The locals loved Tony.'

'You're right.' Maddie peered through the glass walls as a few customers meandered past. 'We'd better talk to Sabi and Ed – he's giving the new gate that links our land and Dennis's farm a coat of preservative. It's one of hundreds of jobs that's long overdue. If we are going to have a celebrity in our new and not-at-all-ready garden – then at least we can stop it looking tatty.'

'It's true?' Winded, Sara headed to the nearest bench.

'I never bullied Hazel, or anyone else, when I worked for the council.'

Sara's stomach muscles clenched as Jo spoke.

'Hazel misunderstood things. I didn't mislead her on purpose – but somehow, I managed to mislead her anyway.'

Knowing it was too late to back out of discovering a truth she was no longer sure she wanted to hear, Sara muttered, 'You're not making a lot of sense, Jo.'

'No. Sorry.' Yanking his beanie from his head, Jo played it through his fingers. 'Hazel didn't recognise me when she came to work at the council, you see. I recognised her though – and as soon as I saw her, I was afraid.'

'Afraid of what?'

'That she would remember me – from before.'

Sara had a sense of standing on shifting sands. 'Are you telling me that you knew Hazel *prior* to working at the council?'

'School.'

'Oh.'

'Yes. I wasn't... I wasn't always the nicest back then.'

'You weren't *you* back then.'

'That's no excuse. There's never an excuse to bully another human being. I can't tell you how ashamed...'

As Jo drifted into silence, Sara tried to digest what she was hearing. 'You are physically so changed? Facially, I mean – enough not to be instantly recognisable to someone from your past?'

'Very. I went the whole nine yards – as the surgeon I saw in the US kept telling me. Neck, chin, nose – all had tweaks.'

'Oh.' After a short silence Sara ventured, 'Hazel and you – I can't imagine you being natural friends.'

'We weren't – not really.' Jo paused, trying to work out how to explain. 'I owed her – although she didn't realise that. She was new to the council offices. Shy even – at the start anyway. By taking her under my wing, I saw a way to make my past behaviour up to her.' He exhaled softly. 'We enjoyed helping clients get the plans for their homes approved. We worked well together.'

'And things developed from there?'

'Only in shared lunches during our dinner break and such. Every so often, we'd eat together after work too – if it had been a long day and we'd had a tricky project to work on.'

Sara spoke carefully. 'And then you asked her out?'

'No.' Jo rubbed his head in his hands. 'I never intended it to be anything more than friendship. It began as me being nice to someone I owed... Maybe, if I'd been more comfortable in my own shoes as a child, we'd have been friends back then – but I wasn't. I am partly responsible for making her into the Hazel Cooper she has become – a brittle woman who wears a protective layer around her, so she doesn't get hurt.'

'And while you were at the council?'

'Every day I thought she'd rumble who I'd been before.'

'She knows now though?'

'Yes.' Jo swallowed. 'I didn't defend myself to Henry because I deserve her hate.'

'You don't.' Pausing for a moment, Sara asked, 'How did she work it out?'

'At work it was all first names – you know, in an effort to be customer-friendly, informal and approachable. She'd never seen my surname written down and no one used it – until one day there were some forms to fill in. We did them together – not something that often occurred as we had desks at different ends of our office, but...'

'Ahhh... she saw you write down Dunn – and the penny dropped.'

'Uh-huh.'

'You say you never asked her out on a date, so, did she ask you?'

'It was more that she took it for granted that we were going out already. I was merrily having a nice time with someone I'd started to consider a friend – however unexpected that friendship was – totally unaware that she was counting every meeting outside of work hours as a date and was making long-term plans for us.'

'Oh.'

Jo got up. 'Do you mind if we walk while we talk now?'

'Okay.'

Glad to be able to stride out through his regrets, Jo explained, 'With hindsight, it started to fall apart after I refused her offer of a visit to meet her parents. That was the moment when the penny dropped with me. She thought we were in a relationship. I immediately tried to backtrack – in the kindest way possible. Then, the next day she discovered my surname.'

'What did you say to her?'

'I made the mistake of being honest about why it was never going to happen. Told her that I regretted the past and that I saw her as a good friend who I enjoyed spending time with, but no more than that. We'd never so much as kissed or held hands. We just got on. I honestly didn't see what she saw in me partner wise.'

Sadness swelled in Sara as she recognised how she'd made the same mistakes with Jo as Hazel had. Made the same assumptions.

Jo began to walk faster. 'I'll never forget the way she looked at me – staring at my face as if unlocking a puzzle that had been bothering her for some time.'

'She recognised you as her school bully.'

'She did.'

'Making your life hell at the council offices afterwards was her revenge?'

'Yep.' Jo was almost jogging now, and Sara had to run to keep up with him. His breath shortened as his explanation came out in a rush of words: 'But you can't go on like that for long. In her defence, not once did she spread rumours about my sexuality or my gender – perhaps because she has some principles, perhaps because she felt embarrassed about not having worked that out herself. Either way, I was grateful for that. I don't blame her for being so angry – not for a second. From then on though, when mistakes were made at work, she always put them down to me. Then she started to hint that I wasn't always honest. I might have deserved it to some extent, but soon I'd had enough. My working atmosphere had become one of suspicion. In the end I quit. Better for me – and better for her.'

'I'm sorry, Jo.' Sara slipped her arm through his, pulling at it to slow their pace.

Swallowing against his suddenly dry throat, Jo allowed himself to be temporarily comforted by the closeness of his friend. 'A few years have passed since I last saw her, but she clearly hasn't forgotten, or forgiven – and I can't say I blame her.'

'Even if that was the case, that doesn't make her behaviour alright, Jo.' Sara looked up at the sway of the trees. 'I had wondered if someone else had hurt her, before you. And if your rejection was the breaking point for her.'

'They did – me. *I* hurt her in my earlier incarnation,' Jo mumbled as they trudged through a particularly muddy stretch of woodland. 'When I decided to leave the council, I vowed to myself that I'd adopt a life without personal complications.'

'Which is why you disappeared when I declared more than an interest in you.' Sara's voice faltered as she saw Jo's sad smile. 'But then Hazel came to The Potting Shed.'

'Yes.'

'No wonder you wanted to make sure I understood exactly where you and I stood relationship wise when you came back to Hawthorn Park.'

Jo reached out a hand to Sara, experiencing a swell of relief when she took it. 'I didn't want to hurt you in the same way. I knew you wouldn't be cruel in revenge though. You are very different to Hazel.'

'Thank you.'

Sara negotiated a few more paces through a muddy path, before making it to drier ground and scraping the sludge from her boots. Following suit, Jo asked, 'Is this the bit where I tell you where I've been while AWOL?'

'Almost.' Sara headed off beneath the canopy of oak trees that bordered the pathway leading back to the car park. 'First I should tell you that Maddie has offered me a job at The Potting Shed.'

'She has?' Jo was stunned.

'You told me I would like Maddie and her sister, and so I went to see them. It's a bit awkward with Sabi. I haven't a clue how to treat her, considering what her actions meant for Dad, but Maddie and I hit it off straight away.'

'That's good.' Jo slowed his pace. 'Are they alright?'

'You mean, are they missing you around the place?'

'I suppose so.'

'They are. Very much. The sooner you get your arse back there the better.'

39

'A caravan?'

'A static.' Jo rubbed the toe of his boot against the back of his leg, smearing mud up his trousers in the process.

'Why do you say that like it's a bad thing?'

'Says the woman who lives in a stately home.'

'Only a small one.' Sara was surprised at her friend's resentful tone. 'And since when has how big or small someone's home is made a difference to you?'

'Sorry.' Jo gave her a sheepish glance. 'It doesn't.'

'So, why are you acting as if you're ashamed of living in a caravan?'

Aiming for a bench along the pathway back to their cars, Jo sat down, patting the seat next to him. 'I had a nice house before I went to the States.'

Sara could see a dog walker in the distance, waiting patiently while their Sheltie explored a tree stump. 'So, why don't you live there now?'

'Had to sell up. It was the only way I could afford... I couldn't keep going as who I was.'

'The house sale paid for your operation?'

'Yep. And travel, accommodation during recovery, and so on. More or less cleared me out.' Jo spoke matter-offactly. 'I could have used what I had left to rent a bigger place, but I noticed the static for sale and went for it. It was in a bad way – really run-down – so was at a bargain price. It's always going to be just me, and as it was becoming more likely that I'd need money to help Mum get into a good care home, I thought why not? I was perfectly capable of doing it up, and I don't need much space to live in. It has a decent bedroom, a tiny spare bedroom – which I use as my wardrobe – a lounge-diner-kitchen and a shower room.'

'You never told me much about it – the operation.'

'No need, is there?'

'No. No, I suppose not.' Sara abruptly stood back up. 'I'd like to see your caravan sometime. Where is it?'

'Tiverton.' Jo lifted his hands and showed them to Sara. 'These are the giveaway. Sometimes people comment when I'm serving the coffee. "Haven't you got lovely little hands" or "What beautifully slender fingers."'

'Does it bother you?'

'Depends how it's said.'

'Makes sense.' Sara reached out, gave Jo's nearest hand a quick squeeze. 'Shall we go then?'

'Go?'

'To The Potting Shed. It's Saturday. You're supposed to be there serving coffee. Half a day would be better than not at all.'

Jo stared at his feet. 'I don't think so.'

'What?' Sara couldn't believe it. 'They want you back. They *need* you. I was so sure you'd just go back…'

'But—'

'Jo! People are arriving at The Potting Shed, seeing you

aren't there and leaving again without even looking round. As soon as you explain the reason—'

'That I was a bully?' Jo shouted in frustration, before quickly lowering his tone. 'How do I explain that I failed in my clumsy attempts to make it up to my victim and that she is still hurting after all these years?' Jo tugged his beanie back onto his head. 'I can't see them wanting to take me back after hearing that – because that is the truth, whether I like it or not. If I come back, it'll only be a matter of time before Hazel makes sure someone overhears her complaints about me. And I can't argue – I can't claim innocence. Bullying lasts forever.'

'But Hazel isn't there anymore. I told you, Henry—'

'Told her not to work there. He didn't ban her from The Potting Shed altogether – nor should he. It's a free country ... ish.'

'But, Jo—'

'Come on.' Interrupting with a helpless shrug of his shoulders, Jo gestured to their vehicles. 'I've got to hit the Internet to find other places to sell coffee from, and I'm sure you have work to do too.'

Ed pressed his boot hard onto the gravel that he'd used to fill in one of the many potholes that littered the gap between the far polytunnel and Dennis's field. The ground gave way slightly, so he dug another shovel full of gravel from the nearby wheelbarrow and layered it into the space.

The sound of someone moving one of the six chairs he'd used to block the area from the public, made him swing around. 'Dan, how you doing?'

'On good form, young man, thanks.' He gestured to the wheelbarrow. 'No rest for you on your weekend off then?'

'Nope.' Ed grinned. 'To be honest, I rather enjoy some physical labour for a change. More doing than thinking, if you see what I mean.'

Dan chuckled. 'I never did understand how you office types could stand being stuck inside all day.'

'It's not all it's cracked up to be – unless it's pouring with rain or freezing cold.'

'Daft bugger, rain doesn't make us shrink, you know, and you can always buy thermals!'

'True.' Ed chuckled as he pressed the gravel more firmly into the hole. 'Amazing how much one small pothole can eat up.'

Dan waved a hand before him. 'How long has it taken you to do the three you've filled so far?'

'All day, nearly.' Ed wiped the back of his hand over his forehead. 'But if we're going to be ready for Ditzy…'

'Umm…' Dan walked over to the new gate that linked the wood and The Potting Shed. 'This looks good. You did a great job of hanging it.'

'Can't take credit for that. Jake's your man there. I just painted it.' Ed smiled. 'Maddie and I hope to take a trip through it later. We've been so busy we haven't explored the wood yet.'

'Best check it's safe for the customers.'

'Exactly. Although, I'm not sure what we can do if it isn't.'

'Just put up a sign saying walkers are responsible for their own safety, and so on.'

'I think I'll suggest we do that anyway.' Ed, finally satisfied that the latest hole was plugged, moved the barrow on to the next one. 'How can I help, anyway, Dan?'

'Other way around.' Dan motioned to the potholes. 'Got another shovel?'

'You sure?'

'Of course. There's muscles in this old frame, don't you know.'

Maddie closed the car park's gate with a sense of relief. Every part of her ached with fatigue while everything she still needed to do somersaulted around her brain in ever-decreasing circles. Rubbing her hands down her jeans, she forced her feet towards the bluebell garden.

'Dan! I thought you'd gone home.' Maddie felt a wave of happiness sweep over her as she saw her boyfriend in happy conversation with her mentor.

'Hey, Maddie.' Dan tilted his head towards the stretch of ground between them. 'Perfect timing. The last shovelful of gravel has just found its new home.'

'You've finished it!'

'The filling up anyway. Thanks to Dan helping out.' Ed laid down his shovel and flexed his stiff arms. 'We still need to turf over the top.'

'It's coming on Monday.' Some of the tension in Maddie's shoulders slipped away. 'I'll get it rolled out once I have Ivan in place.'

'On your own?' Ed frowned.

'I'm perfectly capable.'

'Indeed you are.' Dan chipped in as he heard the defensive tone in Maddie's voice. 'I think what Ed meant was, you'll have a pretty full-on day, and no Jake to help you.'

'I'll manage.'

'Splendidly, I'm sure. Well, I'll leave you to close up and get some rest.' Dan passed his shovel to Ed. 'Don't let her do too much more tonight.'

'Dan, I'm right here!'

'You are, lass, but would you listen if I told you to stop for five minutes?'

'Probably not,' Maddie admitted.

'Let Ed look after you – not because you're weak or feeble, but because he loves you and wants to help and, although you're busy now, come May 1st, it'll be insane in here.'

'Not that bad, surely?' Maddie wasn't sure if the prospect of being insanely busy thrilled or panicked her.

'Trust me. Ditzy will make a difference.'

'For one day.' Maddie bit her bottom lip. 'Sorry, I didn't mean to sound ungrateful, Dan, but Sabi and I have a deal – if this place doesn't turn itself around enough to be out of debt by the end of May, then we'll have to stop the upgrade and just be a nursery with a large shop. We've come so far; I don't want to backtrack now. I love the idea of a café and—'

'You won't have to.' Ed and Dan spoke in unison.

'Thanks for the faith, boys, but we'll see.'

Suddenly the effort of driving to Culmstock, of fitting into her sister's well-meaning but regimented evenings, was too much. Their walk along the wood's narrow but beautifully winding pathway had been magical in the evening light. The patches of leaves showing the imminent arrival of a bluebell crop that would double the blooms already in evidence, had lifted Maddie's spirits, and she didn't want to break the spell.

Ed slipped an arm around her waist. 'Come on, that's enough for today.' He checked his watch. 'And dinner will be ready at exactly seven-thirty. It's already seven.'

'I suppose so.'

Ed opened the gate and let them back onto The Potting Shed's land. 'That was not an enthusiastic response.'

'To tell you the truth, all I want to do is curl up with you in my own home with a plate of cheese on toast, before getting into my own bed.'

'Sounds nice.' Ed smiled. 'So, why don't we?'

'Because Sabi will already have cooked, and I have no idea what state my kitchen is in – nor do I have any cheese or bread.'

Ed laughed. 'As crises go, that one is easily solved. Is the plumbing working?'

'Yes, Robert messaged yesterday to say we have running water.'

'Then you go and have a shower, and I'll nip to the shop. Any wine with your cheese on toast?'

'I'd sooner have a hot chocolate.'

'Your wish is my command.'

'But what about Sabi?' Maddie gave a wistful sigh. 'She'll have gone to so much trouble with dinner and—'

'And I'd put money on her longing for a night with just Henry and Jem. I'll call her. Go and shower. Just for once, allow yourself to be cared for, and leave everything else to me.'

40

'I don't think I've ever eaten so much toast in my life.' Ed smeared a generous swipe of butter across his breakfast.

'Stick with me, and it'll become your staple diet.' Maddie picked up the pot of marmalade Ed had purchased alongside the cheese, butter, bread and milk the evening before.

'I can think of worse habits than serial toast consumption.' Ed took a bite of his breakfast. 'Although, once the kitchen is in proper working order, I'll cook for you if you like.'

'I do like, although, you don't have to. I really am perfectly happy with toast. I'm just delighted to find the kitchen in working order. Robert said it would go from being a mess to being done, with little time in between, and he was right. I can't wait to get my things back in here.' She grinned. 'Now there are a few toast crumbs dotted on the work surfaces it's definitely my space again.'

Delighted to see such a happy expression on his girlfriend's face, Ed asked, 'Feeling better after a night in your own bed?'

'Very much. Even the smell of paint doesn't matter. I'm so glad to be home.'

'That sounds as if you've decided not to go back to Sabi's?'

'Ummm… well…'

'When they start knocking walls out downstairs, you'll need to.'

'Maybe, but that isn't happening until tomorrow – maybe not until Tuesday if they need a day to ponder what to do first, so I think I'll stay here tonight.' Maddie lowered her mug to the coffee table.

A distant click announced the arrival of the Sunday newspaper through the letterbox. 'I'll fetch it.'

Ed's eyebrows raised. 'I think you're the only person I know who still has a newspaper delivered.'

'Only on a Sunday. I like the crossword.'

'Oh my God!' Maddie sat down with a thump as she held up the *Devon and Somerset Times*. 'Have you seen this?'

Ed scanned the front page, which Maddie was holding as if it was a bomb about to go off. The headline was unmissable.

Local nursery declares war on BIG chain!

'Catchy.' Taking the paper, Ed scanned the article as Maddie paced the room.

'Declares war! What is wrong with these people?' She scrubbed a hand over her forehead.

'They must be starved of normal headlines. Maybe no lawnmowers have been nicked from people's garden sheds this week.'

'Don't be flippant when I'm angry.'

Trying not to laugh, Ed grabbed Maddie's hand as she paced past him, and guided her to his lap. 'This is just fluff. Stuff to sell the paper. You haven't done anything wrong.'

'It feels like I have though. We know that Davina wanted to come here, but they make it sound as though her appearing here before going to BIG is an underhand tactic.'

'It is a sort of tactic.'

'Yes, but it wasn't dodgy or sneaky! It was the only day she was free, and it was her idea!'

'I know that, but that won't sell papers, will it.' Ed flicked to page two, where the headline story continued. 'A good old-fashioned local rivalry story is going to do their paper sales good. Let's face it, distribution of regional papers isn't what it was. They need a sensation every now and then to… Oh, here we go, listen to this, "The Potting Shed nursery is expanding fast, and will soon be able to proudly call itself a small garden centre – but from little acorns forests grow – and who can say how long it will be before Madeline and Sabrina Willand's horticultural empire will rival that of the newly planted Big In Gardens (commonly known as BIG), garden centre, which opened this Easter, only twenty miles along the M5."'

'You have *got* to be joking!'

'Nope.' Ed put the paper down. 'It's a rehash of what the other paper reported the other day, but with the addition of championing the underdog.'

Maddie peered down to see what Ed was reading.

'The paper is clearly on your side, love. "With Davina Ditz appearing at both establishments this May, it will be interesting to see which event draws the most interest, although this paper imagines both will be well attended, perhaps by an overlapping crowd. What is certain is that the *Devon and Somerset Times* will attend each occasion, talking to the visitors, and – hopefully – with the lady herself. Davina Ditz is, after all, fast becoming a national treasure."'

'A journalist is coming to our event?' Maddie went pale. 'I haven't invited them. I was going to call a few papers today to see how much it would cost for an advert for the event.'

'No need now, they are advertising the tickets already.'

'What do you mean?'

'Listen. "To obtain your ticket for these events call…" And then they give BIG's email access ticket line, followed by your shop's phone number.'

'Oh my God!!' Maddie leapt up. 'Come on!'

'Where are we going?' Ed put down the paper.

'The shop! If we've read the paper, then so have lots of other people. We could be sat here missing ticket sales.'

'But it's seven in the morning, on a Sunday, and you are in your pyjamas! Sexy though they are, I can't see them being practical gardening wear.'

Maddie picked a cushion up off the sofa, and threw it at Ed. 'Well, we'd better get dressed then!'

'Fifteen.'

'Already!' Sabi hugged her sister as they read the list of names and email addresses Maddie had written on the pad by the shop phone. 'How many tickets are we selling? I mean, how much space is there to do this Ask Ditzy thing?'

Maddie's mouth dropped open. 'Oh hell. I was so excited at selling tickets that I just kept going. The phone has barely stopped ringing. What if we can't get fifteen people in the garden?'

'I'm sure we can.' Sabi spoke bracingly, just as the phone burst into life again. 'I'll get it. You go to the new garden and see if you can picture the layout of the event. I'll join you in a minute.'

'But we can't leave the phone unmanned. It might ring again.'

'Yes, we can. And anyway, if we don't want to sell more than, say twenty tickets, we're nearly sold out already.'

'I can't believe you're leaving today.'

Maddie found Jake tending to his fruit canes as she passed the fruit polytunnel, on the way to the bluebell garden.

'Nor can I.' Jake tenderly ran a hand over the raspberry plant before him. 'I'm going to miss it here.'

'You aren't here that much these days, with college and everything, I suppose, but...'

'I know, but this is different.'

'It is.' Maddie admired the row of plants. 'But exciting different. This is what you were born to do, Jake! Arlington has got itself a fabulous new gardener.'

'An apprentice.'

'For now, but they'd be mad to ever let you go.' Suddenly finding herself choked at the thought of Jake's departure, Maddie changed the subject. 'I wanted to pick your brains. How many people do you think could sit in the bluebell garden to listen to Ditzy?'

'Three.'

'Excuse me?'

'There is just one bench. No way would you sit more than three people on it.'

'I ought to call Sara. Make sure if she is still okay about us borrowing some picnic tables.'

Sabi stood next to her sister in the bluebell garden. 'It's always smaller than I picture it in my head.'

'I know what you mean.' Maddie examined the stretch of ground. 'When I had the children gardening here it felt bigger – but then they are small, and we were all on our hands and knees, or were jumping around splashing in puddles. Once we have picnic tables all spread out, the space is going to be eaten up.'

'I sold another three tickets.'

'So, that's eighteen people.'

'Plus, the press.' Ed called out as he walked up behind them, Jake at his side. 'The *Devon and Somerset Times* just called. I assumed you were okay with me agreeing to them coming.'

'I can't see how you could have said no. I saw the paper this morning.' Sabi looked satisfied.

'But they might want to talk to us if they come here.'

'That's sort of the idea of them coming.' Sabi rolled her eyes. 'It's like Dan said, the work we are doing since Dad died – making his dream come true – it's newsworthy on a local level. And they are on our side and not BIG's – which makes a change!'

'On our side unless it goes wrong!' Maddie squeaked. 'What fun they'd have if the evening was a disaster. What if no one comes, or Ditzy is ill and can't perform, or if people get narky because there's no refreshments or—'

'Whoa there!' Ed put a hand out to his girlfriend. 'What if nothing goes wrong and it is a roaring success? You're telling people to bring a picnic when they book tickets, aren't you?'

'Yes – well, saying they can if they want to.'

Sabi nodded. 'And asking them to email their gardening question ahead of the day, so Ditzy can have a pre-event ponder?'

'Yes.'

'There you go then. So, for now, all we have to do is work out numbers, and get some tables sorted with Sara.'

'We'd need to hire a van to collect them.' Maddie chewed on the end of a pencil she was carrying.

'If Jo was here then...'

'But Jo *isn't* here, Sabi, and even if he was, we couldn't get picnic tables in his van.'

'Sorry. No, of course we couldn't.' Sabi added "hire a van" to her list of jobs. 'Do you mind calling Sara, Mads? I'm not sure I should.'

'Umm...' Remembering that she hadn't had chance to talk to her sister about her connection with the Northcott family, Maddie agreed. 'No problem. I want to see whether she's decided if she wants to work here.'

Jake looked up. 'You've filled my boots already?'

'Oh, Jake – it isn't like that! I...' Maddie paused, a surge of relief hitting her as she saw a playful gleam in his eyes. 'You swine, I felt guilty as hell then!'

'Only joking. Course you'll need to replace me.' Jake rubbed his hands together. 'And I think you can get twenty-four people in here on eight benches – that way, you'll have an average of two or four people on each one – some groups will have to share. Then, you could have the Little Acorns on rugs or chairs from the house, at the side.'

'Oh God! I'd forgotten about the children! The paper said they'd be there. I'd better email their parents today.' Maddie was regarding Jake with a new level of respect. 'When did you work all that out?'

'After I'd read the paper, you left in the shop. Had a feeling you'd be panicking about it.'

'Oh, Jake, what are we going to do without you?'

41

'What are you going to do all day then?'

Sara found Jo sitting on a fallen tree trunk, staring out across the main bulk of Hawthorn Park's woodland.

'I'm going to clean the caravan and start working out what supplies I'll need for the May bank holiday.'

'Uh-huh.' Sara sucked in her bottom lip as she sat down next to him. 'And I still can't persuade you to go back to The Potting Shed before then?'

'We've been through that.'

Sara said nothing more on the subject. 'If you want to stay here another night you are very welcome, but I'm off out.'

Surprised by the lack of offer to accompany her to the garden centre, Jo muttered, 'Thanks, but I should go. I'll see you soon. Yes?'

Sara smiled as she waved her hands out to either side of her. 'Of course, I live here.'

'The forecast is still dry for the 1st of May.' Maddie stared at the weather app on her phone. 'I've been checking every day, just in case the forecast changes, despite Davina's conviction it'll stay dry.'

'If it did rain, we'd have to move the event into the polytunnel.' Sabi didn't sound particularly enamoured of the idea. 'We'd not get so many people in.'

'Wouldn't be quite the event the papers are advertising inside, would it.' Maddie looked across to the bluebells planted so lovingly by the Little Acorn group. If any of them did come along, she could imagine how disappointed they'd be if the celebrity guest didn't get to talk from their garden.

'Let's assume it will be a dry evening and go from there.' Ed checked his watch. 'But for now, shouldn't we get this place open? It's almost ten o'clock.'

Sabi took a key from her bag. 'Would you be a star and undo the car park, Ed? We'll be right with you.'

Guessing that Sabi wanted a private word with her sister, and hoping Maddie wasn't about to get a hard time about not turning up in Culmstock last night, Ed headed off towards the car park.

'How was staying over here?'

'It was lovely. I'm sorry I left it to the last minute to decide to stay and—'

Sabi held up her hand. 'It's okay, I'm not about to bite your head off. I just wondered how the flat was, now it's a flat.'

'To be honest, Robert, Kevin and Ahmed have been great. The kitchen is lovely. It's gone from being a disaster zone to being clean and functional. I need to find time to restock it now. I don't see why I can't move back. Both the water and electric are on.'

'Was it strange not going downstairs to the kitchen or living room?'

'A bit. I haven't even thought about sorting out a new living room yet. We're in such a muddle.'

'And the bathroom? The builders must have been using it. Was it left clean?'

Maddie couldn't help but laugh. 'That was a very Sabi question.'

Sticking her tongue out, Sabi countered, 'Hygiene is important.'

'It was spotless. They hadn't even left the toilet seat up.'

'Hello?' Sara peered around the polytunnel. 'Can I come in?'

'Oh, hello.' Jake gave the newcomer a smile as he checked the temperature of the polytunnel. 'Come for some training?'

'Training?'

'You're taking on my job, aren't you? You'll need to know what I do and when I do it?'

'I suppose I will.' Sara joined him at the potting bench. 'Actually, I haven't accepted the job yet. I was going to see Maddie, but she's helping someone in the shop at the moment.'

'You are going to take it though, aren't you?' Jake looked at Sara properly. 'I don't like the idea of leaving Maddie so short-handed.'

'I am, but only for a while. And I can't do the bank holiday.' Sara gestured towards the thermometer in his hand. 'Checking to make sure the fruit doesn't get too cold?'

'Exactly.' Jake gestured along the row. 'Raspberries, blueberries and blackcurrants in the first two rows. Then, at the back we have gooseberries.'

'When are you watering, and how often? Or is there an automatic system set up?'

Obviously impressed by the question, Jake walked along the row of canes, with Sara close behind him. 'There's no automatic system. I water daily at this time of year, but not heavily. Usually just before the gates open. Obviously, as they weather heats up, then it's a twice-daily task, pre and post customers. I can show you where the hose system is set up if you like.'

'Great.' Sara paused. 'Do you have this all written down somewhere, Jake?'

'Well, no – I just sort of, do it.'

Sara opened her mobile. 'Do you mind if I make notes? I'd hate to forget to do something vital.'

Jake's eyebrows rose. 'No problem. I'll give you the whole tour of what I do if you like, although we might get interrupted if people need my help.'

'That would be fabulous.' She waved her phone at him. 'I can't wait to get your wisdom down.'

'Wisdom?'

'Yeah. Jo said you're the best gardener there is.'

'Jo did?' Jake paused in the act of pruning a few unhappy-looking leaves. 'You've heard from him? Does Maddie know?'

The intense gaze of Jake's eyes made Sara take a step

backwards. 'I have. That was the other thing I wanted to talk to Maddie about.'

Having confirmed with Ditzy what time she'd be arriving on the 1st of May, Maddie relaxed against the potting bench as she rested the phone against her ear. 'Can I ask you something my dad always wondered about?'

'Sure.'

'Davina Ditz – is that your real name?'

'It is!' The gardener chuckled down the line. 'The capacity for parental cruelty knows no bounds – hence preferring Ditzy. You should read my biography.'

'I will read it – but I won't be getting a copy from BIG.' Maddie pulled them back to the point of her calling Ditzy. 'I'm a bit concerned about this local rivalry thing the press have got going between us and BIG. I'm not their biggest fan, but I don't see myself as being at war with them.'

'Don't worry, it'll blow itself out. One of the journalists I spoke to cottoned on to the fact that I'd been booked with BIG for a while but had added you onto my tour at the last minute. He must have put two and two together, made five, and run with a local interest story. I'm doing a full UK garden centre tour for the book – stopping at the odd Royal Horticultural Society venue along the way. It's so much fun – but hard work too.'

'Because you have to be upbeat and happy all the time?'

'More, being seen to be happy all the time. I suppose the title of the book says it all – Being Ditzy – it's great, but it's not real.'

Maddie wasn't sure what to say for a second, but rallied with, 'I'm so glad Dan asked you to come here. I take it he appears in the book?'

'He sure does! I'd be lost without that man. A man who has spoken very highly of you over the years.'

'Really?'

'Sure. He rates you.' Ditzy laughed down the line. 'Don't you worry about the journalists. Just give them free tickets to the event and leave them to me.'

'Thanks, Ditzy, that's… Hang on, did you say journalists – plural?'

'Sure.'

'But I've only seen stuff in two papers.'

Ditzy chuckled. 'I'm thinking we'll get all the Devon locals, as well as the Somerset ones. The advantage of The Potting Shed being placed on the county border – more or less. But don't worry, there won't be more than half a dozen of them – you'll have room, won't you?'

'The important thing is not to panic.' Sabi addressed her sister from across the till desk, clear signs of anxiety in her own voice.

'But if we can only fit twenty-four people in the space, and Davina is expecting journalists, then…'

'They won't all come.' Ed pushed up his sleeves as he leant back against the table they were preparing for Ivan to use the following day. 'And if they do, they won't hang around. They'll interview Ditzy and then hop it.'

'I hope so.' Maddie wasn't convinced. 'I haven't been

able to get hold of Sara to one hundred percent confirm we can borrow the picnic tables yet and...'

'You can.' Sara waved as she followed in a customer, her arms full of fledgling raspberry canes. 'Hi, everyone.'

'Sara?' Maddie stepped back to let Sabi jump into shopkeeper mode.

After Sara had made sure the customer would be alright carrying their purchases to the car once they were boxed up, she headed towards Maddie. 'I meant to say hello as soon as I arrived, but you were busy, so I went to find Jake. I've been helping him for the past couple of hours.'

'Does that mean you're working here?' Maddie tried not to get her hopes up. 'Or are you just popping by and helping out?'

'I'm here to work, if that offer is still open.' Sara peered around the shop. 'It's such a great place, although... didn't there used to be a seed rack and more houseplants in here?'

'There did. We're mid rearranging things as we have a cheese seller and some high-end handmade beauty products coming in tomorrow.'

'Ivan and Elspeth?'

'You know them?'

'Jo's friends. Sure.' Sara lowered her voice and wandered to the far side of the shop, away from the customers waiting at the till. 'I'm here about Jo too.'

'You've heard from him?'

'Yesterday. We met up, and he stayed over. He is adamant you won't want him back.'

'But we do!'

'I know – but...' Sara felt awkward '...his reasoning is

sound. He may even be right – you might not want him back when you know the truth, but I think you deserve to know the full story before he finds himself coffee selling gigs elsewhere.'

'Where?' For the first time, Maddie realised she hadn't believed Jo was gone for good. That he was just working something out and would come back.

'I imagine somewhere far away. Somewhere where his past will leave him alone.'

42

'Can I help, Aunt Maddie?' Jemima jumped over the step into the herb greenhouse.

'Hello. I didn't think you were coming in today.'

'I wanted to be here so I could say goodbye to Jake.'

'I'm going to find it weird here without him.' Maddie took her niece's hand. 'Sara's going to work here for a while instead. You met her at Hawthorn Park, I think?'

Jemima raised her eyebrows. 'She's nice. Mum dated her dad – which is a bit odd.' She paused before asking, 'Have you heard from Jo?'

Maddie cleared her throat. 'I was going to message you about him later. Sara has heard from him. He's okay.'

'When's he coming back?' Jemima's face lit up. 'I miss his smoothies almost as much as I miss him.'

Maddie's heart sank. She'd hoped Jem wouldn't ask, but she supposed the question was inevitable. 'He isn't. At least, I think it's highly unlikely he'll come back. I need to talk to your mum about—'

'What!?' Jemima's hand stilled over the tiny linked leaves of a maidenhair fern she was stroking. 'But he has to come back. He's my friend.'

Putting down the peace lily she'd been checking over for

damage, Maddie put her arms around her niece. 'I'm sure he misses you too, but it appears that Jo feels his hands are tied. He thinks his being here could dent our reputation.'

'But that's ridiculous. Nothing that horrible Hazel said was true and...' Seeing the expression on her aunt's face, Jemima stopped talking. 'It isn't true – is it?'

Her knees tucked under her chin, Jemima wrapped her arms around her bent legs and stared out across the field behind The Potting Shed. Between the wild grasses she could pick out where a spattering of poppies would be opening in the weeks to come.

Every word her aunt had told her replayed itself in her head. She obviously hadn't wanted to tell her, but she'd pestered and pestered, and Jemima knew she'd not left Maddie with any choice but to tell her the truth.

I shouldn't have gone on at her. I preferred not knowing.

The idea that Jo had been a bully when he'd been at school did not sit well with her. She couldn't visualise the man she knew acting in any way other than nice.

'Something happened – something changed him.' Jem uncurled her arms and pushed her legs out in front of her. 'And that something has to be Hazel. But I can't believe that she'd spread rumours about him around the customers like Jo seems to think. She's already tarnished her reputation with Dad, why would she risk making it worse? I wish I knew how to make Jo see he's just being paranoid. I don't even know where he is and couldn't go to him if I did.'

Restless, Jemima got up from the bench. She needed to

do something – something that would make Jo see that whatever had happened, he could come back.

Suddenly she stopped moving. *Do I dare?*

Deciding there was nothing left to lose, and that no one would be cross with her if it worked, and she could hide at boarding school until the flak died down if they didn't, Jemima set off in search of her father.

'Maddie!' Robert's booming voice broke through the gentle customer chatter that filled the polytunnel, as three separate couples browsed the vegetable seedlings on offer.

'Oh, hello. Everything alright?'

Robert chuckled. 'Every time one of my clients asks me that, they always sound worried.'

'I bet. I'm just surprised to see you on a Sunday.'

'Keen to get you up and running lass.'

Maddie beamed, 'That's' wonderful. So, how can I help?'

'By coming to see if you're happy with how we've left things upstairs.'

'You're done upstairs?' Maddie was already contemplating fetching her belongings back from Sabi's and bringing Florrie home from Ivan.

'Yep.' Robert pulled a battered mobile from his back pocket and scrolled through his calendar. 'Now then, we'll need tomorrow to fetch the tools and materials required for the conversion of downstairs, but then we'll be back on Wednesday to make a start on knocking through and putting in the new doorway, keeping us on course for 1st May ... ish.'

'That's fantastic. Thank you.'

'Let's see, it's the 17th of April tomorrow, so, although I can't promise we'll be finished in time for you to be operational on 1st May, it's not impossible. If we can, we'll have your new shop space structurally sound and useable, if not fully decorated.'

'Thank you.' Wondering whether they'd be able to combine the opening of the new building with Davina's visit, Maddie checked to make sure she wasn't needed by a customer before turning to the tunnel's exit. 'Do you need me to do anything downstairs, preparation wise?'

'Just move everything out. You've got all day tomorrow – shouldn't take a tick.'

'Mr Willand-Harris?'

'Um, no.' Jemima spoke in a rushed whisper, holding the phone she'd pinched from her dad's jacket while he was helping Ed unload some large terracotta flowerpots from a delivery lorry.

'Then who is this?' Hazel's tone was almost imperial. 'Mrs Willand-Harris?'

'No – it's Jem. Jemima.'

'Who?' Hazel's tone was sharp.

'Their daughter.'

'Oh. What do you want?'

'I'd like to talk to you please.'

'You do know it's a Sunday! The weekend. As in days off work.'

Jemima crouched between the back two polytunnels, hoping that her dad hadn't noticed his phone was missing. 'Yes, it's about Jo.'

'I don't think so.'

'Why not?'

'Why are you whispering?'

'Because no one knows I'm calling. I just need to know what you intend to do next?'

'Next?'

'Aunt Maddie says Jo won't come back to The Potting Shed because you'll destroy his reputation, and therefore all my aunt's and my mum's hard work, if he does. I don't want you to. We need him here... I'm sure he can't have been that bad so...'

'Silly girl!' Hazel snapped. 'Although not so silly if you managed to break into your father's phone to call me.'

Not liking the accusing tone – especially as it was accurate – Jemima said, 'For a good cause! I'm worried about Jo. He's my friend.'

'He's a bully! Not someone who you should be friends with.'

'Maybe he was – but that doesn't mean he still is!' Jemima started to shake as she heard the anger in the voice of the woman on the other end of the line. 'He's changed. If you'd just let him explain and—'

'Damn right Jo's changed – but that's not the point! Jo Dunn made me very unhappy. Twice!'

'But please...' Jemima felt tears welling at the corners of her eyes.

'Goodbye, Jemima. If you don't contact me again, then I won't tell your father about this call. Jo Dunn is *not* worth your friendship.'

★

Henry gave Jake a friendly slap on the back. 'Thank you so much for helping Ed and me lay the turf in the new garden. It looks great.'

'No problem. I'm glad it arrived early so I could help.'

Ed echoed Henry's thanks. 'This place won't be the same without you, Jake.'

'I'm only going to be forty miles away!' He sounded casual, but Maddie could see he was trying to cover his emotions. 'And I'll be back soon. I mean, I'm assuming you'll want some help on May Day?'

'Really?' Maddie gave him a hug. 'Would you? And Petra?'

'Of course – we aren't going to want to miss out on Davina, are we?' He hesitated. 'Will we have to buy tickets? I'm not sure I can afford…'

'Don't be silly.' Maddie let go of him. 'I'm not going to go sickly sweet on you, 'cos you'd hate that.'

'I would.' Jake shuffled his trainered feet.

'I'm sorry we can't give you a proper send-off at the pub, as you have to head to your new digs tonight so you can start work tomorrow, and I have to morph into a furniture removal person so that Robert and crew can crack on, but I wanted to give you this.' Maddie held out a small velvet-covered box.

Jake's hand hesitated over his employer's hand. 'You don't have to give me anything.'

'We want you to have it.'

Sabi echoed her sister. 'We are sure it's what Dad would have wanted.'

Jake's soil-stained fingertips rested on the velvet lid. 'This was your dad's?'

'It was.' Maddie could see how much this meant to Jake, and knew they'd have to proceed carefully, as he'd hate to cry in front of them. 'You can open it on your own if you'd rather.'

'Oh.' Jemima sounded disappointed. 'I wanted to see what Grandad has left him.'

'It's okay, Jem. I'm curious too.' Jake levered open the tightly hinged box. It was a few seconds before he was able to speak. 'I can't take this.'

'You can.' Maddie put her hand on his. 'You've earned it – and more. Please, it would mean a lot to us.'

Sabi stood with her sister as they watched Jake take their father's wristwatch from its box and lay it over his arm.

'Tony wore this every day.' Jake spoke with awe.

'It's a bit battered.' Jemima looked anxiously at her mum. 'Is that okay?'

Sabi nodded, not quite trusting herself to speak.

Jake fastened the catch around his wrist. 'It's more than okay, Jem. It's battered because he wouldn't take it off, whatever he was doing, because he loved it. Almost as much as I loved him.'

43

Maddie flopped onto the sofa as the third loud crash of the day made the building shake.

She wasn't supposed to be there, but the need for five minutes' peace had driven her into the newly converted flat while Robert and his team had been on their lunch break. A break that was clearly over – as was her moment's quiet.

Due to Robert and Kevin catching flu at the same time, the demolition of the connecting walls downstairs hadn't started on the 17th of April after all. Now, almost two weeks behind schedule, they were knocking out the walls below, prior to constructing some safety pillars to support the ceiling until they could fix some permanent steel beams in place. The previous day they had knocked out a space that would house a set of double automatic doors, removing her former front door in the process. The way in and out of her flat was currently protected by little more than a thick tarpaulin sheet.

'I should never have asked Ditzy to open the new-look Potting Shed.' Maddie glared at her mobile phone, knowing she'd have to warn the presenter that the official launch of The Potting Shed as a garden centre was off.

'I bet she's told people already – and if she's told the press...'
Maddie shuddered. The last thing she needed was to have
to explain why they wouldn't be operating as a full garden
centre during the Ask Ditzy event, when she'd promised
they would be. She could just imagine the people at BIG
smirking at her failure to fully open on time.

Robert had asked if they could come today, even though
it was a Saturday, to try and claw back some time – but with
only forty-eight hours before Davina Ditz's visit, she knew
there was no way they'd catch up enough to pull off a last-
minute 'we'll be open after all' miracle.

'It doesn't help that Ed isn't here,' Maddie told the fern
that sat in the windowsill.

*He'll be back this afternoon. You know he'll help once
he's arrived.*

'I know.' Maddie wiped some dust off the fern's nearest
leaf. 'I'm just feeling dismal because he's gone back to
Bristol for a chat about his options job wise.'

He may not take it, even if they offer him the job.

'Maybe not.' Maddie picked the fern's pot up and weighed
it in her hands. 'You need some water.'

As she moved to the sink, Robert's tuneless humming
could be heard from below, between the bouts of falling
masonry and the sound of sweeping and clearing. Maddie
didn't want to think about the dust that would be escaping
from the house and floating over The Potting Shed, which
she Sabi and Sara had scrubbed to within an inch of its life
the evening before, in the hope that they'd only need to do
a surface clean before Monday's event.

She checked her watch. It was almost three o'clock. There

was no way she could hide for much longer. There were two hours of trading left and, although the number of customers tended to trail off from three o'clock onwards, there was plenty to do. For a start, they were expecting a delivery of picnic tables from Sara at four-thirty.

With a final look at the list that she'd come inside to work on – of new plants she wanted to buy in or grow from scratch – she gave a heavy sigh, before replacing the refreshed fern back on the windowsill.

Looking outside, she could see a satisfying number of people down below. The regulars seemed to have adjusted to the lack of refreshments – which was good in the short term, but not a situation Maddie wanted to live with for much longer. Yet, despite Sabi's efforts to find a replacement – even a temporary one – for Jo and his van, they'd had no luck.

Many of the shoppers and browsers she could see below her were now familiar faces; several had been terribly disappointed to learn that all the tickets for Ask Ditzy were sold out before they'd even heard it was happening.

'I'm still not quite sure how we'll get everyone in.' She pictured the forty tickets they'd ended up selling – more by accident than design, with Dan and Ivan, both promising tickets to friends; each thinking they were being helpful, unaware that the ticket limit had been met almost on the first day of sales.

Sara declared that the answer was to place more people around the same number of tables – claiming six – maybe even eight small bottoms – could be put around each picnic table. She made no comment when Ivan pointed out that not all bottoms were as small as hers.

Maddie's gaze roamed on towards the polytunnel containing the fruit and then to the one holding the vegetables. It was strange not seeing Jake popping in and out of them, clucking over his produce like a mother hen. She'd had a few texts from him and Petra, both saying how well he'd settled into the team at Arlington Court, and confirming they'd be there to help on Monday.

She was about to move away, when Maddie spotted Ed crossing the garden centre, a holdall in one hand, his suit folded in a bag that hung over one arm. She smiled as she saw him waving to some customers. He looked so much at home.

I need to ask him to move in properly. The pace of life at The Potting Shed had been nonstop since Sara had replaced Jake. *I wonder how his work chat went.* There hadn't been time to talk about their future beyond the 1st of May. Beyond him suddenly announcing on Friday that he had an afternoon meeting in Bristol, and that he'd been asked to stay overnight to have a meal with the firm's partners, the potential job in Bristol had barely been mentioned. 'I should have asked him how it went last night.'

The fern rustled its leaves up as it ventured: *You haven't asked because you're hoping it will all go away.*

'Always quick with the unhelpful truth.' Maddie stroked the delicate leaves. 'I also fell asleep on the sofa after work and didn't wake up until morning, missing his text saying he'd gone to bed in a hotel room that was far posher than he was used to.'

Maybe he'll be able to take you to posh hotels if he gets the job.

'I'd rather have him here.'

The fern became silent, making Maddie wonder if relying on her favourite houseplant for advice meant she'd gone mad. *Perhaps I have.*

The sound of sweeping up below began again, and Maddie took her chance to creep downstairs, hoping that no customers noticed her coming out of a building that was surrounded by 'Keep Out' signs.

The moment she got outside Maddie was hit by a cloud of gritty dust that billowed from where Ahmed was sweeping the contents of the fallen masonry out of the recently knocked-out double doors. Coughing sharply, she soon alerted Ed's attention.

'How are they doing?' He frowned. 'Aren't you supposed to wear a hard hat when you're in there?'

'I wasn't in there – you're imagining it.' Maddie waved a dismissive hand towards the door. 'How was it? Sorry I didn't reply to your text last night. I dropped off.'

'I'm not surprised. You look like you could fall asleep now. You okay?'

Knowing that there was a real danger she'd be too tired to enjoy the event on Monday if she didn't have a full night's sleep soon, Maddie avoided admitting she'd been working seventeen-hour days all week. 'I'm always alright. So, Bristol?'

'Fine. Nice people. They certainly know how to impress a client. I can't imagine my current boss wining and dining anyone like that.'

'Ronald is lovely though.'

'He is.' Ed gave Maddie a kiss on her cheek. 'And he's been ever so good about all this. I really don't like leaving him in the lurch.'

Maddie felt herself go cold. 'Is it definite then? Are you moving away?'

'It was just a chat. But if I did get it, well... You see, I don't want the job as such, but if—'

'You don't want it?'

'No. I want to be nearer you. However, if—'

Maddie's forehead puckered with confusion. 'Then don't go.'

Ed dropped his holdall to the floor and laid his suit bag over the top. 'Could I possibly finish my sentence, do you think?'

'Sorry.' Maddie blushed.

'I am contemplating Bristol because it would bring us a bigger income. That would help The Potting Shed – wouldn't it?'

'But you can't pay for things here! That would be so unfair. You do heaps around here for no reward as it is. I could never—'

'Even if I lived here? With you. I know we've talked about it – but always as just a future possibility.'

The intense gleam to Ed's eyes made Maddie's insides melt. 'I was thinking about that just now. I keep meaning to ask you – officially ask you – if you'd like to come and live with me here, properly, but there's always something going on and now—'

A well-timed crash from inside the house made them both jump.

'...they are pulling my house down, from the inside out.'

'I'm glad Robert, Kevin and Ahmed are back. Did you sleep at Sabi's again last night?' Ed looked over at the space where the old front door had once been, taking in the roughly knocked-out brick wall.

'No. I stayed here. It's structurally sound, so it's okay.'

Ed's eyebrows rose. 'I'm surprised Robert would say it was okay until the ceiling supports are in.'

'Well... he didn't say I couldn't so... I'm happier here, and Sabi is enjoying having time to plan the interior décor of her house without me under her feet, so I'm just being careful.' Maddie glanced at Ed out of the corner of her eye. 'Before you tell me off for staying here – I would love it if you moved in with me. Please – will you?'

Pulling her closer, Ed murmured softly, 'You're sure?'

'One hundred per cent. Let's live together. From right now! Yes?'

'Absolutely yes!' Ed gestured to his luggage. 'I should have enough stuff to keep me going until Monday night, then I'll head to the flat and think about what I need to bring over and what I can get rid of.'

Finding herself scooped up into a giant hug, Maddie snuggled into her boyfriend's shoulder. 'I love you, Mr Tate.'

'You too, Miss Willand.'

As Ed let her go, so he could pick up the few belongings he had with him, Maddie grinned. 'Welcome home! What better declaration of love than finding someone who'll break health and safety guidelines with me!'

44

'I'd rather like to have had a very, *very* long lie-in with you on our first night of officially living together.' Maddie switched off the alarm.

'I'll second that.' Ed pushed back the duvet. 'At least we know we'll have lots more mornings to be lazy together.'

Maddie laughed. 'Together yes, but if you're looking for lazy, you're in the wrong bed.'

'Ain't that the truth! In all those adolescent dreams about waking up with a beautiful woman every day, I never dreamt it would be one who gets up at seven o'clock on a Sunday morning.' Ed pulled on a pair of boxer shorts. 'On the plus side, the advantage of this being a flat now is that I don't have to go downstairs to make our morning tea.'

Ed had only been out of the bedroom a moment, when a text from Henry arrived, sending Maddie rushing into the newly refurbished kitchen after her partner.

'I've gone off newspapers.'

Dropping a teabag into a mug, Ed asked, 'What are they saying this time?'

'The *Western Daily Press* are reporting that not only is Davina doing the event tomorrow, but she'll also be presiding over the official opening ceremony.'

'Oh hell.' Ed paused over their tea.

'What can we do?' Maddie gnawed at her bottom lip. 'I know it was our intention, but you've seen downstairs – it's a hollow shell with no front door!'

Ed fetched some milk from the fridge. 'Right, so let's be sensible about this.'

Maddie couldn't help but smile. 'You sounded like a solicitor then.'

'Funny that.'

'Go on; you were going to be sensible.'

After passing Maddie a mug, Ed took her free hand and towed her back to the bedroom. 'First of all, we aren't going to panic. Robert and co. didn't intend to be ill; it's no one's fault things are behind schedule, so people will understand.'

'I guess so.' Maddie wasn't convinced.

'They will. Especially, if we do all we can to make it work with what we've got.' Climbing back onto the bed, Ed rested back against the bedhead, lifting his arm so Maddie could snuggle into his shoulder. 'If we work like stink, we could still have an official opening – albeit one without all the stock in place.'

'But Ed, the shop doesn't even have any doors!'

'True, but we do have a lot of friends...'

Jemima jumped around the empty shop, enjoying the echo her boots made on the bare floor. 'It's so weird without Grandad's old carpet down.'

'And no walls.' Sabi took hold of her daughter's hand. 'Could you stop leaping about? You're as bad as Florrie.'

'Sorry, Mum.' Jemima gave her toes one more satisfying

tap on the concrete floor as she fiddled with her hard hat. 'What does Aunt Maddie want us to do?'

'Make The Potting Shed nice by tomorrow afternoon.'

Sabi stared around the space, familiar and yet alien. The wall that had once divided the lounge and dining rooms was gone, as was the wall that had formed the hallway leading to the old front door. Despite the thick tarpaulin, the breeze that was cutting through the early morning air was making its presence felt through the expanded doorway. It was already hard to picture the cosy family gatherings that had once taken place in that very space.

'It's quite tidy.' Jemima looked around. 'I was expecting bricks everywhere.'

'The builders are good at cleaning up after themselves.' Sabi spoke with a sense of satisfaction. 'They'll be back soon though, so there is no point in doing anything much yet – I just wanted to see the lie of the land – get a few ideas.'

'What are they going to do in here today?'

'We need four steel joists to support the ceiling, and then the walls need rendering.'

'Rendering?'

'Plastering, and then painting.'

Jemima walked up to the nearest wall and ran her hand over it. 'Grandad liked this colour. Are we going to paint it the same, but all over?'

'I don't think it would work for a garden centre, love.' She placed her own hand on the pale blue wall. 'It feels like we're removing him somehow.'

'Mum? Are you okay?'

'I miss him, that's all.'

'Me too.' Putting her hand back into her mum's palm,

Jemima said, 'This is what he wanted though. You're doing this for him.'

'Thanks, Jemima.' Kissing the top of her daughter's head, Sabi steered them to the door.

Henry rolled up his sleeves and lifted one end of the bench, as Ed took hold of the other. 'Over by the fence?'

'Just by the gate into the woods.' Ed walked backwards, guiding the way until the old seat was repositioned. 'It should be both useful and out of the way here, if you see what I mean.'

Henry brushed his hands together as he looked beyond the sprinkling of bluebells already in flower, towards the new gate. 'Many people heading into the wood yet?'

'A steady trickle according to Maddie. Word hasn't got around about it yet, but I'm sure after tomorrow night, it'll become popular. Maddie decided not to charge to walk through it in the end.'

'Sensible, that way it'll become an attraction that brings people to The Potting Shed again and again.'

'Hopefully buying something as they pass through.'

'Exactly.' Henry regarded the space before them. 'Any idea how we're supposed to be positioning the picnic tables?'

'I think it's just a case of making sure they are all angled in the direction of the new garden. Maddie's plan is to have a focal table and chair, where Ditzy can stand or sit for her session. It'll be first come, first served seating wise, so those who get here early enough will get the best view.'

'Is there a microphone?'

'What for?' Ed tried to imagine all the picnic tables, currently stacked together in a haphazard fashion at the side of the car park, in place. It was going to be something of a jigsaw to get them in place, and still leave enough room for people to move between them.

'When people ask their questions, it's important Ditzy can hear them – and that they can hear her.'

Ed opened the notebook that held Maddie's incredibly long to-do list. There was no mention of microphones. 'Don't suppose you have a couple – one for Davina and one for Maddie?'

'Afraid not.'

'Perhaps it'll be okay.'

'Maybe.' Henry didn't sound convinced. 'But the sound might not carry too well, and it would be good if Maddie could go from guest to guest and relay the questions to Ditzy in a way that everyone could hear.'

'Let's not add it to Maddie's worry list.' Ed put his phone away as they strode towards the car park. 'Microphones are a low-priority problem right now.'

Henry acknowledged the point as they rounded the herb greenhouse and reached the car park as Robert drove his van in through the gates. Kevin had Ahmed jammed next to him in the three-man cab. 'Ah good, they're here.'

'What do you think the chances are of them getting the ceiling supports in, and making the building safe enough for the public to enter by tomorrow night?'

'Next to zero.' Henry grimaced. 'But at least they've promised to try.'

*

'Maddie! We're here!' Petra stuck her head through the plastic doorway. 'Oh – different!'

'You could say that.' Maddie dashed towards her former employee, so that they could talk away from the building site. 'It feels like a totally different place to my old home.'

'I bet.' Petra radiated positivity. 'It's going to be fabulous! Jake has gone to do the veg – although between you and me, I think he's checking up on you and making sure everything is being looked after!'

'He's more like my father than he knows.' Maddie gave Petra a hug. 'I'm ever so grateful for you two giving up your weekend off again.'

'Are you kidding! We love Ditzy. Can't wait to see her. So...' Petra took the keys to the shop out of Maddie's hand '...how are you? Is Ivan settling in okay? What can I do to help while I'm between customers, and do you want me to put the kettle on?'

'I'm happy but exhausted; Ivan is doing well, and Elspeth's goods are selling too, but less so as they are expensive; and I'd love it if you could hit the social media marketing between serving people.' Maddie threw her arms around her friend. 'Thank goodness you're here.'

Petra chuckled. 'And I take it that is a yes to a cup of coffee then?'

'That goes without saying!'

'I have to go.' Sara pointed towards the growing line of cars already parked up, ready for their occupants to walk up the driveway, once she opened the gates in ten minutes' time.

'If I don't leave now, there's a chance I won't be able to get my car out.'

Regret gnawed at Jo as he said, 'You aren't expected at The Potting Shed today. They'll assume you'll be here. This is Hawthorn Park's biggest weekend of the year. Just look at the bluebells.' He gestured around him, showing off the stunning carpet of purple and green that surrounded them. Each leaf and petal shone proudly in the early morning sunshine. 'It's a perfect Bank Holiday Sunday.'

'It is, but everything will happen here, whether I'm here or not. It's a different story at The Potting Shed.' Knowing Jo felt bad about not going with her, Sara let him off the hook. 'You have no choice. You *have* to stay here – your coffee van is part of the reason people come, but I don't need to be around. Tickets to come in were presold online, and – frankly – if people just come in and wander for free, I really don't care. Not just this once.'

'What if someone needs help that I can't give, or asks questions I can't answer?'

'Tell them I've dashed off to help a friend in trouble.'

'Right.' Jo pulled at the edges of his beanie, as he heard the excuse he'd first used to desert The Potting Shed repeated back to him. 'Do you think Maddie'll be ready for tomorrow night?'

'I've no idea, but I'm going to do everything I can to help. I've only worked there a fortnight, but I love it already.'

'The Potting Shed has that effect on people.' Jo acknowledged the point. 'It's not like being staff, it's like being...'

As Jo's voice trailed off, Sara finished his sentence: 'Family?'

'Sort of.'

'Did you see your mum yesterday?' Sara looked at him properly.

'Yes. Not that she'll remember I went, but she was on good form at the time.'

'I'm sure she remembers it in her own way.' Sara reached out and squeezed Jo's arm. 'I must go. Just call if you need me.'

Watching her walk away, Jo headed towards his coffee van, preparing himself to make hundreds of drinks for total strangers, wishing for the thousandth time that he'd never met Hazel Cooper.

45

'We must be mad.' Maddie adjusted the hard hat Kevin had plonked onto her head as she'd walked into the cavernous space that had once been her living and dining room.

'Quite possibly.' Robert chuckled as he adjusted his ladder.

Ed wiped a smutter of dust off his nose. 'It'll be worth it.'

'And we don't have much choice, do we.' Sabi lifted up a pot of paint with an air of satisfaction that belied her tone. 'Ditzy has told the papers we'll be fully open – so open we'll have to be.'

Kevin gave a thumbs up from the opposite side of the space. 'Okay, this one's done.' He tapped the thick telescopic metal ceiling support pole. 'Now, as we said, this is a temporary fix. We've checked with the authorities, and providing we use eight of these, you can have people in here. But to be honest, this home is as sound as – well, houses! You'll be safe enough.'

Sabi found herself in the unusual position of wanting to hug a tradesman. 'We can't thank you enough for this.'

'Pleasure.' Kevin wiped a grubby hand down his overalls, 'But um, well... we wondered...'

'Go on.' Maddie came to her sister's side as she saw Kevin struggle for the words.

'Young Ahmed there, his gran is mad keen on gardening. Don't suppose there's a ticket left over for tomorrow is there?'

'Of course! It's the least we can do. Would that be two tickets – one for Ahmed and one for his gran?'

'Um, well, yes, unless...'

Maddie grinned. 'Four tickets? One for Ahmed, his gran, you and Robert?'

'Now you're talking, lass.' Kevin rubbed his hands together. 'A bit of alright is that Davina.'

Maddie's eyebrows rose. 'Are you telling me we're gifting you a hundred pounds' worth of tickets so you can come and ogle her?'

'Yup.'

'Honest, at least.' Maddie laughed. 'They're fair exchange for saving us in our hour of need and all your hard work, but I'm afraid we can't offer you reserved seats or anything – we're already fully booked.'

'Doesn't matter, lass. We'll just enjoy the moment.' Kevin sent a thumbs up across the room to his colleagues. 'Fear not, we'll be well behaved. Although I'd be lying if I said we won't be enjoying the view. Ditzy is a fabulous gardener – Rob and I both have allotments. Follow her tips on veg on the radio every week, don't ya know.'

Ivan took the offered mug of tea, as Sara came by with a loaded tray of drinks.

'Thanks, lass. I'm surprised to see you; thought you'd be at your place.'

'Maddie doesn't know I'm here yet. Jo can cope at home.'

Looking up from his mug, Ivan said, 'Jo turned up to serve coffee at your place?'

'Yeah.' Sara felt her cheeks flush. 'I'm sorry that he'll come to me but not here.'

'No need to be. I'm glad he didn't let you down.'

Sara shrugged. 'In his mind, he has a good reason for staying away from The Potting Shed, but...'

'You've done your best. It's up to Jo now.' Ivan spotted a customer heading his way. 'Duty calls. Can you let Maddie and Sabi know I'm happy to take on any little jobs that need doing if I can do them from here?'

The smell of paint wasn't as bad as Maddie feared as she levered the lid off a giant tin of magnolia emulsion. It wasn't the colour they'd have in the end, but, as Sabi had pointed out, it was dense enough to cover the current, rather faded, pale blue paintwork and refresh the walls. Plus, it was cheap. While there would be no time to render the walls that had newly exposed brick edges as they'd planned, Robert had confidently told her that they'd treated them with a temporary glaze, which would hold the brick dust back until the job could be done properly.

As she plunged her paintbrush into the pot, Maddie looked round at her family. Ed was next to her, his longer reach meaning he didn't need to stand on a stepladder like she did. Sabi was working on the opposite wall, Henry next to her, while Jemima was on her hands and knees, running a brush along the bottom of the wall.

It's happening, Dad, not quite as I expected, but we're all here – together. A prickle of tears threatened at the corners of Maddie's eyes as the rustle of the tarpaulin being pushed aside made her turn round.

'Break time!'

Seeing Sara, a laden tray in her hands, Maddie put her brush down. 'You're a welcome sight, but shouldn't you be at home?'

'Jo's keeping an eye on the place…' Sara faltered. 'Sorry.'

'Not at all!' Sabi took off a pair of disposable gloves and waved them towards the haphazard doorway. 'How is it out there, customer wise?'

'Ivan has customers and the greenhouse and polytunnels all have people in – oh, and Ivan says he's happy to do any little jobs that want sorting between customers if you need him.'

'That's great.' Maddie extracted a crumpled list from her back pocket. 'Could you ask him to call Dan for me – he knows the number – and double-check what time we can expect Davina to arrive here tomorrow and find out if she is a tea or coffee girl?'

'On it!' Sara held out the tray of mugs towards the builders, who each murmured their thanks. 'When I left Petra, she was helping pack a box of assorted veg seedlings for a customer, and Jake is making up more hanging baskets in the far tunnel, as there are only three left.'

'Three!' Maddie turned to her sister. 'There were nine when we opened.'

'Didn't you want to sell them?'

'Well, yes, but I didn't think they'd go so quickly. I imagined them helping to decorate the place while Ditzy was here.'

'Fear not, Jake is on it.' Sara added, 'He's taken a few plants out of stock though. I made a list of them, so the accounts didn't get messed up. Oh, and we've sold the final pot of primroses – I'm assuming you won't get in more of those now?'

'No, their season is definitely over. I'm amazed that pot held out, to be honest.' Maddie clutched her coffee cup. 'I haven't seen Jake yet today. I'd like to make sure he's okay.'

'I'm sure he'll find you later.' Sara smiled. 'He seems very content.'

'That's good.' Sabi sipped her tea. 'Please thank Jo for holding the fort for you, so you could come to us.'

'Yeah!' Jemima clambered to her feet; her hair was matted with paint in places, from where she'd accidentally brushed it against the wall. ''Cos if he wasn't there, you couldn't be here bringing them tea.'

'Oh, that reminds me.' Sara reached inside her overcoat and pulled out a small green bottle. 'Jo sends his love.'

'A smoothie!' Jemima held it close. 'I miss Jo's smoothies.'

'I'll tell him.' There was an awkward silence for a moment, before Sara said, 'He does know you need him back here, that you haven't been able to get anyone to replace him – if it helps, I know he's not happy about it.'

'We know. We're not angry with him – or disappointed in him – or any of the other things I'm sure he's assuming.' Maddie exchanged a reassuring glance with her sister. 'His reasons for not coming back... we appreciate them, but they aren't sound. Hazel could tell every customer who walks through the door what Jo did in the distant past, but it won't mean much to them, will it?'

'Some people won't like it.' Jemima glanced up from her smoothie. 'If you're bullied, you don't forget – not ever. My tutor told me that. But for lots of people, his coffee will be more important than his past – so he could come back if he could face the occasional fallout. Make *that* his punishment, rather than not being with his friends.'

Sabi regarded her daughter. 'Your tutor said all that?'

'Uh-huh.' Jemima focused on her paint pot. 'I was a bit down about Jo. I talked to Mrs Stevens. I think maybe she was bullied too – but she didn't actually say so.'

Henry came to his daughter's side. 'I always liked her.'

'Me too.' Jemima put down her brush. 'Can I get some fresh air please? I could go and see if Jake needs help.'

'Good idea.' Maddie watched her niece leave before saying, 'If Jo isn't coming back...' she glanced towards the one remaining internal wall that divided the former lounge and hall from the original kitchen '...we'll just have to make a fortune quickly and get the café converted and open, won't we?'

She'd been sure it would be there, but it wasn't.

Hazel sat in the driver's seat of her car and watched as customers milled in and out of The Potting Shed. The papers had been full of the forthcoming event – not to mention the opening of The Potting Shed as a fully-fledged garden centre. Surely, they'd need refreshments, and that – she'd assumed – would mean Jo.

Risking getting out of the car, Hazel rested against the door. Straining to see as far as she could, knowing there wasn't enough space to park a camper van beyond her visual range, she forced herself to accept the obvious. There was no bright orange coffee van here.

What would you have done if there had been? Resentment boiled inside Hazel. She'd worked so hard to get a better job – and up popped her past. A past that had belittled her not once – but twice and—

'What are you doing here?'

Batting away the tears that had threatened to fall, Hazel swung around to see the owner of the timid but angry voice that was addressing her.

Jemima clutched her bottle of spinach and kiwi fruit tighter as Hazel glared at her. 'You aren't supposed to be here. My dad—'

'Said I couldn't work on the redevelopment of the house. He did not ban me from visiting the site.' Hazel reined in her temper as she looked down at the child addressing her. 'I'm sorry, I didn't mean to snap at you.'

'Did you want to buy a plant?'

'Not really.'

'So, why are you here?'

'It really isn't any of your business.'

'Jo isn't here. You chased him away.'

Hazel felt triumphant, until she looked back at the girl's face. 'He did this to himself, you know.'

'Did he?' Jemima shook her head as she remembered her teacher's parting words when she'd confided in her about Jo. 'Or are you as mean an adult now, as he was when he was a child?'

46

Florrie wagged her tail with such enthusiasm that it fleetingly crossed Maddie's mind that it might drop off. But her puppy didn't jump up at her, nor did she run around in overexcited circles.

'Ivan! You have worked miracles.' Kneeling to praise Florrie for being such a good girl, Maddie hugged her, inhaling her comforting scent. 'I've missed you so much.'

'It's been a joy having her around.' Ivan bent down to fuss his own dog. 'Sheba has been a good influence on her. If she hadn't been, I wouldn't have brought her back today of all days.'

'I'm glad you did. It wouldn't be the same without her.' Maddie straightened up. 'Although I'm not sure where to put her for a moment. I can't take her into the new shop space and you can't have her by the cheese stall, and she isn't used to the flat like it is.'

'No problem, lass.' Ivan held up a hand in reassurance. 'Already sorted. Dan and Elspeth are going to take Florrie and Sheba for a gentle Bank Holiday Monday stroll. They'll be here to collect her before we open at ten.'

'That's wonderful. Thank you.'

'It's the least we can do. I sold three pots of Elspeth's

body creams yesterday – no mean feat as they are pretty pricey. I'm already getting regulars to my stall too.'

Maddie gestured to the house behind her. 'Hopefully, you'll do even better once you are installed in there, although it might be a little while longer than planned before you move over.'

'Not a problem, lass. All you need for now is to be seen to be open – then you can close briefly for upgrades – everyone will understand.'

'They'll have to.'

As Ivan took the dogs towards the car park to wait for Dan and Elspeth to arrive, Maddie pulled on her hard hat and headed into the new shopping space.

All eight ceiling supports were in place, and the walls had received one coat of paint. There was a light smell of emulsion and dust that clung stubbornly to the atmosphere that Maddie wasn't sure would ever leave, let alone be banished within the next few hours. The biggest problem, however, was the doors – or lack of. The blue tarpaulin was still in place, and although it would be removed for the opening ceremony, it still formed a rather incongruous opening, with its ragged brick formation.

Maddie checked her watch. It was almost a quarter to ten, and there was still no sign of Robert, Kevin, or Ahmed. Davina was due to arrive in six hours, and the Ask Ditzy session started in eight.

Their friendly builders had promised they'd be there with a temporary door system before lunchtime, as the automatic door fitter hadn't been able to reschedule his timetable so he could come this week, after they had to cancel his earlier appointment.

JENNY KANE

'How's it going?' Maddie hailed her sister, who was busy winding rich maroon ribbons around the furthest ceiling support pole, in an effort to make it appear less industrial.

'Fiddly, what do you think?'

'Looks good – I wasn't sure when you described your plan, but it works.' Maddie blew out a long breath. 'What about the rest of the space though? It's so empty it echoes – and we haven't set up the till yet.'

'That won't take long, but as we want it by the doorway, it isn't worth putting it in place until there are doors.'

'I can't see how they are going to fix a door in anyway – the space is huge, and the surround is all awkward.'

Picking up a huge roll of ribbon, Sabi passed it to her sister. 'They haven't let us down yet. It'll be alright.'

Maddie couldn't help smiling at the reversal in their roles. 'Aren't you supposed to be the pessimist and me the one who blunders on in faint hope?'

Carrying a stepladder to the next pole, Sabi grinned. 'Maybe. But look at this – all of it – we're doing it, Mads! We're living Dad's dream.'

Maddie passed the ribbon up to her sister as she climbed the ladder. 'I love your positivity when you're in interior décor mode.'

Sabi stuck her tongue out at her sister. 'So, when were you going to tell me that Ed and you are now living together?'

Jo had lost count of how many drinks he'd sold by one o'clock. He hadn't had time to think about Sara's absence – or the significance of where she was. No sooner had he

BLUEBELL SEASON AT THE POTTING SHED

ground one set of coffee beans than he was refilling the grinder, ready to start the process again. He was almost out of pastries, and there was only one packet of biscuits left.

Without exception, his customers were in high spirits, each one happily extolling the virtues of the park and, in particular, its stunning display of bluebells. His cash box was already heavy, and his card machine had been in constant use since the doors had opened at ten o'clock.

You should be thrilled. You've already sold more today than you did yesterday, and that was a good sales day too.

As a customer approached, he plastered on the fake smile he'd been using all weekend, and set some hot water running into a large teapot as he collected a bottle of orange juice from his cooler.

So why do I feel as if I'm just going through the motions?

Jo's eyes fell on the few remaining smoothies he had in stock, and the lurch of his heart answered his own question.

Because I want to be at The Potting Shed too.

The guilt he'd experienced over letting Maddie and Sabi down was nothing compared to how he felt about walking away from Jem and Henry without any real explanation.

They thought I'd leave if they asked me for rent money.

Handing out the tea and orange, Jo swallowed hard against his own thoughts. *They used the need for more income as a test – they were testing me – which meant they believed Hazel. I know Sara thinks I'm wrong about that, but...*

Grabbing up a cloth to wipe the nozzle of the coffee machine, Jo was arrested by the sight of his next customer. 'Oh.'

'I don't want to be here.' Hazel hugged her handbag to her chest.

Glad that no one was behind her in the queue, Jo muttered, 'And I don't particularly want you to be here, so...'

'It was something Jemima said.'

'Jem?'

'Can we sit down?' She gestured to a free table, which was still strewn with used cups.

Unable to hide his surprise, Jo picked up a tray and cleaning spray bottle. 'You want to sit with me?'

'No, but I don't want us to be overheard.'

Pilling up the empty cups, Jo gave the table a generous dose of antibacterial spray. 'Coffee?'

'No thanks.'

Jo sat opposite Hazel. 'I might have to dash off at any moment.'

'I'll be brief.'

'Before you start...' Jo peered over his shoulder to make sure the couple at the nearest table were too engaged with one another to be paying them any attention '...I want to say sorry for being so awful at school.'

Hazel's set expression wavered. 'You laughed at me.'

'As I said, I'm really sorry.'

'And then, later... why didn't you tell me who you were? Do you know what an utter fool I felt? Not only did I think I was having a relationship that I wasn't having, but I was – well, *wasn't* – having it with *you*!'

'I know. I'm sorry.' Jo fiddled with the cloth in his hands. 'I was so sure you'd recognise me, despite everything. When you didn't... I hoped I could be the friend that I'd failed to be before.'

'I don't want anyone to be my friend out of pity!'

'I didn't mean that – I never meant that! I...' Jo dropped

the cloth onto the table. 'Oh, what does it matter! I was in the wrong, I said sorry – I wish I could turn the clock back, but I can't.'

A silence cast a shadow over the otherwise sunny table before Jo went on. 'Anyway, you've won – you've got what you wanted. My friends at The Potting Shed started to believe you. And as I can't deny what I did…' Jo was glad to see a teenager heading towards the van, a ten-pound note already in hand. With a brief nod in Hazel's direction, he got to his feet. 'I'll be back in a minute.'

The solo customer became a steady stream of customers. Jo kept moving, all the time aware of Hazel's eyes on him. She hadn't told him what she wanted, or what Jem had said to her to make her come to Hawthorn Park.

As time ticked by, and his queue of customers showed no sign of abating, Jo caught a movement out of the corner of his eye. When he finally had the chance to go and see what Hazel was doing, she'd gone.

'Are you absolutely sure?'

Ed was close to exasperation as his girlfriend asked him for the third time if he thought there was enough seating. 'Maddie, I have triple-checked. I've even gone so far as to sit on every seat, to make sure there is room, and that the majority of people have a good eyeline to the front of the action.'

'Sorry.' Maddie threaded her way through the picnic tables to the chair and table that had been placed ready for Ditzy. 'I'm just so nervous.'

'I know.' Deciding not to mention the lack of microphones, Ed admired the arrangement of flowers on the tablecloth-covered table, alongside which was a jug of water and a glass. 'It's great.'

'Thanks. Sabi has worked wonders, and Jake's created three fresh hanging baskets to put up outside Dad's old shop, alongside some extras to sell.' Maddie turned towards the main body of the nursery. 'Shame about the new shop though. All that work, and the doorway looks like a caveman has attacked it with a club, and we haven't had a chance to consider lighting. I'm afraid it is going to be pretty dark inside.'

'It's not that bad.'

'Ed!'

'Okay, so the doorway's not great, and we do need more light, but there's still time.' He checked his watch. 'It's only half-one. Have you heard from Robert?'

'A quick text saying they were waiting for supplies.'

'There you go then. They'll make it.'

Maddie stared up at the cloudless sky. 'At least the weather is being kind. One less thing to worry about.'

'Come on. There's nothing else we can do here.' Ed spoke with a sense of satisfaction. 'The picnic tables are in place, the bluebells look incredible, Ditzy's spot is sorted, there's a set of travel rugs near her for the Little Acorns to sit on... How many of them are coming, by the way?'

'All of them.' Maddie felt a new hit of anxiety as nerves for the event spun in her stomach. 'They are very keen to show a famous person their garden. I hope Noel and Kayleigh don't think they can ask lots of questions.'

Ed laughed. 'Maybe you should sit Jem with them as crowd control.'

'That's not such a silly idea.'

They were just putting up a 'No Entry' cordon, when the sound of Jake's boots running in their direction made them spin round.

'You should come quick. The builders are back.'

47

'Wow!' Maddie and Sabi watched as Robert and Ahmed, directed by Kevin, carried a huge wrought-iron, hinged fence panel from the back of a lorry. Painted a crisp white, the panel was formed of a latticework of twisted and curled vines, with leaves occasionally "growing" out of them. The whole effect was of a wealthy Victorian's decorative garden panel of a sort that might bedeck an orangery or outhouse.

As she got closer, Maddie saw that it was hinged in two places, splitting the piece into three, and making it possible to bend as required.

'This is beautiful. Like an exaggerated dressing screen.' Sabi ran a finger along the smooth metalwork. 'But, umm… it's not actually a door, is it.'

Robert ran a hand over his stubbled chin. 'Drew a bit of a blank there, lass – hence the delay, but as screens go, this is sort of garden centre-ish. Obviously, if it's no good…'

'It's perfect.' Sabi examined the panels closely.

Maddie wasn't so sure. 'It is beautiful, but how can it be used as a door? I don't mean to sound ungrateful.'

'Not at all.' Robert gestured back to the lorry. 'We can take it back if it won't do to shield the entrance.'

'Oh, please don't.' Sabi stroked some dirt off the side of the panel. 'This could be amazing.'

'But Sabi, look at how rough and ready the surround to the doorway is!'

'Jemima said it looked like "Diagon Alley" when it first opens up for Harry Potter.'

'I suppose it does a bit.' Maddie reappraised the pattern of bricks around the largely roughly rectangular opening.

'Trust me. Give me an hour, and then come and help me set up the till and get the temporary stock in.' Sabi turned to Robert. 'I don't suppose you happen to have any of that tubular isolation pipe covering plumbers use – the really wide stuff – in your van?'

Sara was carrying an armful of assorted herb-filled flowerpots from the polytunnel to the greenhouse, when her mobile vibrated in her pocket. Waiting patiently for a customer to move from examining a coriander plant near the doorway, she refilled the empty spaces before checking her texts.

The moment she'd read it, she left the greenhouse and headed to the far polytunnel, the only space she could guarantee to be empty, and made a call. Sara had been close to hanging up when the line finally connected. 'I take it you're busy then?'

'Insanely. Died off a bit now.' Jo tucked his mobile between his chin and shoulder as he stacked a tray with empty cups. 'Sorry I took ages to answer. Last-minute hot chocolate request.'

'Last minute? You've got an hour yet.' Sara checked her watch. 'It's only three, Hawthorn doesn't close until four.'

'True, but I'm going to have to close now. I'm all out of tea and coffee. I've never known anything like it. Talk about a swarm of locusts! Albeit a friendly one. I loaded up way more stock than usual this morning, knowing you wouldn't be here to fetch top-ups for me, and it's all gone but for the hot chocolate.'

'You have had a good day!' Sara smiled, before the memory of his text made her frown. 'Has Hazel really been there?'

'She has – but she left before we could talk properly.'

'She *wanted* to talk to you?'

'Because of Jem.'

'Jemima? How come?'

'As the Americans would say, she staged an intervention. Hazel left me a note. I have to talk to Jem, but I can't just appear after...'

'Yes, you can.' A list of all the things that she'd promised Maddie she'd do while she was getting ready to launch The Potting Shed ran through Sara's head. She couldn't possibly leave now... but on the other hand... 'Pack up your end. Do you have more stock in the house?'

'Just drinks. No more food until I get to the wholesaler tomorrow.'

'Go and restock the van with tea and coffee. I'll be there in an hour.'

'But no one there will want me to—'

'Don't argue, Jo. I'll be there in an hour.'

Petra wasted no time. The moment Sara explained the situation, she called Jake on his mobile. Five minutes after that, her boyfriend finished making up the hanging basket he was working on at top speed and carried it towards the shop. Hanging it on a hook that had been used for that purpose for as long as he could remember, Jake went straight to the old shop, waving across the space to Petra, as he headed to Ivan.

'Sara's had to nip back to Hawthorn Park, so I'll be doing the jobs Maddie asked her to do until closing. Petra said the first thing was to make sure you didn't need any cheese stock from the fridge in your van.'

'I'm good thanks, Jake.' Ivan surveyed his counter. 'I've enough to last the final hour. Is Sara okay?'

'She needs to be there to help close Hawthorn Park for the day.'

'Makes sense.' Ivan flexed his legs, stiff from where he'd been sitting for so long. 'It's quiet here now. Do you want to ask Petra if she'd like me to take over the till? Then you two can go and help the girls get ready for our special guest.'

'Last question, Miss Willand.' The final journalist due to visit The Potting Shed that afternoon pushed his mobile phone closer to Maddie. 'Do you think your father would be proud of the work you and your sister have put in here today? From what you have already said, you've certainly had one or two obstacles in your path since you decided to honour his wish to expand from a nursery to a garden centre.'

'Dad always believed in hard work. As you say, there have been some adventures along the way, and I'm sure they aren't over yet – but yes, I think he'd love what is happening here today.' She looked around her. 'Just having so many customers here – many of whom my father knew, along with lots of new ones, not to mention a sold-out gardening event tonight – would make him grin like the Cheshire cat.'

'And we're done.' The journalist moved his mobile phone away from where he'd been recording Maddie's voice and clicked it off. 'So, a photographer will be here this evening to take pictures of Ditzy. Otherwise, we have all we need.'

'That's good.' Maddie, who'd been itching to get back to helping arrange the new shop, jumped up from where they'd been perched on one of Sara's picnic benches. 'I'll show you out.'

However anxious she'd been about what was happening in her absence, Maddie knew she had to hand it to her sister. If anyone was going to be able to make an entranceway stunning, it would be her. The brick edge to the doorway was now hidden beneath the padding of thick lengths of pipe covering, giving it a smooth protective surface. The greyness of this curved polystyrene covering was disguised with lengths of the same ribbon Sabi had used to cover the ceiling supports within. The wrought-iron screen was placed in front of this, two-thirds of it flat against the open doorway, the third part opened out, as if in welcome, to form a passageway, big enough to pass through comfortably, while also giving the feel of an open doorway.

'This is incredible.' Maddie couldn't believe the transformation. 'I love it! You're so good at this, Sabs.'

'All we need is a length of ribbon hung across from the screen to the hanging basket that Jake's fixed up, and

Ditzy can cut it as she declares us open.' Sabi nodded to her helpers. 'I can't take all the credit. The boys have been fabulous with helping me get everything into position.'

Robert, Kevin and Ahmed raised their mugs of tea in a uniform gesture of appreciation, before Kevin said, 'If you two are okay, we should get this lorry back to the chap we borrowed it from.'

'Of course. Thank you so much.' Sabi beamed. 'We'll see you later.'

As the sisters watched them head towards the exit, Maddie asked, 'Have you seen Ed? He said he'd take Florrie for a walk to wear her out before this evening.'

'He's already done it. Florrie's asleep in the back of his car – with both windows rolled down, I should add.'

'She'll jump out!' Maddie immediately turned towards the car park.

'No, she won't.' Petra appeared from through the temporary doorway. 'She's with Jemima. They're snuggled together, one asleep, one buried in her mobile phone.'

'Excellent. Thanks.' Maddie felt flustered. 'Um, so is the old shop shut now then?'

'Fear not, all our customers are being looked after. Ivan's on the till. He can keep an eye on his stall too from there.' Petra moved closer to Sabi. 'That's all the ceramic flowerpots in place. I have to say, you were right – they do make a fabulous visual feature as you go in.'

'Flowerpots?' Maddie was beginning to feel as if she'd taken a wrong turn and missed something vital. 'We weren't going to have those in there, were we?'

'We weren't.' Sabi took her sister by the hand and led her inside. 'But the space is much bigger than we imagined. We needed something so it didn't look too empty. Come and see.'

Maddie's mouth dropped open as she stepped inside. 'How long was I with those journalists?'

'An hour.' Ed straightened up from where he'd been plugging in an extension cable, so that the till could be set up. 'Like it?'

The first thing she noticed was how bright the space was. Strings of fairy lights left over from the Santa's grotto they'd had at Christmas were draped across every wall. Lanterns, each containing a battery-controlled tealight, sat either side of every table. These, along with the ceiling lights that had been there for years, illuminating the old lounge and dining room – plus some standard desk lamps (discreetly hidden amongst a display of black and purple grasses) – gave the space a cheerful, semi-enchanted feel.

Petra, her ponytail tucked into her jumper to keep it out of the way, was placing pots of double begonias and calibrachoa. Their rainbow-coloured petals reflected warmth in the fairy lights as they nestled next to tubs of freshly cut tulips and tubs of sweet peas, whose scent was perfuming the air with a welcoming sense of calm. All of these sat proudly on a trestle table, which had been covered with a maroon tablecloth that complemented the colour of the ribbons around the ceiling props.

'It's incredible.' Maddie gave her sister a hug. 'Wherever did you get so many matching tablecloths?'

'Jemima's school. I called the head and collected them last night. We have them until tomorrow. They usually only see the light of day for award ceremonies and posh dinners.'

Sabi's cheeks blushed in the grotto-type light. 'To be honest, I picked the ribbon first, assuming that it would be okay to borrow the tablecloths.'

'Sabs, you are priceless.' Giving her sister a hug, Maddie whispered, 'I haven't had the chance to ask – are you okay now, about Simon's death and meeting Sara?'

Sabi drew in a sharp breath. 'You knew?'

'Sara told me – she assumed I already knew. Why didn't you tell me?'

Lowering her eyes to the ribbon her hands, Sabi murmured, 'I was ashamed – and well, you're so fond of Henry. I didn't want you to think I didn't love him.'

'So, you carried all that sadness on your own until you were brave enough to tell Henry?'

'Maybe.'

'Oh, Sabs. What are you like?'

'A dreadful snob – but...' she gave a brave smile '...I'm much better than I used to be.'

'Sabs, you are wonderful, and I wouldn't have you any other way.'

Giving her sister another big hug, Maddie led the way to Ed by the till. Only then did she notice Jake at the far side of the shop, crouched on the floor, filling three huge wicker baskets with his home-grown vegetables.

Picturing her father, wondering what he'd say if he'd been there, Maddie's words were suddenly choked with emotion. 'I can't thank you enough for all this.'

'Our pleasure.' Henry arrived through the door with an armful of cash to load up the till. 'Shame it is only temporary, I think it looks great.'

Maddie nodded, overwhelmed at the effort put in by her friends and family. 'It does.'

'All we need is to make enough money tonight to pay for it all.' Sabi regretted airing her dose of reality the second the words had been spoken. 'Sorry.'

'Don't worry – it's the truth after all.' Even the twinkle of the nearest string of fairy lights didn't diminish the nagging doubt that, fun as it would be having Davina Ditz there, they still might not make enough money to break even by the end of the month.

48

Jo drove into The Potting Shed with a sense of trepidation. Sara had told him over and over again that everyone would be pleased to see him, yet he couldn't stop the voice at the back of his head muttering: *But what if they aren't?*

Wishing he didn't drive such a conspicuous vehicle, he eased it into the far side of the parking area – a space that was empty, but for Henry and Ed's car, plus an old-school Nissan Micra, which he presumed to be Petra's.

Pulling his beanie over his head, Jo caught his reflection in the rear-view mirror. Even now, the sight the greeted him could sometimes catch him by surprise. He'd always avoided mirrors in the past – he wasn't a great fan of them even now – but at least he could bear them when he had to.

You need to tell Jem. You owe her.

As if she'd heard his thoughts, suddenly, there Jem was climbing out of Ed's car, Florrie at her side. He had the impression she'd been asleep.

'Jo?'

'Hi.' Jo saw Jem's small chin jutted up in self-defence as, despite Florrie trying to persuade her to the contrary, she stayed where she was. *She really is Sabi's daughter.* 'I'm glad you're here. I wanted to say sorry for not telling you I left The Potting Shed. And I wanted to thank you.'

'Thank me?' Jem ruffled Florrie's head.

'For talking to Hazel.'

'How did you know about that?'

'She came to see me.'

'She said she wouldn't.' Jem rubbed the toe of her left boot against the back of her right leg. 'She talked to me as if I was a child… I know I am a child, but – oh, you know.'

'Yes, I know.' Jo gave a quiet sigh. 'Well, whatever it was you said must have made her think, whether she considered it childish or not.' Jo passed a folded piece of paper to his friend.

Jo, I can't forgive you for what you did to me at school – or for not telling me who you were when we met at the council, but I don't want you to think that I've sunk to your level.

I won't make things difficult for you if you want to work at The Potting Shed. I can't imagine I'll go there again.

Hazel

Jem's face lit up, her eyes shining as she held the piece of paper out to Jo. 'Does that mean you'll come back?'

'I'd like to, but I haven't behaved brilliantly. I've messed Maddie and your mum about a fair bit. They might not want me back.'

'Rubbish.'

'Maybe.' Leaning against the side of Ed's car, Jo took a deep breath. 'Jem, do you remember when I got cross with you when we were talking about school?'

'When we talked about bullies?' Jem peeped up at him through her fringe.

'I'd like to tell you why I was sad – why I reacted like an idiot although I knew you were trying to help.'

'I think I already know. Hazel's right – I am only a kid, but I'm not stupid.' Jem put down her drink. 'After you'd asked me about those sorts of girls – the popular ones at school. There are one or two at my school – perfect hair, perfect intelligence, perfect skin, perfect lives – and a cruel streak a mile long.'

'That's them.' Jo found he couldn't look at her, not wanting to see any judgement in her eyes.

'You were like them, weren't you, Jo. Mean like them – in an undercover, sneaky way?' Jem put her had on his knee to show she wasn't cross with him. 'A bit bully-like maybe.'

'No, Jem.' Jo didn't know he was going to say the words out loud or not until he heard them come out of his mouth. 'I wasn't *like* those girls – I *was* one of those girls. It wasn't a boarding school like yours, but it was a *girls'* school.'

Keeping a tight hold of Florrie, Jem gazed at her friend for a while, working out what he was saying. 'So, Hazel?'

'Was at school with me. She desperately wanted to be one of the gang – to be a popular girl. It wasn't like the comfortable school you go to. It was cold and dark, and the staff seemed to work on the principle that a cross word was better than a kind one – at least, that's how it felt at the time. Hazel tried so hard to be one of us – *too* hard – it was painful to witness. And I didn't help. I could have been nice to her – but I wasn't. I mocked her efforts to join in. And she never forgot.'

'Oh.'

Afraid of what Jemima might say, Jo ploughed on. 'Then, when I saw her later, she didn't recognise me. Why would she? I'd become who I was always meant to be. Even my face was different, thanks to the surgeon's skill at changing the shape of my chin – and with a different haircut... I was happy. Content – all the anger had gone and... I wanted to make amends when Hazel came to work at the council.' He gave out another ragged sigh. 'I was so pleased when we got on.'

'But it didn't work out.'

'You noticed, huh.' Jo risked a glance in Jem's direction. 'I would understand if you didn't want to know me anymore. I'm not the greatest role model.'

Standing closer to Jo's side, Jem asked, 'Is that why, when Hazel told Dad you were a bully, you didn't argue? You believed you deserved to be punished?'

'I wasn't nice at school – I really wasn't.'

'You weren't you at school – the *you* who you were supposed to be.'

'That's kind of you to say so...' Jo shrugged '...and as true as that is, Jem, it is no excuse – no excuse at all.'

'It's a reason.'

'A poor reason. No bullying is excusable. Ever.'

Jem rested her head on Jo's arm as it hung loosely by his side. 'Do the others know about you not always being the right version of you?'

'Only Ed officially – but he told me Maddie has guessed, so I expect your parents know too.'

'I didn't guess. You look like a boy.' She sat quietly for a while, before saying, 'I'm glad you told me.'

'You're my friend.'

'Thank you.'

'You are also a demon smoothie recipe designer.'

Jem burst out laughing, the tension that had existed only seconds ago forgotten. 'I sure am, and don't you forget it, mister!'

Maddie placed the recipe cards that Jemima had created, and Henry had printed, between a few fledgling blueberry and spinach plants. Running a finger across the laminated sheets, designed so that stray soil could be easily wiped off them, the emotion that had been bubbling near the surface all day begin to get the better of her.

'Jem's going to be as good a gardener as you were, Dad.' Whispering the words, Maddie wiped a stray tear from her eye. 'Ed's gone to wait for Dan and Ditzy. They'll be here soon. I think you'd like Ed – he lives here with me now. Not that we've had time to think about that, but he does. He loves this place. I don't really want him to go to work in Bristol.'

Wiping her tears away with a tissue, Maddie sat behind the till, taking a moment of total peace while she could. It was hard to picture where the sofa and bookshelves had once been as she took in the eight tastefully placed tables, the till waiting by the makeshift door, the heady scent of a mix of flowers and soil filling the air.

Checking her phone, making sure she hadn't missed a text from Ed to say their guests had arrived, Maddie saw it was four-fifteen already. The customers had gone, Jake was sweeping out the polytunnels and Petra and Sabi were cashing up.

'In five hours, it'll all be over, Dad, and I'll have to move all of this to somewhere lockable overnight.'

She optimistically patted the loaded till. 'I hope we sell a few things. Everyone has worked so hard to make this look like it isn't a building site. I know Davina will be brilliant, but what if our guests assume there'll be refreshments, even though I've told everyone to bring their own picnic?'

No good worrying about things you can't control. It's going to be perfect.

The echo of her father's voice felt so assured, that Maddie got up off her chair.

'You're right. We've all worked hard; it's just a case of doing our best now.' She made one last survey of her new domain and smiled. 'Thanks, Dad.'

49

As Maddie crossed from the newly arranged shop space towards the car park her heart thudded in her chest. Petra and Jake were stationed by the old shop, ready to tick people's names off their ticket list. Sabi was busy on the other side of The Potting Shed, making sure the new garden was at its best, and Henry was in the kitchen slicing a huge cake he'd made, ready to offer their special guest a treat on arrival. She could see Ed in the distance talking to someone, although she couldn't see who.

What if that's Ditzy already?

'Come on, you've spoken to her on the phone, and she was lovely.' Maddie was still muttering to herself, when Ed stepped to the side. *Jo!*

Breaking into a jog, Maddie called out, 'It's *so* good to see you, Jo – but if you're going to tell me you are here to sell drinks this evening that would be even better.'

Jo's cheeks flushed. 'Ed just said the same.'

'Not that you aren't welcome without your van.' Maddie backtracked, realising how tactless she might have sounded.

'It's okay, I know what you meant. I'm fully equipped hot drinks wise – but not for food. And I don't have much in the cold line left. Hawthorn Park has cleared me out.'

Jo sucked in his bottom lip. 'I didn't come here assuming I'd be welcome. Sara said I would be, but... I came to thank Jem. She spoke to Hazel on my behalf.'

'Jem did?' Maddie was amazed.

'That niece of yours is one incredible young woman. She'll be ruling the world by the time she's eighteen at this rate.'

'The world could do a lot worse. Have you seen her to say thanks yet?'

'Yes.' Jo swallowed. 'Adults should never underestimate the understanding qualities of children.'

'Amen to that!'

'Sara will be here soon.' Jo gave his friends a shy smile. 'She's closing up at Hawthorn Park instead of me, so I could come here.'

'We'll have to make sure we hold her back a slice of Henry's cake as a thank you.' Maddie grinned. 'So, Jo, do you fancy getting set up so you can provide coffee for our celebrity? She'll be here very soon. Apparently, she likes it black with one sugar.'

'Then black with one sugar is what she will have.'

'I can't believe I didn't think of that!' Maddie's insides did a backflip as her sister and Ed looked at her. 'I just assumed Ditzy would do all the talking. Why do I have to be the one who introduces her? Can't you do it, Sabs? You're far more confident than me.'

'No way.' Sabi shook her head. 'This is your event. I've just done the cosmetic stuff.'

'You've done way more than that.' Huddled behind Jo's

van, the familiar fingers of panic gripped Maddie as she realised she was going to have to join Ditzy – who was currently in her kitchen with Dan and Henry, devouring a slice of Victoria sandwich cake – on the stage.

'You'll just be talking to customers – and you're good at that.' Ed slipped a hand into hers. 'And luckily, Ditzy foresaw our microphone issues, so she's brought a twin headset.'

Maddie blanched a paler white. 'Everyone will be able to hear me!'

'That is sort of the point, Mads.' Sabi checked the time. 'Come on, it's filling up out there. I'll go and make sure Jemima is coping with the Little Acorns.'

As Sabi left, Ed opened his arms. 'Come here.'

Burrowing herself into his chest, Maddie's voice was muffled by his thick navy jumper. 'It'll be okay, won't it?'

'It will be amazing. All you have to do is introduce Ditzy, and then walk to each of the people who have questions to ask. Repeat their questions so everyone can hear them clearly. Let Davina do the rest.'

'What if no one wants to go into the new build afterwards?'

'They'll all want to. Trust me.' Ed took both of her hands. 'Kiss for luck?'

Maddie didn't recall much of Davina's opening talk. Occasional lines hung in the back of her head, waiting for digestion later.

I've just had the best coffee ever – and if Henry Willand-Harris ever starts making cakes for a living, then I can thoroughly recommend them.

I never had the pleasure of meeting Tony Willand, the founder of The Potting Shed, but I've heard so many lovely things about him today, from his old friends and regular customers here...

Chalky soil... always an issue. More a problem in the Home Counties of course, but...

Impatiens – often known as Busy Lizzies – they're my favourite bedding plant. Marvellous in hanging baskets as well of course, and slugs aren't too keen on their taste...

The evening simply dissolved. The final question from the audience, all packed, sardine style, onto the closely placed picnic tables, had been answered and Maddie found herself joining everyone in a round of applause. She felt she was floating on a soft cloud of kindness and goodwill.

Her eyes roved over the younger members of the group. The Little Acorns had hardly fidgeted, thanks to Florrie and Sheba, lying amongst them, enjoying having their fur stroked by eager little hands. They'd positively glowed as Ditzy had praised their fledgling bluebell garden and extolled the virtues of starting children gardening from an early age.

Now, as Maddie regarded the audience, all jammed cosily onto their benches, picnics in evidence on almost all the tables – alongside hot drinks provided by Jo, she geared herself up for the final official part of the event. She'd meant to rehearse what to say, but somehow there had never been time.

Just say what comes to mind. You'll be fine.

With her father's imagined reassurance echoing in

her head, Maddie raised her hands to make sure she had everyone's attention.

'Ladies and gentlemen, boys and girls, thank you so much for coming along this evening. You are welcome to stay and finish your picnics. However, if you would like to head over to the main building, I am delighted to say that our very special guest, Davina Ditz, has agreed to cut the ribbon, officially opening The Potting Shed as a garden centre. Once the ribbon is cut, you are welcome to head inside. Although the current arrangement of goods inside will change as we add to our stocks, everything in there is on sale, and the till is open.'

An unusually shy Noel climbed off Davina's knee and ran towards his mum, a signed photograph in his hand.

Maddie, light-headed with relief that her time in the limelight was at an end, and the ribbon cutting and posing for the local paper's photographers was over, rested next to the till with Petra. 'So, that's the secret of stopping Noel talking? Get him to talk to his dad's favourite celebrity.'

Petra chuckled. 'He's a bit of handful then, is he?'

'In a good way. Noel is keen with confidence.'

'He and his fellow Little Acorns were as good as gold.' Petra waved a hand at Jake as she saw him in the distance, helping Ed carrying a large Ali-Baba-style pot for a woman, who was muttering about not knowing what her husband would say when she got it home – while simultaneously glowing with pleasure at her new purchase. 'Jake and I will need to go soon. I'm sorry we can't stay to help you clear up, but if we don't go it'll be dark. That link road is a swine to drive down, even in daylight.'

Having driven the A361 towards Barnstaple on many occasions, Maddie could only agree. 'I totally understand. It's a hell of a helter-skelter.'

Seconds later, as Henry took over the flowerpot-carrying from Jake, Maddie found herself the focus of a fierce joint hug while Petra thanked her for everything.

'I'm so glad you could make it this weekend. The customers are always asking after the pair of you. It goes without saying that if you ever need jobs in the future, you only have to ask.'

'Here.' Ed slipped a coffee next the till as Maddie waved off their final customer. 'Extra caffeine to get you through the clear-up.'

Running around to the front of the till, Maddie engulfed Ed in a cuddle. 'This is why I love you.'

'Love you too.' Kissing the top of her head, he murmured, 'You did it! Davina was a massive hit. And look around you – you've sold loads of stuff.'

Not wanting to leave the security of Ed's arms, Maddie said, 'But did we do it? The till has barely stopped ringing, but did we make enough? Have costs been met? I hardly dare cash up.'

50

Jemima lifted her smoothie and gave the straw a long suck. 'I hope my smoothies taste as good as Jo's when they've grown.'

'I'm sure they will.' Sara smiled. 'You've very fond of Jo, aren't you?'

'He treats me like a grown-up.'

'And so he should.' Sara knocked a heap of empty recyclable cups into a cardboard box.

'You're fond of him too.' Jemima knocked her straw against her lips.

'Yes.'

'He loves you.'

Sara hid her face by bending down to pick up a fallen crisp packet. 'Jo will always be my best friend.'

'I think he gets lonely.'

Sara turned in time to see Jo serve the final coffee of the night to their guest of honour. 'He likes being alone; he needs space.'

'You've got loads of space at Hawthorn Park, but I bet you get lonely on your own.' Jemima lowered her eyes, wondering if she'd overstepped the mark. 'Sorry, I didn't mean to be rude.'

'It's okay.' Sara watched Ditzy give an appreciate sniff of the drink Jo had served her. 'The house does feel a bit empty sometimes.'

'Then fill it.'

The matter-of-fact way Jemima spoke made Sara laugh. 'Actually, I'm thinking of using some of the en-suite rooms for an Airbnb. It was Jo's idea.'

'You'd need help with that. Jo would help if you asked him. I bet he'd cook a fabulous bacon sandwich for breakfast.'

'You're probably right, but it's a long drive for him every day.'

'It doesn't have to be though, does it.' Jemima threw her hands up in despair. 'Honestly, why are adults so dim sometimes?'

'You blend this yourself, Jo?'

'Only this past year or so. It's become something of a passion to be honest, but I don't have a great deal of space at home, so I'm a little limited as to what I can achieve.'

Ditzy took another sip of coffee. 'I don't even need sugar with this one. What gives it that sweet edge – or is it a trade secret?'

'Definitely a trade secret.'

'Fair enough.' Smiling as she picked up the bunch of flowers the Little Acorns had presented her before their parents had escorted them home, Davina gestured to Jo's coffee machine. 'You know, if you ever consider making up a gardener's blend, I'd happily endorse it.'

Jo's eyes widened. 'For real?'

'One hundred per cent for real. You don't have a business card, do you?'

'It's been a fabulous evening, but I should go.' Ditzy hugged Maddie and Sabi as if they'd been friends for years. 'This place is a real treasure.'

'Thank you so much for coming.' Maddie beamed as her sister held out her hand to their guest.

'It's been amazing.' Sabi smiled. 'We should do it once a year.'

'I'd love to.' Ditzy gave an awkward clap, encumbered by flowers and coffee cup as she was. 'Seriously, let's get it in the diary.'

'Do you mean it?' Maddie couldn't believe it. 'You don't have to be nice to us just because—'

'I mean it!' Davina waggled her mobile at them. 'Call me tomorrow – but after ten; I'm planning a lie-in!'

Maddie zipped up the last polytunnel and followed Ed towards the bluebell garden to make sure the gate to the wood had been padlocked. 'The evening's gone so quickly.'

'Because it was a huge success. If it hadn't worked, the time would have dragged.'

'That's true.' Maddie smiled.

Ed picked up the travel rugs the children had sat on and carried them to the bench that overlooked the field. Patting the space next to him, he placed them over their legs as Maddie sat with him. 'There's something I have to tell you.'

Tucking herself in, Maddie savoured the chill of the spring evening on her face. 'Don't tell me, Sabi has been monitoring how often I eat toast on a secret app, and she's worried I'm going to give you rickets due to vitamin deficiency.'

'You guessed!'

Maddie tilted her head up so she could see him properly. 'So, what did you want to tell me?'

'I told you a lie. A small one – and with good reason.'

Some of Maddie's euphoria dipped. 'Go on.'

'The meeting in Bristol. It wasn't just a dinner. I had the interview. I didn't want you worrying about that when you had all this going on.'

'But I have been worrying about it anyway!'

'I know. Sorry.'

Maddie focused her gaze on the wood. 'You got the job.'

'Yes.'

'Congratulations.' Despite her best efforts not to, Maddie realised she felt as flat as she sounded. 'Are you pleased?'

'To be honest, I've no idea how I feel about it. I'm used to working for a small family firm. These guys are a very different proposition. City lawyers in the proper sense of the word.'

'You don't sound keen.'

'The money is good.'

Determined to be as supportive of him as he was to her, Maddie asked, 'When will you need to start hunting for somewhere to live in Bristol?'

'Are you mad?' Ed took hold of her hands. 'We've only just started living together. I'm not moving anywhere.'

Maddie's gaze swung from the calming balm of the bluebells to Ed's face. 'But won't you hate the commute?'

'Be worth it to come home to you.' Ed tucked a stray hair away from Maddie's eyes to behind her ear. 'I could get a bicycle. Cycle from here to Tiverton Parkway each day. Better for the environment.'

'Promise me though, Ed, you'll only take the job if you want it. *Not* because the money would be handy this end.'

'Promise.' Ed cuddled Maddie to his side. 'You see those bluebells?'

'Yes.'

'They are almost as beautiful as you are.'

Sara's nervous system had gone into overdrive as she watched Jo stack a pile of unused cups into a box in the back of his van. Waiting until he'd put them away, she marched up to his side and blurted out, 'Do you like living in that caravan? An honest answer please.'

Surprised by the question, Jo said, 'It's a means to an end I suppose. There are lots of worse places.'

'That's not an answer.'

'Okay then, no. It never gets warm in winter and it's too hot in summer. Despite my best efforts, it's never felt like home.'

'A temporary measure.'

'That was the plan. But I've no hope of paying a mortgage on a house the way prices are rising. I'm just grateful that I have a roof over my head.'

Before she could bottle out, Sara gabbled, 'There's a

job going – some cleaning, some woodland work, some cooking. Comes with accommodation.'

'Sara?' Jo's hand stilled on the camper van's door as he went to shut it. 'Are you asking me what I think you're asking me?'

'I'm going to give the Airbnb idea a go. I'll need help. I don't fancy having a stranger in the house – so, how about you help me?'

'But if you open as an Airbnb, you'll have lots of strangers in the house.'

'They'll come and go. A member of staff would always be there.'

'But Maddie's asked me to come back to work here, and I've said yes.'

'I'm only asking if you'll work for me when you aren't here.'

'And live with you?'

'No.' Sara spoke firmly. 'Live at Hawthorn Manor – alongside me.'

Jo caught a glimpse of Jem out of the corner of his eye. She was sat on a bench waiting for her parents, Florrie at her feet – and she was staring knowingly in their direction. 'Was this Jem's idea?'

'Let's just say, she planted the seed.'

'A born gardener, like her aunt.' Jo brushed his fringe from his eyes. 'The job, is it real, or was it a way to ask me if I wanted to share your place without it sounding like you were asking me to live with you?'

'The job is real, although I would like you to live with me – in a non-romantic, but in a very close friends way.' Sara fiddled with the cuff of her jacket. 'The arrangement could work both ways, as you'll need help when it comes to testing new coffee flavours when you accept Davina's offer.'

'She might not have been serious.'

'I don't think Ditzy's the sort of woman to say things she doesn't mean. It'll be much easier in my kitchen rather than the caravan. So…' Sara pushed her hands deep into her pockets '…do you want to live with me, rent-free, in exchange for helping when my Airbnb people come?'

'Yes please.'

'Good.' Sara grinned. 'And now, I think I need a coffee.'

'Me too – unfortunately, this shop has just closed.'

As they stood together, overlooking the bluebells that swayed in the light evening breeze, Henry gave out mugs of hot chocolate from a laden tray.

Thinking back over the evening now past, Sabi tapped into her mobile as she said, 'Did you see how red Robert went when Davina signed a photo for him?'

Jo laughed. 'Kevin told me his brother's smitten with her.'

'If she comes back next year, we'll have to remember to invite him and Kevin along.' Maddie took a large bite of the cake Henry had kept back for an after-event celebration.

'And Ahmed and his gran,' Ed agreed. 'She's a game old bird.'

'You sounded just like Dan then!' Maddie gave her boyfriend a friendly shove.

Draping a travel rug around Elspeth's shoulders, Dan chuckled. 'Here, is that so bad?'

Elspeth tutted. 'Don't you be fishing for compliments, Daniel!'

'As if I'd be so reckless.' Dan nodded to Ivan. 'So, are you looking forward to moving your cheeses into the new building?'

'Absolutely. I can just picture them all laid out in a proper refrigerated counter near the old kitchen.'

Jemima readjusted her position on the grass, where she'd was fussing Florrie. 'Once there's a café, it'll be better still.'

Maddie's sense of euphoria dipped abruptly. *We're talking about next year as if we'll still be expanding. But we might not be – we might be cutting back or...*

Seeing the cloud that had cast over her sister's face, Sabi reached out a hand to Maddie. 'I need to have a quick word. In private.'

With a worried glance at Ed, Maddie let go of his hand and followed her sister into the nearby tunnel.

'Mads, you can stop worrying.'

'I can?'

'You see this.' Sabi held up her phone. 'This accounting app is linked to the till. I've been monitoring sales for the past two weeks.'

'What?' Maddie's forehead creased. 'You never said.'

'Didn't want to worry you.' Sabi wrinkled her nose. 'If we weren't going to break even, I'd never have let things get this far. Let's face it, it would have looked awful if Ditzy had opened this place and then we'd had to tell everyone that, despite all our talk, this was as far as the expansion would ever go.'

Maddie's mouth open and closed. When her words did

eventually form, she muttered, 'I could kill you, Sabi! I've been worried sick about finances.'

'I know, but you hate talking money, and you've been so busy. The Potting Shed only broke even loan-wise as of yesterday afternoon. We needed to do well tonight to be more secure. And we did! The original bank loan can be declared paid off. Three weeks before our deadline!'

'We can keep going… we really can?'

'We really can.' Sabi engulfed her sister in a hug. 'Dad would be so proud of you.'

'Of *both* of us.'

Stood next to the new garden, Maddie addressed her friends. 'As we have – miraculously, with all your help – managed to pay off our first loan, Sabi and I now feel secure enough to dive back into debt and take out a second business loan. For the café.'

'Already?' Sara shuffled closer to Jo, who was sat on the floor next to her. 'Congratulations.'

Sabi beamed. 'We were going to concentrate on buying stock, but having researched lots of garden centres, we've decided that having a café, sooner rather than later, is a must.'

Jo raised his mug in a salute. 'I can't say I'm surprised that this place has done so well so fast. It's so friendly. It's just as well Sara has offered me a job, now you won't need my van.'

Maddie's cheeks flushed. 'Actually, we were going to ask you to run it, but if you've got a new job then…'

'Me? Run your café? After all the trouble I've caused?' Jo was stunned.

Henry shook his head. 'You caused no trouble – trouble was caused for you. The matter is closed. Hazel emailed me this morning. She won't be working off her probation period. She's gone.'

'You never said.' Sabi's eyes widened.

'I didn't want to cast a cloud over the day by talking about that young woman.'

Jo sucked in his bottom lip. 'Well, I wish her well – I really do.'

'Me too. But I'm glad she's gone.' Jemima moved closer to Jo. 'Are you going to run the café then?'

'I'd love to, but Sara offered me a job and—'

'Of course, you must run the café!' Sara raised her mug in salute. 'You belong here. And what better place than a professional café to develop coffee blends endorsed by the most famous gardener in the country?'

The smile that crossed Jo's face – so wide it woke muscles he'd forgotten he had – dimmed for a second. 'I'd love it run your café – but...'

'But?' Maddie asked softly.

'I need you to know that I would have been more than happy to pay for my pitch here. Hazel may have been right about a few things, but I'd never...'

'Say no more.' Henry held up his hand. 'We never doubted that for a moment. I blame myself for not making that clearer up front.'

Jo pulled his beanie from his head. 'In that case, thank you – once it's ready, I'd love to run your café.'

'Excellent. Providing you'll keep bringing the camper van

until then.' Maddie pushed herself to her feet, turning back on the bluebells, to survey The Potting Shed. 'This used to be one of Dad's favourite spots. He'd stand here and view his land. It seems fitting to be here as we raise a toast to Ed, Sara and Jo's new employment ventures, to remember two much-missed fathers, Simon Northcott and Tony Willand, and – of course – to wish The Potting Shed, now officially a garden centre, lots of luck.'

'A garden centre *and* a bluebell wood!' Jemima added.

'Of course!' Maddie beamed. 'Soon to be joined by the Forget-Me-Not Café.'

'That's a great name.' Jo laid a hand across Sara's shoulders. 'What made you chose that?'

'You'll find out when it's built.' Putting down her mug, Maddie yawned. 'Now, however, I think we'd all better get some sleep. We open again in ten hours!'

Acknowledgements

To all the lovely folk who work at The Old Well in Willand, Devon – these people were as much an inspiration behind the writing of The Potting Shed stories, as the garden centre itself.

Also, to Steve, Lucy, and Isaac, who have supported my nonstop need to create fictional versions of our reality with understanding, coffee, and chocolate for the past eighteen years.

Special thanks must go to the team at Aria (Head of Zeus), especially Martina, for being so enthusiastic about The Potting Shed series.

Finally, to my agent Kiran, of Keane Kataria: thank you for your constant help, valued input, and kind guidance.

About the Author

J ENNY KANE is the bestselling author of many romantic fiction series. These include the Mill Grange series, Abi's Cornwall series, and the Another Cup series. She has had bestsellers in the Amazon Romance, Contemporary Fiction and Women's Fiction charts and multiple other bestsellers. If you enjoy Jenny's writing, then why not follow her author page for updates on all of her new releases!